Unbreakable
BOND

Desmaligan Archives

Book One

Stella McAfee

 Celestial Trails Publishing

Published independently by Stella McAfee, Celestial Trails Publishing

Cover Art: Markee Books

Editor: Jessica Fortenberry, www.enchantedinkwell.com

Map: Inkarnate, Stella McAfee

Chapter headers: Canva, Stella McAfee

ISBN: 979-8-9947123-0-6 (paperback)

ISBN: 979-8-9947123-1-3 (ebook)

To all the girls who refuse to surrender to the shadows of chaotic doubt

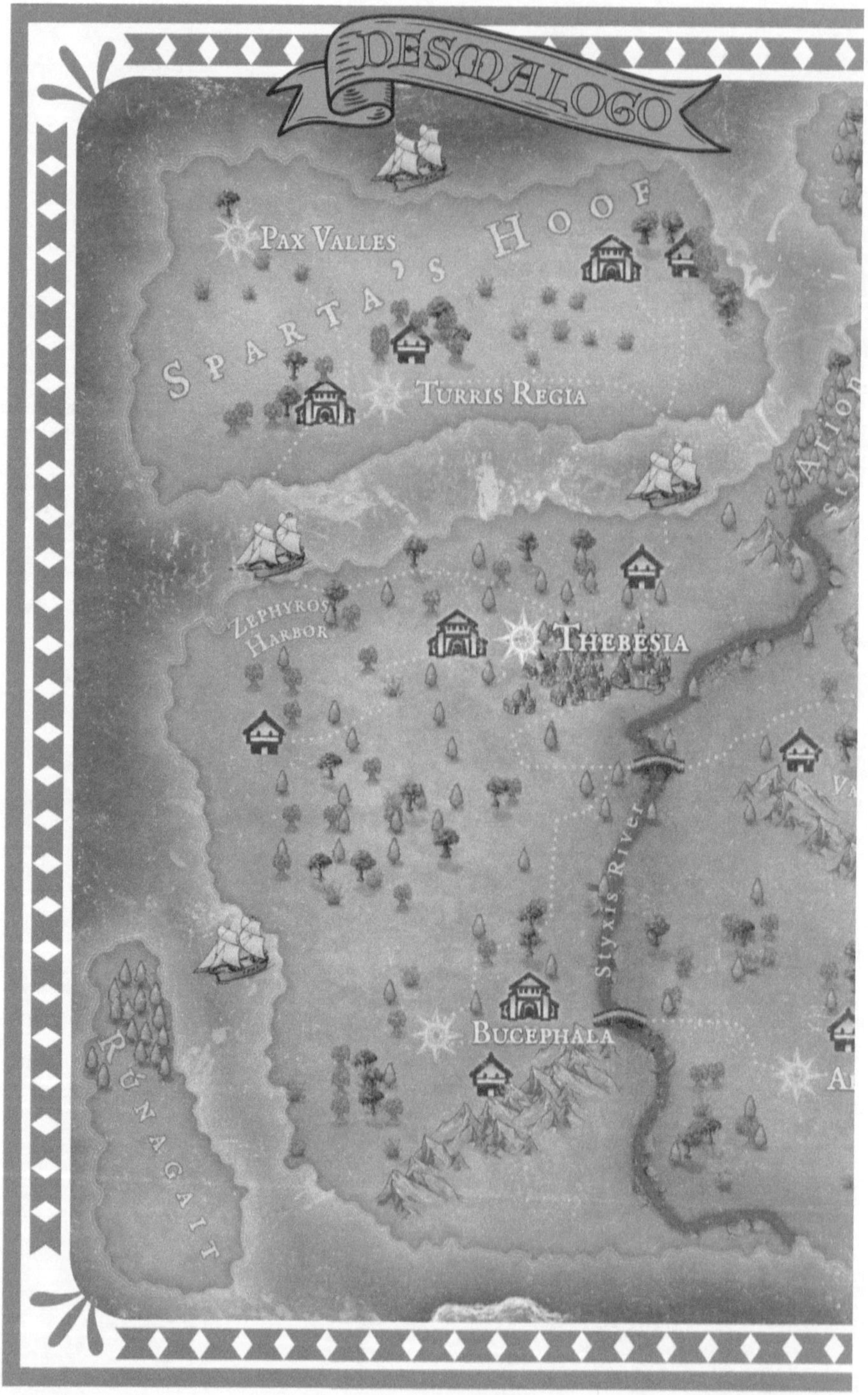

DESMALOGO
SPARTA'S HOOF
PAX VALLES
TURRIS REGIA
ZEPHYROS HARBOR
THEBESIA
BUCEPHALA
Styxis River
RUNAGAIT

Woodlands
Thebesia's Crown
VALLUMVIS
CORINTHAR
DIONYSIAN
FALLS
Satyrian Meadows
VALLEY OF VATHIS
Ombros Silvae
River of Naiad
ETHERPOLIS
MYSTICO GROVE

AUTHOR'S NOTE

Dear Reader,

Cassie's story began with a single scene. What would happen if one day you awoke to an empty mind? It's a scary thought, I'll be the first to admit. One would need perseverance and courage to move through life and a certain kind of drive to never give up. However, I'm a firm believer that everyone is always in the right place at the right time. Cassie losing her memories has purpose, and fate brought her to the island of Desmalogo for a reason.

While this story is suitable for all ages, there are mentions of amnesia, mental struggles, and death. There are no graphic depictions, and I tried my best to address these topics with care.

All the best,
Stella <3

1

"I do hope your reason for calling me out here is as good as you made it seem," the cloaked figure muttered, tugging his hood lower over his face. The dark brown fabric concealed most of his features, rendering him unrecognizable to anyone but the doctor.

"A very good reason, I assure you." Dr. Lykaion's voice held a touch of rarely expressed emotion, piquing the curiosity of his companion. The staff at the clinic ignored them—the doctor was one of the most respected in the field.

"None of them care about my presence?" A whisper came from the hooded man.

"They'll talk, of course, since the cloak gives you a mysterious air. But as you're without the usual robe, they won't know who you are. Not the first time I've brought a fellow doctor to work on a case." The doctor dismissed the snort of disagreement from his companion and pressed on. "It's quite the special case. I'm sure you will enjoy it." He opened the door to a small room at the end of the hall. The shades were drawn to prevent sunshine from spilling into the room. A young girl lay on the bed, an intravenous drip attached to her outstretched arm. "I hope you took my warning seriously that this is a case of utmost confidentiality. No one of your kind knows you are here?"

"No." He stood in silence, allowing his eyes to take in the girl. "I still don't understand why you chose me for this. You know I've not healed—"

"That's enough," Dr. Lykaion interrupted, directing his attention toward the patient.

Her face was ashy gray, her breaths so shallow they had to look closely to notice. Hand-drawn charts on the wall displayed her recent heart rate measurements, never once reaching the sixty beats per minute required for healthy functioning. Another noted the lack of brain activity and movement of the nervous system, and the third graphed a pattern of heavily unstable blood pressure. Medically, she was as close to dead as she could be without truly dying.

"I don't see what's so special." The cloaked figure scanned the room before fixating on the girl. "Stars, it's dark in here."

"I wasn't sure if the light would bother her. Given her status, she might be from a place where the dark would be more familiar to her."

"Status? What could you possibly be speaking of?" The sharp words severed the stillness in the room as the cloaked figure stepped closer to the doctor, whose hand hovered over the blankets.

"Jakobi," the doctor warned, "one thing at a time. We must be careful." He reached out to lift the edge of the blanket, revealing her legs. Carefully tilting the right one, he exposed a strange pattern on the back of the calf.

Jakobi's demeanor changed in an instant, his scowl flattening into an unreadable line. Slowly, his finger reached out to trace the unique pattern on her chilled skin, his thoughts nearly audible in the dead silence of the room.

"It's confirmed to be a birthmark, not a tattoo." The doctor reassured him, but he second-guessed his decision to invite Jakobi here. Would the man be willing to bring the girl back to a state of consciousness?

"She is not from Káto. It is unheard of for someone to cross to the underworld or back here without the knowledge of the Fýlax." The matter-of-fact statement from Jakobi did little to soothe the doctor, who gestured in a pleading way toward the charts on the wall.

"She has been unconscious for the month she's been here, plus however long she was at sea before being found."

"You want me to heal her?" Jakobi clasped his palms together behind his back, the slight shake of his head betraying how conflicted he felt on the matter. He met the doctor's pleading gaze with soft brown eyes.

"What options remain?"

A moment of silence ensued, both men shifting their gazes to the face of the girl as she sighed lightly, her eyes fluttering in a rare display of vivacity.

"She's hardly alive, but it is as if something is keeping her from dying. I hate to see her suffer like this, on the edge of consciousness without any guarantee of recovery." The doctor's voice fell silent as his eyes landed on the exposed birthmark on the back of her calf. "Had this been anyone else, I would have made my demands earlier. You don't recognize her at all?"

"No. I've seen the face of every person banished from our island, and hers is unfamiliar." Jakobi paused as if he had already said too much. He pressed his lips together, his gaze tracing the mark on her leg one more time. "I can help, but there are risks," he finally uttered, stepping back from the girl.

The doctor breathed a sigh of relief, replacing the blanket gently over her lower legs. "Whatever you need, I can supply it."

"I can't do my work here. We would have to transport her to someplace more private. Concealed from any eyes, outside the realm of the island." Jakobi took a step away from the bed, his posture stiff. "I couldn't tell anyone about this, for if I am discovered helping the enemy, the consequences will be harsh."

"I've considered everything to minimize the risk of discovery." The doctor nodded, focusing on the cloaked figure. "You think she has a chance at life?"

"I cannot promise anything. You know quite well healing is not my area of expertise. What have you learned about her?"

"There seems to be an intense amount of head damage. So much so I doubt she'll remember anything upon waking up."

"I will have to wipe everything regardless, to the point where she should not be able to access her—" He cut himself off, gesturing loosely toward the birthmark obscured by the blanket. "She will have a fresh start and hopefully stay out of trouble." Jakobi's statement lacked confidence, and he pulled the hood even lower over his face.

"Relax. No one can see you here, and besides, that hood won't help you if your location is discovered." The doctor chuckled, rubbing his chin thoughtfully as he turned toward the girl, ignoring the conflicted expression brewing behind the young man's eyes.

"So many risks associated with this. What if she has family that comes looking for her? What if she did this on purpose to escape the wrath of the Fýlax? Some think death is preferable to banishment." Jakobi held back a sigh, his knuckles whitening from clasping his hands so tightly. The questions stirred turmoil in the doctor, who had fought with all those questions before calling the only one he could trust to betray his own kind.

"The Desmaligan Rangers have asked nearly everyone on this forsaken island about her. There are no family, no relations, not a single soul that has recognized her."

"If her family were aware of the consequences of hiding

an Opposed, I doubt they would be so eager to reveal themselves."

"I tried everything before reaching out to you. See yourself as her last hope. I have a peculiar feeling that she won't die, yet she isn't alive. It haunts me." The two men allowed their eyes to meet, the gravity of the situation heightening the anxiety of both.

"And if I am successful, and she returns to consciousness?" Jakobi's voice dropped to a whisper, as if he were worried someone could hear him. An irrational fear, given that the hospital had been built on one floor, spanning a large area with several wings for patients that were kept isolated for various reasons. Nurses kept a strict schedule, only entering rooms when necessary.

"I've already reached out to an older woman in allegiance with the Fýlax. I kept my message short, telling her we have an older teenage girl who needs a place to live while recovering from a brain injury. She never had children of her own and has been known to foster a few. I'm willing to sponsor her out of my own funds during this time until we can discover her family or place of origin." The doctor paused for a moment, reaching to adjust the blanket on the bed. "I like to see it as a sign from the land or the sea. She was very much meant to be here."

"It doesn't seem right for me to leave without helping." Jakobi stepped back, his head shaking slightly. "I'm hanging on by a thread regardless. I suppose nothing better would be expected from me." He squeezed his eyes shut for a moment.

"I'll take the blame," the doctor interjected. "I doubt she knows anything about the Opposed. She was found in the water, wearing what any equestrian wears for a ride."

"Then why wasn't she recognized? If she were a Desmaligan citizen, the odds of someone not looking for her are very, very low," Jakobi countered.

"If you can sever her connection to Rhiza and deem her

untraceable, she will have a chance to live a normal life, free from their influence or the need to hide."

"Unless she's recognized," Jakobi stated in a flat tone. The doctor turned to him, his disappointment palpable. He started to object, but Jakobi stepped forward, his hood slipping back. "I will help."

"Thank you." Tension fled from the doctor's face.

"But, I will wipe her past clean, and none of the Fýlax will be able to trace her to her origins. It will not be easy for her to restart her life completely."

"Better than death. How shall we proceed?" Dr. Lykaion asked in a hushed whisper, pleased with the turn of events. It was rare that he let a patient down, always going above and beyond to ensure the health of the people.

"A ship," Jakobi grumbled, making his way toward the door. "We'll take her out on a ship. I'll do my best, then bring her back. Ensure there are enough sedatives to keep her down until it is finished."

"Of course. I'll arrange for transport tonight."

"Does she have a name?"

"Yes. Cassie."

"Very well. We shall meet soon."

A handshake in the dark sealed the pact, and the two men parted ways.

Chapter 2

er eyes fluttered open. She lay there motionless, unsure of her name, scared to breathe. The sudden stillness was a stark contrast to the soft rocking sensation just out of reach in her mind.

An unexplainable calm enveloped her body, distinctly separate from the swirling in her mind and blending in with the flashes of indigo light hidden beneath her eyelids.

Slow blinking brought the room into focus, a place that enclosed her with four patterned walls, a ceiling, and curtains that blocked out something bright. Her hands reached toward the source of illumination, and she shivered in shock at the pale skin of her thin limb.

The beginnings of questions threatened to flood her mind. Who was she? She searched the depths of her mind, finding nothing to give her an answer or a single clue about the before.

Why couldn't she remember anything? Taking great care to avoid the dizziness again, the girl lifted her head and gazed around the room.

What was this place? Nothing looked familiar; everything

was achingly meaningless. A dresser stood to the side, a desk nestled in the corner.

Leaning back down on the pillow, she caressed the soft blankets keeping her warm. They felt heavy, constricting, and paralyzing. She tossed them to the side, instantly regretting the motion as a cold draft nipped at her toes.

Lifting one hand, she watched her limbs as they curled and straightened out. Those were her fingers—she could use them to move things, and her legs could be used to move her. Glancing down at her body sprawled out on the bed, she studied the loose pajama pants and oversized shirt she was wearing. It had something on it, and she pulled out the edges to get a better look.

It was a sketch of a horse running with its mane flowing freely behind it. The horse was attached to nothing, suspended on her shirt without an anchor. Something skittered across her mind, reminding her that she had been floating in the darkness like the horse on her shirt. She closed her eyes for a minute, trying to see the indigo color again, but her mind was unyielding.

A strange thumping reached her ears, the steady increase indicating that it was coming closer to the door from outside the room. Her eyes shot to the door, sweat collecting on her palms as they came together to stop the trembling within. She narrowed in on the door handle as it turned. Glancing around for something to stand between her and whoever would enter, she grabbed the pillow and held it in front of her defensively.

Fear. She was finally able to name the emotion crawling inside her. She didn't like it.

The door slowly creaked open, and the girl scrambled backward to the far corner of the bed. A shriek escaped her lips when a strange figure stepped into the room. Without a thought, the girl threw the pillow as hard as she could, pressing herself against the wall. Her heart hammered in her chest. She would run, if only she had an exit. A single door, blocked, and a single window, closed tight. What was this prison that had no escape?

The figure easily caught the pillow and continued toward her. Her cocoa hair complemented her warm skin, streaks of gray highlighting dark locks. Aged eyes were crinkled with worry at the edges as she slowly advanced toward the girl, the hem of her dark skirt nearly brushing the floor with each step.

She didn't seem menacing, but the way she drew ever closer was enough to alarm the girl, sending a foreboding dread through her in shockwaves.

"Go away," the girl hissed, her mind flipping in confusion before registering the meaning of those words. This wasn't home, and this woman she had never seen before kept inching closer.

"Please," the figure said in a low and soothing voice, "I won't hurt you." She raised her hands, dropping the pillow to the floor. The words were familiar to her, but in a different language than the threat that escaped from her lips. She met the gaze of the lady head-on, fighting between saying harsh words and submitting to the woman.

"Let's start with something basic." The lady was still speaking, drawing the girl back to her. Her lips curved upward, a peace offering. "Hello."

"Hi," the girl said in the second language, lowering her head. She needed time to process each word, but she could speak and understand the strange language of the woman. Strange, yes, and unfamiliar.

Her hair fell over her eyes, and she peeked out from behind the orange strands. She knitted her fingers together, preferring to stare at her freckled skin than the woman.

"You understand me?"

The girl nodded, reaching up to push her hair back, but it swept forward again, brushing against her shoulder.

"Good, good. My name is Yvonne," the lady said, pointing to her chest.

The girl pointed to herself and lifted her chin slightly in anticipation of learning what she could call herself.

"You are Cassie," Yvonne stated.

"Cassie," she whispered, her finger still on her chest. "Cassie." She smiled. It was fitting. She was a Cassie. "Why am I here?"

"You . . ." Yvonne sighed, moving closer. She sat on the edge of the bed, her eyes full of pity. "Do you want something to eat?"

At the mention of food, Cassie's stomach growled. She nodded, shoving her hair out of her face. Did her face look like Yvonne's? A memory of another caregiver surfaced, but this one was different. She lunged at it, wanting more, but her mind went blank. She shook her head in frustration, annoyed that she couldn't grasp any memories.

No, Yvonne did not look like her mother would have. This woman's skin was a rich bronze, a contrast to her own pale and freckled one. The girl pulled down a strand of hair, noting the soft red color. Yvonne's was nearly black, cascading down her back as she made her way out of the room.

The door closed, leaving Cassie alone again. An aching pain was left behind, the realization that she was missing someone very dear to her.

Cassie scanned the room, annoyed at the stark unfamiliarity of each item. Clattering from the hall drew her forward with curiosity, and she lifted her chin.

Swinging her legs over the bed, a gasp escaped her lungs when her feet hit the cold wooden floors. She shoved the warm and inviting blanket further into the corner and grimaced against each step on the cold flooring.

Following the sounds, Cassie found herself in a space that doubled as the kitchen and dining room. Exhausted from her journey through the halls, she collapsed into a wooden chair. It was flat and hard compared to the bed she had woken up in, providing little comfort. She felt Yvonne's gaze on her but ignored it, allowing her eyes to roam over the walls and counters, with pictures of horses hung in an attempt to brighten up the lonely home. The paint had faded and cracked, yet the passage of time could not dim the beauty of the creatures.

"Horses," Cassie whispered, her fingers stretching out as if they wanted to stroke one. "I like horses." The word was deliciously familiar on her tongue, bringing with it a wave of happiness that rippled down her spine. Horses called out to her in a way that made her certain they were part of the before, and she ached to remember what it felt like to be near them, to brush her fingertips through the silky hair.

Yvonne plated up a simple meal for her. Some scrambled eggs with toast on the side, butter slathered on top.

"How do you feel?" the lady asked, easing into the seat next to her.

"I—I don't know. I try to grasp something in my brain, but it's so empty. Why is it so empty?" Cassie turned her wide, hopeless gaze toward Yvonne. The woman's eyes were warm, a streak of sympathy in them as she placed her hand over Cassie's. It was a kind gesture, enough to start breaking down the wall of uncertainty between them.

"I'm so sorry for what you have been through. I can tell you what I know and help you with anything you need. Unfortunately, I cannot bring back what's lost." They held eye contact for a few moments, and then Yvonne pointed to the food on her plate and commanded her to eat.

"What happened?" It was the appropriate thing to ask. Cassie knew she came from somewhere, and it wasn't here. This place was cold and unfamiliar, and the only things that brought her comfort were the pictures of the noble horses on the walls. They offered windows to another world, the one she came from.

"A ferry travels along the water to bring passengers to the mainland."

"From where?"

"Sparta's Hoof. It's a sizable island off the northwestern coast of Desmalogo. It's part of our country, just separated by a strait."

"And where am I now?" Cassie pointed to the floor of the house.

"We are in Thebesia, the capital of the main island of Desmalogo. Arguably one of the biggest and busiest cities you'll come across. The port is well established and is used to trade with other places." Yvonne's tone was patient, but the slow words grated against Cassie's nerves, frustrating her because of her lack of understanding.

"That doesn't tell me anything."

"The people on the ferry found a body floating in the water and rescued you. The doctors put in a lot of effort to bring you back to life. Throughout all the time you spent in the hospital, the Desmaligan Rangers were unable to discover your identity or where you'd come from. I was asked to take you in and volunteered willingly." Yvonne ended her statement with a soft smile.

"I don't remember being in the water. I don't remember anything." Cassie let out a pent-up sigh, her hands balling into fists. The only thing she did recall was something dark, damp, then a flash of light and being brought to the surface. And now this lady, who appeared kind and reassured her there was nothing to be concerned about. How was that possible, to be expected to live without knowledge of how one appeared in a mysterious place?

"I know. The doctor said your head was severely damaged." Yvonne continued speaking, and Cassie loosened her hands when she caught the lady's gaze on them. "The most probable cause is that you fell off a ship unnoticed. You nearly drowned but stayed alive long enough for the ferry to catch sight of you. I know it's difficult when you have no memories, but I am impressed."

"With what?" Cassie asked bitterly, pushing the plate away. "The fact that the sea spit me out?"

"With how well you understand everything. You must be grateful you have a full understanding. There were worries the brain damage might have negatively affected you. You can talk, communicate with me, and move freely. So many things might have gone wrong." Yvonne let out a deep sigh, her gaze falling to the rough grain of the table. Cassie watched her, taking in the information.

If what the woman said was true, then Cassie was at her mercy.

There was no before; there was only now.

"Cassie, I will do my best to make your life as comfortable as possible, but you will have to cooperate as well. Desmalogo is an amazing place, and soon you will make many friends. You can ride the horses in the fields, maybe even join some competitions. In addition, you are welcome to live with me for as long as you need. Should we discover your family, I'm sure they will be delighted to see you again."

Cassie rubbed her temples, trying to process what was being said. "Is it possible that I might remember?" she asked in a faint whisper, searching the emptiness in her mind.

"It is. The doctor said you might recognize things as time goes on."

"Thank you," Cassie said, picking up her plate. "I need to see as much as I can, because the emptiness in my mind is going to drive me crazy." She deposited her dishes in the sink as Yvonne let out a soft sigh. When Cassie returned to the table, a map was laid out in the center. She scanned the words and symbols, a pout developing on her lips.

"The doctor wanted you to see the map when you awoke, to see if anything is familiar to you."

"No." Cassie stared at the formations scattered on the paper before tearing her eyes away. The black ink had faded from years of use, the paper crinkling at the edges. The map had been drawn many years ago, yet it was so achingly new to her. She longed to see something that would comfort her senses, to remind her of the life she had before this moment.

"I see it will not help us. Instead, we can start by going to the city to shop around," Yvonne stated. She stood, rolling up the aged paper and setting it to the side.

"I'd like that," Cassie affirmed. "We walk?"

"Yes. Horses are the primary method of transport, and with time, you are welcome to get yourself a mount as well. I used to own a horse, but the hassle of taking care of her became too great with my age. I walk to the city as it isn't far, and if I need to go further, I call out a buggy."

Cassie slipped her feet into the shoes pointed out for her, finding them a touch loose but deciding not to complain. She pressed her lips together, noting that none of the items she had seen so far were hers. It reiterated the coldness of the place around her, but the frigid feeling stayed inside the house when she stepped into the sunshine. Her hands flipped upward to soak in the warmth, the simple gesture providing comfort. She kept her palms up as she trudged alongside Yvonne, taking note of the cottages they walked past and taking one final look behind her to imprint their house firmly in her mind.

A young man dressed in a black uniform caught her eye. The indigo and white stripes on his sleeves and back were a heavy contrast against his deep gray jacket, making him easy to identify amongst the passersby. His horse was completely focused on his task, ignoring everyone as he trotted deeper into the city.

"What is he?" Cassie's face lit up at seeing a real horse, not just a picture. The tail flowed just like she imagined it would, the strands dancing in harmony with a slight breeze tugging at them.

"One of the Desmaligan Rangers. They are everywhere and keep the city safe from any harm," Yvonne explained, steering her away. "It isn't polite to bother them unless something is wrong, as they serve as mounted police."

"I want to do that," Cassie whispered, her eyes following the horse and rider until they were out of sight. Withholding a sigh, she caught up to Yvonne's side.

"Ride?" the woman asked, pausing in front of a rustic store. Wide windows allowed natural light to flow freely into the space, inviting Cassie deeper inside.

"Yes, ride," she replied with a nod, her eyes growing distant. Something about a horse, a soft chestnut in color, struck a memory in her mind. A memory she couldn't place or see, but it was there. Not the pale mane and tail—just the orange.

Cassie lifted a strand of her hair, studying the color carefully. Yes, this kind of orange.

"This store has plenty of clothes to choose from. You'll need some things to wear," Yvonne said patiently, swinging open the door.

The girl continued fingering her strand of hair but nodded, stepping inside. A vast array of clothing items met her, the vibrant colors and sheer number overwhelming. Cassie sucked in a short breath, allowing her eyes to take in the sights before a splash of deep green caught her eye. It drew her closer until the fabric was in her hands.

The softness of the hoodie was akin to the blanket on the bed, and she measured it against herself.

"How's this?"

"Suits you well." Yvonne nodded in affirmation. "Anything else you noticed?" she asked, and Cassie squirmed under her watchful examination.

"I don't know. I like green." Cassie stared at the soft fabric in her hands.

Yvonne leaned in, scanning Cassie's eyes. "Matches your eyes nicely. Come along, I'll help you find more."

She followed Yvonne around the store, nodding, shaking

her head, or shrugging at the options presented to her. She found her eyes constantly trailing to the windows on the side of the store hoping for another glimpse of the noble steeds that trotted back and forth with their arched heads.

One side of the store was lined with mirrors instead of windows, and Cassie froze for a moment, catching the reflection of a girl just a hint taller than Yvonne with bright green eyes that seemed unnaturally juxtaposed against her sickly pallor. A neat nose sat above upturned lips, decorated with a dash of freckles. She frowned, the image staying in her head even when she turned away and counted the shiny coins laid out by Yvonne in exchange for her wares.

It was a relief to be outside in the sunshine, and Yvonne took her down a path leading deeper into the city until they reached the city square. A large horse had been sculpted as the centerpiece, smaller models of ships positioned around it to resemble them being at sea.

"The statue was built in honor of Eileen Thetis, the founder of our island. She and her husband . . ." Yvonne trailed off, her gaze moving toward a person standing near the fountain.

An elegant white robe clothed her, leaving her face concealed from prying eyes. Curious glances from the public went ignored by the feminine figure, her stillness akin to the statue.

"Who is that?" Cassie's curiosity was piqued when Yvonne turned away in a rush.

"A member of the Conservation Society of Desmalogo. We mustn't disrupt their work. What do you say we drop off your items, change into something more comfortable, and head to the stables?"

"To the horses?" Cassie grinned, momentarily forgetting about the robed character. "I would like that."

"Yes. To the horses."

"Thebesia Stables are set to the west of the city. We follow the main road until it branches into two, then take the path to the stables. The other leads north toward the ports," Yvonne explained, pointing out the directions. Cassie kept her pace brisk as she walked along the road, staying away from the people milling back and forth. The road changed from neatly placed cobblestone to a dusty and worn path that had seen hundreds of people and horses cross.

Fields spanned the area behind the city, boasting rich soil. The golden-green stalks of young grain waved silently in the wind, beckoning visitors closer to the barn full of horses. Near the stables, they came upon a grove of trees that were planted in neat rows along the walls of the stables and arenas. From the entrance point, Cassie gazed up at the tall metal gates, reading the carved words: "Welcome to Thebesia Stables."

"It's a nice place, don't you think? One of the oldest in Desmalogo." Yvonne smiled, taking the lead further down the path. Cassie slowed, reaching out to brush her fingers against various surfaces: the bark of an ancient tree, flowers growing along the wall, the crisp white fence.

The main barn stood in the center of it all, grand and imposing. Cassie's eyes widened in wonder at the intricate architecture, the attention to detail making it clear just how much the citizens loved their steeds. A grand hall rivaled the size of the barn, windows lining the top and displaying the many housing quarters available to the public. On the other side, a covered arena protected several riders from the sun as they moved through memorized routines.

"Yvonne!" An older man rushed over to them. He had an athletic build and wore a black polo tucked into white pants, indigo boot socks stretching to his knees. "What brings you to the splendor of Thebesia Stables?" His eyes dropped curiously to Cassie.

"Good to see you, Henrik." Yvonne gestured at Cassie. "Cassie here is new to Desmalogo, and we would like to set up some riding lessons for her."

Cassie plastered a smile on her face, awaiting his reply. The horses were too familiar for her to have never ridden, and anticipation sat at the edge of her fingertips, growing with every moment.

"Welcome to Desmalogo, where horses and competition are the drivers of life! Have you ridden before?" His bold voice was obviously used to commanding people. Cassie's eyes fluttered, and her gaze dropped to the ground. She felt that she had, but she had no proof.

"I—I don't remember," she murmured, her fingers curling into fists. Her blank mind offered no support, and she refused to glance up at the nice man lest he see the storm of doubt behind her eyes.

"Cassie, why don't you run down to the barn and meet some of the horses?" Yvonne asked, a smile pressed on her face. "I can work out the details with Henrik here."

Cassie's frown deepened. Being shoved away from the decision made her feel akin to a child. Her being new to the island did not equate to being unable to make her own choices. She wanted to be there and participate in the conversation, to understand where she was.

But arguing with Yvonne, who had done so much for her, was out of the question. Even if the retort was on the tip of her tongue.

Cassie suppressed a sigh as she stepped inside the large building and walked down the aisles, glancing inside each stall. Some were empty; others housed horses munching on their hay.

Something about being there and listening to the horses' sounds was comforting: a grunt, the chewing of hay, a bucket kicked over and its resonating echo throughout the space. It calmed her scattered thoughts, and she was able to arrange them in a straight line.

She liked horses. It was impossible to ignore the growing realization that she had come from a different place and needed to adjust to her new surroundings. But the horses, they offered peace.

Her solitude lasted a few minutes before it was interrupted by a crowd of girls laughing with each other and leading a horse in through the side entrance. Cassie's gaze fixated on the stunning black horse with a kiss of white on his forehead. His still-damp coat shimmered in the midday light, muscles rippling under his skin.

She hardly realized her fingers had stretched out toward the horse, but the group of girls didn't seem to notice, moving away from her and further down into the barn. They settled the horse into a stall and covered him with a light sheet before they disappeared through the back.

The group was cohesive, jabbing at each other and making jokes they all seemed to understand. A pang of home-sickness washed over her, a ridiculous notion since she couldn't remember her home, much less miss it.

A wheelbarrow thumped against the floor near her, and Cassie jumped.

"You look new. Are you from a different city?" A girl leaned on a pitchfork and stared at her from under her base-ball cap, hair messily sticking out the sides. Cassie sucked in a breath.

"Yes." It was an easy enough answer. "I want to learn how to ride." The girl grinned and stuck her hand out. Cassie awkwardly accepted it, unprepared for the firm handshake.

"I'm surprised you don't know how already, unless you mean ride well enough to compete. I'm Mitchie, by the way. I work for Henrik in exchange for room and board at the stables."

"I'm Cassie." She attempted to smile, clasping her hands in front of her. "I will go see if Yvonne is finished talking to that guy. Henrik." Cassie stumbled over her words, rushing away before Mitchie started asking questions about her past. Questions she couldn't answer and didn't want to deal with.

"It was nice meeting you. Hopefully, you'll come again soon!" Mitchie yelled out after her, her confusion coming through in the last few words.

"Cassie!" Henrik called as she walked outside, taking a few steps toward her. "I talked with Yvonne, and this is my offer: you will do some duties around the stables, and as compensation, we can teach you to ride if you want. Then you can be around horses as much as you like. How does that sound?"

"Can I start now?" She breathed the words, flexing her fingers in anticipation.

Yvonne shook her head, casting a disappointing shadow over the glimmer of sunshine. "I've already scheduled your test ride for tomorrow. We'll go home and rest. Then tomorrow bright and early, you can go to the stables."

"Don't worry. The horses will still be here," Henrik said in a light tone.

"Ok." Cassie nodded. She knew he was trying to be kind, but concern gripped her chest as she wondered if tomorrow she would remember the events of the current day.

She waved farewell to Henrik as she followed Yvonne back to their home on the outskirts of the city. Each time she closed her eyes, the soft swirl of windswept tails tugged at her mind, calling her back to the horses.

C assie popped her eyes open as soon as sleep departed, and she cautiously scanned the room. It was the same one as yesterday, and she remembered the events of the day before. She couldn't help her smile as she washed up, greeting Yvonne as she sat at the table.

Memories of something different swirled in her mind, tainted with streaks of indigo lights. They had faded from the day before, settling in the depths of her mind like a shadow.

Yvonne set a plate of oatmeal on the table next to a basket of fresh blueberries. Cassie eyed the soft blue color, a wave of familiarity washing over her. She tossed a handful into her mouth, the sweetness bursting through her senses.

"These are delicious," Cassie murmured, eyes half closed at the flavor. It tasted almost like home and not a strange land. Picking up another handful, she sprinkled them over her oatmeal and finished it off with a drizzle of syrup.

"Blueberries have quite an extensive season here in Desmalogo. These are the first fruits off my bushes and will only get sweeter with summer coming soon." Yvonne placed a cup of milk on the table, and Cassie drank half the glass before setting it down.

"I'll have to taste and see." Cassie grinned, wiping her mouth with a napkin. Yvonne smiled, picking at her smaller portion of food. "Yvonne, is it possible to have a memory of something that happened only in your head?"

A moment of silence ensued, and Cassie looked back and forth between the food and her guardian, the seconds ticking in her mind louder than usual.

"Perhaps like a dream?" Yvonne asked, setting her spoon down, curiosity shining from her eyes.

"Yes. A dream."

"Do you want to share?"

The light prod was all she needed to open up. "Everything was dark, no matter which direction I turned. I was scared until I saw some kind of bright light very, very far away. I moved toward it, but with each step it only became further from me. I started running, desperate to have it in my reach, but it was too far away." Cassie used the blueberries as an excuse to cut off her thoughts, her mouth full with the bright taste. They reminded her of warm sunshine beating down on her, soft grass caressing her bare feet as she ran through a field. The mere thought of running brought back her dream, her legs aching from exertion, her mind screaming in protest. Such feelings she wasn't ready to share.

Yvonne gazed at the wall behind Cassie. "That might be how your head feels about your memories—far away and out of your immediate reach." Her gaze moved back to Cassie, thoughtful.

"You're probably right." Cassie forced a grin, tilting her head to the side. It was a simple enough explanation, and maybe that's where the problem was. Too simple. The light had called out to her, bringing her to the surface from the depths of darkness. "I don't think I would have figured that out myself. Thank you."

Wherever she was now, without the light, was a dark and lonely place. She distracted herself by finishing her food and carrying the plate to the sink, thinking of the beautiful horses instead.

"You will come with me to my lesson?" Cassie asked over her shoulder.

"Of course, dear. The doctors advised me to keep a close eye on you for the first few weeks to make sure you are doing fine. As you might expect, I won't let you go anywhere unsupervised until I'm confident you know your way around the city. After your lesson, we can head to your first doctor's appointment."

Cassie's stomach dropped at the words, her smile wavering.

"Go get dressed. I have this covered." Yvonne ushered her away, and Cassie retreated into her room. She had nearly forgotten that she had to face the doctor today, a casual statement dropped by Yvonne the day before. Would he be kind? She was sure of it, having yet to meet someone that she instantly disliked.

She scanned her new wardrobe and picked out an outfit to match her brown riding boots. Due to the limited selection of boots in the store, hers ended up being a touch too tight, but she couldn't complain. Not when Yvonne had counted out so many drachmas for the purchase.

Cassie tucked a deep green polo into tan pants, pulling on matching boot socks before threading a belt through the loops of the pants. The outfit was made complete with loafers, which Yvonne had explained were much more comfortable for walking. With the boots in hand, she waited patiently for Yvonne to put on her own shoes.

"It's good to see you so happy. I was worried, I'll admit, how you would settle in, but it seems you are doing well." Yvonne shooed her out of the house, turning to lock the door behind her.

"Yes, I'm happy." It was true to an extent, more so when

she stepped into the bright sun. Inside, she still felt cold, but with each second of natural light, the darkness receded.

Cassie walked ahead, pausing at the end of the path leading to the main road. A sense of familiarity washed over her, reminding her of yesterday. Her brain was building memories of this place, easing away the shadows of doubt.

Yvonne tried to keep a conversation, but Cassie was less than interested. She clasped and unclasped her fingers, taking measured breaths as she made her way down the path to the stables, her mind jumping between the horses, her upcoming appointment, and the constant question of who she was before.

"Are you nervous?" Yvonne asked, placing a comforting hand on Cassie's shoulder.

"More excited, really," Cassie said, trying harder to reassure herself. "I love horses." Her voice dipped into a whisper, her words nearly carried away by the spring wind.

"When I was younger, I rode plenty. Nothing in the paddocks, though, as it was too restricting for me. I loved to gallop bareback through the Arion Woodlands. That is the forest northeast of the stables." Yvonne pointed to a canopy of trees hardly visible past all the buildings peeking out from the flat fields surrounding the area.

"What color was your horse?" Cassie asked, giving Yvonne her full attention.

"I had a gray mare. She was a very sweet horse, always sneaking more food than she needed." Yvonne chuckled at the fond memory, glancing around as they walked into the stables of Thebesia.

"I'm still trying to decide what color I like best." Cassie sighed, tossing her head up to look at the sky. Chestnuts seemed to stick out to her, perhaps because they matched her hair.

"The color of a horse is a trivial matter." Henrik's voice was unmistakable, a welcoming smile on his face as he approached the ladies. "Is my new student ready for her first lesson?"

Cassie nodded eagerly, her eyes snagging on the same black horse from the day before. A girl about her age was exercising him in the ring, attempting to go over a set of poles. The black horse snorted, sidestepping and avoiding his rider's commands.

Henrik followed her gaze, shaking his head with a tsk.

"Never mind her. She struggles at times. The girl you met yesterday, Mitchie, can help you get ready." He shooed her off, and Cassie started walking toward the barn, then paused.

"What does it mean when you say the color of a horse is a trivial matter?" she asked as she turned back to him.

"Well, Cassie," Henrik grunted, folding his arms over his chest, "here at Thebesia Stables, we breed horses for performance. The goal is to raise jumpers of the highest quality. So for me, it doesn't matter if they are black or white. If it jumps, it stays."

"Thank you." Cassie treasured each word, mulling over the statement in her head. She didn't want to disagree with someone who knew so much when she couldn't even remember what happened the day before yesterday. But to her, color was very important. Especially if it was the orange that seemed so familiar to her.

Cassie stepped into the barn, and the girl with the baseball cap grinned, waving her over.

"Oh, you came back! That's so exciting! Here, come with me. I will show you the horse you will be riding today!" Mitchie enthusiastically tossed the pitchfork to the side and grabbed Cassie's hand, leaving the girl with no choice but to oblige.

"Isn't Cookies the cutest?" Mitchie squealed, standing in front of a stall.

Cassie nodded. She surveyed him carefully, taking note of his strong, powerful legs. Cookies was tall and handsome, pale brown with black hair, a patch of white on his shoulders. The horse warily glanced at her out of the corner of his eye, then resumed munching his hay.

"The crossties are just over there." Mitchie pointed out the grooming bays. "We can get him stationed and then I'll explain the tools we use to get them cleaned up. There is a halter and lead for you."

Cassie picked up the halter hanging on its hook and set her boots on the floor, then stepped inside the stall. Clipping the lead to the halter, she backed the horse into one of the grooming bays. Mitchie appeared with a caddy filled with brushes.

"This one is the curry comb. Use it first with circular motions, like this." Mitchie slipped the rubber piece with little teeth on her own hand and began demonstrating how to use it.

Cassie smiled, unfazed. She knew what the tools were, but they sat at the edge of her mind out of reach, frustration mounting with every passing moment of not remembering. Mitchie handed her the comb and Cassie brushed vigorously, ignoring the girl's compliment on how well she was doing.

"It loosens the dirt so that the other brushes can take it out of the hair." Mitchie patted Cookies in a comforting way, holding one of the ties in her hand.

"I know," Cassie quipped, moving to the other side of the horse. Mitchie's smile faded slightly, and Cassie feigned not to notice. The comb, as small and unimportant as it seemed, felt as natural to hold as if she had been born with one attached to her hand. It was more than just a familiar object—using it seemed to be ingrained into her very mind. She had no doubt that the stables were where she belonged. Whatever was part of the before, there were many horses. And perhaps Mitchie's assumption was right, that she simply was from another city.

"The next tool we usually use is—"

"I don't know what it's called, but I know what it is,"

Cassie interrupted, rummaging in the bucket until she found the stiff brush and showed it to Mitchie.

"Oh!" Mitchie took a step back, her hands open. "Forgive me if I'm being over-informative. Henrik told me you might need a lot of help because you are a beginner."

Cassie narrowed her gaze, ignoring the urge to roll her eyes. She allowed them to drift toward Mitchie, and a twinge of guilt fluttered in her chest. The girl was only trying to be helpful, and she had cut her off so sharply she might as well have used a knife.

"The tools are not new to me, I just—" Cassie blew out a breath, staring at the brush in her hand. She needed to explain that hovering over her like she was a child was unnecessary. "I had a bad head injury and have forgotten some things. But I didn't forget what they are. My body knows what it's supposed to do, and my brain is left behind. I'm sorry. If I make a mistake, please do correct me." She tossed the brush back into the bucket, sure she wouldn't make any mistakes, and her shoulders relaxed when Mitchie's face softened.

The group of girls from yesterday had all been friends, and Cassie knew she wouldn't make any by being rude.

"I'm sorry to hear that." Mitchie ducked her head, stroking the horse's face and holding him steady with the other hand.

"There's no need." Cassie picked up a soft brush and worked the hair until it shone in the low light. Once the hooves were done, she stared at the horse in front of her. "Where's the—" She grasped at the word just out of reach, pointing to Cookies's back.

"Tack?"

"Yes, tack." Cassie shook her head, annoyed at herself for not being able to remember something so basic and fundamental.

Mitchie led her to a small room, showing her the proper things and naming each one: saddle, numnah, girth, and the bridle with its bit. Cassie watched with fascination, more interested in the kindness of the girl than in the technical names, which her brain picked up after hearing once.

Could Mitchie tell her more about the Rangers, or better, would Mitchie know anything about the figure by the fountain? She seemed to be a reservoir of knowledge, but she might have the same response as Yvonne.

It couldn't hurt to ask, but only when the right moment came.

Cassie shoved the questions away for another time and accepted the helmet Mitchie handed to her, buckling it under her chin and grabbing her boots from their place on the floor and shoving her feet into them. She tightened the laces, then straightened out.

Cassie couldn't contain her grin as she led a fully prepared Cookies down the barn aisle and outside, shadowed by Mitchie. Henrik was waiting for her, talking to the girl with the black horse. The girl gave Cassie a tight smile before moving away.

Henrik opened the gate, a kind expression on his face.

"This first lesson will be private, but we can always put you into a group if you would like that better."

Cassie nodded, fingers wrapped around the soft leather of the reins. She was the last person to know what she'd prefer.

"Thanks for helping her, Mitchie." Henrik nodded at the girl, who grinned and leaned against the fence.

"Is it ok if I watch?" she called out, and it took Cassie a few moments to realize the question was directed at her. She nodded, patting the soft face of the horse next to her. If Mitchie stayed, she could ask her a few questions later. Fingering the lead rope, she waited for Henrik to say she could climb on the horse.

Her hopes shattered at his next sentence.

"Why don't you lead him around the ring? Get to know

each other a bit?" Henrik folded his arms across his chest, one foot propped up behind him on the fence rail.

Cassie glanced around looking for Yvonne and frowned when she was nowhere to be found. Putting her grumbling aside, she led the horse around the ring as asked. The least she could do to show her gratitude for the lesson was obey and ignore her rebellious mind.

"It would help to talk to him," Henrik offered, turning to say something to Mitchie. The girl laughed, drooping over the fence. Cassie glanced sideways at the horse, the frown still there.

"Well, I'll be flat-out honest with you, buddy. I don't have anything to say, because this—" she pointed to her temple "—is about as empty as my stomach before breakfast." The horse ambled along. His ear flicked at her once. "Do you think this is enough 'get to know you' stuff?" Cassie paused in front of Henrik with her nose scrunched up against the direct sun beaming down on her.

"The mounting block is right there. Go for it." Henrik pointed out the plastic block on the other side of the pen, and Cassie led Cookies to the spot, ignoring the two sets of eyes watching her. She refused to ask for help and appear unskilled, gently tugging the horse back and forth before moving the block closer to the horse. Muscle memory kicked in and she hoisted herself into the saddle, a deep sigh escaping her.

Cassie tilted her face toward the sun, eyes closed. For a heartbeat, she remembered doing this before, wind tugging at her hair, sun warming her face. It was enough to make her smile before the thought scurried away to the depths of her mind, out of reach like all the other memories.

Without waiting for Henrik's command, Cassie encouraged Cookies forward, her hands out neatly in front of her, back straight. She relaxed in the saddle, guiding him a few steps to the right, then to the left.

"Your posture is perfect. Keep those heels like that."

Henrik nodded, again turning to Mitchie. Cookies dragged his feet against the sand with a lazy walk.

Cassie clicked him forward, encouraging the horse into a trot, following his movements up and down.

"Very good. Do you know about your diagonals?" Henrik asked, scratching the back of his head. Cassie gave him a blank look, and he explained the concept. Glancing down, she remembered: post to the outside leg.

Once she was comfortable with trotting, she asked Cookies to canter. It was a smooth gait, one that was easy to follow. She noted Henrik shaking his head out of the corner of her eye, an amused smile on his face.

Shifting her attention back to riding, Cassie cut through the ring and switched directions, asking for a lead change. After that, she slowed down, needing some time to process exactly what had happened in the ring. She moved on muscle memory, her mind trailing like a shadow. Her legs knew what to do at the exact moment, but the why behind it was swept away with the wind. Shaking her head in an attempt to reorganize the muddled mess of her thoughts, she rode up to Henrik and Mitchie.

"Where's Yvonne?" Cassie leaned forward, ruffling her horse's hair.

"She said she had some urgent business to attend to. I'm sure she'll be back soon." Henrik pushed away from the fence with a thoughtful face.

"Can I try a jump?" Cassie was unsure but asked anyway. She met Henrik's surprisingly friendly ice-blue eyes, noting how intensely they were analyzing the situation. He appeared bemused that she could ride at all, and Cassie pressed her lips together. It wasn't his fault he assumed a blank mind meant she knew nothing.

"You've ridden before, and you're very good. You might not remember it, but it's there." Henrik patted the neck of the horse.

"I have, yes, but I was struggling at times to keep my balance and felt almost weak."

"I wonder how long you were in the coma before coming to," Henrik mused.

Cassie shrugged in response, knowing the question was not aimed at her but not able to ignore how it grated on her nerves.

"If you come here and ride, Cassie," he continued, "you'll grow very strong, building back everything you must have once worked hard for. Has anything in Desmalogo struck you as familiar?"

"Horses, and that's it. I did a lot of riding before. I realize that now." Cassie sighed. "Blueberries." She turned her face toward the sun since the visor on her helmet kept it mostly out.

"Remember anything about your own horse yet?"

"No. But it wasn't like this one."

"How do you know?"

"Riding feels a little off because of the gaits. I don't know. Can I try a jump?" Cassie lifted a lock of thick black hair from Cookies's mane, straightening it out.

"Sure. I'll get some set up." He turned to Mitchie, who nodded.

"Just one," Cassie said. She knew how to jump, but she simply wanted to capture the feeling of it again, have it tucked away in her memory for her mind to toss around until she got sick of the feeling and moved on to something new.

"Mitchie, grab those two poles." Henrik pointed to a pole striped with lovely indigo, reminding Cassie of her dream again, and Mitchie dragged it across the sand. Cassie kept Cookies moving, allowing him to amble freely without direction.

"How high can Cookies jump?" Cassie frowned at the cross pole that nearly touched the ground in the center point.

"He can go higher, some." Henrik scratched the back of his head.

"Do the highest he can," Cassie countered, encouraging Cookies to pick up a canter. She only had one chance to do this, to prove to herself and Henrik she had done this before.

"You sure?" Henrik called out, his gaze flipping from the jump to the girl on the horse. Cassie nodded, not a trace of doubt in her mind.

Cassie took another loop around the ring and turned squarely toward the jump. She didn't hesitate, and neither did Cookies. Together, they neared the obstacle, his powerful feet pushing off the soft sand to launch them over two wooden poles.

Her smile stretched across her face as Cookies's front feet touched the ground and he collected himself for the next command from her. She loved the feeling of flying through the air more than anything she had encountered yet. The higher the jumps, the more power involved, the freer she felt. Free from the shackles of darkness that threatened to drown her, free from the endless questions that bombarded her.

Cassie rode up to Henrik with a soft smile, kicking her feet out of the stirrups to stretch her ankles back and forth.

"Well, I'll be . . ." Henrik scratched the back of his head. Mitchie grinned, walking up to pat the neck of the slightly sweaty horse.

"You're such a good rider! Here I was thinking you're a noob but turns out you're a pro!" Mitchie was clearly impressed, shoving her hair further under her baseball cap.

"Cookies is nice, but it doesn't really feel like he's mine," Cassie said in a low tone, fingering the reins and hoping she didn't sound ungrateful.

"You'll get a horse," Henrik nodded. "And not just any horse—one good enough to compete with. You have it in you to get to the top with proper training."

His words brought a surge of hope and purpose, throwing

Cassie's mind back over the obstacles set up in the ring. But they were higher, there were more of them, and a fiery orange horse moved in harmony with her. Each jump was tackled with an ease and grace that could only belong to a certain steed, her powerful legs rippling with each step. Cassie's smile stretched wider at the prominent color displayed in her mind, a color only comparable to her hair.

She snapped out of her daydream when Yvonne approached, beaming at Cassie. "Why, you look like you belong on that horse."

"That she does. Tomorrow, Cassie, I'll put you on a more advanced horse. I'm sure you can handle it." He winked. "We can practice more jumping."

"I'm not as strong as I need to be yet," Cassie countered self-critically.

"Naturally, given your long break. We will work at whatever pace you want to set," Henrik reassured her.

Cassie slid off the horse, patting his neck. He nuzzled his face against her, enjoying the attention. He obediently followed her back to the stable to be cleaned up, and Mitchie appeared again. Cassie studied her for a few moments, deciding not to ask about the figure at the fountain just yet. She had a more important task at hand: determining who the horse her mind kept conjuring up was.

It was the most beautiful horse Cassie had never seen.

Chapter

4

Cassie followed Yvonne back to the house, pleased that the woman allowed her to ramble on about her lesson. Had Yvonne not listened, she would have told the passing birds about her happiness, knowing she might burst if she kept it inside.

Yvonne had laid out an appropriate outfit on her bed, making her a quick snack while she changed. Cassie did her best to wash her face and wrangle the mess of hair on her head, smoothing out the top so that it didn't scream "helmet hair." She ate her sandwich as she followed Yvonne into the city for her doctor's appointment, apprehension mounting with each passing step.

"He's a kind man," Yvonne said gently. "You can tell him things that are bothering you. Communication is important for him to know how to best help you."

"Ok." Cassie nodded, schooling her features. It was hard for her to trust anyone, especially when she first met them, but if Yvonne said he could be trusted, she would try to be accepting. This was a doctor, after all.

They headed deeper into the city, passing the tall buildings of Odos Kentriki, the busiest street, before reaching a long, low building with the doors propped open. She stepped ahead of Yvonne, noting a sizable waiting area with a desk in the center and seats on both sides for waiting patients.

It was quiet here compared to the bustling city, instantly leaving her at peace. A lady glanced up from the main desk, colorful beads hanging down from her glasses. They momentarily distracted Cassie as she studied the lady.

"Can I help you, miss?" the woman asked, the beads dancing in rhythm to the movements of her head.

"I'm here for an appointment? I'm Cassie."

"Last name?" The lady picked up a file, her finger going down the list. Cassie gulped, stiffening when Yvonne appeared at her shoulder.

"I don't know." Just when she thought she was getting used to this new environment, this question dumbfounded her. Her response echoed in her brain, rattling it. The number of times she had said those very words in the past two days rivaled every other phrase that crossed her lips.

"She is a special case," Yvonne filled in.

"Well, that's helpful." The lady sighed, then her finger paused. "Ah. I see now." She set the file to the side and stood from the desk, walking around carefully. "I can take you to your room now."

Cassie glanced at Yvonne.

"I can come along or stay here," Yvonne offered, her face truly neutral.

Cassie's fists clenched, and she closed her eyes for a fleeting moment. No, she was not a child. She could do this herself. She bit her lower lip, shaking her head to convey she would be fine by herself.

The receptionist led Cassie down the hall and to a small room. At the lady's command, she clambered up on the exam bed, wringing her hands together nervously.

"The doctor will see you soon." A click of the knob sealed the door shut, leaving the girl alone on the table.

She didn't know why, but the worry crawling through her only increased with each passing moment until she was nearly trembling. The door swung open, making her jump inside. She reminded herself that doctors were here to help, and she had nothing to fear.

"Cassie, hello." A middle-aged man with a white lab coat draped over his shoulders stepped into the room. His dark brown hair was short and neatly combed, sharp hazel eyes taking in the situation. "My name is Dr. Lykaion. How are you doing?" He stretched out his hand, and Cassie gently accepted. His hands were cold, sending another shiver down her spine. "Did Yvonne not come?"

"She's out waiting," Cassie said after she finally found her voice, clasping her hands together again. The doctor glanced over the girl, then settled into a chair a short distance away.

"How is your head? Any pain?"

"No." Cassie swung her legs slightly to get the nervous energy out, forcing another deep breath before continuing. "Sometimes it's hard to think. I can't remember the names of many things, but when someone mentions it, it clicks." She glanced around the bland room with its monochrome walls, then allowed her gaze to meet the doctor's. He was patient with her, and she felt like she could trust him. After all, this was the same doctor who'd done everything he could to make sure she made it alive and well to this moment.

"What about now? Are your new memories holding in place?" His voice was low and gentle, very different from Henrik's. A coaxing voice, encouraging her to speak to him.

"Yes. I have woken up in the same house for two days now. I am recognizing some things, like that I love horses. I dream of the lights only at night." Cassie sighed, pressing her finger against her temples.

"Lights," Dr. Lykaion repeated, leaning forward with a newfound curiosity flickering across his features.

"Yes. Something about my memories, Yvonne thinks. I

don't know. I do know that I want my horse back." Cassie smiled as the familiar orange filled her mind again. The idea of the horse being fictional never even crossed her mind. Her horse was somewhere, she was sure of it.

"You have a horse?"

"Yes."

"Cassie." The doctor sighed, leaning back in the chair, his hands on his knees. "How do you know you have a horse?"

It wasn't until she spoke the words that she was sure, and all the pieces in her mind fell into place. The dreams of something missing, the bright orange color calling out to her. Dead or alive, she'd had a horse before, and now she had to explain to the doctor how she knew.

"The same way you know you once had something you lost. I remember my horse, and I have no other reason to remember having a horse unless I did have one." The words came forth in a hushed whisper, locks of red sweeping forward to cover her face. The doctor nodded.

"Have you adjusted well?"

"Maybe." Cassie shrugged. "I don't have many friends. I don't like telling other people about myself. They don't understand. I don't understand."

At her words, the doctor's eyes softened with a wave of sympathy.

"One day, when you're comfortable, you can meet the Rangers that found you out in the water. Is Yvonne treating you well?" His tone became serious at the mention of Yvonne, and Cassie's head snapped up.

"I guess. I have a place to live, and today we were riding horses in the morning. Well, I was. She left for somewhere but came back for this. She has blueberries though, and I like blueberries. And horses."

"Riding at the stables?" the doctor guessed, and the girl nodded.

"It's a lot of work, but Henrik likes how I ride, and I like it at the barn."

"Good." Dr. Lykaion glanced up at the clock. "I will be right back." He left the room and returned within a few moments, a small box in his hands. "For you."

"A gift?" Cassie gasped, unable to contain her curiosity. The doctor grimaced, handing it to her. The top half of the box opened with a hinge mechanism, and inside the box was a silver chain and locket nestled on a satin pillow.

Cassie was stunned. Fingering the clasp, she pulled the tiny chain necklace out and set the wooden box to the side. Her fingers moved to pop the locket open, which revealed two names etched into either side of the metal. The letters were illegible at first, the words clicking in her head after a few blinks.

"Cassie and Tenille." She whispered the words, clutching the metal close to herself. "Tenille." For a brief moment, a light in her memory flickered. It was her horse, her closest friend, her other half. Without Tenille, she was a hollow chasm.

Somewhere further in the back of her mind, she felt the haziest fragment of a memory. Being with her horse, getting the locket, someone gifting it to her. Why couldn't she remember the details?

"Thank you." Cassie sighed, unclasping the chain and placing it around her neck. She froze, making eye contact with the doctor again. "Where did you find this?" Her voice was laced with suspicion, and she made sure the clasp was firmly in place before letting go. Was it truly hers? It had to be. She was Cassie, and the name Tenille was too close to her own heart to even be questioned.

"It was on you when the ferry captain found you in the water." The doctor's words were slow, his gaze too intense for comfort.

"Oh." Cassie wrapped her fingers around the locket, the small action confirming that it was still there.

The doctor tapped his fingers against each other. "Do you know who Tenille is?"

"My horse. I knew I had a horse, but I don't—" She cut herself off.

"Do you think she could be on this island with you?" Dr. Lykaion asked in a low tone, only receiving the slightest of shrugs from the girl on the bed. Cassie opened the locket and closed it a few times, trying to see if she could trigger any more memories. The doctor observed her for a few moments before changing the subject. "When you saw the necklace, what did you remember?"

"Nothing. I almost did, but my mind is stupidly empty." The doctor seemed taken aback by her harsh words, but he nodded. Cassie clenched her hands together, a rising discomfort at the back of her neck. She wished she did remember something, if only to not disappoint the doctor.

"Interesting. I did want to see if something familiar would spark any memories from the past. Alas, it has not. Now the horse, tell me about her."

Cassie hesitated, then shook her head. She had nothing to share, nothing to tell him yet. She only had a feeling at the edge of her mind, not even a memory to go by. Her horse was just a whirlwind of feelings that she could either spill out to the doctor or wait until she— Wait until what? Perhaps if she told the doctor, he could help her.

"She is someone close to me, a friend like none other." Her eyes swept upward, meeting a steady gaze that managed to assure her it would be alright.

"If she feels the same and is on the island with us, I am sure you will find her." The doctor paused, reaching behind him to get a paper from the desk. "Before I forget, the receptionist mentioned you did not know your last name, which of course you don't. However, you'll need a last name. It will make everything easier. Until we find your real family, I thought it was best to give you my own name, Lykaion."

"Lykaion? As in, Cassie Lykaion?" She tested the combination of names.

"Yes. That way, if anyone has questions, they can come to me."

"Ok." Cassie nodded, hopping off the bed and accepting the paper. As she headed out to where Yvonne was waiting, she had to admit to herself that the check-up did wonders in alleviating her fears.

She simply couldn't decide if she was being too hopeful about her horse or if she should prepare for the worst.

She had only fallen asleep when her eyes opened again, slamming her with the harsh reality that unfamiliarity with her surroundings was becoming a very common feeling for her. This time, she was not in a hospital or house, but outside. A bleary mist spread across the terrain, settling around her. She was lying on the ground, her eyes on the open night sky above. This was not anywhere she had been before.

Scrambling to her feet, Cassie glanced around. Soft grass reached past her waist in every direction, rolling up and down in harmony with the land. Her eyes landed on a barn in the distance, hardly visible in the fog. The warm light flickering from the lamps was the only bright spot in the darkness, enticing her forward.

Cassie started running, the long grass preventing her from picking up speed. A root reached out and grabbed her ankle, tugging her to the ground, hard. Gasping for breath, she picked herself up, trying to orient herself.

The barn had only gotten further away, smaller now than when she had seen it a moment ago. Behind her, she felt the strangest sensation of being pulled toward something. She spun around, and there in the distance stood a horse.

At least, she thought it was a horse. It bore no color or distinctive shape, yet it beckoned to her. The horse-figure shifted almost as much as the grass around it, appearing and disappearing into the layers of misty fog surrounding her.

Cassie took a tentative step closer to the alluring horse, and the grass parted in front of her. She stared at the path opening up, leading her away from the barn and the safety it promised. Cassie broke into a run, grasping at the only familiar thing in this strange land.

Familiar? She tossed her head back at the stars twinkling above her, as if they could give her an answer. Yes, the horse was something close to her own soul.

A shrill whinny split the silence as the horse reared, tossing its powerful hooves into the air. Cassie froze in place, marveling at the sheer sight of the display. The horse seemed to fade out of view for a moment, and she pushed forward again.

Her lungs burned with exertion, her mind screaming in confusion when she was not getting any closer to her horse. She spun around to stare at the barn, heaving deep breaths in the cool night air. The building had not moved, the twinkling lights above laughing at her futile attempts.

Cassie.

The grass whispered her name. Cassie closed her eyes, anticipating its next words.

Cassie.

It wasn't the grass speaking. It was the horse, coaxing her closer.

"I can't." The words slipped past her chapped lips, cold wind tearing her voice away. She could not be heard over the whisperings of nature; speaking was as futile as running. But she couldn't stand the thought of doing nothing and moved toward the horse one last time. Slamming her eyes shut against the lies of the world around her, she ran to the horse, the sound, the call.

Fear gripped her when she opened her eyes, paralyzing her in place. A young man with a hungry smile appeared out of the grass, dragging a dark brown horse along with him. He approached the ghost horse, holding something in his hand.

"No!" Cassie shrieked, pumping her legs against the ground in a desperate attempt to reach the horse before the man did. "Don't touch her!"

The man didn't notice her, creeping closer and closer to the figure of the horse.

"Please." Cassie collapsed on the ground, small rocks digging into her knees. She couldn't run anymore, her lungs burning from the effort of taking in a single breath. "Don't take her."

A cruel hand reached out toward the silhouette of the horse, and the ghost vanished as soon as the man reached out to her. Cassie blinked rapidly as all three figures faded from her view, and the world shifted under her feet. The brilliant flash of light blinded her for a moment, and in the next, she was standing in a barn.

The beams were a breath lower than in Henrik's stables, the stalls wider to accommodate tall, shiny horses. Cassie sighed in relief, rushing toward the one with the whisper of a horse. As she approached, the horse materialized into a beautiful orange mare, the soft glow of moonlight still outlining her.

Cassie smiled and reached out to stroke the soft muzzle, her fingers a hair away from contact when her body was torn away from the dream and slammed back into reality.

Cassie tumbled out of bed, slamming her head against the floor. She yelped, fighting with the covers blocking her sight. Throwing the pillow across the room, she groaned. A dizzy sensation tingled through her body all the way to her fingertips as she attempted to stand and straighten her mind.

The dream from the night before was too real to ignore, nothing compared to the random and shapeless dreams from before. It was more like a vision, showing her where to find her horse.

Fibers of the blanket tickled her legs, reminding her of the tall flora from the dream. She jumped away from the pile of fabric, noting the wooden floorboards of her room. No grass here.

Cassie picked up the pillow and drew the blanket over the bed. No, she remembered that yesterday she spent most of the day at Henrik's barn, riding a horse named Cookies and getting oriented with her work, then went to her first doctor's appointment. She didn't have time to travel anywhere or find magical horses in the dead of night.

But none of the horses at the stable yesterday had felt like her own, and now she knew why. The horse in her dream had been her horse. She was sure of that. Certainly, she was somewhere out there, waiting for her. The chestnut had been too real, too vivid in her mind for the horse to be dead. Not a memory, but a gateway into a different reality.

Cassie swallowed against the strange lump in her throat, remembering how fleeting the image of the horse had been. One moment a ghost, the next materializing into a real horse. Either her mind was playing tricks on her or her horse was truly waiting to be found.

She shivered. She had to identify the source of the dreams to know if the horse was real. Cassie couldn't just ignore her, not if the horse continued to haunt her mind.

Picking up the smells of breakfast wafting from the kitchen, Cassie shoved the dream out of the way, unsure who she could share such an intimate detail with. Yvonne was a possibility, given that she had helped her before, and so was the doctor. He had wanted to know more about her horse, and now she had more to share.

Tenille. Cassie could almost picture her, even though some of the details were still fuzzy. She reached up to the locket wrapped around her neck, comforted for a moment as she made her way down the hallway and to the kitchen.

But a deep thought struck her heart, and she squeezed her eyes shut at the possibility of her horse being dead. She could have died in the accident, leaving only her memory to haunt Cassie.

No, she shoved the thought away again. She had to believe her horse was here and waiting.

"Good morning! I made muffins if you'd like, but I do have a better idea." Yvonne smiled and counted out several silver coins. "I'll give you these drachmas, and you can pick up breakfast at one of the many vendors around the city square. I can come with you if you wish, or you can go alone if you feel comfortable enough."

"Thank you." Cassie's fingers wrapped around the drachmas, her mind conjuring a mental map of the city. "I think I'll be fine on my own, thank you." Her lips stretched into a hesitant smile as she picked up one of the muffins, taking a careful bite while heading toward the door and finding her shoes. The crumbs were tasteless in her mouth, and she squashed the rest of it into her pocket.

Cassie closed her eyes and opened the door. Carefully peeling one eye open then the other, she breathed a sigh of relief. No stranger was waiting to catch her like he had been trying to catch the horse. The house had not moved, the street was still the same, all visual cues pointing to the fact that she was still in Thebesia.

She headed deep into the city, taking the road that led away from the stables. In the center of the city, a statue of a tree rose up from a fountain, the bubbling water hardly heard over the chatter of people and clip-clop of hooves on cobblestone. Cassie sniffed the air, picking up the mesmerizing smells of breakfast being made throughout several stalls placed strategically with crowds forming around each one.

Horses were tied to the side, a black one catching her eye. She wasn't sure, but he seemed to be the same one she had seen several times at the stables. He tossed his head nervously against the reins that held him to the post.

Cassie walked toward the closest food vendor, squinting her eyes to read the hand-scrawled menu up on a board. Making no sense of it, she stood in line and waited her turn. A girl that looked slightly older than her poked her head out of the window, a half smile on her face.

"What'll it be?"

"Um." Cassie hesitated, fingering her drachmas. "I don't know. Maybe you could recommend something for me?"

The girl sighed but nodded. "Alright, our most popular item is the flatcake with berries and cream. Does that sound ok?"

"I like blueberries." Cassie shrugged and offered a handful of coins. The girl counted some out, then gave the rest back to her.

"Go have a seat at one of the tables, and we'll bring it right out." The girl waved her hand dismissively, and Cassie walked off, picking a table close to the street. She fiddled with the edge of her sleeve, ever watchful of her surroundings. Several girls sat at a table a few rows down, faces she recognized from Thebesia Stables. People and horses bustled nearby, no doubt on their first errands of the day.

Two matching horses trotted by, their heads held high. Cassie's eyes dipped to the coordinating jackets of the riders, dark with the colors of the Desmaligan flag tied around their upper arms and sewn onto their backs. The two riders were deep in conversation, not acknowledging the people who moved out of their way or tentatively greeted them. She sighed wistfully, wondering if either of them rescued her from the water.

"Here you go, miss. And I threw in a lemonade, too, since the last customer changed her mind and I didn't want to throw it out." The girl set a plate piled high with steaming flatcakes on the table. The drink had blueberry syrup on the bottom starting to swirl with the bright lemonade and leaving tinges of indigo between the two colors. "Besides, you said you like blueberries."

"I love blueberries. Thank you." She tore her eyes away from the indigo color of the drink and used a straw to fully mix the liquid. It reminded her too much of the lights from her dreams, sending a tremor through her.

"When you're done, just bring the dishes to the back." The girl had a bright smile, and she left to continue her work.

Cassie picked up a flatcake with her fingers, making sure it had ample berries and cream on it. She sighed deeply after taking a bite, savoring the flawlessly combined flavors. Crispy edges were freshly fried and softened by the light and airy cream.

Wrapping her fingers around the cold glass, she took a tentative sip before downing half the lemonade. It was the most refreshing drink she had tried, tart lemons blending with the bright sweetness of blueberries, reminiscent of the sun and cooling shadows.

She made a mental note to thank Yvonne for the drachmas and for the recommendation to eat here. Oatmeal was good, of course, but it paled in comparison to such rich foods as the ones on her plate. And the lemonade! It tasted like sweetened sunshine in a glass, encased for her enjoyment.

Cassie slumped against her chair, half the stack of flat-cakes untouched on the plate. The black horse whinnied in distress, tossing his head back against the loosely tied reins. She scanned the tables, not finding a single person who seemed to notice the nervous horse. He pawed the ground, then kicked his feet up into a rear, the sudden action causing the reins to snap.

"Kismet!" The shriek echoed between the buildings, and one of the girls from several tables down leapt into the air, her eyes wide with horror as the black horse tore away from the post and charged down the city street, reins flapping and his hair catching in the wind. The girl ran to wave down a Ranger, but Cassie wasted no time. She sprung from her chair, dodging several people in her pursuit of the black gelding.

"Kismet, come back here!" The voice rang out, but Cassie ignored it as she pushed herself to run faster. Her legs pumped to the same rhythm as they did in her dream, but this time, no one tripped her and the buildings moved past her. She tried whistling to get the horse's attention, but he paid no mind, tail raised high as he dodged another crowd.

The main road stretched out further, with several horses heading into the center of the city. Kismet swerved to the right into a narrower street, then ran himself into a compact alleyway. Cassie skidded to a stop right in front of the alley-way, her heart pounding as the horse halted in the dead end. A fence blocked his way, too high to jump over. The horse eyed it, snorting against the barrier in his path. He turned and tossed his elegant head, rearing up toward the sky.

"Steady boy." Cassie spread her arms out in front of her, inching closer to the horse.

"He went this way," a masculine voice called out, and someone approached from behind Cassie. It must have been the Ranger the girl waved down earlier. She ignored him, prolonging eye contact with the horse. He tossed his head again, his rear half-hearted as his hooves landed against the cobblestone with a resounding clop. His eyes didn't show any white, and the slow movement indicated he wasn't too worked up, most likely having spooked himself when he tugged the reins free.

"Steady," Cassie repeated in a low tone, closing the distance between them with each step. The horse backed away until his hindquarters bumped up against the fence, still-ing. "There's no need to run. Here, I have something for you." She retrieved the half-squashed bran muffin from her pocket, holding it out like a peace offering. His nostrils quivered with curiosity at the scent of fresh bran, ears flicking forward.

A low nicker rumbled in his throat as he lowered his head in response to Cassie's outstretched arm. She was surprised when he pressed his head against her, asking for a pat as he chomped away at the muffin, his sticky tongue catching some crumbs and knocking the rest to the ground. Cassie giggled, scratching the tiny white patch on his forehead.

"Aren't you stunning?" Cassie whispered, patting his cheek as her fingers moved up to grip the reins dragging along the ground. He didn't seem to mind, nibbling on her shirt in search of more treats. Only when the leather was securely in her hand did she tilt her body to face the people at the entrance to the alley. A Ranger leaned on his horse, the girl who had originally called him Kismet by his side. She had dark brown hair straighter than a fence board that swept down to her waist. It was the same color as her eyes, complementing her sun-kissed skin effortlessly. Between her crossed arms and set facial expression, Cassie did not know if the girl was pleased or annoyed. The girl muttered something under her breath, and the Ranger's mouth hitched into a smile.

"Say, do you know this horse?" he called out, slowly moving toward the two.

"I don't know." Cassie swept her gaze across the gleaming black gelding, gauging his reaction to the Ranger coming closer. The horse was still unbothered. He was a sense of comfort to Cassie, her hand on his neck and the specific white patch on his forehead triggering a blank memory in her mind. Had she known a horse similar to this one before?

"His name is Kiss Me Kismet. I'm Selene. I don't think we've— Oh!" The girl's eyes brightened. "No, I do know you. You're that new girl at the stables."

"I think my work here is done. Keep a tighter rein on him, Selene." The Ranger tipped his hat and spun his horse around to exit the alley. He showed no signs of recognizing her, leaving Cassie to deduce that he was not involved in the search party for her family.

"Thank you, I'll try." Selene smiled, then turned to Cassie again. "What stables did you ride for before transferring to Thebesia?"

It was an innocent enough question, but not one she was willing to answer. She forced a smile as she fiddled with the reins. "I don't know." Kismet bumped his face against her, and Cassie's smile tipped to something more genuine.

She faced the waiting Selene and handed her the reins, rolling her shoulders back against the knots building up. Questions like these couldn't be avoided forever, not if she wanted to make friends while being on this island.

"A couple days ago I woke up from a coma. I got into

some kind of accident and it damaged my head, and I really don't remember much." Cassie stared at the ground, surprised when Selene placed a hand on her arm.

"I'm sorry. I didn't know. There was a lot of gossip going around, but it— Never mind that. It makes sense now. You truly do have a way with horses, you know that?"

"Maybe." Cassie shrugged, inching away from the conversation. "So far, they've been easier to deal with than people."

"You do." Selene laughed, the sound surprisingly warm. "I really appreciate you catching him. Maybe now my father will send him back to the cursed place he came from."

"Why?" Cassie gasped, stopping dead in her tracks. "He's one of the most beautiful horses I've seen yet."

"Perhaps. But it doesn't change the fact that we don't get along."

"Maybe you need to adjust your training. I think—it would be a mistake to let him go." Cassie kept her voice low.

"I'll consider it. Do you need a ride to the stables?" Selene pressed her lips together, and Cassie hid a grin when she realized she was not the only one avoiding certain topics.

"I haven't finished my food yet. I can walk."

"I didn't either. What do you say we go and finish our breakfast, then we can double to the stables? Oh, and when we get there, I'd love to see your horse." Selene's gleaming smile only served to increase the sinking feeling inside Cassie.

"I don't—" She sighed, rubbing her temples. "We can double to the stables, but I don't have my horse with me."

"Oh." Selene opened her mouth to ask another question, and Cassie stared at the ground. Nothing could compare to the relief that washed over her when Selene didn't say anything further and mounted her horse instead. Cassie accepted her hand and climbed on behind her, her legs wrapping around the barrel of the horse.

The street they exited to was sizable compared to the cramped alleyway, yet it only served to provoke the gelding.

He tossed his head, fighting nearly every command given to him by his rider. Cassie stayed silent, not wanting to say something that would harm whatever tenuous friendship had formed between her and Selene. She found a desire to laugh like Selene did, to act as if she wasn't constantly plagued by wondering what the right thing to do was. After a moment of contemplating, Cassie spoke up.

"I don't remember a lot after the accident, but I do know that my horse was separated from me." Cassie swallowed tightly, appreciating the fact that Selene was busy with her own thoughts and didn't prod. "She might be somewhere on this island."

"I'm sure you'll find her." Selene stopped the gelding in front of the post, allowing Cassie to dismount first.

"Thanks." She smiled, making her way to her now-cold flatcakes.

Cassie thanked Selene one more time, sliding off the horse and stepping inside the shady interior of the stable. Henrik was busy conversing with someone else but made his way over to her when he saw her, frowning at a patch of wayward straw in the center of the aisle.

"Cassie!" He grinned, his hands clasped together. "Do I have a surprise for you!"

"For me?" Cassie echoed.

"Yes, yes. Come." He waved his hand, and Cassie followed, her curiosity piqued at the stable owner's excitement.

They turned toward a quieter wing, darker, with the lights hanging low.

"What do you think?" Henrik patted the inhabitant of the stall, a smile stretched across his face. A horse nibbled at the hay net, his big brown eyes shifting to watch the people invading his space.

"He's beautiful," Cassie whispered. His coat was the color of a flatcake, a dollop of whipped cream dripping down his forehead. Shiny black hair cascaded down his neck, flowing back and forth as he shook himself. With a swing of his elegant head, he turned to sniff at Cassie.

"They call him Denny at the stables, but his show name is Denny's Rhythm. He's eight years old, still in training but incredibly talented. I purchased him several weeks ago for one of my top riders to show him this season. But then—" Henrik turned toward Cassie. "There's you. What do you say—you think you two could get along?"

Cassie hesitated, her thoughts on the orange mare, the one she couldn't fully picture, the one she couldn't place. Her eyes flitted from Henrik to the horse, knowing this was a grand opportunity but unable to fully jump in.

"Is it possible to have more than one horse at a time?" Her voice wavered, and Henrik stepped closer.

"Of course, many of my riders keep multiple horses. Was there another one you liked?" Denny poked his head over the stall, arching it slightly.

"My own horse," Cassie whispered. "If I find her."

"Ah. You remembered?"

"Something like that." She leaned forward and pressed a gentle kiss on the horse's soft muzzle. His breath came out in a snort, an ear flicked. Long lashes framed his brown eyes, the grace and gentleness around him making it impossible for Cassie to dislike him.

"I got him settled back here for the first day while he adjusts. We're a little busier than Aetherpolis where he came from, less of a racket there." Henrik shook his head, amused. He picked up a halter from a nearby hook and handed it to Cassie. "Off you go."

Hardly able to suppress her smile, Cassie stepped into the

stall and gently fitted the halter over the golden-brown head. She wondered what she would do with two whole horses. It would take so much time to be with both that she might end up living at the barn instead of with Yvonne.

Henrik followed at a distance as Cassie led the tall gelding into the main barn area and backed him into a grooming bay. He was nearly spotless already, but she quickly brushed him down.

"His saddle and bridle are labeled with his name, any numnah will do. Oh, and boots please," Henrik commanded, stopping in front of the horse and patting his head.

Cassie nodded. She would have run to the tack room but knew plenty of horses spooked easily. Taking the necessary items, she dodged a few girls and their questions about Denny on her way back to the horse. It only took a few minutes to get him ready, and Cassie led him down to the ring, Henrik shadowing her. He held open the gate to one of the smaller riding rings.

Instead of stepping inside with her, Henrik closed the gate and leaned against it, a smirk tugging the side of his mouth. Cassie led Denny toward the mounting block in the center and climbed up. Turning Denny toward Henrik, she waited.

"Go on." Henrik encouraged, chuckling to himself. "Try him out, however you feel necessary."

Cassie dipped her shoulder, adjusting her position. Nudging the horse forward, she was instantly impressed by his smooth gait. His movements were fluid and graceful, his gait flowing like a river from one to the other. Denny kept flicking his ears toward the fields behind the barn, fighting the bit at times.

"He's getting distracted, and we can't allow that. If he goes to a new place for a show, we can't allow him to be preoccupied as it will ruin his performance!" Henrik called out. Cassie spared a glance in his direction. He had climbed the fence and was balancing on the top board.

Her focus back on the horse, Cassie tried to find contact again. Denny was young, and his attention span was almost as short as hers. She constantly needed to remind him to keep his pace, and in doing so, reminded herself about it as well.

She pressed for a canter, satisfied that he picked up the correct lead. His ears flicked toward her words of praise as he strived to please his rider. Cassie leaned back in the saddle, relaxing slightly, and Denny slowed to a trot, his rhythmic two-beat pattern soft against the raked sand.

"Much better. He gets bored easily, so you need to engage with him or else he will float off somewhere and forget what he's supposed to be doing. But he was trained very well. I'm impressed."

Cassie jerked her head in Henrik's direction, having forgotten he was there. She nodded, slowing down near Henrik. Riding Denny was like getting lost in a forest without a need to be found. The world had been shut out only to be brought back in when the ride came to an end.

"I am too. He listens very well." Cassie leaned down to pat his sleek neck, then kicked him forward. They circled the ring a few more times, alternating between a figure-eight pattern and simply going around the perimeter. After trying out a circle in a trot, she brought Denny to a stop next to Henrik.

"Could we try a jump? He'd do beautifully," Cassie pleaded. One jump, and she'd be happy.

"I don't argue against that, but not today. You must build up a solid foundation before going anywhere." Henrik squinted up at her through the sun. Cassie nodded, hiding her disappointment. "Cool him off for about a quarter hour, then we can get him settled into a stall. There will be another day for jumping."

Cassie fingered the reins, nudging the horse forward. Denny picked up his feet lazily, wandering over to Henrik instead of around the ring like he was asked. Henrik patted the horse's head, one hand holding the side of the horse's bridle.

"You did very well. I'll go as far as to say you might be one of the most talented riders I've trained." Henrik sounded proud of her, and Cassie smiled as she turned to face him.

"Thank you," she finally whispered.

"We have about two weeks until show jumping season starts, and you both need to be in tippy-top shape to compete. If that's what you want." Henrik finished his statement with another glance at the girl, still stroking the golden horse.

"Compete." Cassie wrinkled her nose, trying to imagine what that would be like.

"The first one is always held in Vallumvis. They wouldn't have it any other way. All the riders, representing their barns, go against the same course. The fastest without faults takes home a trophy and prize money. A hefty sum of drachmas." Henrik said each word slowly, and Cassie allowed them to seep into her brain. She flipped them over in her head, weighing her options.

Expanding her horizons beyond Thebesia could mean unlocking a memory if she had come from a different city. She was tired of the emptiness, and even though the past few days were nothing but perfect, she couldn't ignore the questions about where she was from or what had truly happened to her. Better yet, Rangers from another city could answer her questions.

Henrik was watching her carefully, and Cassie nodded, her hair swinging back and forth underneath her helmet.

"Yeah, I think I'd like that."

Chapter

6

Taven Thespios considered it an honor to be selected to help with the shows on the island of Desmalogo. He jumped at each chance he got to visit a new city, every opportunity to work with different stations. The show season was limited, starting when the weather cleared up and the racetrack finalized its championship. He had no idea why the horses were raced in the rain, but he understood that the citizens of Desmalogo did not want to be forced to choose between visiting a race and visiting a jumping show.

Smaller ones, of course, were held at liberty, most often sporting the youngest of riders to give them some undivided, albeit limited, attention. Even those he would willingly help set up and take down, anything to be of assistance.

Instead, the letter dropped off at his door that morning confused him more than the lack of instruction regarding the shows. He made his way down the main street of Thebesia, stopping in front of the large building that served as the head-quarters for District One. Each district had no more than three stations, with one chosen as a head. All heads reported to the Proedros, who currently resided at Vallumvis.

Leaving his mount outside, he headed into the old building, the well-oiled doors slamming silently behind him. It was empty most days, the Rangers being out and about for their duties. Luke Katsaros, Head Ranger of District One, stood when he entered the office.

"Thespios. I appreciate you arriving on such short notice." His handshake was firm, then he settled back into his desk, pulling out a file. It was new, beautifully smooth and without the crinkles that came with being handled many times. Taven's interest was piqued. "How has Arion been treating you?" It was more of a statement than a question. Luke knew him too well to care about the response.

"Well enough, though you know I am not there most days."

"Correct. You've always been keen on running around elsewhere."

"And you wouldn't have it any other away." Taven lowered his voice, not wanting to come across as disrespectful. More often than not, he was Luke's choice to run errands despite being placed in Arion due to the Thebesian station being full.

"Taven, you're suited fine where you are at." Luke paused and pushed the file across the desk while keeping a finger on it. "Something's come up that I think I can trust you with. Instead of you dilly-dallying at Vallumvis next weekend, I have a better assignment for you." Luke met his gaze, and Taven straightened out, hands clasping behind his back.

"Yes, sir."

"We have received a complaint about a horse on the loose," Luke began, flipping the file open. The stack of papers was smaller than expected, and Taven couldn't help but lean forward to glimpse the words written inside. "There are a few discrepancies that do not sit well with me. First, there is very little information submitted on what kind of horse this is. Says here, 'chestnut mare with white legs.' That was the first detail that caught my eye. Dozens of horses at each stable fit this description. But whatever, that doesn't bother me much. I have no copy of the pedigree, and when I requested it, I was told there was none. Now how do you have a horse without a pedigree? It's more important than our birth certificates." Luke scoffed.

"Either she was purchased illegally, or the details were lost, or—" Taven racked his brain, trying to find a suitable answer for the missing information.

"Or she is simply not from this island. Wouldn't be the first time a horse was snuck in." Luke had a stoic face, handing the file to Taven. His eyes scanned the paper, landing on the name of who had submitted the report: Reginald Xiphias.

"The jockey?"

Luke nodded.

"Sounds a little shady."

"My thoughts as well. Therefore, you'll go investigate the matter. If he is abusing the system and trying to sneak a horse into Desmalogo, the report was a stupid idea. Sounds to me like he's trying to throw us into a vain pursuit." Luke paused, his light eyes narrowing. "Edmunds thought it would be best to have someone outside of Vallumvis investigate this, privately. I don't need any distractions for the Rangers."

"Agreed," Taven said firmly. "With the general public flooding toward the city for the event, we need as many as we can patrolling the show instead of running around aimlessly."

Luke nodded. "Precisely. I knew you would understand."

Taven hid a smile, swelling with pride. Of all the Rangers, Luke asked him to do this, meaning he trusted him. District Two, Vallumvis, only had a single station, but it was so big it could have been split in half and was considered the most prestigious place a Ranger could be accepted into.

"The Vallumvis Rangers will expect you tonight. I told them you'll be an extra pair of hands for any fillers they need. I will be quite busy with the Dasos Academy interns. They will make up the brunt of the workforce, so I will have my schedule full. I expect you to make most decisions yourself.

Now, unless you have more questions, I suggest you make preparations to leave."

"Yes, sir." Taven left the office before he could break into a smile in front of his boss. Not only was he put in charge of an investigation, he was explicitly told not to bother Luke, which was another way of saying Luke trusted him enough to handle this on his own.

Rophon, his mount, nickered when his rider walked outside. Taven scratched the gelding's forehead, finding his thoughts wandering to the last time an uninvited guest appeared in Desmalogo. He considered the community of each city tightly knit, most people knowing each other by name. Even in the great capital of Thebesia, the events were set in place to forge bonds between citizens. But that girl had lain on that bed, unrecognizable. Not a single soul who walked past could identify her, and no reports for a missing girl had been filed. Was she also from outside Desmalogo? It was the only reasonable answer.

Unlike the horse, she had been real, tangible, half dead. The doctor had never followed up with him on her, and most likely she was still in a coma. Taven sighed, running a hand through his light brown hair before placing the cap firmly on his head. It had been two weeks since Luke had allowed him to check with the doctor about updates, and he'd had none. Taven couldn't leave the matter, though, and needed to know if the girl had woken up.

The hospital was as stoic as ever, the old building greeting him with surprising warmth as he sought out the doctor at hand.

"Taven Thespios, District One Ranger." Dr. Lykaion waved off the formal introduction and led him to his office.

"You're not that forgettable. What brings you in today?"

"Nothing work related, actually," Taven admitted, fingers gripping his hat. "I wanted to ask if there were updates on the girl found in the water."

"Ah. Cassie." Dr. Lykaion steepled his fingers, his eyebrows pinching together. "Yes, she is doing better."

"Has she awoken?" The question escaped his lips, his fingers holding his hat so hard they were sure to leave a mark. The doctor hardly blinked at the unbidden question, gently sliding a file to the side of his desk.

"Taven, I appreciate the concern you have for my patient."

He backed away a few steps, dipping his head.

"I understand. Thank you." He turned to go, but the doctor's voice stopped him at the door.

"I remember the accident with your sister well, Taven."

The mention of his sister sent a tremor through him, and he swallowed tightly.

"I know you see the matter of Cassie as something personal. When the girl is ready to have a conversation, I will be sure to contact you."

"Thank you." He couldn't manage more than that past the lump in his throat, so he shoved his hat back on his head, tipped it at the doctor, then distanced himself from the hospital and the memories it held.

Taven swung by his apartment and picked up a few essentials, then headed out of the city along the all too familiar road through the Arion Woodlands.

Truth be told, he still wasn't sure how he ended up there, training for years at the Academy to be a Ranger in Thebesia. He had always counted on being in Thebesia, and though his work often carried him there, the forest still felt constricting.

The river flowed at his side, a fish jumping out of the water to taunt him. He forced a wry smile, glad when the road and river separated.

Taven reached into his pack and pulled out an apple, eating half of it, then leaning forward and offering the other half to his horse. Rophon turned his neck and accepted the gift, chomping away happily as he trotted toward the passage in the mountains. His horse knew the road quite well, both taking as many shortcuts as they could to get there faster. The sun was nearly setting when they reached the only Ranger station in Vallumvis, a massive building that could house dozens of horses and riders at once. The assigned Rangers even had their own personal grooms, something unheard of at other stations.

"I'll take care of my own horse, thank you." Taven waved away one of the grooms, who frowned. Ignoring him, Taven led his gelding to an empty stable, removing the tack and carrying it to the designated locker. He found some brushes and rubbed down his horse, fitting him with a light sheet before heading toward the main room.

Edmunds was supposed to head the station here, but with him getting on in years, fierce competition had sprung up to determine who would replace him. Several hopeful candidates greeted Taven as he entered, introducing themselves. The Proedros himself appointed the heads for the station based on recommendations or complaints made by other Rangers. And it was no secret that Taven and Luke had a closer friendship than most Rangers and that Luke tended to influence Edmunds more than the other heads.

Taven grabbed a dinner plate, scanning the dining room for options of where to sit. The Proedros was sitting at a table in the far corner of the room, and Taven took a gamble by sitting next to him.

It made sense that Edmunds was waiting for him, Taven's hunch confirmed when the old man greeted him warmly.

"Taven, good to see you." Edmunds smiled, his eyes framed by tanned wrinkles. "Luke told me you were coming."

"Yes, sir. Happy to be of service." Taven dipped his chin respectfully.

"I hope he made it clear that this needs to be kept away from my Rangers. Reginald is a popular man, more so as he is expected to take the championship win tomorrow, and I have no desire to create division within my ranks."

"I understand." Taven's voice was steady, unaffected by his escalating heart rate.

"Here is a rundown of the situation. About a month ago, Reginald Xiphias visited Sparta's Hoof. He returned with a wild horse that he claimed he found on the plains there, gloating about how he was hardly able to wrangle her down. He also claimed that he had asked around at all the local settlements, looking for an owner, and everyone he spoke with pronounced the horse as unfamiliar. Upon arriving back home, he took her down to the racetrack and confined 'the demoness,' as he called her, to a stall. A week ago, I believe, he made the mistake of taking her out for a run. Before this, she was lightly exercised by hand but mostly kept inside. As you can probably imagine, he was thrown off and she ran away. He filed a report for the missing horse, which I assume Luke showed you, and threatened one of my Rangers about the consequences of not finding her. Of course, I have spoken to him about that. Your task will be to find the horse and determine its origin. If indeed no one claims it, Reginald will need to register her with the Desmaligan Archives for record-keeping and obtain official paperwork of ownership. He should have done this beforehand, alas." Edmunds waved a tired hand. "I just see this all as a waste of time."

All those years of academy training proved useful as Taven maintained an even expression and tone in his reply, ignoring the hurt of Edmunds's last statement. Edmunds simply needed a useless Ranger to fill a useless role.

"I assure you, sir, the horse will be found, and the situation dealt with. It will also be kept under wraps, as you wish."

Chapter

7

It was the crack of dawn, the sun not quite ready to make its appearance for the day. Cassie strolled toward the stables, stifling a yawn. Sleep had evaded her over the excitement of her new horse. Not hers, really, but one she was entrusted to ride.

The stables were a little quieter than Cassie expected for a weekend, and she caught sight of Mitchie entering the feed room with her hands full. Walking past the rows of stalls, she stopped in front of Kismet and watched the stormy gelding munch through his hay. The mare next to him seemed to be more interested in receiving human affection, and Cassie moved to the side, stroking the face of the horse gently.

"Morning, Cassie!" Mitchie sang as she walked by, oats rattling at the bottom of the bucket.

"Morning," Cassie mumbled back, moving toward the back of the barn where Denny was sheltered. His stall had less natural light flowing in, the darker atmosphere relaxing her nerves. She stopped when she heard Henrik and Selene talking around the corner.

"—someone to be her friend as she has no one," Henrik finished in a low voice, and Selene huffed.

"Very well." She tucked her hands into her back pockets, her eyes on Denny. Cassie waited a few more moments, then joined them at the stall.

"Hello, Henrik," Cassie stated, her attention on the golden-brown horse in front of her.

"How are you doing?" he asked politely in turn, his gaze shifting between Selene and Cassie.

"Fine, thank you."

"Selene here wanted to invite you someplace," Henrik continued with a pointed look at Selene. The girl smoothed out her facial expression, a slight smile appearing on her lips.

"Cassie, yes. Some of us girls are heading to Vallumvis to watch the last race of the season. Would you like to come with us? That way you can visit the city and will feel more comfortable next week when we show."

"Yes." Cassie clasped her hands tightly behind her back, schooling her expression to hide the giddiness building up inside of her. She would get to see more of the island and perhaps even uncover some details about herself. The invitation was too special for her to care that Henrik had prodded Selene into it. The girl hadn't seemed against it, and they could find something in common if they chatted more.

"Henrik?" Selene called out. "Do you have a spare horse?"

"Well . . ." Henrik scratched the back of his head. "Denny is due for a visit with the vet. You can take Athena, just don't overwork her."

"Thank you." Selene smiled. She headed down the barn aisle with Cassie following and stopped in front of a stall housing a lovely bay mare. "Get her ready."

Selene walked off with a toss of her dark hair, calling out for Mitchie. The groom stepped out of the feed room at the command to tack up Kismet. Cassie brushed her borrowed horse down, her attention on how Selene snapped at Mitchie for any minor mistake.

Part of it was Kismet's fault, not being able to stand still for more than a few moments at a time. Kiss Me Kismet. Something about the name triggered a hazy memory, and again, the ridiculous thought that she might have known this horse from before crossed her mind.

She shoved it away quickly, placing a saddle over Athena's back. She had no use entertaining silly thoughts. There was no way she could have known Kismet if he lived on the island since she had only been here for a short while. If Selene did not recognize her, her horse must simply be similar to one she'd known before.

Athena and Kismet were ready at the same time, and Cassie led her horse out to the yard. Even though she had not ridden her before, the horse was well trained and used to many different riders, chomping on her bit as Cassie settled herself into the saddle. Two other girls were waiting with their horses, and Cassie briefly greeted them. With a wave at Henrik, they rode away from Thebesia Stables.

"You've never been to Vallumvis before?" Selene broke the silence, pushing her horse into a brisker pace.

"Not that I remember." Cassie sighed, her horse matching Kismet's speed. She stuck to the back of the group, where only Selene was close enough to speak to. The other two girls chatted between themselves a few paces ahead, not bothering to include Cassie in their conversation.

"Ah. About that. If we hurry, we might make it to the prerace parade."

The group traveled through the city of Thebesia, following a path that led them into the beginnings of a forest. Selene explained that this was the Arion Woodlands, public land belonging to the government of Thebesia.

"There are two Ranger stations in District One, plus an office in the center of Thebesia. One is on the outskirts of the city, and the other is further in the forest. It's very peaceful here." Selene droned on about the forest. Cassie found herself tuning out the sounds of chatter, admiring the trees with their low-hanging cover and soft greens throughout.

The trees began to space out, and looming mountains peeked through the foliage above their heads.

"We're going there?" Cassie pointed at the wall of mountains that appeared. Selene kicked Kismet into a smooth canter after the rest of the girls, gesturing at a gap between two mountain peaks.

"That's the road to get across. It's relatively flat. Funny though." She turned Cassie's attention to the tall mountain a short distance away from the gaping valley. "That's the tallest mountain in Desmalogo: Thebesia's Crown."

The passage through was uneventful, the sure-footed horses knowing the path well.

"Anywhere to stop for water?" Cassie asked, scanning the sweat lathering up on her horse. Beyond the semblance of a town ahead of them, a tall iron fence surrounded a glamorous city.

"I don't want to stop here." Selene flicked her eyes toward the small houses standing away from the road. "We're almost at Vallumvis. The stable there is lovely. In fact, I think their stable might be bigger than Henrik's."

"Bigger?" Cassie breathed the word. Thebesia Stables rivaled everything within sight with its splendor and glamor.

"And there's a second stable just for the racetrack." Selene laughed at Cassie's incredulous facial expression and picked up the pace until they reached the iron fence. She slowed to a walk along the fence, allowing the horses to catch their breath.

"The city is surrounded by a fence all the way around it?" Cassie asked, squinting through the bars at the pastures close by. In the distance were the stables Selene had mentioned. If they were bigger than Thebesia Stables, it was not by much.

"There's only one entrance," Selene explained. The path curved toward the open gate, but a Ranger stood at either side of the entry. One stayed completely still, he and his horse a singular statue. The other dipped his head toward Cassie, and she gulped.

"We can simply walk in? You sure?" She leaned close to Selene with her whisper. The dark-haired girl nodded, patting her tired horse. Athena's ears perked up at the sight of the stable. One of the girls turned her head back to Cassie with a hint of a smile across her face.

"Don't let them scare you. Most of the Vallumvis family are harmless if you don't mess with them, and they love it when people come to admire their stronghold." The girl led them down a path to the barn. The stable did not have its own gate, seamlessly flowing with the rest of the architecture. Selene slid off her horse, and Cassie followed her lead. The other riders ignored them, stopping by a long water trough close to the edge of the large stable. Selene's friends broke off from them, leading their horses into the stable and handing the reins to one of the many grooms bustling about.

Cassie patted Athena's sweaty neck, admiring the talented riders of all ages in the rings, some being observed and trained, others on their own.

"Tie her up here, and we'll walk to the racetrack. It's on the other side of the city, but trust me when I say it's so hectic that you'll be glad you left your horse here." Selene loosened the girth of her horse, patting him gently. After kissing his cheek, she led the way deeper into the city. "My friends have some errands to do, but we can go straight to the races, if you'd like."

Cassie nodded, following the girl along the main street. She noted many similarities to Thebesia in the layout, though plenty of things were still new to her. Two Rangers trotted past on the opposite side of the street, their uniforms sporting different colors.

"In Thebesia," Cassie said, frowning, "all the Rangers had indigo and white on their sleeves. But these are different?"

Another Ranger trotted by with deep red and black stripes on his jacket.

"Oh," Selene said, glancing around. "They're apprentices at the Academy. Most Rangers are trained here in Vallumvis, but they wear the colors of the stations they hope to get into."

"Thanks." Cassie smiled at a bright chestnut crossing the road in front of them. He was a leggy gelding with one white sock on his front leg.

"Here we are." A hedge separated the racetrack grounds from the city, lifting up into an archway to allow people to freely move back and forth. Vines and flowers entangled with the shrub, offering pops of color in the midst of all the green.

Pushing through the crowds dressed in elegant clothes, Selene led the way into the barn. Cassie glanced down at her breeches and hoodie, swiping away at a piece of loose straw and bits of horse hair. She kept close to Selene, only glancing up once to see a scowl aimed her way. No, she didn't belong here, but she was just trying to reach the barn.

Cassie's breath hitched. Something about the layout of this stable was achingly familiar. Lower beams, longer stalls. Horses with long legs, shining from the efforts of the grooms.

"Selene!" A young man called to her with a smile as he brushed his horse, a medium bay color without a single white mark.

Selene smiled, twirling her hair as she leaned against the stall. "He's hot."

"A real beauty, though his chances of winning today are pretty low." The man's grin expanded, and he ran a hand through his dark hair.

"Shame. Who's the favorite?"

"The wild one claimed that title until she broke out of her stall. Not that anyone would actually race her." The man tossed his head back with a laugh. "Running on Desire is the actual favorite, of course. Everyone expects Reginald Xiphias to take the win." He glanced at Selene and then finally registered that she wasn't alone. "Who's your friend?"

"Cassie. She wanted to see the racetrack." Selene spared her a soft smile, then turned back to the man in the stall.

Cassie forced a smile, his words still ringing in her head. What wild one? Could it be the horse in her dream? It seemed too similar to be a mere coincidence, with the barn exactly the same as the one in the dream with the ghost horse.

"Theo." The man gave her a polite, though somewhat disinterested, smile.

"We'll be heading to the bleachers now. Just wanted to say hi." Selene gestured for her to follow, but Cassie was rooted to the spot.

"Wait," Cassie said sharply, surprising herself. "I'd like to know more about the wild horse that was the favorite."

"Ooh." Theo laughed again, hardly sparing her a glance. "Rumor has it Mr. Xiphias found her in the plains of Sparta's Hoof. He asked everyone at the stable, the ranch, even went to Pax Valles. No one claimed her, so he took her to the track. I guess she's his now, unless they find her rightful owner." He peered at Cassie, his eyes focusing as if this was the first time he was paying attention to who stood there. "Do you know about her?"

"No—" Cassie nibbled on her lower lip, her mind spiraling with doubts. She needed to see the horse, needed another confirmation that she might be hers. Even if several factors seemed to indicate that the missing horse from the racetrack could be her very own Tenille, she could not tell Theo without proof.

"She's a chestnut?"

"Yeah." The man muttered out his statement. "Kind of matches your hair."

A burly man interrupted them by stopping a short distance away.

"Theodore? Is the horse ready?"

"Yes, sir," Theo mumbled, and Cassie slipped away from the stable, glancing around for Selene. The girl was near the entrance, her eyes narrowed at Cassie.

"What was that about?"

"I—" Cassie hesitated, not sure how to begin. "I had a horse before my accident, and when he mentioned someone found a horse, I had to ask about her."

"Is she?" Selene asked in a flat voice, only serving to increase Cassie's worries.

"I don't know. I have to see her to be able to tell." Cassie clenched her clammy palms, her mind far away from the race. "It seems too much of a coincidence that I show up on an island the same time an unclaimed horse does."

"Hmm." Selene gestured toward the bleachers with pursed lips. "We can find our seats, then you can tell me more."

Cassie nodded and followed after her, glad that Selene's friends' seats were still empty.

"So, you remembered your horse from before your . . . accident?"

"Not really. I had a dream, maybe a memory, that she was taken away from me. I don't remember exactly what she looks like, but I believe she is here." Somehow, being positive about the horse made Tenille feel more attainable.

"We could check the archives. All horses are registered, and when sold, their previous owners must note all information." Selene was only trying to be helpful, but Cassie grimaced.

"I don't even know my true name. Cassie, yes, but the doctor gave me his last name to use."

Selene arched an eyebrow. "So you want me to believe that some random horse on the loose is yours?"

"What if, Selene, what if she is truly mine?" Cassie countered, her frustration rising. "I have to find her." The dismissal in her friend's voice angered her to the point of hurt. She had only shared something so personal because Selene asked, yet now she was acting as if she never wanted to help. Her fingers curled into fists, and the desire to see the race vanished. She should be asking people more about the horse, but if the answers were anything like Selene's, it would be futile.

"I don't know if you'll be able to do that. How about we wait until she is captured and then come back and see. You know, just in case it's the wrong one. We don't want to go on a wild goose chase." Selene nibbled her lip, her statement cautious.

"Ok." Cassie swallowed a sigh, turning to face the horses parading out onto the racetrack. She could live with that. If Tenille was here, another week would make little difference.

"You seem so certain she is yours. Please don't tell me you think this is your soulmate horse." Selene rolled her eyes, tilting her head away from Cassie.

"What's that?"

"Here in Desmalogo, some citizens believe in some kind of soul bond nonsense. Horses that connect to their humans on a deeper level. I think it's made up." Selene scrunched her nose. Cassie stayed silent, a burning sensation on her calf where a strange half circle overshadowed by wavy lines was centered, the birthmark being unique enough that she assumed it was a tattoo of sorts. She wondered if she should bring it up to the doctor, who no doubt had seen it.

"But I did lose my horse." Cassie's voice was weak, and she pulled out the locket the doctor had given her. She opened the heart and showed it to Selene in a final effort to convince her, and the girl let out a long sigh in response.

"I'll ask Theo to send us a message when she is found. How's that?" Selene swept her hair back, her voice low as her friends approached and sat next to her, laughing about something.

"Ok," Cassie whispered, watching the horses on the dirt again.

Selene didn't have to believe in anything, but Cassie knew that her horse was indeed connected to her on a deeper level. A bond that hovered beneath the surface, just out of reach. Just like in her dream, just like in her memories.

She watched the race with dwindling interest, her mind on her horse. If indeed the runaway steed was Tenille, they were a heartbeat away from being together again.

Chapter

8

Henrik was serious about training with Denny. Cassie started each morning preparing him for whatever exercises her trainer set up. Even in the cool days, both horse and rider were dripping with sweat by the time they finished.

Denny's feet hit the ground, and Cassie wrapped her fingers around the sleek mane to steady herself as they cantered toward the next jump. He snorted, his hind legs pushing against the arena sand, and the two glided through the air to clear the obstacle.

Henrik called out in the background, but she ignored it. She guided Denny toward the highest jump in the course. The gelding picked up speed, going even faster than before as he launched over the poles with an excited snort. His hind legs clunked against the top pole, but she kept her focus as she moved toward the last obstacle. Turning around to check was only a distraction that would ruin their laser focus.

The last jump was a shorter triple bar, and Denny had no trouble clearing it. Cassie slowed him, surveying the course with a growing smile. The poles were still up, meaning they had not made enough contact to knock any down.

"Cassie!" The irritation was evident in Henrik's voice, and she trotted closer. "Didn't you hear me telling you to slow down between jumps? That is why he touched the poles." He shook his head.

Cassie avoided his glance, busying herself with Denny's mane falling through her fingers.

"No, not really. I was focusing on the course." Her voice was hardly above a whisper.

"Your riding style is admirable, but it doesn't fit with Denny. He doesn't need to go faster; he needs to slow down and keep an even pace. A knocked pole will get you time penalties. He's still young and doesn't need to be rushed."

Cassie bit her lip to refrain from talking back. Henrik sighed.

"Sometimes," Cassie said quietly, then made her voice bolder, "sometimes it feels like we don't agree on how to ride the course. Is that . . ." She groped for the right word. "Normal?"

Henrik had a small smile on his face as he stroked the tall horse.

"Yes. There will be a horse, Cassie, that you might find. Your thoughts and her thoughts will be synonymous, and it is quite the experience. But even more valuable is the skill to ride any horse well. You almost have that." He paused, waiting for the girl to meet his gaze. "You and Denny are a magical team, but you must think about him and not only yourself. Why don't you try the course again, and this time don't allow him to rush."

Cassie tugged on the reins, Henrik's words tumbling through her brain. A magical team would be her and Tenille, but she couldn't argue that Denny was a dream in his own way.

Denny tossed his head against the bit, and Cassie reminded herself to focus on the jumps ahead of her. Curbing

Denny's excitement, she held him tight until he could jump, leaning forward in sync with the horse.

"Much better!" Henrik shouted as the two finished the last jump flawlessly and trotted toward the trainer.

"I don't know who trained me before, but it was very different from this." She sighed, pulling the reins backward to ask for a halt.

"You've adjusted quite well. But yes, each trainer has a different style of teaching and adapts it slightly to fit their students. You know, in life, sometimes change is good," Henrik offered. "Do you think if you visited all the stables, you might find one familiar to you?"

"Perhaps. I'd like to visit Vallumvis again." A smile tugged at her lips, for more reasons than one. "But I do like training here."

Henrik smiled, slapping Denny's sweaty neck.

"Glad to hear, because we like having you here. Off you go, now, cool him down. I'll have Mitchie hose him down when you're done. No more jumping until the day of the show, just flatwork exercises. With two days left, we don't want to overwork him."

Mitchie was waiting at the entrance of the stable with Athena, handing the lead rope to Henrik before taking Denny off Cassie's hands. Henrik led Athena to the blacksmith and his makeshift forge created near the stables.

Cassie found herself following, the loud banging intriguing her. The blacksmith was a heavily built man, forehead dripping with sweat. She wondered if it was from the labor or the proximity to the fire set up not too far away.

"Ah, Cassie." Henrik motioned toward the blacksmith. "Meet Conrad. He's the best on the island."

"Hi," Cassie said in a soft voice. The man set his tools to the side and extended a hand to her. He had a kind face, which put her at ease.

"How's Desmalogo treating you? Henrik told me about

you, a fascinating case." Conrad's handshake was surprisingly gentle, not matching his build.

Henrik tied Athena to the post, and Conrad moved around to the side, lifting her front leg.

"Good. Yvonne takes good care of me, Dr. Lykaion is kind, and Henrik is amazing." Cassie narrowed her eyes as the blacksmith pulled nails out of the hoof.

"He really is." Conrad glanced up at the stable owner with a grin. "If we didn't live on opposite sides of the island, I'd bring my girls here to ride."

"I'm sure the stable at Vallumvis has everything your daughters could possibly need," Henrik replied with a chuckle.

"You're from Vallumvis?" Cassie blurted out, her mind darting to her horse. Was it possible this man had seen the mare?

"Yes. I am a Vallumvis." Conrad had a wide grin, setting the foot down and reaching for another horseshoe. "I'm only here as a favor to an old friend, as Henrik's usual blacksmith fell ill."

"Oh."

"My wife is a Vallumvis, and when we married I took her last name." A hearty laugh escaped from his lungs, and Cassie felt the need to join in without quite knowing why. "A small tradition they have there, to preserve the family line. Have you visited our lovely city?" Conrad asked, talking loudly over the resumed banging of his hammer.

"Yes. I watched the race," Cassie replied.

"She'll be there again Saturday, competing with Denny." Henrik had a touch of pride in his tone, and Cassie shyly ducked her head.

"He's a good horse. You're lucky to have him." Conrad set down the second shod foot.

"He's not mine. Mine is . . ." Cassie shut her mouth, not

wanting to say more. Conrad seemed like a person who wouldn't care much for her fantasies.

"Yours isn't worthy of competing?" Conrad pressed, moving toward the other side of Athena. Cassie clasped her hands behind her back, noting how Henrik eyed her with curiosity. She hadn't told him about what happened last week at the racetrack and was struggling to determine if the blacksmith was someone who would listen to her.

He could be like Selene, dismissing her dream. Yet Conrad's presence was comforting, and nothing about him struck her as odd. Henrik was more professional and strict as his stables were his life.

"I had a horse before my accident, and we were separated. I only know that her name is Tenille." *And that she was orange,* but she kept that thought tucked away in her mind. She wasn't sure, not quite yet. Her mind was not a reliable source of information, as blank as it was.

"Do you think she's on the island of Desmalogo?" Henrik asked with a frown. "Given that you were found here."

"I had a dream." The words slipped out like a confession, and the two men had vastly different reactions.

"Cassie, that's hardly—" Henrik scratched the back of his head.

"You don't think she's right?" Conrad paused his hammering, straightening to look at Henrik. The man folded his arms across his chest, lifting a shoulder.

"I didn't give it much thought."

"What does your horse look like?" Conrad asked, returning to his work.

"She—" Cassie was uncertain how to explain. After a few moments, she continued, not caring if she sounded ridiculous. "She has a coat that matches my hair. A horse broke away from the racetrack that was bright orange, and I was wondering." Cassie gulped. "She might be mine."

"Indeed." Conrad was silent for a few moments, and when

Cassie met his gaze, she realized how grave he looked. "I do believe I saw her running across the city."

Cassie's breath caught in her throat, her emotions torn between excited and angry. She wanted to go there now, not wait until tomorrow.

"A loose horse, and no one caught her?" Henrik voiced his doubts quite loudly.

"She's—" Conrad paused to choose his words carefully "—quite the handful. Several Rangers could not tame her. She was fast. I can see how she would race well."

Henrik's lips twitched, yet he did not comment.

"Stars, it's getting hot out here." Conrad wiped his brow.

"I'll have a groom bring you some water," Henrik said, stepping away to find someone. As soon as he left, Conrad dropped Athena's leg and turned toward Cassie.

"You best be careful when you find your horse. She is a Pneúmós, which explains why you formed such a strong bond. You should sense her in your heart and mind, at least to an extent. Though I am not sure just how strong the bond is." His voice was hushed, his eyes never leaving hers. "Henrik won't have an issue with it, but there are plenty of people in our city who would love to take her off your hands."

"What's a Pneúmós?" Cassie asked, her memory refusing to yield anything. It sounded familiar, but she couldn't place it. His statement of caution bounced around in her mind, sweat collecting on her palms as she thought about the danger they both might be in. She needed to know more.

"A spirit horse." Conrad raised an eyebrow and turned back to Athena as Henrik returned, accepting the glass of water.

"Henrik, what's a Pneúmós?" Cassie feigned indifference when Henrik turned with surprised eyes and a slight tilt to his head.

"An old Grecian word meaning your spirit horse. We sometimes use that term to congratulate a person who forms a special bond with their horse." He quirked an eyebrow at Conrad, clearly dubious.

"Have you ever bonded like that with a horse?" Cassie challenged.

"Yes, many, many years ago. I still remember every detail of it." Henrik chuckled. "He couldn't jump like my champion, but it's a shame the sickness took him like it did." He shook his head, sadness glazing over his eyes.

"Sometimes," Conrad continued, "the bond is even stronger. In rare cases, horse and human can join together to—"

"That's nonsense, and you know it, Conrad," Henrik scoffed, waving his hand. "We're far too old to believe the fairy tales we tell to put the little ones to sleep. Forgive me, though, I'm sure your girls enjoy hearing about them."

Conrad smiled in what seemed like agreement, but it was more strained now.

"Of course, Henrik. I assumed Cassie would be interested in hearing more about our land." He handed Athena's lead rope to Cassie without another word, draining the rest of the water in his glass. Cassie gripped the soft rope, annoyed at Henrik for being on the wrong side of the conversation.

Cassie didn't argue when Henrik told her to lead the horse back to the stable, then she busied herself with her chores before heading home.

The hammering echoed as she walked down the path and through the entry gate of the stable, but she didn't dare go to Conrad again. Not with Henrik hovering over him overseeing the shoeing of the horses. She finally found someone who could answer her questions and wanted to kick herself for not mentioning the robed figure she had seen in the square so many days ago.

But if Henrik wanted nothing to do with it, she had to respect that.

Horses and people could be friends, it seemed, but that was where the line was drawn.

Cassie rubbed her temples at the onset of a headache as she hurried home hoping for a hearty dinner. Yvonne usually put in more effort for the last meal of the day, and Cassie looked forward to them.

She pushed open the door, pausing in the doorway when she caught voices speaking in low tones.

"I'm sorry, I cannot stay here." It was a feminine voice, flowing like a stream in the forest.

"Whyever not?" Yvonne was aghast, and a long sigh followed.

"I have detected some traces of corruption and need to find the source. It is no longer safe for me to stay."

"Nora, I don't understand why—"

"Yvonne?" Cassie slammed the door behind her, stepping into the main room.

She froze in place when a lady in the main room lifted a hood to cover her dark hair, her back facing Cassie. Yvonne's eyes flickered between the two girls in alarm.

"Cassie! You're back early."

"I was told to go home and rest, since tomorrow we pack up and go to Vallumvis for the first show of the season, which is on Saturday." Cassie's eyes pointed meaningfully at the girl, presumably named Nora.

"Ah. You best be going to bed then."

"I will go as well." Nora slipped past Cassie, leaving only a shiver in her wake.

Unless she was mistaken, the woman's robe was the exact same one she had seen in the city square her first day out with Yvonne.

"Who was that?"

"A member of the Conservation Society of Desmalogo. You needn't worry about her." Yvonne waved her hand dismissively. Cassie didn't miss the way her eyes were unsteady and how her face seemed to be distorted. Had Yvonne not realized Cassie would see the lady if they spent the night in the same house? "If you're hungry, there's dinner, just please wash up first."

Yvonne retreated to her quarters, leaving a hollow chasm in the room. Cassie stood still for a few moments before snapping out of her daze and heading down the hall.

Closing the door to the washroom behind her, Cassie turned on the spigot just enough to wash her hands. Yvonne often scolded against being wasteful of resources, so she was careful not to use more than necessary. She grabbed the hairbrush, which dislodged a piece of aged parchment tucked to the side of the counter. She stared at it for a moment. After double-checking that the door was still shut, she picked the paper up delicately and ran her finger along the folded edge.

It was probably something of Yvonne's, and she shouldn't touch it.

She placed it back on the counter, but her curiosity grew too strong.

Retrieving the paper, she unfolded it to reveal dark ink looping in very neat handwriting. She blinked slowly, letting her mind adjust to the words.

Nora will be continuing her investigation in Thebesia this week. She might need to stay a day or two. In addition, you are expected to return with her on Saturday to discuss urgent matters.

The letters in the note matched the ones in her locket, but not the letters scrawled on the board selling flatcakes and blueberry lemonade. Two different languages in Desmalogo, but only one seemed to be common.

She racked her brain, deciding that asking Yvonne about it would not prove useful at the moment. She would save the question, tuck it along the other ones nestled in her brain, and ask when a better opportunity presented itself.

Cassie reread the note with a deep frown, the message unsettling her. Refolding the note, she placed it back where she found it and ran the brush through her hair. First she avoided questions about the robe in the city, and now a strange message. Yvonne was clearly working with these people. So why didn't she want Cassie to know?

Cassie slipped into her seat at the table, surprised to see Yvonne there again. Nothing about her betrayed their confusing conversation from earlier; she had slipped back into the role of a doting, caring, older woman.

"Thank you very much for dinner."

"Anytime, dear. Did you have a good time at the stables?"

"My first show is on Saturday," Cassie said slowly, trying to see if Yvonne cared enough to remember.

"That's a milestone to be proud of."

"Thank you." Again, Yvonne had hardly noticed anything about Cassie's life. She provided food, drachmas, and a place to live, and that was where she drew the line.

Cassie finished her meal as quickly as she could before retreating into her room. She would simply have to make friends elsewhere.

9

Cassie pushed open the windows of her room, sticking her head out into the cool dawn air. She closed her eyes against the nausea building up, trying to forget the restless sleep behind her.

The day before had been a whirlwind of last-minute preparation and lessons, then the entire stables packed up and headed to Vallumvis. It was dark when they arrived, with only enough time for a simple dinner before everyone settled into their rooms. All night, she could nearly feel her horse, a sensation so strong that when she reached out her fingers and felt nothing, a frown developed on her face.

She popped her eyes open, facing what she assumed was the direction of the racetrack, tucked in near the coast across the city. If Tenille had run from there, would she still be within the gates?

The question was more important than the show, and she hardly spoke as Selene awoke and joined her at the window, saying something about dark circles under Cassie's eyes. She submitted herself to Selene to fuss over her hair and makeup, everything passing in a daze.

Hours later, Cassie found herself outside a training ring, staring at the influx of riders. Henrik appeared by her side after finishing a conversation with a handful of other students.

"Cassie! Sign-ups begin in half an hour. I want you to warm Denny up in the arena and sign up as soon as you can. Your class will probably be first." Henrik sighed at the blank look on her face. "Actually." He glanced around and hailed a Ranger trotting by. "Adria?"

"Henrik." The Ranger slowed her horse, turning toward him. "Good morning."

"Could you please show Cassie where the warm-up arena is, the sign-up booth, everything? This will be her first show at Vallumvis."

Adria's warm smile surprised Cassie.

"How exciting! Here, let me tie my mount to a post and we can get started." She made quick work of the task and was soon by Cassie's side. "My name is Adria in case you didn't hear." She offered a handshake, and Cassie accepted.

"I'm Cassie," Cassie said softly.

"It's a pleasure to meet you. I assume you've already seen the barn. Let's go straight to the most important aspect of the showgrounds: the main arena. The outdoor arena of Vallumvis is the biggest within all of Desmalogo and a source of pride for local citizens." Adria stopped near the arena. The bleachers towered over three sides, the fourth sporting both an entry gate and a judge's tent.

"It's not that much bigger than the Thebesian arena," Cassie commented, slightly annoyed by the arrogance of the people of Vallumvis.

"Oh, I know." Adria rolled her eyes. "It's like a meter more on both sides, only done so they could brag."

"Are you . . . not from Vallumvis?" Cassie asked.

"I am not. I am a Ranger stationed at Arion Woodlands, which is the prettiest woods in all of Desmalogo. You traveled through them on your way here. Come along."

"It is nice there," Cassie agreed, following the Ranger. "And I'm probably the only dunce here who doesn't know the layout of a Vallumvis show."

Adria's laugh caught Cassie off guard, revealing a row of pearly white teeth.

"That's far from the truth. Everyone has a first time here, especially if they're from a smaller stable or are new to competing. The warm-up rings, you should be careful. Stables tend to be possessive over which one belongs to them, so stick to where your riders are." Adria pointed to several food stalls being set up on the other side of the rings.

"If you want a snack during the show, there are plenty of options. My personal favorite is a strawberry milkshake." Adria paused for a brief moment as Cassie looked at the different offerings.

"I like lemonade." Cassie shrugged.

"Lemonade is good."

"Blueberry."

"Sounds heavenly. Let's go." Adria smiled, leading her to the registration booth. "Here, I'll help you sign up."

A young girl shuffled papers inside the small cubicle. After setting them aside, she leaned forward with a smile. "Welcome to the Vallumvis Debut Show! Which stables are you riding for today?"

"Thebesia," Cassie replied.

"Name?"

"Cassie Lykaion." She winced at the false last name.

"Your horse?"

"Denny's Rhythm."

"Thank you." The girl finished writing everything in neat little boxes under Cassie's scrutinizing gaze. The letters were the same the food vendors used, the same language they were all speaking. She racked her brain, trying to determine if she had seen more of the language from her locket anywhere in Desmalogo. Her memory failed her, and she could only recall the Desmaligan language everywhere.

"I need the fifty drachmas for the entry fee, and then we can place you in the right class."

"I'm in advanced," Cassie said, placing a small sack of drachmas onto the table. "Show jumping."

The girl glanced up in surprise.

"Did you compete last year?"

"No." Cassie shrugged.

"I'm afraid that in order to qualify for the advanced class, you must reach top ten in at least five shows during the previous season. Only the panel of judges can change it, but you would have had to submit your request to them weeks ago and auditioned," the girl apologized.

"Henrik said I can apply for advanced," Cassie said stubbornly, looking between Adria and the girl.

"I'm afraid I can't do that. Vallumvis rules are rules, and they do not change for anyone." The girl gave her a tight smile and wrote the word "intermediate" next to Cassie's name.

"Fine," Cassie retorted. She started walking toward the lemonade stand, trying to think how to approach Henrik after this. If the auditions were weeks ago, then she had still been in a coma.

"Cassie?" Adria called out, running to catch up to her. Cassie's face heated with a flood of shame. She shouldn't have left the Ranger like that.

"Don't worry about it." Adria placed a gentle hand on Cassie's arm. "I'm sure at the next show they will allow you to compete at a higher level. Henrik probably forgot to set the audition up. The last few weeks before a show are hectic. Did you want to continue the tour?"

"I think I've seen everything I need," Cassie said, forcing a smile. "But thank you." Henrik had not forgotten; it was simply not an option.

"Of course. If you need anything, find one of us Rangers. We're here to help." Adria waved goodbye, her ponytail swinging as she made her way back to her horse. Cassie watched her go with a hint of a smile on her lips. Another Ranger that was nothing but kind, yet she didn't know her. Which station were the Rangers from that had tried to identify her?

Shaking her head at her own musings, Cassie ordered a blueberry lemonade. The iced cup in her hands already made her feel better, and she headed back to the barn.

"Signed up?" Henrik called out when she approached.

"Yes and no. They didn't allow me into the advanced class. I'm in intermediate," Cassie replied, swirling the last of her lemonade to meld the flavors together. The glasses were altogether too small. Cassie would have purchased it by the bucket had it been sold that way.

"Ah. Sometimes they are stricter with the rules. Regardless, you'll do well. Mitchie has Denny waiting for you."

"Thank you." She found her horse and asked Mitchie to run the glass back to the stand while she led the steed to the training ring. Selene was there with Kismet, the duo struggling with some basic maneuvers.

A pulsing headache began to beat in the back of Cassie's head, and a pain developed in her lower calf. Cassie pressed a hand to her forehead, her pulse humming beneath her fingertips. Mild headaches she had experienced before, but this was something more powerful.

After the show, she should march up to the doctor and demand an explanation. Most likely her headache was related to the accident, and he could help her manage future ones.

Hoping to distract herself from the throbbing, Cassie focused on the names being called out for a lower-class show. The arena started with the poles hardly above the ground that would be moved up with each class, allowing the elite riders to compete later in the day when more people were around.

"Two more riders, then they will set up the intermediate course. We do the course walk and then the show begins," Selene said nervously, fingering the reins of her horse. "Let's head to the main arena." She reached forward and ruffled the black hair of her horse, his ears flicking in response.

"Fantastic. I can't wait until it's over." Cassie sighed, her emotions conflicted. She had been looking forward to this day, but it was proving to be overwhelming.

"Same." Selene shivered. "I don't think I'll do that well."

"You will," Cassie countered.

She wanted to tell Selene that she didn't care too much about the show. To an extent she did, knowing this would help her fit in with her friends at the stables and build common ground with the riders. But more important to her was the search for Tenille, which she planned to begin as soon as her ride was over if her headache lessened.

"It's time to walk the course," Selene said, leaving Kismet tied next to Denny. The two geldings seemed fine next to each other, and the girls joined the line of intermediate riders. They were allowed in one at a time to walk the course, the whole procession overseen by a handful of Rangers.

Cassie's headache morphed into a strange buzzing sensation, and she found it impossible to concentrate. The strangeness of the procession unnerved her, even when Selene reassured her it was so the riders knew the course but the horses didn't. That way, it was a display of the rider's ability to maneuver the course, not a test of if a horse could memorize a pattern.

"Cassie Lykaion, next. Don't rush, but please, don't take too much time." A Ranger handed her a paper map of the course layout and opened the paddock gate. Cassie stepped inside, the world going hazy around her. She was not sure how much more of this she could take before passing out, but backing away was not an option. Or was it? Would Henrik understand if she explained how she felt?

She blinked furiously, staring at the paper and trying to concentrate. The obstacles were numbered, a line tracing the path she was to take. She walked toward the first jump. Something in the back of her head told her to count strides, but Cassie didn't care. It took too much effort to simply walk.

Jump three, jump four. The edges of her vision blurred, the pangs of pain growing sharper. Jump nine, jump ten. A few more. Cassie gritted her teeth and walked past the last jump, stumbling out of the arena. She found Denny, gripping his reins to ground herself.

"Are you ok? You look pale," Selene asked as she approached.

"I'm fine. Just a headache." She forced a painful smile.

"I have some meds for that. Be right back." Selene ran off and came back with a few pills and a glass of water, ignoring Cassie's effort to wave them away.

She was being pulled somewhere, and it would drive her insane if she didn't figure out where.

"Really, everything will be ok. Even if you completely mess up, it's ok." Selene offered a comforting smile, placing a hand on Cassie's arm.

"Thank you." Cassie blew out a short breath, the remains of air hitching in her throat when she heard her name. She didn't expect to be the very first one to do the course, but perhaps it was better this way. She could only hope her headache was somewhat related to nerves and would lessen once this was over.

"It's ok. Go dazzle them." Selene's grin didn't help ease her fears, but her boosting Cassie up into the saddle did. She closed her eyes and could almost picture the course setup, the loopy lines showing where to go.

The arena hushed as she entered, ready to see what kind of performance the newcomer would bring. Cassie paused and bowed, taking a few spare moments to regulate her breathing.

She could do this. Jumping was second nature to her.

A tap of her heel against his side was his cue, and Denny launched into a buttery smooth canter toward the first jump. Cassie relaxed as she pictured his knees folding perfectly under him, clearing the first jump, then the next few, without so much as a snort.

Cassie . . .

The wind whispered her name, and she whipped her head around to see where it came from. Denny nickered, unsure why his rider was distracted, and sped up his pace.

Cassie scolded herself for losing focus and slowed him just in time to sail over the fourth jump. Taking a deep breath, she refocused, and they cleared the next group of obstacles without a hitch. She gritted her teeth against the sensation sweeping over her, making a mental note to thank Selene as the pain of the headache softened around the edges.

Cassie . . .

The voice was louder, harder to ignore, harder to pretend she was imagining things as the pounding around her increased with each step. This wasn't her headache or her heartbeat but a forceful presence enveloping her. Cassie blinked furiously, something wet traveling down her cheek.

With only a few jumps left, she couldn't lose focus. Not even with the indigo lights flashing in her mind, so bright against everything else.

Denny only needed the lightest of cues to head toward the next jump, and he cleared it. One more. One more and this nightmare would be over. She would head back to Thebesia and distance herself from this strange place with its pains.

Cassie . . .

Tenille?

Cassie snapped her head toward the other side of the showgrounds. Something was there, watching her, waiting for her. She could feel it deep in her bones, a force impossible to ignore.

Time slowed. Her mind was now completely focused on the place where the voice in her head originated. Her horse.

With a flash of indigo lights, Tenille appeared with her orange mane flowing gently with the wind, powerful legs pushing against the ground. She weaved through the crowd, deftly dodging the outstretched hands of those brave enough to try and stop her. Others ran from her as she bolted straight for Cassie. Someone shrieked as the mare jumped over the arena fence and finally stopped with a rear. Her front legs kicked against the sky, showing that she didn't care she had interrupted an important performance.

Cassie gripped Denny's mane as he stumbled, crashing to a halt in front of the last obstacle and nearly flinging her off in the process.

She slid off Denny and ran the short distance to Tenille, her shaking arms wrapping around the solid, pulsing neck of her horse.

"Tenille." She was real—real in flesh and blood, standing in the arena with all the regalness that belonged to her. It was too much to handle, tears of joy mixing with emotions she couldn't name. No longer a ghost, but a living, breathing creature. She was here, and she was hers. A missing piece of her soul clicked back into place, all the throbbing sensations melting away like butter on a hot flatcake.

Her heart thrummed with adrenaline as she pulled herself onto her horse's broad back, warmed by the sunshine, and turned her away from the arena. She needed to get out of here before someone came to take her away. Needed to run from the pressure, run from the commotion of confused crowds trying to decipher what had just happened.

Under Cassie's lead, the mare barreled out of the city, past the iron gates that provided protection, and back to the woodlands that separated her from Thebesia. The steady beating of hooves was the only thing Cassie heard until they were well away from any people; only when they were in the safety of the forest did the two of them slow their pace.

Her thoughts settled, and Cassie smiled. For the first time since waking up in Desmalogo, she felt truly at peace. Whole and complete, with a taste of freedom she never knew existed.

Chapter

10

Taven kept himself as busy as possible the morning of the show, nearly exhausting his vast knowledge in small talk with every citizen in town. Enough people mentioned something about a wild horse with chestnut hair running through the city and thwarting all the Rangers' attempts at catching it, but not a single person had seen anything firsthand.

The first class began, a younger group of beginner competitors. For most, this would be their first ever show, and nerves were abundant. Taven retreated into a shady corner under the trees, watching the groomed horses walk by, their shiny coats glistening in the sun. His own mount waited for him, nuzzling his shoulder in a friendly way.

The lower classes were not half as fun to watch as the advanced riders, and Taven climbed up onto his horse, heading closer to the arena. The intermediate course had been set up, a slew of riders waiting nearby.

He kept one eye there, the other scanning the crowds for any trouble. It didn't take long to spot it.

A familiar scowling face strolled onto the showgrounds. Taven drew in a sharp breath. Reginald's dark eyes met his.

"Morning, Reginald. How do you fare on such a wonderful morning?" He tipped his hat out of respect, though truly, he wasn't a huge fan of the man. However, with him here, it was the perfect chance to dig deeper into the case.

"Another useless Ranger. Where is my horse?"

A very kind man, indeed.

"What horse? What does he look like?" Taven asked.

"She," Reginald spat the word, "is a chestnut mare. She has a blaze and four white stockings."

"Is this something you've already reported?"

"Of course." Reginald threw his hands up in the air. "I've already alerted the Rangers about this. The entire island should be searching for her!"

"I'm sorry, sir, but certainly, you can't expect everyone to drop their business and look for a horse that isn't even yours." He steeled his voice, refusing to be talked down to by someone as disrespectful as Reginald Xiphias.

Reginald's face reddened as he took a step toward Taven. Rophon snorted in warning, and Taven was glad for his trusty mount always at his side.

"You are not the only one in Desmalogo who has misplaced their steed," Taven continued in a firm tone, straightening his posture.

"Cassie!" A shout pierced the peaceful air, jolting his attention to the people behind him. A bright orange horse barreled through the crowds, nearly knocking some people over.

"There she is! My horse!" Reginald grinned for a split second, then his face returned to its normal scowl. "She's right in front of you. Are you so stupidly useless that you can't even wrangle her for me?"

Taven gritted his teeth, keeping his tongue in check. With a light tap on his sides, Rophon broke into a canter after the taller mare, Taven shouting a warning to the people in her way. The crowds parted to allow the horse through, her path aimed straight at the main arena of Vallumvis.

A girl riding in the arena turned her head to look at the orange horse as her mount approached the next jump. Taven halted Rophon as the scene in front of him unfolded. The orange horse was too focused on her task for it to be random. Taven's eyes flicked to the girl, the world slowing for a moment.

She looked almost like . . .

He shook his head. He had to be imagining things.

The girl's horse stumbled at the last jump, nearly knocking her off. At the same time, the orange horse leapt over the fence and came to stand in the arena near her. Taven's heart skipped a beat—he couldn't believe what he was seeing.

Leaving the bay horse by itself in the arena, the girl ran toward the chestnut, her hands wrapping around its neck. It was touching; the two clearly cared about each other very much.

He nudged Rophon closer to the nearest gate, prepared to step between her and Reginald. The girl didn't give him a chance, mounting the chestnut horse and running away from the arena as if being chased. She jumped over the fence a short distance from him, heading straight to the main road of Vallumvis. The very one that would lead them out of the city.

For once, Taven was at a loss for what to do. His many years of Ranger service had not prepared him for the choice of chasing after the girl or staying here to ensure no citizens were harmed. He needed instruction.

Taven whipped his head around to see if anyone else knew what to do. Thebesia Stables owner, Henrik, scrambled over the fence and approached Denny with an outstretched hand. The gelding trotted up to him, and then Henrik's eyes landed on Taven.

"Ranger."

Taven turned and was surprised to see Dr. Lykaion, Thebesia's most renowned doctor, trying to catch his attention.

"What are you doing here?" he asked, dumbfounded. The last time he had seen the doctor, he had been swamped with work at the Thebesian clinic on the other side of the island.

"There's no time for that. Find the girl. And be careful," he said calmly.

Taven held eye contact for a moment and then kicked his mount into a gallop. If only he had a spare moment, he would have asked if this was the same girl as before. Was that why the doctor told him to go after her? He took in a shaky breath, the memory of her pale body being pulled out of the water fresh in his mind.

He had agreed to run a letter to Turris Regia on a whim, not realizing that his presence on the ferry would save her life.

Cassie. That was what the doctor said her name was.

The road led him through the mountains, and Taven scanned the countryside in case she had stopped somewhere with the horse.

As the mountains grew near and trees began to close off the landscape, Taven allowed his horse to slow down. He surveyed the trees, hoping to see a flash of chestnut hair.

He didn't even know if this was the same girl, Cassie. He could call out her name, but if it wasn't her? The doctor should have given him more information before sending him off on a fruitless chase.

Without any other option, he decided to let Rophon lead the way. The horse ambled between the trees, then his ears perked up and he headed down a stray trail, overgrown and hardly ever used.

"I swear, if this is you going on an adventure for a tastier patch of grass," Taven muttered under his breath, removing his hat and shoving sweaty hair off his forehead. He slowed his movements, leaning back in the saddle to halt his horse.

The girl and her horse stood a short distance away, half hidden by a large tree. Her hands clenched the orange mane of her horse, her slitted eyes watching his every step.

"Never mind. You always seem to know better than me." Taven dropped his voice to a whisper, waiting a few moments before stepping forward again. Approaching too fast would only tempt her to run again, and he didn't want to be perceived as a threat. Her stance displayed how distrusting she was, and he had to surmise her horse was stolen from her, fear of it happening again overwhelming her.

It brought forth the wave of protectiveness he always had toward the citizens of Desmalogo, especially the girls. After his failure with his sister, he vowed to do better, to somehow make it up to her.

"My name is Taven," he said, gentling his voice. "I am a Ranger of Desmalogo. What's your name?" He held his breath.

With a rustling noise, the girl slowly emerged from the shadows.

He nearly choked on his next breath, her face fully visible now.

It was her, as he'd originally thought. Whole and alive. Her face was missing the ashen grayness he remembered and was now full of vibrant life. She was thinner than she had been, but a radiant glow surrounded her face, even now when she was clearly displeased with him.

He understood why the doctor was hesitant to share about her case. She needed time to adjust to her new surroundings. Taven bit back the questions burning his tongue, knowing she might not respond well to a question about her head damage.

"She's mine." Cassie spat the words, her fingers woven in the orange mane. He noticed for the first time that the horse matched her hair perfectly, another silent confirmation that the two belonged together. Taven's eyes collided with Cassie's bright green ones.

"I believe that. No one will take her from you." Taven smiled, hoping he sounded more confident than he felt. It was his job to fix problems, but it wasn't often they were such difficult ones.

"How do I know that the stupid thief, whatever his name is, won't take her again?"

"He won't. I will make sure of it." Taven nudged his horse forward a few steps, pulling up alongside the girl.

He drew in a sharp breath.

Freckles.

"We should head back." Taven reached out with hesitant fingers to pat the chestnut horse, drawing back when teeth snapped dangerously close to him.

"Tenille!" Cassie scolded, patting the neck of her horse gently. "Mind your manners." She pulled at the orange mane. "No." She glanced up.

"No?"

"I'm not going back," she clarified. "I want to go home."

"You found your family?" Excitement crept into his tone. That would resolve many of the problems brewing on the horizon, yet the dark expression crossing her face told him he was wrong.

"I did not. I live with—with Yvonne." The girl narrowed her eyes at him. "Did you know me before?"

Taven shook his head. The doctor said when she was ready to have this conversation, he would let him know. Yet here she was, asking him directly.

"I had been running errands in Thebesia and then went to the harbor. I was on the ferry when I spotted a body in the water. The ferryman was already heading toward you. I knew Dr. Lykaion would take the best care of you—" he nearly choked on his own words "—so I took you directly to him. After examining you, he said you only had a small chance to live. That's when we ramped up all efforts to find your family before you—" Taven swallowed, uncomfortable with continuing under her scrutinizing gaze.

"Passed away? I didn't. I woke up at Yvonne's house.

Empty." Her voice dropped to a whisper. "I can't remember anything from before."

"I'm sorry," Taven said in a low tone, placing a hand on hers. He had inched closer during the conversation, wanting, *needing* to know more about her. He had only wanted to touch her to make sure he wasn't somehow dreaming this, that she really was alive.

Cassie looked down at their hands with a slight frown, and Taven drew back, hoping he hadn't crossed a line.

She scrunched her nose at him, leaning closer to him. "You're the Ranger who found me."

"Yes." He was not expecting her to look so disappointed or to toss her hands in the air.

"So you know nothing. I'd hoped you would know." She paused, her hands busying themselves with her horse's chestnut mane.

"Cassie." Taven said the name slowly, trying to find words to comfort her. "I can only imagine how difficult it is for you, not knowing your family and thrown into a cold world." Was she smiling? He couldn't see with her head bent down, her choppy hair swishing past her shoulders to mask the corners of her lips.

"No one knows where I came from?" It was a whisper, so soft he nearly missed it to the rustling trees overhead.

"We will figure it out." It was the least he could say to help her. "Shall we return to the show?" Her head snapped up, the fiery expression in her eyes returning. "Dr. Lykaion expects you to return, and I assume Henrik does too. It's not very . . ." He searched for the right word, not wanting to offend her. "*Nice* to leave everyone like that. To bolt from the arena, it paints you in a bad light."

"Good grief." Cassie rolled her eyes, then her expression softened. "My horse was stolen from me and then we finally reunited. I'm sorry I overreacted." She wrinkled her nose, not seeming truly apologetic. "The show will be over anyway. I'd rather go back to Thebesia."

"You wouldn't like to see how everyone placed?"

That seemed to catch her attention, her green eyes brightening.

"I can lead the way."

"What do you think, Tenille?" Cassie leaned forward as if listening to her horse. She glanced at Taven with a grin. "We'll go, but if you dare take us anywhere but the show, I'll run and you will never find us again." She nudged her horse forward, falling into step beside him as Taven led them out of the forest and back to Vallumvis. They rode in silence for a while, Cassie balancing on her horse with an air of grace around her, as if this was her most comfortable setting.

"Apparently I'm Cassie." After a moment's thought, she pulled a necklace with a locket from under her show jacket. "The doctor gave me this locket. It says Cassie and Tenille on it. Did you see it too? Is that why you know my name?"

"Dr. Lykaion told me, and yes, I saw the locket. I'm Taven," he said, unsure if she heard him the first time. "My horse is Rophon. I'm stationed here at Arion, but most days you won't find me here." He sucked in a breath, not wanting to ramble. A glance her direction proved she was occupied with her horse's mane again and hardly reacting to anything he said.

"I am Cassie," she said again, and he smiled at how important her own name was to her. "Tenille confirmed it."

"She did. Seeing how you two reunited, I have no doubt that you were made for each other."

A smile lit up her face as she turned toward him, and for a split second, time slowed. He swallowed, unsure why he liked her happy face so much. After all those hospital visits seeing her gray, near-dead face, this one was sunshine after a rainstorm.

"You think Tenille likes carrots or cookies more?" Cassie asked, a frown twisting her face.

Taven blinked, thrown off by the random question.

"Probably carrots. They are similar to her color." It was a wild guess, something he didn't even know about his own horse. Rophon took up any snacks offered to him, and Taven did as well.

"That might be right. Tenille says it depends on the type of cookies." She squinted at the path ahead. "Race you back?"

He nodded without thinking, being left in the dust within a few seconds. Only when he reached the gates of Vallumvis did her statement from before truly register with him. Tenille spoke to her? Surely that was nonsense. Horses didn't speak.

He shoved his thoughts to the side, straightening as he approached the showgrounds. Henrik was waiting for them, the doctor a few paces behind.

"Cassie! What is the meaning of this?" Henrik's eyebrows furrowed together, his tone harsh.

"This is my horse, Henrik. She is the only familiar thing to me on this island. I'm sorry we fumbled the last jump. Surely you understand we had an unconventional distraction. I'll do better in the next show." Cassie faced him directly, not an ounce of remorse in her voice as she delivered what sounded like a rehearsed speech. It was impressive, in a way, how little she cared about the scolding she was receiving.

Henrik sighed, pinching the bridge of his nose.

"Mr. Xiphias has told everyone that the horse is his. He says that you have stolen her."

"I can vouch for her," Taven cut in. A single glimpse of Cassie's face was enough for him to know he needed to speak before she did. "I was there when Cassie was rescued from the water. Mr. Xiphias said he found Tenille on the plains of Sparta's Hoof. Cassie was found in the water of the channel nearby around the same time. Reginald never asked Cassie if this was her horse, nor did he ask the Rangers to find the owner of the horse; he overstepped here. The Rangers side with Cassie." He was sure Luke would agree with him once he had a chance to explain everything.

"Very well." Henrik sighed and turned to Cassie. "I do not expect you to leave Denny like that ever again." Shaking his head, he muttered something and rushed away. In the background, the advanced class winners were announced.

"I've been dreaming of Tenille almost every single night." Cassie spoke quietly, and Taven snapped his attention toward her. A light breeze played with her chestnut hair, the sun reflecting from her eyes intensifying their green. "I suppose I should thank you for convincing me to come back here and for following up on your promise." With a soft smile at him, Cassie turned her horse away.

Chapter

11

Leaving Tenille at Thebesia Stables had been torturous that first night, and Cassie was up with the sun running toward her the next morning.

"Morning!" Cassie said cheerfully to a groom outside, slowing to a walk as she entered the barn. She stopped at Denny's stall in the main aisle, pressing a kiss to his muzzle and ruffling his forelock before leaving him to his hay. Tenille had been given his old stall in the quieter wing of the stable since Henrik said it would be better for now.

The mare lifted her head from her hay, stretching it toward Cassie when she approached.

"Hi," Cassie whispered, wrapping her arms around her neck in a firm embrace. A strange pain began to develop in her left calf, just like the day before, sending her heart racing. Would the headaches return? Selene's pills had helped the day before, and she might have to take some again. She would have to bring this up at her doctor's appointment tomorrow evening.

The pain was eclipsed by a wave of peace and harmony. With Tenille, she felt safe, whole and complete. Simply being in her presence was enough to overcome any physical pain, and the longer she hugged her horse, the more the pain slipped away.

Cassie adjusted the forelock of her horse, reaching past to grab a fistful of hay and feed it to the mare. She wanted to tell her everything, but it was as if the horse already knew every thought that appeared in her mind, every idea she wanted to share.

It was strange, ridiculous even, but she felt that if Tenille really wanted to, she could tell her some things too. They understood each other's thoughts perfectly.

"Would you still be willing to work with Denny?" Henrik leaned against the stable door, startling Cassie. Tenille flicked an ear in acknowledgment.

"Willing?" Cassie frowned. "You said riders have multiple horses."

"Wonderful." He smiled, but it was strained. "You two get along so well."

"I like the stables. The more I can do here, the less I have to be at home." Cassie's eyes grew wide after the statement popped out. She hadn't meant to say that out loud, especially not to Henrik. "I'm sorry again about what happened at the show yesterday."

"Are you and Yvonne having problems?" Henrik ignored her subject change. His voice was surprisingly soft, curiosity mixed with a sort of concern. Cassie bit her tongue so she wouldn't say something she shouldn't, running her hands through Tenille's messy locks.

"No. Everything is fine." She forced a smile, pushing her lips upward. So fake, she knew she wasn't convincing anyone.

Henrik was silent, his gaze moving over the bright chestnut horse.

"Home is for resting, and I have little to do there." Especially with strange robe people staying the night.

That night had been torturous in more ways than one. Staying at Vallumvis for a few days had opened a door into a world she was more than willing to step in to. She had hardly seen Yvonne after returning home and suspected that the older woman was still upset over the Nora situation. The lady had run from the house even though she was supposed to stay. Was it somehow Cassie's fault?

"I suppose, for today, you could ride this beast instead of Denny. I want to see how you two get on. Regardless, with the show this Saturday, you should prioritize the gelding. I think you'll do well."

Cassie grinned, fitting a halter over Tenille's elegant head. His words were like sunshine breaking through after a thunderstorm, flooding her soul with warmth. She was glad he didn't prod more about Yvonne, but she was even more grateful she could ride her horse today.

"There is another matter as well." Henrik stepped out of her way as she led Tenille into the aisle. "Selene kept commenting on how well you did with all the pressure around you, and if it wasn't for the mishap at the last jump, you would have likely placed second."

"Really?"

"Yes. Alas, the rules state that all jumps must be complete, which resulted in your disqualification. However, one of the judges was impressed. You're free to compete at a higher level this time around."

Cassie grinned. "And the fact that I ran off right after?"

"Bah." Henrik waved his hand. "Personal matters are separate from the competition."

"Ok."

"But Selene," Henrik started again, and Cassie paused. "Well, she could use some additional help with her horse. If she asks, do consider."

"Sure." Cassie nodded, unsure what her answer would be. Right now, she wanted to focus on her own horse, not run around and solve everyone else's problems. She liked Kismet, though.

Cassie led Tenille to the grooming bay and did her best to ignore a bouncing Mitchie. She groomed her horse until she shone brighter than a new coin.

"She's so pretty!" Mitchie gushed for the umpteenth time. She reached out to pat her and drew her arm back with a gasp as the horse snapped at her outstretched fingers.

"She's not very friendly," Cassie said apologetically.

"Like her owner," a groom dropped as he walked past. Cassie rolled her eyes, prompting a laugh from Mitchie.

"Don't mind him," Mitchie said.

"He's a dunce and he knows it." With utmost carefulness, she placed the saddle she used with Denny on Tenille's back. She took a step back, and they both frowned.

"Her withers are narrower than Denny's. That saddle won't work." Mitchie stated the obvious, and Cassie nodded.

"Morning." Selene yawned, taking Cassie by surprise when she wrapped her in a deep hug.

"Hi," Cassie said awkwardly, flinching from the embrace.

"I'm sorry I didn't believe you," Selene whispered into her ear.

"It's ok. I hardly believed myself." Cassie smiled, her eyes flicking to Mitchie. The groom made no indication that she had overheard the conversation.

"She really is beautiful. Almost as beautiful as Kismet." Selene shot her a teasing smile, and Cassie grinned.

"I was going to ride her today, but I guess I will have to wait. The saddle doesn't fit her."

"Try Kismet's," Selene replied without hesitation. "He had the same problem, so I had a saddle custom made." She turned to Mitchie with a raised eyebrow. "Go on. Bring it."

Cassie squirmed at the obedient way Mitchie nodded and went to do Selene's bidding, but she didn't want to mention it. Perhaps it was normal for the two of them.

Cassie traded Denny's saddle for Kismet's when Mitchie returned.

"Much better." Cassie nodded. "Thank you, Selene."

"We need to get you one of your own. I will arrange for the saddle fitter to come tomorrow." Selene put up her hand before Cassie could protest. "There isn't another option. We can't share a saddle."

"Thanks." Cassie breathed the word, hurrying to adjust the stirrups and girth. She led Tenille to the indoor arena, knowing there would be fewer distractions inside.

Once mounted, she slowly walked around the arena, waiting for Henrik to join her. Walking was incredibly boring, though, and after one lap the pair moved into a trot.

Tenille picked up a canter as soon as the thought crossed Cassie's mind. If a jump had been set up, Cassie would have guided Tenille toward it without waiting for Henrik's approval.

When Henrik walked into the arena, Cassie slowed down, approaching him with a wide smile. His lips were pressed into a thin line, and Cassie's grip on the reins tightened.

"She's an aggressive horse, Cassie. I think you are the only person she hasn't tried to nip. I would have preferred you did some groundwork with her first. I'd hate to see you hurt."

"Tenille would never," Cassie retorted.

"I understand you have a relationship with her, but by the looks of it, she's very young and very green. And—" Henrik met her gaze, solemn. "A horse is a horse. Young ones are prone to bolting or bucking or misbehaving even when they like their rider." He wanted to say more but cut off his statement as Cassie, still holding the reins, crossed her arms.

"Tenille would never hurt me," Cassie repeated firmly, uncrossing her arms and heading off. She started trotting in circles around the arena again, catching his last words before the distance became too great.

"Rash. Horse and rider alike."

Cassie ignored him, dipping into a blissful world of her own. It was a world where she and Tenille were one, and no one else was included. She'd do anything to remember the adventures she had with her horse before the accident, but for now, the new memories they made together would have to suffice.

"Keep a tighter rein on her, but be gentle. She's very sensitive," Henrik called out, dragging a pole to the center of the arena. Four more followed, set out on the ground a stride apart. "You can try this with her. I would say if you want— but I know you probably want me to bring out our tallest oxers." He grunted, stepping to the side.

She had no hesitations with Tenille. Her horse would go willingly wherever she led because she trusted her. It was worlds apart from riding any other horse, even Denny.

Cassie smiled to herself. Trust.

"You handle her very well. I am impressed." Henrik gave an approving nod, and to Cassie, it was much more meaningful than he'd ever know.

"Do you think," Cassie began in a quiet voice, "that this Saturday we can enter a show? The lowest class, the short jumps, to get her used to it? Denny of course would be the real star of the show." Cassie held her breath, hoping he'd say yes.

"You've had your horse for a day and you're already jumping into a show." Henrik shook his head, lips flattening into a grimace before he straightened his expression. "I can't stop you, but I would be very, very careful." Henrik patted Tenille's rump, aiming for a place far away from her snapping teeth.

A pit settled into her stomach as she led Tenille back to the grooming bay to untack her. Shows did have a lot of pressure, and internally she had nearly crumbled during the last one.

But only because of Tenille. They were together now, and neither her calf nor her head were bothering her like the day before.

Removing the saddle and bridle, she walked across the hallway to the tack room, nearly bumping into Taven.

"Hi! Cassie, right?" His bright smile illuminated the aisle, and Cassie smiled back, contagious as it was. His eyes crinkled at the edges, obscuring the warm honey-brown color behind thick lashes. He was without a cap this time, his soft brown hair swept to the side.

"Yes." She suddenly felt small, only reaching up to his shoulder. Up on their horses, the height difference wasn't as palpable as it was when they were on the ground.

"Here, let me help with that." Without waiting for a response, he took the saddle and bridle from her.

"Why are you helping me?" she asked cautiously, clasping her hands tightly together. His attention was flattering, but Yvonne's strict warning that the Rangers were not to be bothered echoed in her mind. Both Adria and Taven had proven to be exceptions.

"Because!" Taven smiled, a flash of white teeth visible. "I've told you before: I'm a Ranger. It's my duty to help you." She followed him inside the tack room and watched as he placed the saddle on an empty rack. Cassie grabbed a spare rag and wiped down the supple leather, his presence a breath away.

"It's Selene's saddle. She let me borrow it." Her voice quivered, her mind needing to say anything to fill the empty space between them. He nodded.

"Has your horse settled in well?"

"She came here yesterday," Cassie said defensively, backing out of the tack room. "She hasn't had time to get to know anyone yet. After the way she was treated at the other stable, it might take her a while before she trusts anyone." He followed her to the grooming bay where Tenille was waiting impatiently. Cassie picked up a curry comb and ran it over the sweaty spot on her back.

"I hope she can learn to trust me." Taven reached into his

pocket for a cube of sugar, offering it to the mare. Her careful mouth picked up the treat, her head bobbing up and down as she chewed.

"She says thank you."

"Ah, that's right. She talks to you?" he asked with a grin. Cassie didn't know if he was curious or mocking her.

"We simply understand each other." Cassie huffed, tossing the brushes to the side. She needed to take Tenille back to her stall, and the way the Ranger was lingering was not natural. "Why are you here?" The question was direct, and quite honestly, bordering on rude. Not that she cared, with him getting in her way.

Taven's smile didn't shrink.

Her disappointment didn't lie with him but with how useless he had been the day before. He knew nothing about her family or how the accident had happened. She was grateful he had rescued her from the water, truly she was, yet the sinking disappointment in her stomach only served to remind her that he couldn't offer her more.

"Cassie." Her name rolled off his tongue. "I can get so much more done when I travel than when I'm tied down in Arion. Luke, my boss, lets me run around on occasion; other days I'm not so lucky. Currently I'm taking advantage of my freedom." His eyes darkened into something more devilish. Cassie raised an eyebrow, not believing he'd ever broken a single rule in his life.

"Were you sent here to spy on me?" There, his smile faltered. Cassie lifted her chin and cracked her own half smile, reaching up to unclip the side ties.

"Cassie." The number of times he said her name made her wonder if he really liked it or if he had no other way to start a sentence. "No one is spying on you. You're perfectly safe here in Desmalogo. But if you want the truth . . ." He no longer held his smile, his thin lips set in a line. "Yes, Luke wanted me here today to make sure everything was alright. It's not only because of you. The scandal with Reginald, the stir you caused running off with Tenille like that; he wanted to press charges against the Rangers." Taven let out a frustrated breath. She locked eyes with him for a few moments, hardly breathing. "I'm glad we got it all sorted out," he finally managed.

"Who's Reginald?" Cassie demanded, her hand suspended in the air.

"You don't know him?" Taven asked, falling into step with her as she led Tenille to her stall.

"No," Cassie replied. She considered sharing her dreams but decided against it. Selene's reaction had been difficult to process, and she did not want the Ranger to think she was crazy. For whatever reason, she wanted him to be her friend.

"He's no one you should worry about. That's my job." He winked with a lopsided smile, and Cassie looked away, heat crawling up her neck.

"Whoever he is, I hate him," Cassie said through clenched teeth, releasing Tenille into her stall. Taven reached out to pet the silky mane and Tenille, who was apparently satisfied with the treat, made no attempt to nip.

Tenille was happy to be left alone with her fodder, and Cassie went outside for a wheelbarrow.

"Hate is a powerful emotion." Taven had a smirk at the edge of his lips, angering Cassie further.

"I have to clean the stalls now. Is your interrogation over?" Her forehead puckered as her eyebrows shot together, pinning him with a stare she hoped translated to "please leave." He was a distraction she didn't quite know how to deal with, and by the looks of it, he would prove useless about the robes as well.

"I'll help." He grinned as if he actually liked shoveling manure.

"You can't." Cassie frowned. "I am doing chores for Henrik in exchange for extra lessons and Tenille's board."

Taven reached past her and picked up a pitchfork, his arm brushing against hers. Her breath caught at the touch of contact, eyes snagging on his muscular arms. He probably never shied away from extra work.

"I'll explain to Henrik that my help will count toward your needs." He winked. Again. Her stomach flip-flopped. Her mouth went dry.

Taven walked beside her to the first stall. For several minutes, they worked quietly together, but then Taven started telling her about himself. Cassie liked the sound of his voice even if most of what he said went over her head. She learned his father was a Ranger, as was his father before him, going all the way back to when the Rangers were founded in Desmalogo.

It was hard not to believe he was simply here because he was nice. However, he had told Cassie he was here to ensure no one would take the horse, and he was following through.

They had only finished half the stalls when Henrik appeared, glancing over at Cassie.

"That will be enough for today. I know you have a doctor's appointment in a few days, and I don't want to catch flack for overworking you." He chuckled to himself, turning to Taven. "Thanks for the help."

"I'll be fine." Cassie sighed, internally relieved to be sent home early, not even finding the energy to correct Henrik that her check-up was tomorrow.

"You will if you head home." Henrik's voice was firm, leaving no room for arguments. Cassie handed him the pitchfork, too stubborn to admit how tired she was and too tired to argue.

Taven waved to her as she left, his smirk replaced with pinched lips.

Selene approached her the next day with the saddle fitter, doing most of the talking while Cassie held Tenille very still. He took several measurements, wrote them down on a paper, and promised to be back within a week.

When he left, Selene lingered, the question hanging in the air between them.

"Henrik said you wanted someone to help with Kismet?" Cassie asked, her gaze on her own horse. It was only right for her to bring it up, since Henrik forewarned her.

"Yes." Selene shrugged. "I would like that. You'll be paid, of course."

Paid. Her own source of income and a step toward becoming fully independent.

"When would you like to start?" She hoped she didn't sound too eager.

"Today."

Mitchie had Kismet prepared, and Selene led him out to one of the round training rings. She stood hesitantly, her hands gripping the reins with unsure fingers.

"Is everything alright?" Cassie questioned when Selene refused to give her the reins.

Selene was silent for a few moments, but when she glanced up, her eyes were wet with tears.

"No. It isn't alright. My parents expect me to take top placing at the show, but lately everything has been going downhill between us." She nibbled on her bottom lip, eyes drifting to the ground. "I want a different horse, but they won't hear of it. He was imported from Sparta, and Pa says I won't find a better one in Desmalogo. But look at our last show. We placed far from the top ten."

"You don't need a different horse. This one is perfect," Cassie reasoned. "He's the most beautiful horse in all of Thebesia Stables."

"And? Kismet doesn't like jumping. He doesn't like dressage. He doesn't like groundwork. He doesn't like flatwork," Selene lamented with a sniffle, finally handing the reins to Cassie.

"He does. He's overwhelmed and doesn't know what to do. Your cues can be a little rough and confusing." Cassie's voice dropped to a whisper, not missing the flaming glance Selene gave her. It was true, what she said. Selene often showed little patience toward her horse, and it became evident in the show ring.

"You're accusing me of being a bad rider?" Selene said, the pain clear in her voice.

Cassie sighed, tilting her face toward the sunshine. "No."

"If you're so good, then you ride him." Selene stomped off but not before Cassie noticed a single tear trailing down her cheek. Cassie swallowed, her gaze moving to the helmet in her hands. She wasn't trying to prove anything. She wanted Selene to do her best at the show too. But if Selene needed space right now, she could respect that.

Clipping her helmet into place, Cassie led an anxious Kismet to the mounting block and clambered into the saddle.

The stirrups were a little short for her, but she didn't bother with the adjustments.

Kismet sidestepped nervously, champing at the bit. Cassie settled deeper into the saddle, relaxing her legs. She'd wait until he calmed down a little before asking things from him.

"You're such a handsome boy," she cooed, his ears flicking toward her. Patting his neck with a gentle hand, she tightened the limp reins for a better connection to the bit and bridle. "You could walk on in a circle around the ring." Ever so slowly, the horse relaxed and allowed Cassie to guide him in a walk around the arena. With several words of encouragement, he picked up a lazy trot.

Cassie steered him toward the middle but not at the poles. Instead, they trotted by them. Then circled around them. She slowed him to a walk and allowed Kismet to stop and sniff the poles.

Once Cassie was confident Kismet was not scared of anything, she asked him to walk toward the poles and then over them several times. After that, she approached them at a trot.

Kismet's ears kept flicking back and forward, and Cassie kept a steady stream of chatter going.

"You know, horses are so different from humans. They don't talk back to me, yet I feel like they understand me better than any human ever could." Cassie sighed, tapping her heel against his side and cantering toward the poles. She could feel his hesitancy but kept consistent pressure, patting his neck when he crossed the last one.

"There you go. That's enough for today. You deserve a break for being such a wonderful pony." A grin developed on her face, then she glanced at Selene at the side of the arena. The girl's arms were crossed, her slitted eyes following Cassie's every move. Sucking in a tight breath, Cassie urged Kismet to walk over to her. The overeager horse burst into a trot, stopping right in front of the fence.

"You look like you belong on him."

Was that a hint of bitterness in her tone? Cassie wasn't sure. "He's a wonderful horse, but perhaps not as comfortable in the arena as he should be. He needs a lot of repetitive training to increase his comfort level. It takes him a while to adjust to change."

Selene dropped her chin to rest on her knuckles, her eyes trailing the black mane rippling in the wind.

"Ok."

"I like riding him. He feels familiar to me." Familiar enough to convince her she had ridden him before, even though it sounded impossible. If she had ridden Kismet before, would that mean she'd been on the island before?

"I think his build is similar to Tenille's. Which, by the way . . ." Selene squinted her eyes against the sun to meet Cassie's eyes. "I'm surprised you were able to walk away with her like that."

"But she's mine." Cassie gaped at the statement, unable to understand why Selene would say that.

"You wouldn't be the first to make something up to get your hands on a good horse," her friend continued, unbothered.

"You thought I was lying to get my horse back?" Cassie shook her head violently, her red hair whipping her across the face. "Even Taven could tell we belong together."

Selene nibbled on her bottom lip and stroked the soft muzzle of her horse.

"I suppose you do. Thank you for this." She reached into her pocket and handed Cassie a couple matching silver coins. "There's just, a group of people." Selene's jaw stiffened, and she wouldn't meet Cassie's gaze. "And there have been cases of horses going missing, people taking them away, and even a case where a girl was killed over her horse. I wouldn't want you to be entangled in all that."

Cassie's heart dropped, her mind a whirlwind of indigo

lights clashing with thoughts and words. A group of people. Secretive. Taking things without permission. Nora at Yvonne's.

"Do these people wear robes?"

"Yes," Selene whispered. She snapped her head up as someone approached, grabbing the reins almost forcefully. "Kismet needs to be taken care of. Let's go find Mitchie."

Selene said nothing else of the robe people and was silent when Cassie asked if she could share anything else. Cassie dropped the subject, intending to pick it up with the doctor.

The door to the clinic swung open, and Cassie stepped inside. The lady at the front desk smiled.

"Welcome, Cassie. You are just in time." She scratched away at some papers, then stood and led Cassie to the empty room. Cassie thanked her and sat atop the exam table, her hands clenched together.

The air smelled too clean, too sterile. Nothing like the barn with its welcoming atmosphere and soft ambiance.

Cassie gulped a breath of the bitter air, her mind churning over how to approach the doctor. Flat out ask? Wait for him to bring it up?

The door opened, and Cassie nearly jumped out of her skin. The doctor frowned, lowering himself into a chair on the other side of the room.

"How is your horse?" he asked in a quiet voice, folding one leg over his knee.

"She's mine," Cassie quipped, surprised at his choice of opening question.

"Yes." Dr. Lykaion nodded, running a hand through his hair. "How are you feeling now that you've reunited?"

"Better." Cassie rolled her neck, her spine popping. "I spent all day at the stables yesterday and missed lunch."

"That's not good. You should be putting on weight, not skipping meals. Try to eat more." He reached toward the files on the desk behind him, absentmindedly flipped through them, then set them back. "Anything bothering you? Your head better?" The questions seemed hollow, and Cassie shrugged.

"It hurt so bad when Tenille appeared. Selene gave me pills, and they helped, but I thought my head was going to split in two. It's been two days, and the pain has not returned. Not even in my leg. I still can't remember anything, stupid head of mine." She bit her bottom lip to stop herself from saying things she shouldn't, then took a deep breath.

"The pain was associated with your horse coming back, though it is unclear why. Your bond is deeper than you realize." The doctor leaned forward.

"I understand quite well," Cassie retorted. The doctor's eyes dipped to her left calf, where it hurt when she was with Tenille. He seemed to know a lot of things about her.

"You have a birthmark there, hardly visible."

"I've seen it, but what does it mean?" Cassie sucked in a shallow breath. The birthmark was a half circle with wavy lines on top, etched so lightly into her skin that it was only visible in good lighting.

She almost didn't want to know what it meant if it would turn her world upside down. Learning something new felt like plunging her head underwater and not knowing how much time she had until she could breathe air again. The very thought of being sent back to the cold state of nothingness sent shivers down her spine. And those indigo lights never seemed to leave her mind either.

"I think it's best for it to remain a mystery. Not something you want to tell people. Certain ones will not take it well." Dr. Lykaion locked eyes with her, waiting to see if she understood.

"Like the people with the robes." The statement came out blunt and harsh, and something flickered in the doctor's gaze.

"The people with the robes understand very well what the bond between a girl and her horse can create."

"Henrik said there is a bond stronger than none other, but it doesn't mean much. To me, Tenille is as close to me, as familiar as my beating heart."

Dr. Lykaion smiled. A kind smile, one of a proud guardian.

"That's why it's so special. And certain people, well." He sighed, steepling his fingers. "You can't expect them to understand something so deep, so personal. Desmalogo has an air of enchantment around it that connects people with horses. But some people, like you, Cassie, experience it even deeper. Most citizens prefer to live in a fantasy rather than in truth, but I am afraid you will discover that truth for yourself. It wasn't what I intended. I wanted you to live a normal life. Like Selene, or the other friends you have made. But I'm optimistic about the future." Dr. Lykaion was staring at the wall, eyes clouded in thought.

"Who are the people with the robes, the ones who claim to conserve the island?" Cassie asked, tired of being in the dark. Here she was again, underwater, trying to decipher everything said. She wanted to live peacefully with Tenille, but she couldn't ignore what was happening under the surface. The lights, the language, the birthmark. Surely they were all connected.

Dr. Lykaion's eyebrows shot upward.

"Have you met any?"

"The first day I awoke in Desmalogo I saw someone. And then another time, it might have been the same person." Cassie kept her voice low.

"Can you tell me about it?"

"Very well," Cassie muttered, giving up trying to maintain secrecy. "A lady, Nora, was at the house one time when I came back from the stables. She was wearing a robe, a light-colored one, with gold stitching along the edges. Yvonne said she could stay, but the lady said something about traces of corruption in the house and left in a rush. I never asked Yvonne to explain, but I find it hard to believe this was the first time she harbored robe people." Cassie glanced up to find the doctor leaning forward in his chair, his jaw slack.

"A Fýlax," he grumbled, running a hand through his hair. "No, it is alright." He let out a slow breath through his lips. "They visit the cities to ensure everything is in order. After all, they are a conservation society. But Yvonne would prefer to be secretive, I know, as there are enough people who mistrust them."

The information lined up with what Selene had shared, and Cassie tucked away the doctor's words. If Dr. Lykaion knew about Yvonne, he would not have been so surprised when he heard one had visited.

"Henrik doesn't like them, I suppose." Cassie sighed, itching to remove herself from the room and return to the stables. "Conservation" was a word that could encompass a wide range of ideas.

"No. And you are free to form your own opinion too." The doctor had a strained smile, and Cassie already felt herself negatively influenced against the group.

"The language they speak, I saw it on a note written for Yvonne. It matches the letters on my necklace, but not the letters of the island."

"It is called Grecian. It used to be more prominent throughout the island but has faded with age. Cassie, do you know Grecian well?" he asked in a low tone.

"I can read it, understand it. As much as the current language, if not more." Cassie drew her knees up to her chest.

"Not many people in Desmalogo know the language of the Fýlax." He ran a hand through his hair, which did little to calm Cassie's nerves. "Right now, we are speaking Desmaligan. It makes me curious how you learned it."

"I don't know. Maybe go into my head and tell me instead." Cassie's voice turned bitter, annoyance woven between each syllable. She had started to feel as if she could belong on the island, with Selene and Taven, even Adria and Mitchie. Was there so much more below the surface?

"Does Yvonne know?" The doctor eased into a hint of a smile, taking up a more relaxed posture.

"If she knew, she wouldn't leave her stuff around." Cassie shrugged, shaking her hair back behind her shoulders. She turned to the doctor with a harsh glare.

"I won't be the one breaking the news to her." Dr. Lykaion lifted his hands in a sign of peace. Cassie rolled her eyes, then hopped down from the exam table with a frown.

"Her other friends are much more important than me."

"Cassie, it's not like that," Dr. Lykaion began, clasping his hands behind his back.

"Are you also acquainted with her Grecian friends?" the girl challenged, and the doctor took a moment to collect himself.

"When is your next show?"

"This Saturday."

"Good. I'll be there. Anything else you'd like to ask about?" The doctor studied her for a moment, and Cassie nibbled her lower lip. Was it right to trust him more than Yvonne? He was more open with his thoughts but no less secretive about matters of the island. Unless he didn't know.

"Not today, thank you." Cassie smiled, pausing at the door. "And I will be expecting you at my show."

"Of course."

13

L okiir's eyes were colder than the icy seawater as the ship passed his for the seventh time in the last two days. So close, he was tempted to reach out and touch the edge. His jaw set with annoyance as the man on the other ship scanned the sea, seeking but not finding.

Despite crossing paths so many times, not once had the other ship spotted his.

Lokiir ground his teeth in a grimace as sharp talons dug into his shoulder, announcing the arrival of Mnemosyne.

The raven, dark as night, stared at the man with beady eyes. Had there been a speck of light in his forbidden haven, her feathers might have gleamed.

Alas, in the foggy air with low visibility, her feathers merely rippled in the darkness.

"Well?" Lokiir asked, lifting his free hand to stroke the top of the bird's head. "Do share. It's been too long since we have been together." Mnemosyne's silence unnerved him.

"Lokiir, I've missed you," the raven cooed, dropping from his shoulder to his wrist resting on the edge of the ship. "How have you fared whilst I was away?"

"I have lived each day in agony." Lokiir wrapped his

fingers around her fragile neck, applying pressure until he could feel the bones.

"As have I." The raven slipped her neck from his unrelenting grasp, landing on the ship railing an arm's length away. "Ah." She lifted her head, amusement in her beady eyes. "You have no interest in removing the shroud for your dear brother to see you?"

"He'll wait." A smile tugged at the edge of Lokiir's mouth, and the bird croaked.

"Doubt he's in a rush."

"Not that he has a choice," Lokiir added, shifting his weight from one sore foot to the other. He braced himself as a particularly strong wave hit the side of the ship, rocking it from side to side. Rare were the days that the ship was peaceful, the weather usually driving him mad.

"Should I mention he wishes to update you about the situation with the horse?" the raven continued, her voice nonchalant.

"Mnemosyne! You wonderful little bird. How long have you known?" Lokiir gripped the railing with enough force to whiten his knuckles, a ghost of a smile on his face.

"Nearly a day. I saw him and then went back to the horse. Then I came back to you. The horse, which by the way—" Mnemosyne launched into the air, looping around Lokiir's head slowly "—is nothing but a horse. Well, a Pneúmós, as claimed, but really. She reunited with her owner. Your lovely kinmate watched and stormed here." She landed on Lokiir's wrist again, tossing her head back to caw in laughter. It was a cold laugh, void of any emotion. Not because birds didn't have emotion, but because she was his bird.

"He thinks we care that he lost his toy." Lokiir sighed, scooping up the bird with both hands. He was careful not to crush her, though he so badly wanted to. The fragile bones would break with a snap, and the beady, taunting eyes would forever lose the light illuminating them.

"You best let him in so you can tell him to go away. And—" Mnemosyne tried to wriggle out of his grasp, but his grip was too tight. She resorted to pecking sharply at the sensitive skin between his thumb and forefinger, drawing blood.

Lokiir grumbled, releasing the bird but following it with his sharp eyes.

"And?" he pressed. The thought of leaving Reginald waiting outside his shroud for a week was appealing.

"And tell him we no longer wish to see his face. He's after nothing but shiny coins to line his pockets with." She scoffed, the caw echoing through the ship.

"If you insist." Lokiir lifted his hand, lazily moving the shroud near the entrance of the ship. He would be seen now, but the darkness he would never relinquish. "Have someone bring him to my quarters." Releasing the railing right as another wave slapped against the ship sent him flying, and his hands smashed against the wooden boards, nose an inch away from being crushed. Blasted boat. It almost made him want to go back to the underworld, but Káto was worse—so much worse.

Besides a cabin for sleeping, he had a sizable conference room in the center of the ship. Those two were the only rooms off limits to everyone else on the ship, his bedroom and his throne room. There, he didn't feel completely useless, having the power to unleash all the chaos and evil he wanted toward the cursed island he hated so much.

He made himself comfortable on the throne in his conference room. He didn't have to wait long before two young women led Reginald into the room and deposited him in the center. Both ladies he found so detestable that he couldn't decide who he disliked more.

"Ah, what a surprise." He raised his eyebrows, contempt drawn over his face as he gazed down on his brother. A few years older than him, yet coming here to grovel on his knees like the coward he was.

"Lokiir, hello." Reginald knelt, his head bowed. "I am sorry to inform you I was not able to capture the horse you requested."

"Indeed." Icicles were not as cold as Lokiir's voice. "Previously, I was told you had captured her and would deliver her to me in a timely manner."

"She is an unruly demoness. I had captured her, but she broke the stable door and ran away—"

"Nonsense!" Lokiir roared, standing. "These are mere excuses. I do not believe for a moment that she broke away." He paused, staring down at the man he had once called brother. "You must be keeping her for your little racing hobby. You are seeking to back out of our agreement."

"She did run away," Reginald pleaded. "I would never do that to you!" That statement was bogus enough to make Lokiir laugh, a hollow sound against the wooden walls.

"You promised me you would deliver the horse, yet here you are making excuses as to why you don't have her. I don't tolerate empty promises!"

Reginald dropped his eyes even further to the ground, if that were possible, the slight contraction of his shoulder blades betraying him.

One of the women, her dark hair curling over her shoulders, tossed Reginal an annoyed glance, taking a step away from him. A malicious smile grew across Lokiir's face, uninvited but not unwelcome.

"I tried." Reginald groaned. "The horse was driving herself mad because she was away from the girl. I should have taken both, but it's too late now," Reginald finished in a pathetic tone. Lokiir imagined he well regretted ever trying to strike a bargain with him.

"You received your end of the bargain, did you not?"

Reginald nodded.

"What about mine?"

"Won't any other horse suffice?" he begged.

Lokiir refused to indulge in his inward delight. He had no use for a horse that would end with him being discovered. The girl could keep her horse. He would rather target the ones left alone for too long. They had tried to banish him once. If he was found, they would do it again.

"No. You promised me the chestnut one. You told me that one holds a lot of power. You think a mere average steed would be a match for someone like me?" Lokiir spoke each word slowly, eyes narrowed with suspicion.

"No, of course not."

"Precisely," Lokiir mocked. "I should have you killed right here, dear brother, but I will never stoop to your level." The man beneath him squirmed, adding to his delight. "You fought for years to rid the island of my presence, and you got what you wished for. Was that not enough? No, your endless drive for power knows no bounds." He thrust out his wrist to catch the raven sweeping toward him, gritting his teeth at the pain of her talons. Pain he would take any day over the emotions swelling inside of him. "You got rid of me, as you wished, then all the Opposed. Silly of you to come back here, being so afraid of our power. So afraid that a single horse is enough to throw you off balance. I tire of this, Reginald." Lokiir turned his empty eyes to the girl with the dark curls and darker eyes. Merel, he remembered. Her hatred for him was so strong he wouldn't be surprised if it could be sensed from outside the shroud that kept them hidden. So different from the white-haired one, Daz, who would bend over backward to please him.

Merel hated being here, but stars. No one hated being here as much as he did.

"Merel. Open a portal back to the cursed island."

She complied, only because she had no other choice, and a swirl of indigo lights materialized all around Reginald.

"You have one last chance, Reginald. If you do not get me the horse within a week, it will be the last week you live."

Chapter

14

Cassie hurried to the stables after another night of avoiding Yvonne. Too much conflicting information had created distance between them, especially about the robe character. What had the doctor called her? A Fýlax.

According to the doctor, she wasn't supposed to know Grecian. Cassie frowned, passing Taven and Selene without acknowledging their presence. With a certain hurry to her step, she entered the far wing of the stable and leaned on Tenille's stall door. When the mare lifted her head from her hay and ambled over to Cassie, the girl pressed a kiss on her soft muzzle. The world around her was changing again, but Cassie rested in the steady presence of her horse.

"I'll be back to ride you, but I have to get to Denny first today." Leaving her horse with another kiss, Cassie entered the main aisle, sputtering in anger at the riders and horses clogging the alleyway.

She stopped in front of Denny's stall, her frown deepening. It was empty.

"Henrik?" she called out, pushing past several riders in the barn. He was in the arena, coaching another rider. "Henrik?" she repeated, and the man turned toward her voice.

"I have about a quarter hour left here."

"Where's Denny?"

"Out in the paddocks." He gave an approving nod, going back to the girl on the deep bay horse. His several white socks and large blaze paired with fluid movements made him a flashy mount, and his rider took him through the fences with ease.

Cassie walked away, noting a tiny detail she would have changed if that had been her atop the horse. She was good enough to be on the advanced team as well. She simply needed more practice. A thought of doubt crossed her mind. Was she truly ready for the next level of jumping? She quickly squashed it. Yes. She was.

Picking up a lead rope, Cassie went back outside and jogged toward the paddocks. Denny was in the south one, munching on grass and not at all happy to be dragged back to the barn.

After struggling to find an empty crosstie, she brushed Denny down vigorously. He was gleaming, barely dirty from his time in the outdoor paddocks.

Cassie weaved through several riders, stopping when a girl a few years older placed a hand on her arm.

"Cassie, isn't it? Your horse is stunning. Do you mind me asking where you purchased her?"

Her mind scrambled, eyes slowly blinking as she tried to avoid saying "I don't know."

"Same place I came from."

Ignoring the confused response, she stepped into the tack room. Cassie picked up everything she needed and pushed out of the room, hardly able to see over her stack of items.

She nearly yelped when someone removed the saddle from her arms.

"You look overloaded," Taven commented, his usual smile in place.

"I'm not," Cassie huffed, marching toward Denny, his bridle slung over her shoulder. "I like riding in the early morning when there's nearly no one awake. I oversleep one morning. One, and there's too many people in the barn. So I made one trip to the tack room to avoid them all."

Taking the saddle back from Taven, she placed it on Denny, straightening out the white numnah underneath.

"People are not a threat to you." Taven tried to reason with her, handing Cassie each boot as she fitted them onto Denny's legs.

"They ask questions." Cassie sighed, straightening and reaching out to the horse to steady herself.

"Are you alright?" Taven asked, his eyes scanning hers.

"Overwhelmed, possibly, with so much on my mind." She shrugged it off, fitting the bridle over Denny's face.

"That's not good. Maybe you could get checked out by the doctor—"

"Where do you think I was yesterday?" Cassie snapped, then froze at his shocked reaction.

"Sorry, I—" Taven swallowed, running a hand through his light brown locks.

"No. I'm sorry. I snap at everyone." Cassie rubbed her temples with a sigh, rolling her neck back and forth. "Every time I go he tells me to eat more, then we talk about things that don't relate to health at all. Last time it was languages and certain people. Apparently I know more than one language, and he was really surprised to hear that."

"What language?" Taven asked curiously, taking a step back as Cassie led Denny down the barn aisle.

"This is why I don't like people. They only know how to ask questions." She rolled her eyes and dragged her horse away from the Ranger, frustrated with herself more than with him.

He was trying to be nice; she appreciated his efforts. But it wasn't enough for her to lower her guard. The doctor's words sat in the pit of her stomach, conjuring warnings even if that hadn't been his intention.

If Taven learned Yvonne harbored a Fýlax, would his kindness toward her change?

Denny yawned as she mounted, perking up when Cassie kicked him into a brisk walk. Though a bit lazy at times, he liked his work, always eager to listen to his rider.

He was too easy to please, dutifully going through his warm-up movements. So much so that Cassie found it hard to concentrate, her thoughts wandering down roads they shouldn't go down.

She could ask Taven if he knew anything about Grecian and what he knew about the robes. But that would mean revealing how she knew about those things, and she wasn't ready for that.

The hair on the back of her neck tingled as her thoughts jumped from robes to languages to the very locket nestled against her chest.

Why was she here? What had really happened before she woke up in Yvonne's house, stripped of all her memories?

If she came from the island, wouldn't someone recognize her? She shuddered, wild thoughts galloping across her brain as she considered all the possibilities.

"Cassie, your riding is very sloppy." Henrik's voice broke through her thoughts, and she instantly straightened out. "Better. Keep your legs steady. We don't want them sliding away." He stood next to the fence, about to leave but staying for a few moments.

Cassie ground her teeth, her eyebrows dipping together in focus. She guided Denny through several complicated lead changes, forcing her raging mind to be quiet.

"I don't want to put more pressure on you than you already have." Henrik hesitated, and Cassie slowed down, turning to see what he would say. "That was quite the uproar in Vallumvis. I expect Bucephala to be better, but there will be many, many people watching you. It isn't often someone new shows up and causes a scene."

"We'll win in Buce-whatever," Cassie said, her mouth set. "Denny is good enough to be a champion."

"So is his rider." Henrik almost smiled, a shadow crossing over his face. "The judges will be blown away." He hurried to another riding ring, a young man on a gray waiting for him.

Cassie pushed Denny into a canter, shaking away the clouds of doubt in her mind. They would do well. She simply had to believe it.

After half an hour, the girl cooled down her horse and walked him for several laps before heading back inside the barn. She handed the horse to Mitchie with a stifled yawn, aware of the hunger pangs in her stomach.

She thought about getting lunch, but Selene approached her. Cassie smiled with a wave. They'd last parted on a good note even though the subject was touchy.

"Hi! Do you have time to work with Kismet today?"

"Is two days in a row not too much?"

"We won't have any more time this week. I would ask you to ride him tomorrow and the following Thursday, but that's the event."

"What event?" Cassie asked.

"We're going to Arion on that day. It's an all-day event, then on Friday we rest our horses. Saturday is the show."

Cassie forced a smile, thinking it was nice for Selene to go to Arion. Taven would be there.

"I'll ride Kismet," Cassie said forcefully, walking up to the horse and taking his reins into her hand. Selene nodded and followed her out to the riding ring, preferring to watch their sessions.

Kismet was a saint, and yet Cassie struggled to keep him under her control. The feeling of being all alone in this cold world continued to grow stronger. Even Tenille's presence did nothing to fix the gaping hole in her mind where her memories should be.

At one point during their session, Selene hopped off the fence and jogged back to the barn, concern on her face. Cassie waved it off, assuming she needed to use the restroom or had forgotten to remind the grooms to double clean the gelding's stall.

The riding ring they were in had several poles set up in a X shape, and Cassie weaved through them, Kismet snorting in excitement at the challenge. With the right handling, he was nearly perfect. His movements reminded her of how it felt to ride Tenille, and she swallowed against the rising guilt.

Her horse was always on the back burner since she had to complete her work first.

Because it was her work, Cassie reminded herself. Selene promised to provide her with drachmas, enough to fund her flatcake and blueberry lemonade addiction with plenty left over. Riding Denny and doing chores was her arrangement with Henrik, and he had happily accepted Tenille into his barn without asking for anything in return.

Feeling a little better about herself, Cassie slid off Kismet and led him into the barn, bumping into Selene.

She smiled, taking the reins from her.

"I'll get your wages tomorrow, ok? Thank you." She led her horse away, and Cassie couldn't stand being hungry any longer. Her next chore was feeding the horses their evening meal, which was hours away.

Nearly jogging even though that wasn't allowed in the barn, she skidded around the corner and rushed to her stall.

Taven was leaning against the door, feeding her horse sugar. He turned to her with a twinkle in his eye, jutting his chin toward Tenille.

"I think she likes me now." His voice was triumphant.

"Anyone would like you if you fed them sugar," Cassie grumbled, and Taven chuckled.

"Funny you say that." His smile grew wider as he handed her a paper sack and a blueberry lemonade. "You said you needed to eat more, and after being here for two days, I realized you always skip lunch. It's not good."

Cassie accepted the items, wanting to give him a soul-crushing hug but at the same time feeling incredibly shy. He'd gone out of his way to get her lunch.

"I thought you'd only be here yesterday, then go back to Arion," Cassie stammered, needing to fill the silence. Taven blinked slowly, his long lashes catching her eye.

"I'm here to advertise," he said with a grin.

"Advertise?"

"For the Arion event." There it was again, an event everyone knew about except for her.

"I don't know what that is," Cassie said blankly, finally feeling brave enough to take a sip of lemonade.

"No one's told you? I was waiting for you to ask me about it, since I am a Ranger, one of the main drivers of the event and all." Taven laughed, like he was amused at himself for thinking she would know. "It's Arion Fun Day, where the Rangers host an informational day for the public that's loads of fun. We play games, then have a picnic. Everyone is welcome, but the riders especially have a good time. Friends are pitted against each other in games on horseback, bringing out the true competitive spirit of any good Desmaligan. I don't think there's anything we love more than proving our worth to each other." Taven motioned to the paper sack. "There's a sandwich inside. Please eat it. Or at least try it and tell me if you don't like it."

"Oh." Cassie pulled out two soft slabs of bread, colorful ingredients wedged between them. "This means I'm invited too?"

"Not only are you invited, you must come." Taven reached

out to pet Tenille, whose teeth were reaching toward Cassie's sandwich.

"With what horse?" Cassie asked, her stomach dropping in disappointment. What if she had to take Denny?

Taven's laugh unnerved her.

"Yours." He patted the orange horse's neck. "Tomorrow, the group will leave the stables around eight or nine in the morning, depending on how long it takes for everyone to show up." His eyes dipped toward the nearly gone sandwich. "Next time I'll get two."

Cassie grinned, shoving the last of the bread into her mouth.

"Thank you," she said, the streak of self-consciousness still there. Taven flashed his brilliant smile, giving her horse a final pat.

"See you then."

Cassie opened the door to her house, scanning the dimmed rooms. Yvonne was frugal with her lighting, often leaving a singular candle in each room. It wasn't quite dark outside, the setting sun casting long shadows across the floor. It was quiet too. Either Yvonne was outside or she had left to run an errand.

Cassie stepped into the kitchen. There was no food on the table, only a piece of paper with ink and a freshly trimmed feather nearby. Like a moth to candlelight she was drawn to it, curiosity drowning out the small voice that whispered this might not be for her.

She squinted at the letters; this note was written in Grecian, the same as the previous letter she had found in the washroom. Was Yvonne writing a letter to the strange people?

Dear Aurelian,

There is a matter we must urgently discuss. I am being pressured into something I do not want to do, and I'd like your opinion . . .

Footsteps at the back door had Cassie scrambling to the nearest cupboard for a snack.

"Good to see you, dear," Yvonne called out as she entered through the back door with a basket on her arm. She shed dirt-stained gloves. "How was your day?"

"Good." Cassie picked up an apple, thinking her day would be better if she could have finished reading the letter.

"Wonderful. I was going to make a salad for dinner. Would you care to join me?" She set the basket on the counter.

"Yes." She couldn't keep her eyes from shifting toward the letter, and Yvonne smiled.

"Ah, that is a letter I was writing to my friend. It is good practice for my Grecian." She selected a sharp knife from her cupboard and peeled the tough skin away from a cucumber.

"Grecian?" Cassie echoed curiously.

"It is a foreign language," Yvonne said. "Few people around here practice it anymore."

Cassie cast a long glance at the vegetables in the basket, clenching her jaw as a recent memory surfaced.

The blacksmith. He had used a Grecian word when she was talking about her horse. Cassie rubbed her temples. It was all too much to process.

"I have a show on Saturday," she said, not knowing how to change the subject to something more palatable.

"That's wonderful!" Yvonne smiled kindly, placing the chopped cucumbers into a bowl. She moved on to radishes. "We're getting an early crop this year, and it's certainly a blessing."

Worry wrinkled Cassie's brow. Yvonne had changed the

subject again. Cassie glared at the scraps of vegetables on the counter. Yvonne didn't know about Tenille yet. She supposed her foster mother could learn about the horse when she cared enough to attend the show and watch her take the first-place ribbon. If she bothered to show up, what with her deep friendship with the Fýlax.

"Oh, Cassie. The doctor left a note saying he wants to visit us tomorrow at the house. Is that alright?"

"I'm not sure when I will return. There is an event at Arion."

"Ah, that's right! I nearly forgot. I will let him know about the change. Take these outside, will you? Scatter them in the compost bin." Yvonne handed her the scraps wrapped in a cloth, and Cassie nodded, stepping outside. The sun was level with the horizon. It cast beautiful rays of colored light through the sky, leaving a final impression before tucking in for the night.

Cassie scattered the peels of the cucumbers and other rinds evenly over the dirt, then used a shovel to sprinkle some dirt on top to ensure it was mostly covered. Being outside seemed so freeing, away from the pressures of the stables and the pressures of her own home.

Was it wrong to think Yvonne would provide more than basic care for her? Cassie sighed, realizing she wanted someone to care about the shows as much as she did.

Instead of going inside she stood in the gardens, watching as the colors faded from the sky and bright, twinkling stars came into view.

Twinkling stars flickered and reminded her of the way Taven winked at her in the stables, and the memory brought a small smile to her face. Tomorrow would be a good day.

Chapter

15

Echoes of hoofbeats swirled in the air, a steady pattern that reflected the beating hearts of the riders. Cassie's heart rippled with excitement, Tenille picking up on her mood and prancing alongside Kismet.

"I hope this year goes better than last year." Selene sighed.

"What happened?" Cassie asked immediately, wanting to know what had dampened her friend's mood.

"Well . . ." Selene leaned forward and patted her horse's gleaming black neck. "Kismet was in a terrible mood the whole day, spooked at everything, and ran off into the forest. Taven found him eventually, coated in sweat and tearing off my nice stirrups." Selene's face dipped into a sour frown, then she laughed at Cassie's expression. "It happens often, like when he ran off in Thebesia and you caught him."

"That's not good." Cassie shook her head.

"No, it isn't. But he's getting better. Growing up, I suppose." Selene ran a hand through her dark brown locks, yanking out the tangles. Cassie kept silent as Selene formulated her thoughts. "Or maybe it was my fault."

"How—" Cassie clamped her mouth closed, not wanting to cause an argument. Selene's eyes were downcast.

"I've only had Kismet for a year. I got him shortly before last year's Arion Fun Day. My parents didn't ask me if I wanted him; they just brought him home as a birthday present."

"That's wonderful!" Cassie tried, but Selene shook her head.

"I already had a horse, but she was sold without my knowledge. I'll admit, I did outgrow her, but I was hurt and took my anger out on Kismet. It was wrong, and I am deeply sorry." Selene paused for a moment. "You've helped a lot, made me realize he is a wonderful horse and that losing him would be a huge mistake."

"Selene," Cassie began, then changed her mind. She smiled at her friend. "I'm glad you and your horse get along better now. I was more than angry when Tenille was taken away, so I understand."

Selene looked relieved, her shoulder dropping.

"Welcome, welcome!" the Rangers shouted, waving flags as the riders passed under a wooden arch decorated with streamers and flowers. None of them were Taven, but Cassie waved back regardless. "The Rangers will split you into groups as soon as they can, and as per custom we start off with a tour of Arion!"

Cassie squinted at the girl making the announcement, and she smiled. It was Adria, who had helped her in Vallumvis.

"You'll be with me." Adria approached Cassie with a notebook in hand, also recognizing her. "We'll have a mix of riders from many stables. Come with me and you can meet them all!" There were a dozen riders with each Ranger, their horses varying from the deepest black to patterned paints.

Cassie stood next to a girl with a golden-brown horse similar in height to Tenille, offering a smile when the girl made eye contact.

"I'm Linea," the girl said brightly. "What's your name?"

"I'm Cassie, and this is Tenille." Cassie patted her horse's neck, her focus on the Ranger explaining that everyone could ride in pairs behind her as they followed one of the simple trails around Arion to get better acquainted with the forest.

"I don't remember seeing you last year. This your first time?" Linea asked, and Cassie nodded. "How fun! The trail ride is a little dry, but don't worry. It's all part of tradition." She nudged her horse forward, and Cassie begrudgingly followed. "Waffles loves this forest, for whatever reason I do not know. I think she likes being out of the stable, or maybe I like being out of the stable." She tossed her head back with a laugh, and Cassie smiled.

"I think the forest here is very pretty."

"It is. See those mushrooms growing there?" She pointed to a perfect circle of red-capped mushrooms growing crookedly, almost as if they were all looking at each other. "One of the plants the Rangers point out every single time. They are unique to Arion, not found in any other forest." Linea sat up straighter, rolling her shoulders back. "Sometimes I'm glad my parents didn't allow me to continue my Ranger training. I don't care much for plants or animals."

"But your horse?" Cassie asked with a raised eyebrow.

"I meant studying wildlife. It is fun, but not why I wanted to become a Ranger." Linea pointed ahead of them to a large clearing. "We're almost back to main base. The first game is going to be racing the horses, now that we're warmed up from the trail ride. Bet Waffles is faster than your horse." Her eyes sparkled with the challenge, and Cassie swung her head violently.

"Tenille is as fast as the wind."

"We'll see." Linea urged Waffles faster, almost as if to prove her point, and joined a group of what seemed to be her friends.

Adria was waiting for Cassie, allowing everyone else in the group to pass by.

"I'm sorry, I didn't intend for you to be in the back of the group. Did you hear me at all?" Her bottom lip jutted out. She looked truly sorry.

"Not with that girl talking my ear off." Cassie smirked. "I think she told me enough."

"Ok! If you have questions, ask. I have an entire journal entry about the plants of Arion if you're interested. Right now, I need to go meet with the other Rangers, then we will begin the horse racing." Adria smiled and kicked her mount forward, riding up to Taven. Cassie wanted to call out a greeting, but he seemed busy talking with Adria, leaning close to her to whisper. She laughed freely, tossing her head back before playfully smacking his upper arm.

Cassie tore her gaze away, weaving though the horses to stand next to Selene.

"We're doing better." Selene sighed, her black gelding pawing the ground aggressively. "But I'm not feeling good about this race."

"Then don't do it?" Cassie offered, taken aback by the indignation that flashed in her friend's gaze.

"Everyone must participate. You best find your group. We are starting soon." Selene offered a rushed smile, patting her horse. Cassie joined Linea and her group as Taven approached the center of the crowd.

"Welcome to the Ninety-Seventh Annual Arion Fun Day! The Rangers of Desmalogo take great pride in upholding the traditions of their ancestors, even if the traditions have changed over the years. The first Fun Day commenced as a celebration for the Rangers becoming an official entity within the ruling government of Desmalogo." Taven's eyes scanned the crowd and found Cassie. They lingered for a moment, then he continued with his speech. "Since then, everyone has been welcome to return to this very forest, where the first station was built outside of Thebesia."

"This speech is basically the same every year," Linea whispered, leaning forward in her saddle. Cassie smiled at her, trying to hear what Taven was saying. Adria stood near him with a beaming smile, her eyes never leaving the man.

"As per custom, each team will race against themselves, then the winner of each team will race to decide the final champion." Taven smiled as the crowd roared with excitement, and the first team assembled themselves along the starting line.

Taven lifted a pistol and shot into the air, and the horses launched forward.

"Bet Theo will take the win," Linea said, her eyes slightly narrowed. She pointed to a young man with dark hair on a sleek bay, steadily pulling ahead of several others. As he neared the finish line, he left no doubt about who would be the winner. The crowd erupted into cheers as Theo emerged with a triumphant face, one hand on his horse's neck.

"One more group, then you guys go," Adria informed Cassie, pulling her horse closer to her group. Cassie nodded, allowing her gaze to drift toward the second group lining up at the start. Her desire to win was growing stronger by the minute. Taven stood at the end, his word being final for who won.

She had no idea how fast Tenille was compared to the sleek steeds here, but she was convinced she stood a chance. Tenille had long legs and strong hindquarters, perfect for picking up speed rapidly and also for leaping over fences.

A girl on a dappled gray took the win, her fist pumping the air as she trotted over to where Theo was standing.

"It's our turn now." Linea tapped on the sides of her horse; Waffles picked up a brisk trot. Cassie followed, nibbling on her bottom lip. As she passed Taven, he leaned over and grabbed a rein, stopping her in her path.

"Be careful, and don't be rash." He had a light smile, the worry in his eyes evident.

"I will." Cassie nodded, and he allowed her to line up with the other riders. Linea threw her a curious glance, but no one said a word, adjusting their positions and counting the seconds that ticked by.

Cassie squinted her eyes, staring at the finish line. Tenille internalized her apprehension and tensed in turn, prancing on the spot impatiently.

The shot from the pistol made Cassie flinch, and Tenille launched forward so quickly she nearly lost her balance.

Cassie leaned forward, adjusting her grip on the reins and grasping Tenille's mane for better balance. The wind whipped through her hair, and she tried to find a clear path to get ahead of the other horses.

They passed a bay horse and were neck and neck with Waffles, pulling ahead of the others.

Cassie urged Tenille even faster, unaware that she was slowly pressing up against Waffles, pushing her toward the side of the track.

Waffles stumbled, and Linea launched over the side of her horse. Tenille spooked, ears pinning back as she turned the other way and raced across the track, leaping over the short rope that set out the borders and bolting into the forest.

Cassie groaned, her head spinning. She clung to her horse, gently pulling the reins back.

"Tenille!" She screamed against the wind tearing away her voice. She thought her horse was fast when she was racing the others, but it was nothing compared to how she was pelting through the forest, dodging trees.

She slowed when they reached a bank, jumping over and climbing up the side of a hill. It was enough to wear her out, and she slowed to a manageable speed.

Cassie pulled the reins to a complete stop, annoyed.

"Tenille," she scolded, turning her horse around. "You should not have bolted like that." With a shake of her head, she allowed the horse to trot back to where everyone was waiting. As she grew closer, her shame grew. She was the only one whose horse spooked during the race and ran away instead of finishing.

"Cassie!" Taven was the first one to spot her, kicking his horse into a canter and sliding to a stop next to her. "Are you alright?"

"Yes. Tenille spooked. I don't think she is used to racing," Cassie lamented, finding it difficult to meet the Ranger's eyes. His disappointment in her was evident in how he pressed his lips together.

"She spooked because Waffles tripped. That was not very fair of you, pushing her off the side of the track and into the ropes." She knew Taven was frowning even though she refused to meet his gaze.

"I was not pushing her off the side of the track. Waffles should have been watching where she was going." Cassie didn't recall pushing anyone and refused to be blamed for the accident.

"Cassie!" Taven was aghast, and Cassie finally raised her head. "You could at least apologize for racing unfairly."

"I wasn't racing unfairly! And I would have won if Waffles hadn't spooked Tenille." Cassie clicked her horse forward, refusing to speak with the Ranger any longer. She had been in the lead before Tenille turned away from the track. For all she knew, Linea or Waffles could have done something to thwart her chances.

"Cassie!" Taven called out, chasing after her. He pulled his horse alongside hers, his eyebrows floating higher than usual. "Waffles got hurt, strained her tendon and banged her knee."

At those words, Cassie's wall of stubbornness crumbled, and concern flowed through her. Ignoring Taven, she slid off her horse and left her tied to a post, rushing through the crowds to find Linea.

"Hi, Cassie!" Adria smiled, taking a sip of a strawberry milkshake. "Good to see you back. Is your horse ok?"

"She's fine, but Taven said Waffles is hurt?" Her words were rushed, worried.

"A minor sprain. It will heal in a few weeks. We've loaded her up and sent her back to Vallumvis already. Has the vet glanced over Tenille yet?"

"Waffles will miss the rest of the day?" Cassie asked, so horrified she ignored the question about Tenille. Adria nodded, her eyebrows furrowed together.

"Yes, but accidents happen. It wasn't your fault; don't worry. We'll be having lunch after the scavenger hunt, but you're welcome to get some snacks in the meantime." Adria tilted her head. "You don't blame yourself, do you? I saw how close you got on the track, but with so many competitive riders, small scuffles are inevitable." She smiled before walking off.

With a heavy heart, Cassie ordered a blueberry lemonade, wandered back to her horse, and leaned next to a tree. The vet did glance over her horse and reassured her everything was fine, but the situation left her shaken.

She didn't want to participate in the scavenger hunt, not when Linea had to go home because of her. Adria didn't blame her, but Taven did. He had told her to be careful, and she hadn't been, pushing Tenille past her comfort.

The riders scattered throughout the forest, but Cassie didn't join them, waiting until lunch. She ended up sitting next to Selene and a group of girls from Thebesia Stables. Selene hadn't asked about the race, which only made it worse. She told Cassie about the scavenger hunt and how she was one of the first of the team to finish.

Cassie listened, angry she didn't have a chance to apologize to Linea for what had happened or even ask for her side of what had happened.

"Hey." Adria plopped down on the picnic blanket beside her, a notebook in hand. "As promised, here is some information about the plants of Arion. It's such a unique forest, I could be here for hours simply studying everything."

Cassie took the notebook, impressed by the sketches and neat handwriting. She forced a smile, catching Adria's analyzing gaze.

"You doing ok? You seem upset. I hope it's not over the race still."

Her gaze drifted toward Taven standing in the center of several Rangers, his grin as wide as usual. Adria nodded, half to herself.

"Don't worry about him. He told me you were rash, but in my experience, he just worries too much. It's hard for him, of course." Adria trailed off, shaking her head. "Never mind that. There's plenty of activities left, so why don't you try to have fun? I would rather be in the lab analyzing plants, but I'm out here." She tossed her hands into the air with a small laugh, and Cassie nodded.

She'd ask Adria about Linea later and how she could apologize, but for now, she would try to relax and enjoy the rest of the day. As long as she avoided Taven.

The sky was dark as Cassie headed home from the stables. The unsettled feeling in her stomach only grew stronger, and she was tempted to run all the way to the Ranger station and apologize for her behavior.

Keep people safe.

He had said that so many times, and it was fully her fault Waffles had been hurt. Now Linea would hate her forever, and Taven would never forgive her. Especially when she had ignored him and refused to own up to her actions.

But she couldn't face him for some reason, a reason she couldn't quite pinpoint.

She stopped a few blocks away from Yvonne's house, taking deep breaths to calm her heartbeat down. It had escalated to the point where she was sure anybody passing by could hear it.

What if the vet wasn't honest when he said Tenille was fine? She reached out to her horse, an image of the chestnut mare in her stall filling her mind. Tenille nickered, and even though Cassie was convinced it was only her imagination, she still felt better.

When that faded, Taven's upset facial expression replaced her horse, his soft brown eyes disappointed. She didn't think she'd ever seen someone so unsettled by her behavior. Even at Vallumvis, Henrik had been lenient about her running off.

Adria reassured her that everything would be fine, it was simply a mistake, but Cassie knew it wasn't a mistake. She should have apologized then.

Now where was she supposed to find him? The station was nestled in the heart of Arion, but most of the time he wasn't even there. The Head Ranger of District One, Luke, would know, but there was no point going on a wild goose chase to offer an apology to someone who wouldn't accept it. And Linea deserved an apology as well, if she was willing to hear it.

Cassie dragged her feet toward her house, wishing more than ever that she lived with someone other than Yvonne. She hated the distance that had developed between her and the woman, hated that they were forced to get along.

Next time she saw Dr. Lykaion, she would ask him if she could move elsewhere.

Light spilled out of the front window, a low-lit candle flickering ominously onto the streets.

Cassie smiled to herself, instantly feeling better. If Yvonne had lit a candle, that meant she was waiting for her. Her step brightened, a hand placed on the knob to open it.

She froze. Yvonne wasn't alone.

"Please," Yvonne begged in a hushed whisper, "the girl did nothing wrong. She doesn't have an orange horse, only the bay she rides at the stables."

"Again you lie to me," a male voice snarled, filled with hatred. "Everyone saw her with the orange horse."

"Cassie never told me about another horse. She tells me everything!" Yvonne's voice shook, a sniffle following.

"All you have to do is get her to give me the horse, and no one will be hurt." The voice, so threateningly low, birthed an unexplainable rage inside of Cassie.

No one would take her horse away, no matter what threats they brought. If they tried to hurt either of them, she would fight back with every fiber she had.

Without a sliver of hesitation, Cassie flung the door open and stormed inside, her mind blanking for a second when the man from her dream towered over Yvonne. It was almost impossible, but it was the same man, from the dark brown brows furrowed together to the cunning smile when his eyes landed on Cassie.

"You again," Cassie spat. "Was stealing Tenille once not enough for you?"

"Cassie, no. You must leave, as you are in grave danger." Yvonne stood as pale as the wall, too scared to move.

The man spun toward Cassie with a cold smile on his face.

"Your horse is too valuable to be played with like a toy. Find yourself a different one. She's mine."

"She's mine!" Cassie screeched, surging toward the man. She didn't know what she was going to do; she only knew that she didn't want to see this cold, sneering face ever again.

A breath away from the man, a knife glinted in soft candlelight. Someone from behind Cassie pushed her to the side, and the knife stabbed cold air.

"You little—" The man narrowed his eyes, taking a step toward Cassie. The hands from behind gripped her shoulders tightly, and her knees buckled under her.

"No!" She screamed, unable to even hear herself. Instead of blacking out, she fell through the air, unable to grasp anything.

She was falling, just like she had before the accident.

Falling through indigo lights with nothing around them, nothing tangible, those lights the only thing visible in a sea of darkness.

In her memory, water broke her fall and dragged her into hydrous depths. The hard dirt floor that stopped her fall now was unwelcome, the impact forcing all the air out of her lungs.

Tearing her eyes open, the sharp stab of betrayal pierced her heart. Surely this hurt more than the metal knife would have.

She scrambled to her feet, hating the gray eyes that stared back at her.

Dr. Lykaion.

Chapter

16

Furious pounding on the door of his apartment roused him from his sleep, and Taven grabbed his t-shirt, pulling it over his head as he stifled a yawn.

A Ranger from District One stood on his porch, clearly displeased.

"Luke was expecting you at Arion today."

"No?" Taven forced his eyes open, still groggy from going to sleep so late the night before.

"Nonsense. I've been looking for you for half an hour. You best get to his office. Now." Grumbling under his breath, the Ranger turned away.

Taven nearly slammed the door, marching back to his room for his uniform. Luke had told him several days ago that he could have the day off after the event since he was in charge of most of it.

There had to be some sort of mistake.

Crossing the street to the shed where his horse spent the night, Taven took his time to ensure the tack fit well before heading off to the office of the Head Ranger.

He was sure that when Luke replaced the Proedros, the headquarters would move to Thebesia where it belonged. For now, he was glad there was minimal reason to make the trip to Vallumvis.

Leaving his mount tied to a post, Taven entered the large building and stepped into the main office, surveying the situation.

Luke paced behind his desk, one arm folded across his chest and one propped up, a finger on his chin.

Selene sat in a chair across the room, her face as white as the wall.

"Sorry it took so long to get here." Taven straightened, annoyed at the Ranger for not telling him this was an emergency.

"Rather that then word getting out. The most unusual case we have here. You know Selene, correct?" Luke gestured to the brunette girl in the chair.

Taven nodded.

"Well. Selene here is good friends with a girl named Cassie. Are you aware of such a person?" Luke raised an eyebrow and Taven nodded again, his heart flipping with worry. He refused to jump to any conclusions until he heard what he needed to know. "Here is what Selene told me. Cassie is at the stable every single morning, without fail. She only skips for doctor's appointments, and she did not have one today. This is known because the stables are preparing for tomorrow's show, and she is usually first at the barn. Selene, thinking maybe Cassie slept in after the fun day she had yesterday . . ." Luke paused, his eyes closing as he stopped pacing.

Taven's throat constricted, and he wished they'd never argued the day before. Yes, she had pushed her horse too hard, but maybe he had been too harsh. She was sensitive, after all, given the fact she had ignored him for the rest of the day after the race. The worry that had taken root yesterday blossomed, threatening to choke him. He had only wanted her to be safe and away from harm after her near brush with death, and now his heart hammered in anticipation of what Luke would say.

"Selene walked to Cassie's house, maybe a twenty-minute walk from the stables. She entered the house and Yvonne was lying dead on the floor. The act must have been done quickly, but I think there's enough to indicate some sort of struggle. Though she was deathly terrified, Selene checked the rooms and found no sign of Cassie. She didn't take any of her personal belongings with her. Everything is still at the house." Luke clasped his hands behind his back as he finished his statement.

The world threatened to spin, but Taven snapped himself back to reality. He had to focus if he was to figure out what was going on.

"I firmly believe that Cassie would never turn on the woman taking care of her." At the same time, doubt pierced his soul. Cassie had proven to be rash many times, so why would this be any different?

"No, it couldn't be. She was so excited for the show." Selene finally spoke up, bringing her knees to her chest. "Besides, if she ran away, she would at least take some items with her."

"I also have my doubts," Luke added in, "which is why I don't want anyone hearing about this. Yvonne was a quiet member of society. We can say that she passed away, but we will not be mentioning murder. A trustworthy Ranger is cleaning up the evidence, but Taven, I have a task for you."

"Anything," Taven breathed, knowing well what his boss would ask him to do.

"You're good with people. Set aside all your other tasks and turn your complete focus on finding the girl. Best-case scenario, she killed Yvonne and fled the island to escape prosecution. Worst case," Luke said, grimacing, "someone took her hostage against her will."

"Not a single stone will be left unturned," Taven vowed,

puffing out his chest. "Is there anyone else besides us three and the Ranger that know of this matter?"

"I stopped by the stables to check if she was there and told Henrik she wasn't at the house. I didn't mention anything about Yvonne." Selene sniffled, scrubbing her nose with her sleeve. "I do believe she might be in danger."

"You are sure Henrik knows nothing of the situation?" Taven pressed, already mapping out a list of people he would question. "What known enemies does Cassie have?"

"She didn't always get along with Yvonne, but that isn't surprising. A handful of grooms at the stables didn't like her much, as well as some students. I can't think of anyone who would target Cassie. She mostly kept to herself. I had a hard time being friends with her at first. It takes a while to break through her defenses." Selene rocked back and forth, searching the walls for anything to help uncover another memory. Taven found himself nodding. It was difficult to be friends with her.

"Start with Reginald," Luke cut in. "See if he's still after the horse. I doubt it, but it's a lead." He swung his blocky head toward the girl in the chair. "I'll let you leave now, but with a warning to keep this silent."

Selene nodded, standing on shaky legs.

"And you, Taven. I trust you to keep this silent until we figure it out. No sense throwing the citizens of Desmalogo into a panic when nothing is known for sure. First an unknown girl washes up in our waters, and now she vanishes." Luke gave a light shake of his head, staring at a file on his desk.

"I'll find her."

He could only hope he wasn't too late and this was another chance to make things right. He couldn't bear losing someone again, even though he and Cassie had only recently met. Dr. Lykaion was right. This case was more personal than his other cases.

Taven let out a long breath, making his way out of the

office. He swung up into the saddle, staring blankly at the road in front of him.

If only he'd known her a little better, he'd have a clearer idea of where to start.

She was so complicated, blazing green fire in her eyes one moment, completely passive the next. Her behavior was not normal for an average citizen of Desmalogo, always so defensive, but she was not from the island. She wasn't average either, in his mind.

No, she was highly interesting, and quite pretty as well.

Taven gritted his teeth. He was on a mission to find her, and he intended to do it quickly.

Reginald's house loomed in front of him, strangely silent. Taven craned his neck, scanning the floors. With a huff, he approached the front door and knocked.

He was met with silence.

Frustrated, he turned to the neighbor's house. A lady peeked out, clearly displeased to be bothered at such an hour.

"Yes, what is it?" She stared down at him, too much jewelry clanking on her.

"I'm searching for Reginald Xiphias. He lives next door?" Taven asked in an even tone. His uniform should have been enough to command at least some respect, but maybe that was too much to ask from certain people.

"Yes, yes, of course I know Reginald. If you're looking for him, you'll have to wait. He left on a trip about a week ago, something about meeting his wife from a faraway land. I don't suppose he'll be back until the end of the month." She rolled her eyes as if he should have known this already.

"Very well, thank you." Taven withheld his sigh as the door slammed shut in his face. What a waste of time.

He headed back and reported to Luke, who simply shrugged and directed him to Henrik.

His horse was getting tired from so much traveling, and frankly, so was he. Not from the work, but rather from the fact that he had no leads to follow and everything was so vague.

A girl vanished, not a trace of where she went anywhere. It made no sense.

If she randomly appeared the next day, he doubted she would share where she had been. That posed a problem. Taven let out a soft sigh, regret from the day before deepening. Instead of getting to know her, he had put up a wall between them.

"Morning, Henrik!" Taven called out cheerfully, dismounting his horse. A groom took it without a word, leading him to water. "How are the stables treating you?"

"About as well as can be expected." Henrik grunted, arms crossed against his chest.

"I wanted to stop by and talk with Cassie. Have you seen her?" Taven watched for a sign of reaction, anything to indicate Henrik might be involved.

"No, I have not. Selene came back from looking for her and said the house was empty. She kept it short but sounded worried enough. You Rangers should do your blasted job for once and track down the girl, see if she is doing alright." Henrik was angry, his tone full of accusation.

"The Rangers are already on the case," Taven admitted, knowing he should have been forthcoming with this information.

"And you suspect I might have had something to do with this." Henrik's voice turned even angrier, the emotion directed at Taven.

"And the horse? Is she safe?" Taven demanded, knowing it might be a critical piece of information. Henrik stiffened, his head turning away to the paddocks lining the sides of the stables.

"You're not going to like this, but . . ." He hesitated, and Taven's own anger rose. "The horse is nowhere. She must have broken out in search of Cassie." With a set jaw, he turned back to Taven.

"Great," Taven huffed, lifting his cap and running a hand through his sweaty hair. "Are there any other leads you think I should follow?"

"Might want to ask the doctor. He knows things about her, things that Cassie herself probably doesn't even know." Henrik rolled his eyes. "He was the one that stirred up all the nonsense about inseparable bonds that can never be broken and deep connections with your horse. It's all lies, and she believes them." Henrik spat on the floor, completely shocking Taven.

He had never seen such a display of disrespect from the stables owner.

"You think he might have convinced her to do something she shouldn't have?" Taven forced the words out, his breathing restricted.

"I don't know. All I know is both Yvonne and the girl are gone. So much talent, thrown away to the wind." Henrik frowned. "It is strange that she showed up on the island without any explanation, and no one knows her. Don't you think?" He raised an eyebrow at the Ranger.

Taven lifted a shoulder, not knowing what to think. "She must have come from another place. Outside of Desmalogo."

"And the matter with the memories?" Henrik challenged.

"Henrik." Taven's voice grew impatient. He was ready to end this conversation and go find the doctor. "You're forgetting that I was the Ranger to find her out in the water. The girl was hardly alive, in a coma, all gray and dying." He nearly shuddered at the memory of her lips blue with lack of oxygen, skin void of any life. Under the lighting of the hospital bed, even her shiny hair looked dull. "It's a miracle she is alive."

"You're right," Henrik grudgingly admitted, his eyes trailing away to a paddock where a great black gelding was pacing back and forth. "It is a miracle if she is alive." Without another look at the Ranger he walked away, striking up a conversation with a passing groom.

Taven ground his teeth, knowing Henrik was more than ticked. Everyone was busy getting ready for a show, and one of his most promising riders was missing.

Still, his words sent an ominous chill down his back, and he returned to his horse, climbing on and directing him to the heart of Thebesia, where he would find the doctor.

The clinic seemed busy as ever, nurses bustling about as he approached the front desk with what he hoped was a warm smile.

It wasn't like him to be shaken during an assignment.

But this one felt like a preventable failure, when he should have protected Cassie.

"Hello, I'm Taven Thespios, Ranger with the Arion Unit of District One. Is Dr. Lykaion in today?" He leaned against the desk, his foot tapping impatiently as the receptionist finished scribbling some words onto paper, then finally looked up.

"I'm afraid he is not. He's taking a few days of personal leave. We have several other doctors who can see you. What brings you in?" A string of colorful beads swayed from either side of her glasses, rattling as she spoke.

"Ah, not a physical condition." Taven's smile deepened. A mental one, he wanted to say. "I have questions for the man, not for the doctor." The receptionist reshuffled some papers with a small sigh.

"I do not know where you can reach him at the moment. Being a doctor is a lot of stress. I'm sure he took some time off to refresh himself. He will be back within several days." She turned away dismissively, but Taven thanked her regardless.

Luke's office wasn't far away, and he slipped in, refusing to slump into a chair. The Head Ranger was writing a letter but paused, giving his attention to the younger man.

"Any luck?"

"We're going to need more than luck," Taven said tersely, hands clasped behind his back. "Reginald is away, left long enough ago that we can consider him innocent from the incident. Henrik directed me to the doctor, who is conveniently away from the office on personal leave. Dr. Lykaion that is, the one who helped her recover from her coma." Taven paused, aware of the growing frown on Luke's face. "Shall we take this up to Edmunds?"

"No need," Luke replied, too quickly. "Like I said, we will keep this under wraps. Not many people knew Cassie, so this is a secret mission. Edmunds and I are busy preparing the interns for the Ranger Trials, and this might prove to be an empty case if she returns."

"But—" Taven tried to object, fear rising in his chest. He couldn't just leave like this, not knowing where she was. Did he have a choice?

"Taven?" Luke's voice was sharp but held a note of understanding beneath it. "Do you believe she is in immediate danger?"

He thought about it for a moment. Danger, probably. Immediate danger? He hated to admit it, but it sounded like a hostage situation, and she would be kept alive until the kidnapper traded her for a desired object or information.

"No." He released a pent-up breath, and Luke nodded.

"I'm not telling you to toss it completely, and if anyone gets a lead, we will pick it back up again. I don't want Edmunds involved." A darkness passed over his gaze, and Taven almost smiled.

Luke was eager to prove to the citizens and Edmunds himself that he was the best Head Ranger for Proedros. Should the Ranger Trials go well, the promotion could happen as early as the summer.

17

"I thought I could trust you." Venom laced Cassie's tone as she backed away, slamming against a tree.

Dr. Lykaion took a shaky breath, almost as surprised as she was. "You can," he said simply, not moving.

Cassie glanced at her surroundings, unsettled by the tall trees encircling her. They covered most of the sky but were spaced sparsely enough she could see a string of small cabins in the distance. She whirled on the doctor, but he pressed a finger to his own lips.

"It would not be wise to make a ruckus right now. Come, there is a friend who will receive us." He started off in the opposite direction from the cabins she had seen, and Cassie frowned. For a moment, Cassie stood, her hands clenched at her sides. The doctor paid her no mind, and Cassie huffed, giving up.

She did not know where this place was or how they'd gotten here. She certainly had not been here before, that was clear.

Strange green vegetation littered the ground, climbing the base of the trees and ending with a cluster of tiny pink flowers. A hazy glow shifted around each cluster, providing enough light to see in the dark. Cassie squinted, realizing it came from swarms of lightning bugs huddling around each flower. She sidestepped the weird vegetation, keeping her tracks on the soft mossy grass that carpeted the ground.

With a shudder, she glanced up to make sure the doctor was still in sight. The cabin he was approaching was set apart, vines and other plants obscuring it from immediate view. The doctor knocked lightly on the wooden door, waiting as a candle was lit in the window. The door swung open silently, spilling golden warmth into the forest.

"Mycroft!" the voice inside exclaimed. It sounded male and fairly young.

Cassie picked a tree a safe distance away, leaning against a bare spot on the trunk. Overgrown lichen tickled the side of her face, her eyes narrowing as the events in front of her unfolded.

"What has happened? You do not call often at this hour."

"There's been a bit of a situation." Dr. Lykaion, or Mycroft, she supposed, grimaced. His voice dropped and she could no longer hear him, but in the misty light the doctor stepped inside the small house, and a young man stepped out. His hair, a soft brown, fell over his forehead, his complexion on the pale side. He had a small smile as he approached, stopping before he got too close.

His clothes perplexed her the most, an elaborate robe in a deep indigo color with stitching along the edges alternating between white and gold. They seemed to make patterns, maybe words, but it was of little importance. She frowned at the man.

A Fýlax.

The doctor had made it seem like he was not involved, but he very much was if this was where he took her when she faced danger. And she had assumed the robe characters were the danger!

Cassie dropped her face into her hands, her body going stiff in response to the man's low, melodic voice.

"Hello, and welcome. My name is Vivion. Welcome to the Valley of Vathis." Her head snapped up when he took several steps toward her until he was close enough for Cassie to see his eyes, shining a medium brown color despite the lack of light. "Shall we go inside? I can answer any questions you may have."

"No." Cassie folded her arms.

Vivion's mouth twisted as he tried to hide a smile. "May I ask why?"

"I don't like you, and I don't like the doctor. I don't even know how I got here." Her voice came out too defensive, and she scowled at herself. "You wear a stupid robe, and you are untrustworthy."

"I am very sorry to hear that you received the wrong impression of my kind. As a Fýlax, and especially an Igetis, it is my deepest concern to ensure the citizens of Desmalogo are safe from the forces of darkness." His head bowed, and Cassie rolled her eyes. Now he sounded like he was sputtering nonsense to make himself look better.

"What's an Igetis?"

"A leader of a Kleros." He lifted a palm to stop her next question, the slight smile still on his face. "You have much to learn." He turned his head back to his house. Somewhere in the distance a twig snapped. "Come, it will be safer to talk inside. We do not want to be discovered." He stood as still as a statue, the fabric of the robe heavy enough that it did not shift with the wind.

"Fine." Cassie pushed herself off the tree and walked past him into the house, swinging the door open. The cabin had a very open layout, a bed tucked into one corner, half hidden by a sheet. A kitchen of sorts stood in the opposite corner, a table between them. Closer to the door to her left sat a sofa. Each piece of furniture was beautifully crafted, carved with swirling designs, symbolic lines and Grecian letters. Since the doctor sat at the table fiddling with his hat, Cassie opted to sit on the sofa.

It was surprisingly soft, and she drew her knees up to her chest, unable to right her frown. Vivion had entered behind her, closing the door as quietly as he could. He brought the candle from the windowsill to the table, sitting opposite the doctor but turning his chair to face Cassie.

"First, I'd like an explanation." His voice was commanding, and Cassie stared at him carefully, the youthfulness of his face a stark contrast to the well of wisdom behind his eyes. A leader of a Kleros, he had said. At such a young age, it did not seem fitting. Dr. Lykaion reached into his pocket and placed a candy bar on the table.

"I do believe I've mentioned her before, a special project of mine. Her head was severely damaged from long water exposure, and she was in a coma that resulted in memory loss. It appeared that she had no family, so I found a woman to take of her. That woman was Yvonne." The name was said pointedly, and Vivion nodded in recognition. "Cassie was heading home, and a man threatened her. I got Cassie out in time before she could be hurt, but really, I can't believe no one took Yvonne seriously when she sent several messages about being in trouble." The doctor shook his head slowly.

Vivion sat motionless for a few minutes, then began speaking.

"I doubt anything could have been done to alter fate." Each word was stretched out, and Cassie's patience wore thin. "After all, she never specified what it was, or who. It is difficult to respond to vague pleas." Vivion folded his arms, as if his every action was justifiable.

"You knew Yvonne was in danger?" Cassie spat the words at him, leaping up from the couch. Vivion turned his head steadily, hardly blinking.

"Cassie, you understand little about how we work." He

shook his head, turning his attention to Mycroft. "What request do you have?"

"Cassie needs a place to stay," the doctor stated, his tone mundane as if this were a daily occurrence.

"Do you even know why that man was after Yvonne?" Cassie raised her voice, tired of being ignored. Both men turned in surprise at her outburst. "He wants my horse, and Yvonne told him I don't have one. Because I never told her about Tenille. She is mine." She was angry enough to tear down the entire house and scream at the empty sky above her.

"Cassie, slow down," Dr. Lykaion encouraged, wrinkled lines of worry on his forehead.

Cassie took a step toward Vivion, her eyes narrowing.

"You claim I don't know how the world works, but you're the one here that knows nothing." She paused, deciding that between the two, it was still the doctor she trusted more. Vivion was a nobody to her, a man not many years older with a pompous air about him.

"That man wants my horse. He will not get her. I saw him in my dreams, and he will not defeat me a second time."

"Do you know why he wants your horse?" Dr. Lykaion asked gently, eyebrows pulled together. Cassie shook her head, flumping back on the couch.

The two men at the table shared a worried look, and Vivion clasped his hands.

"We can take her to Conrad. She'll be safe there."

"The blacksmith?" Cassie asked, her interest piqued.

"Yes," Vivion said with a nod.

"Good. I like him."

"But you don't like me?" Vivion tilted his head to Cassie, his lips twitching at her glower.

"Very well. Conrad it is." The doctor nodded, his eyes scanning the room. He shifted in his seat but made no move to stand up.

"I'll go get my horse ready; you can bring yours closer to

the house. We'll meet at the edge of the forest and travel to Vallumvis." Vivion stood but immediately lowered himself back into the chair, glancing at both Cassie and the doctor. "Something else is wrong."

Cassie kept her mouth shut, but it was evident the doctor was not willing to say anything either. Finally, she rolled her eyes at the young man's inquiring glance.

"We did not get here using horses." Her voice was flat, and Vivion's eyes shot toward the doctor, who met him with a steady, if not slightly challenging, gaze.

"You—" Vivion stammered, leaning back against the chair.

"He what?" Cassie demanded, tired of being in the dark for every single conversation.

"I used a portal to get us here," Dr. Lykaion said.

"Like magic?" Cassie gasped, her hands flying to cover her mouth.

"Not quite," Dr. Lykaion clarified, standing from the table and placing his hat squarely on his head. "Think of it as an ability that shows up in times of dire need." He met her gaze, his expression unreadable.

Vivion frowned and also rose from the table to stand next to the doctor.

"Walking will take too long, and I am not sure I can take more horses without being discovered." He used the same tone from earlier, where he stretched out every single word.

Cassie glared at him.

"Simple. We use another portal." Dr. Lykaion lifted his hands, and a circle appeared in the center of the house, growing larger with each heartbeat. It was a stark indigo on the inside, fading out to pale lavender and pink sparkles around the edges. Cassie's mouth fell open in fascination.

Had he created one inside Yvonne's house, right behind her, so fast that she hadn't even seen the colors until she was passing through? He must have, but there had been too many things going on for her to notice.

"Well?" Cassie asked impatiently, glancing between the two men.

"Vivion will go first, giving him a few moments to warn the others. Then you, Cassie. This time it will be of your own free will. I won't force you. I'll go last and close it."

She had to admit, being able to make a portal was intriguing.

Vivion grumbled under his breath, but she couldn't make out his words as he stepped through the circle and vanished.

Giddy with excitement, Cassie stepped through the circle boldly and fell through, as if the earth had opened in front of her. The feeling was too much for her, and she closed her eyes, her body protesting as the memories of her first fall filled her brain again.

A raging storm, her breath taken away as her soul plummeted into a vast vial of nothingness and was consumed by darkness.

Her breath was knocked out of her lungs as she slammed against the hard floor, something sharp digging into her back. Cassie gasped, forcing her eyes open.

Vivion stood over her, concern on his face. A tree overshadowed him, and within a few moments, the doctor appeared.

"Was it like this the first time too?" Vivion asked.

"What?" Cassie demanded, scrambling to her feet and brushing off bits of leaves and twigs from her clothes.

"You're supposed to step through and not feel anything at all, blink and you're in a new place, all upright."

Cassie bit back a laugh, frowning instead.

"Very funny. The portal makes me fall, like I fell into the water before. I'm falling and falling, then I slam against the ground. Or into the water." Cassie shrugged, glancing at the doctor. He stood frozen, mouth open ever so slightly.

"You fell into the water?" he asked, not bothering to soften his tone.

"It's some kind of memory. I don't know." Cassie rubbed her temples. "My head hurts trying to remember."

"Never mind then. That house over there is where Conrad lives with his wife and a handful of children."

"Several handfuls," Vivion scoffed, his eyes narrowing at Cassie, then at the doctor. Cassie didn't miss the murderous look the doctor returned to the robed man, and her guard went up again.

Vivion skirted around the doctor and walked directly up the path to the door, knocking lightly. Cassie walked right up to him, still confused as to why she didn't pass through the portals normally. The damage to her head probably extended further than she thought.

A lady opened the door, a small baby in her arms. She gave Vivion a scrutinizing glance, then her gaze fell on Cassie. For a moment, she thought the eyes of the woman softened.

They were bright green, having more gray undertones than Cassie's, but stunning regardless.

"Vivion," the woman finally said, her grip on the baby tightening.

"Greetings." Vivion bowed his head as the woman sniffed contemptuously. "Forgive me for bothering you at such an hour, but we have a small issue on our hands. Cassie here needs a place to stay. Her previous home is no longer safe."

"Tragic." The lady's voice sliced the cool air.

Cassie turned to where the doctor stood at the end of the dirt path, his hat in his hand. He gave her an encouraging nod, and her jaw loosened into a smile.

"Well, Cassie. Come along."

Cassie did as she was told, stepping inside the house. Vivion followed, as if he were always welcome.

"Make yourself useful," the woman stated, carefully

handing the baby to Vivion. He wrapped it in his robes, staring at the little one with a surprisingly soft face.

"My name is Agnetha, and my husband is Conrad, the blacksmith."

"I've met Conrad before," Cassie commented. Conrad knew about her horse and the Grecian people.

"He's a good man," Agnetha said half-heartedly, leading her down a hall. They entered a large room, a bed nestled along the back wall under the window. Cassie hardly noticed a young white-haired girl amongst all the covers.

Agnetha carefully drew back the blanket, lifting the girl into her arms. She looked to be around eight years old, still easily carried by her mother.

"Mama?" she asked groggily, voice heavy with sleep.

"You'll be with Emine tonight. We have a visitor who needs a place to stay," Agnetha whispered.

"Visitor?" The girl lifted her head.

"You'll get acquainted tomorrow," Agnetha replied, and the little girl didn't argue, nestling her head against her mother's arm.

"I'll bring you a set of pajamas. That door leads to the washroom." Agnetha pointed with her chin to the side door, and Cassie nodded.

"Thank you," she said in a hushed voice, making her way to the washroom.

It had been hard to see from the outside, but the house was extravagant, the bedroom alone being half the size of Yvonne's house.

Touched by the kindness of everyone around her, Cassie changed into the soft pajamas and slipped under the covers, eyes closing in exhaustion.

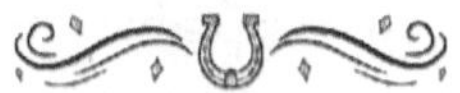

Cassie awoke to Agnetha's hand on her shoulder and the smell of buttered toast wafting through the room. Her eyes adjusted to the low light as she noted it wasn't even dawn yet.

"Sorry to wake you at this hour, but we must get this done soon."

"What?" An unwelcome chill sent a shiver down her spine, and Cassie sat up in her bed, the events of the night before playing in her mind.

The Valley of Vathis. Portals. Vivion.

"Here is a snack." Agnetha handed her a plate with sliced apples and toast, which she accepted and scarfed down in a few bites. "Vivion and the doctor shared what they knew, and we agreed it might be better if you were here under a disguise."

"How do you know Vivion?" And why did she trust him so much?

"Well. It so happens that he is Conrad's younger brother. Not to worry though." A humorous glint appeared in the woman's eye. "They are worlds apart, quite literally. Now, about your disguise. I am a Vallumvis, therefore everyone knows my family. But Conrad is not, so we can claim you are a relative from outside the island who has come to visit. Perhaps even acquainted with my sister. She lives a few hours away by ship." Agnetha stood, motioning to the washroom. "Your red hair must go as it is too recognizable. Blonde would suit you well, don't you think?"

"Blonde?" Cassie sputtered, her gaze catching on Agnetha's pale hair. "Nothing against yours, but—" Tenille was chestnut, their hair matching perfectly. Changing her hair was like changing her identity, severing the connection between her and her horse.

Agnetha waited, her set face and crossed arms an indication that "no" was not an acceptable answer.

Would something as simple as a different hair color really change who she was? Tenille would still recognize her.

They were connected in mind and spirit, not by physical looks.

"Very well." Cassie shut her eyes, squeezing the emotions back.

"Then it's settled, Miriam."

"Miriam?"

"Your new name."

Cassie followed Agnetha into the washroom, keeping her eyes shut through the entire process. She only opened them when prompted by Agnetha, not blinking as the woman lined her eyes with dark liquid that smelled of burnt wood and oil. By the time her makeover was complete, Cassie hardly recognized the beautiful blonde girl in the mirror, her freckles perfectly masked, even her eyebrows losing their red tint under the careful hands of Agnetha.

"I'll leave you to it. Breakfast will be soon, and clothes are on the bed." The woman gave Cassie a reassuring pat on the shoulder, leaving her with her thoughts.

She sat in the chair for a while, getting used to her new look. Through it all, her mind drifted back to her original foster mother and how different she was from Agnetha.

Was Yvonne even alive? She shook her head furiously; her horse was the only thing she needed to worry about. She searched for her in her mind, trying to find any memory of them together.

Instead, a new image filled her mind: her horse grazing peacefully in a field, trees whistling in the wind, not a single soul around.

Tenille seemed safe, and Cassie hopped off the chair, finding a pretty dress laid out on the bed. She smiled to herself, admiring the tiny flowers hand-stitched into it. She slipped into it and twirled in front of the mirror, the peaceful moment interrupted by a thumping across the hallway, furious little-girl footsteps marching back and forth. Cassie frowned and opened the door.

"Finally!" The little girl grinned, her hands placed staunchly on her hips, soft brown hair evidently unaffected by a hairbrush. "Mama said I had to wait until you woke up." The girl's lips jutted out. "Really, I wanted to wake you." Her eyes grew wide and she laughed, scampering down the hall, where the blonde girl from last night caught her in her arms.

"Good morning. Please excuse my sister. She has no manners. My name is Mallika, and this unfortunate creature is Emine. We also have two babies in the house. Breakfast is on the table waiting." Mallika turned to the girl and whispered something, shoving her out of the hallway before turning to Cassie, expecting her to follow.

Cassie gaped at the number of different options before sliding into a seat. Fluffy scrambled eggs sprinkled with cheese, stacks of flatcakes, bowls of fresh fruit, and pungent coffee to top it all off. A toddler already sat at the table, helping himself to a plate of fruit set out for him.

"Do you drink coffee? Of course I can't have any since it's for adults, but maybe you would like some." Mallika pursed her lips, glancing at the coffee pot on the counter as Agnetha burst in from the back door, a tiny baby strapped to her back, Emine on her heels.

"Miriam! Good morning, I hope you slept well. Help yourself to anything you'd like, then we will walk down to the stables. I've already spoken with the manager there. As a relative of ours, I have put in a good word for you, and they have accepted you to clean stalls and paddocks and organize tack. You think you could manage?" Agnetha shook her head at the empty plate, filling it up herself before Cassie could protest.

She ate the food rapidly, both from hunger and because everything tasted so pleasant, then she waited by the door as Agnetha reminded Emine that she must help Mallika watch over the little boy. She ignored the hands-on-hips protest from the little girl, locked the door behind them, and pointed out the path they would take.

"Vivion was the one to suggest a new identity, as the doctor was not sure how much danger you are in."

"I do not wish to bring anything upon your household." Cassie gulped, guilt rising at the thought of the little ones being harmed.

"Nothing will." Agnetha's voice was firm. "You can stay as long as you'd like. I was told about your memories." Her lips pulled downward as she brushed back her pale hair that had come loose in the gentle wind. The baby on her back slept peacefully, unaware of the dangers swirling around her. "After hearing about the situation, most likely someone is after Yvonne, not you, and you shouldn't worry. Regardless, you'll be Miriam. The manager here isn't the kindest, but don't let her boss you around too much." She grew quiet as they approached the bustling stables, and a lady walked up to them, each stride taken with great purpose.

Her deep red polo was detailed with white piping, black breeches nearly blending in with her boots. Sunglasses concealed her eyes, and a cap covered half her head, obscuring her expression. She held a clipboard between her hands.

"Judy," Agnetha said, folding her arms over her chest. "This is Miriam, a relative from Conrad's side. She is a talented equestrian and a hard worker. I don't expect there to be any issues." Her voice was firm, and Judy's pressed lips said she wasn't very pleased about the situation.

"I'm sure not." Judy handed the clipboard to Cassie. "Here are your tasks for the day. Let me know once you're finished, and after I approve them, you may go back home. It that clear?"

Cassie nodded, accepting and running over the list. The most time-consuming and tedious chores were listed with loopy handwriting. This would take her nearly all day to complete.

"If you have any questions, I'll try to answer." With a tight smile at both, Judy left. Cassie glared at her back, already annoyed.

"Don't worry about her. She's an idiot."

Cassie nodded, surprised when Agnetha reached out to ruffle her hair.

"Come by for lunch in a few hours, finished or not."

Cassie nodded again, wandering away to find a wheel-barrow and pitchfork. If she could only get her horse here, she would be completely fine working under a new identity at a new barn with new faces. But really, she would prefer to go back to Henrik's stables, where everything was familiar and there were at least a few friendly faces.

If the doctor didn't check up on her in a few days, Cassie decided she would go seek him out herself, demanding answers about portals, abilities, and secret men in their secret robes.

Chapter 18

Agnetha braided Cassie's hair into a pretty updo, crowning her head. She also reapplied her makeup, and Cassie was surprised by her own reflection.

"If your hair was longer, we would have more options, but it's short." Agnetha sighed, running a brush through her hair as the little girls sat and watched with wide eyes.

"I think I like it short," Cassie countered.

"Has it ever been long?" Mallika asked, her near-white hair plaited into two braids then spun into neat buns at the top of her head. Eminc's hair was similar, but some strands of hair poked out from her plaits.

"I don't remember."

She didn't remember a lot of things, but to her great relief, she could still remember waking up at Yvonne's house and everything that had happened since then.

The list Judy had given her only seemed to grow longer by the day, and Cassie wasn't sure if she would finish everything on it. She had started the morning by cleaning the paddocks, and now with the sun climbing higher into the sky she had moved to the shade of the barn. Another hour or so, and she'd head back to Agnetha's for lunch.

Cassie pushed the wheelbarrow toward the next stall, her eyes catching the name tag.

Waffles 'n Syrup (Waffles). Owned by Linea Vallumvis.

She nearly flinched, stepping inside with a deep breath. Vallumvis only had one stable for all the riders of the city, meaning anyone could be found in the very barn she was currently in.

It had been three days since Arion Fun Day, three days since she had seen any of her friends.

Three days since she had seen her horse, and the ache in her heart grew stronger every day. Did anyone miss her? It only brought more guilt knowing that all her friends thought she was missing. If they even cared.

The stall was empty, but it was clearly being used. Several piles of horse manure, fresh water in the trough, a mostly full hay net. Cassie worked as quickly as she could, but it was not quick enough.

She was pushing the wheelbarrow out of the stall just as a girl and her horse stopped in front of her. Cassie met Linea's inquisitive gaze. She tore away from her work, rushing outside to empty the wheelbarrow even though it was only partially full.

Judy sent a disapproving glance her way when she reentered the stable, and Cassie hung her head, keeping it down as she walked into the stall next to Linea's. She did not look at the girl or her horse, keeping her face turned away and concentrating on cleaning the stalls in the methodical order Judy had told her.

After all, Linea probably hated her for hurting her horse at the race, as she should.

Once she was several stalls away, Cassie relaxed and snuck a glance at Linea, instantly regretting it. Linea was watching her carefully, only pretending to be busy with her horse.

Or maybe comforting Waffles, since she had a light sprain on her leg.

"Judy?" Linea called out, and the stable manager stopped, all smiles as she turned toward Linea. Cassie scowled, moving on to the next stall. "When did we get a new worker?"

"Oh, her." Judy waved her hand dismissively. Cassie's blood ran cold, and she nearly dropped the pitchfork she was holding.

This was it. Linea would rat her out, and her scam would be found out.

"Her name is Miriam, a distant relative of Conrad's apparently. She is staying with Agnetha, and that woman goaded me into giving her a job." Judy laughed, but it was not a nice laugh. It was full of mockery, and it was aimed at Cassie.

"Agnetha? Oh, yes, she always gets her way," Linea said with an uncomfortable laugh in return.

Cassie shoved her pitchfork furiously into the pile of manure, lifting it into the wheelbarrow. She wished she was brave enough to say something to Judy for being so rude to both her and Agnetha, who had shown only kindness by taking her in like another daughter.

Judy was too full of herself, and when she walked by, she paused to watch Cassie work. She said nothing, and Cassie glared at her back as she left.

Cassie finished the last stall and took the final load outside. Leaving the wheelbarrow in the designated spot, she carried the pitchfork back into the barn, stepping into the tool shed. It was right next to the tack room, housing all the items that didn't belong or didn't fit in the other room.

Someone else stepped into the small space, and Cassie ignored them, hanging up the pitchfork along the wall with the others.

The door closed and she rolled her eyes, glad the person had left.

Turning around, she bit back a gasp at Linea standing

there, her hazel eyes bright with curiosity. She pressed a finger to her mouth, a smile curving her lips.

"Shh. I don't want anyone to hear us," Linea whispered, as if this were all a fun game.

"I'm sorry," Cassie blurted out, the first words that came to mind. "I didn't mean to hurt Waffles."

"So it is you." Linea's smile grew wider. "I almost didn't recognize you. The blonde looks good. But the way you glared at Judy gave it away." The older girl laughed, then clapped her palm over her mouth to silence herself. "Waffles will be fine. She is a bit clumsy and you are slightly too ambitious. Do you compete often? You'd be good." Linea tilted her head to the side, genuinely curious.

"I was supposed to." Cassie huffed. She found herself telling Linea about the first Vallumvis show, surprised that Linea had seen it all and had been fascinated by the events.

"I almost recognized your horse at Arion," Linea admitted. "I asked Adria to put us on the same team."

"And I was supposed to be at the show yesterday with my stable, but I stayed at Agnetha's all day instead." Cassie sighed, rubbing her temples.

"Oh. But why? Why are you here? What happened?" Linea asked, befuddled.

"It wasn't safe for me to live in Thebesia. Yvonne was attacked. I escaped, and the doctor helped me find another place to stay." There. That was enough truth without having to explain anything about portals that appeared in times of desperate need.

Linea's eyes widened, and she clasped her hands over her mouth to silence a gasp.

"Oh, I'm so sorry!" She stepped forward, pressing Cassie into a tight hug. "Ok, so you're Miriam now?"

"Yes."

"I'll try to remember. But right now, what's the most

important thing for you?" Linea asked, stepping back, her hand on the door handle.

"My horse." Cassie swallowed against the tightness in her throat, clasping her hands behind her.

"Is she still in Thebesia?"

Cassie nodded.

"Well." Linea steepled her fingers together, frowning when footsteps approached. She swung the door open, her head lifted, her shoulders back.

"Linea?" Judy asked, confused.

"I was telling Miriam that Waffles needs a double layer of straw." Linea smiled, tossing her braid over her shoulder. Her hair was twisted in an elegant manner, starting at the top of her head and ending at her waist. Cassie reached up to her own small crown of plaits.

"That seems like an unnecessary expense."

"Precisely what I thought you'd say. Waffles has a sprain. I want her to be as comfortable as possible." Linea spun around, beckoning to Cassie. "Come, Miriam, I will show you how I want it." Linea strolled forward with importance, ignoring Judy's strained smile. Cassie followed, stepping around Judy and walking toward the stall. "Waffles is very friendly," Linea said pointedly, opening the door to the stall. Cassie stole a glance at Judy, who was moving away slowly. "Oh, and Judy?" Linea called out, stopping the woman in her tracks. "If there is a problem with this, please direct all questions to my mother."

"Very well," Judy replied instantly, rushing away.

"My mother happens to be one of the wealthiest of Vallumvis," Linea said with a sly smile, gently running her hand over Waffles's neck.

"The city is named after your family?" Cassie asked, finally making the connection.

"Yes. It was founded by the Vallumvis family, and we are proud of our hard work in our city, keeping it well protected against any outsiders." She lifted her nose haughtily, glancing down at Cassie.

Then she burst into laughter, nearly doubling over.

"You should have seen your face. Oh, my." Linea giggled, leaning back against her horse. "Most people are nosy and ask too many questions." Her voice dropped as a young man tromped by the stall, directing a curious look at both girls. "Point proven. This Saturday, the stable at Dionysian Falls is hosting a show. I won't be competing since Waffles is hurt and I have no interest in riding another horse, much to the disappointment of my mother. We'll have all the time in the world to find Tenille and devise a plan to get her back. Keeping her at this stable is too risky, but if I recall correctly, Conrad has a small stable at his blacksmith shop, and you could probably keep her there. And don't worry, few people go there. He used to do his work solely at that shop but started traveling now that his skills are considered some of the best. Especially during show season, the poor man is hardly home. He is on the weekends though, unless called out." Linea paused to take a breath, and Cassie took the opportunity to cut through her rambling.

"You think it's a good idea to take Tenille without telling anyone?"

"Yes." Linea's eyes sparkled with excitement, her smile growing. "It will be epic, like a heist. Besides, if you're here under a disguise, your horse should be too. We can give her another name, like Carrots! Waffles is named so because she is the color of a waffle, and it makes sense for your horse to be Carrots since she is bright chestnut."

"Carrots are much too bright of a color," Cassie countered.

"Shame." Linea's mouth twisted into a fake frown.

"Did you truly want more straw for Waffles?"

"Oh." Linea had a dry laugh. "I made that up on the spot,

but we might as well follow through or else Judy Moody will be suspicious."

Leaving the stables, the girls found a wheelbarrow outside and walked to the hay barn, filling it with fresh straw. Linea insisted on pushing the cart, but Cassie shook her head.

"I must do my work or I will be fired."

"I doubt it. Agnetha is my cousin, you know. And Judy would rather keep her job than pick fights with you." Linea shrugged, opening the door to the stall and letting Cassie walk in. "What chores do you have after this?"

"None. I was going to go back and get lunch." She almost said she was going to go back home but stopped herself in time. Agnetha's house was not home.

Linea smiled, taking the pitchfork out of Cassie's hands.

"How about we go and get lunch together? I know a place that makes the best burgers ever." She raised an eyebrow in question, and Cassie nodded.

"Let me go home and tell Agnetha, and I'll meet you back at the stable."

Cassie followed Linea through town, ignoring the people greeting her friend. It seemed like the entire city knew the girl.

They mostly looked past Cassie, and she was more than happy with that, not wanting to be recognized and discovered by someone who would cause problems.

A dark-haired Ranger trotted by, but this one Linea did not greet. She skirted around him bond kept walking, stopping in front of a small pub-style building.

The interior was rustic, with roughly hewn wooden logs for walls and well-built tables decorated with metal accents. A waiter appeared, a practiced smile schooling his features.

"Table for two?" he asked, and Linea nodded.

"A booth, please," she clarified, following the waiter, then sliding into the seat. Cassie sat across from her, accepting an aged parchment menu.

The list of mouthwatering meals was extensive, each paired with a small numerical amount which Cassie assumed would be the price in drachmas.

"I left most of my savings at Thebesia Stables," Cassie commented in a low tone, her eyes on the parchment.

"Is it in a safe place?" Linea asked, thanking the waiter who had reappeared with two glasses of water.

"The craftsman will be back to recheck measurements for Tenille's saddle, and I won't be there." Cassie sighed, leaning back on the plush cushion. Linea studied her for a few moments, her face thoughtful.

"You're not from Desmalogo. Am I correct?"

"No one knows." Cassie shrugged.

"You've been here for weeks now, not counting how long you were in a coma. If someone had lost a girl, they would have alerted all the Rangers on the island. Even if you were orphaned, you wouldn't have been living completely be yourself, isolated from society. Even hermits visit society occasionally." Linea shook her head as if frustrated. "No, I have every reason to believe you are not from this island."

Cassie had known this. She had realized long ago she didn't belong and always felt like an outsider.

Despite this, hearing Linea confirm it struck her deeply, and her heart sank.

"If I had fallen from a ship," Cassie whispered, her eyes growing wide as she realized the depth of the situation, "that means I could be from anywhere. I could have been a prisoner, could have been traveling with my family. What if no one survived except for me?" She blinked back tears, forcing herself to sit straighter as the waiter appeared with his annoying half smile.

"Are you ladies ready to order?" he asked, hands clasped behind his back, leaning forward slightly.

"I am," Cassie cut in, before Linea could answer for her. "I'll have a blueberry lemonade, extra blueberry syrup, double the lemons." She glanced down at the menu, not even reading it.

"And this." She pointed to the first option, then sat back, satisfied. Linea hid a smile, ordering a lamb burger with extra pickled onions and a sparkling black soda.

"Do you like Desmalogo, from what you've seen so far?" Linea asked softly, bringing the glass of water to her lips. It was a loaded question, and Cassie took a minute to consider. Selene was her friend, and so was Linea. Adria was a friend as well, and Taven, despite their argument. Henrik always checked up on her, and Agnetha fussed over how thin she was. The doctor cared about her, even if his intentions were questionable.

"Yes."

"If we don't discover your family, will you stay?"

Cassie laughed, a harsh, bitter laugh. "I don't think I have much of a choice right now, being thrown on this island without any explanation, unable to remember anything. If I remembered my home, yes, I would go back. But I would visit Thebesia."

Linea nodded, satisfied, twirling the glass in front of her.

"I keep thinking about your horse. Is she registered with Desmalogo?"

"Huh?" Cassie frowned. "Registered?"

"Yes. Every horse born on this island is registered and pedigreed with Desmalogo Horse Registry. I wonder if Tenille is there. What's her full name?"

Cassie frowned, leaning forward and resting her elbows on the table, hands moving up to rub her temples. Pain throbbed beneath her fingertips, and she wished the waiter would hurry with her blueberry lemonade. "Linea, I don't know. I don't know anything."

"Don't stress over it. If she is, buyer information will be listed there."

"Like my parents?" Cassie lifted her head, a glimmer of hope in her eyes.

Linea nodded. "Precisely. It would give us a good sense of direction."

"It would, but I do not know her registered name." Cassie caught sight of the waiter approaching their booth carrying two large burgers and drinks on a tray. "Finally," she muttered, eyeing the waiter cautiously.

"Here you are, ladies. Let me know if you need anything else." With a small bow, he left.

Cassie clutched her lemonade, taking a sip to try it before downing half the glass. Linea stared with wide eyes, then she smiled.

"A lot of registries note the barn name as well. It will say, for example, Denny's Rhythm, then Denny in parentheses." Linea tasted one of her fries. "The same way it's written on each stall in Vallumvis."

"I hope Henrik takes good care of her." Cassie sighed, opening her burger and placing a stack of fries inside.

"I hope so too."

Chapter 19

Lokiir gripped the table in the supply room, sick to his stomach. He had sat in his room for the better part of the week as the ship tossed from side to side, the wind merciless, but had crawled out for his duties. The shelves and cabinets threatened to slam into his forehead with each step he took, and he directed his focus to the list he was attempting to make. Enough was stocked to last the crew another few weeks, but he longed for something fresh, something that was not made for the shelf.

A girl popped her head into the room, her white hair glittering in the low light. She said nothing to Lokiir, picking up a box of crackers from the shelf and slipping out of the room.

Daz. Always taking things without permission, assuming that batting her eyelashes was a suitable exchange.

Some of the people on the ship adjusted so easily to the constant rocking, and he hated them for it. Crackers supposedly helped with the nausea, but he preferred an empty stomach.

Grabbing on to walls to steady himself, he clambered back into his room, slamming onto his bed, face flat into the pillow.

Hours passed until he was aware of a steady calm throughout the ship.

Lokiir stumbled to his feet, rushing out to the main deck. For a moment, he dropped the shroud surrounding the ship. A clear blue sky flashed ahead of him, and he quickly brought the shroud back up with a scowl.

He could not allow himself to be discovered. Not yet.

Reaching out with his mind, he connected with Mnemosyne. She was nearing the ship, a bundle of wares carried in her beak. He almost smiled, footsteps behind him making him sneer instead.

The bird passed through his shroud easily, as anyone could if they were brave enough. She flew right over Lokiir, dropping her bundle into his hands. He tore open the cloth, inspecting several bags of fresh fruit and a tiny sack of coffee. It smelled heavenly. This was not something he would share with the rest of the crew. He tucked it into his pocket.

Popping some grapes in his mouth, Lokiir stretched out his hand, allowing his pet to land on his wrist.

"Indeed, there has been a strange turn of events." The raven picked at her feathers, avoiding eye contact.

"Do tell."

"First, address the fair maiden behind you," the raven tittered. Lokiir spun around, locking eyes with the dark-haired girl. Merel scowled at him, her arms crossed over her chest and her dark curls tumbling over her shoulders.

"Today marks an entire year of me being on this ship. One year of you promising to lead us back to Desmalogo so we can be where we belong. I have heard no plans from you, no call to action, nothing."

"If you are so bold," Lokiir began in a low tone, flicking his wrist up. Mnemosyne flapped her wings violently as she regained her balance, landing on a beam a short distance away. "Go, return."

The girl's scowl deepened, but she said nothing, spinning

around and marching back to the lower decks. Lokiir felt the urge to roll his eyes at her outburst, her words only reminding him of how hopeless the situation was. He turned back to his raven, busy picking at her feathers again.

No one cared that he had been the one to seize the ship, the one to collect those who were fleeing from their ultimate demise. He had saved so many from banishment, and what did he get in return? Cold shoulders and blame for them being stuck on this stupid ship.

"I've been keeping an eye on Reginald, to see what the sad lot was up to. He went to the house the girl lives in and yelled at her mother to give him the orange horse," Mnemosyne announced with great importance, breaking Lokiir's train of thought.

Lokiir snorted. That was hardly interesting.

"He killed the woman in a fit of rage. I always knew he had unchecked anger." Mnemosyne shook her head slowly, claws gripping the rotting wood.

"And the girl?" Lokiir asked, growing weary of the tiresome conversation. All the citizens in Desmalogo could kill each other and he wouldn't care. In fact, if they were all gone, he could go back to his home, free of his prison.

"Mycroft swept in and took her to Vathis. I couldn't see her there, but I assume they are keeping her there for safety."

Lokiir smiled, a cold, cruel smile.

"And her horse is still at the stables I assume?"

"Last I checked, yes," the bird cawed, ruffling her feathers.

"Perfect. I have just the person for the job."

If the girl was important to the fools in Vathis, he'd have to get his hands on her horse. Anything to get him more leverage to overturn the useless ruling that had kicked him out for good.

At least he was still alive.

He refused to believe that they all had forgotten him, even though it had been years since his escape. They'd know his work when it was done, but would it change anything? It was a pathetic attempt to return to the island, he knew, but he had to do something.

He'd never tell her, but Merel was right. A year for her, several for him. He wished he could lose count, but each day was ingrained into his mind. Every sunrise prompted him to draw another line next to the rest, a testimony that he was still alive, was given another day given to plot revenge against Aurelian. Three years and counting.

A wave rocked the ship and he nearly lost his balance, swearing loudly. The stairs to the lower deck had a railing, one he gripped with all his strength as he climbed down.

There was a possibility Daz wouldn't be in her room, but he doubted it. Most of her time she spent sleeping the days away, counting them like Merel. That one couldn't be trusted, being new to the ship and looking for any way to escape. It was his fault, yet he did not regret what he did. The rest of the crew seemed neutral, doing his bidding as requested, leaving him alone otherwise.

But this one. Lokiir stopped in front of her door, hand on the knob. If he handled this carefully, she would do anything for him, and he planned to finally exploit her position.

Taking a deep breath, he opened the door to her room and stepped inside, closing it as quietly as he could. Sure enough, she was sleeping, a thin blanket outlining the shape of her body underneath.

Lokiir lowered himself onto the edge of the bed, watching her sleep for a few moments. Even in the near pitch-black darkness of the room, her hair had a certain glow to it, skin perfectly smooth.

Picking up the edge of the blanket, he tossed it to the floor, watching her eyes flutter open. Goosebumps popped up on bare skin as it protested the cold, her thin shift leaving her exposed.

Her eyes met his, and a feline yawn exposed her teeth.

"Hello, dear." It was the breath of a whisper, spun with the softest sugar. He hardly realized that he reached out, allowing his fingers to trail along her arm, stopping at her palm. It surprised him how much he liked the feeling, wondering what it would be like if he left it there.

"Daz." Having crossed enough lines, Lokiir tore his hand away and clasped them together. The girl propped herself up on one elbow, hair tumbling over her shoulders. She stared up at him expectantly, her lips slightly parted, her pupils dilated in an enticing way. "I have an assignment for you," he said in a low tone, noting the way her gaze faltered. "It is of great importance," Lokiir continued, sliding further onto the bed closer to her. He truly hated himself at the moment, but he would do what was necessary to get what he wanted.

Placing a hand on her leg right above her knee, he leaned even closer. He was not expecting her to rise up, to claim his lips with hers.

He shuddered, allowing her to do what she wanted, before she broke the moment to catch her breath.

"Get up and get dressed. You are going to Desmalogo."

Without another word, he slipped out of the room, his heart pounding.

The sooner she left, the better.

Chapter

20

"I'm going to be the best horse rider anyone has ever seen!" Emine shrieked, loud enough for half the island to hear. Mallika shook her pale head, moving closer to Cassie.

"That's wonderful, dear," Agnetha said, holding in a sigh as she led the little girls toward the stable. Conrad had been called out for emergency farrier work, and Agnetha had a nanny sit with the little ones.

"At your current pace," Mallika quipped, "you'll be the one with the most broken bones."

"I've only been thrown off twice!" Emine showed three grubby fingers, and Cassie couldn't contain her smile. It vanished when Judy approached.

"Agnetha! Good to see you. How are the little ones doing?" She flashed a smile at the girls, one politely saying a greeting in return and the other peering upward with a smirk.

"Very well, thank you." Agnetha placed a hand on Emine's shoulder with a curt nod.

Judy turned toward Cassie with a slightly sour expression. "Well, you are quite late today! I think it's best for you to start with the stalls." Her sneer slipped through the facade of politeness, even with Agnetha nearby.

Cassie nodded, hanging her head and rushing to begin her work. She wondered if Judy could see through her scam and knew she was a fraud.

Agnetha led her daughters to two ponies, and Cassie drifted to the far corner of the barn, pitchfork in hand. She worked as quickly as she could, ignoring the glances from the grooms around her.

Cassie wiped the sweat off her brow and watched yet another rider lead her fancy horse down the aisle, freshly shod hooves echoing through the barn. The layout of the stable was similar to Thebesia, but that was where the similarities ended. Cassie couldn't help but notice the stiff atmosphere, as if each person here was in a competition with their next-door neighbor.

With the exception of Linea, she had managed to avoid all riders and horses. She preferred listening rather than talking and overheard a conversation between two girls gossiping about how Linea was always nice to the hired help. It had stung at first until she realized Linea was creating the perfect cover; a simple girl who had no ties to dangerous people.

Five days into the Vallumvis lifestyle and she wanted to say screw the danger, march back to Thebesia Stables, and resume her previous life. But she couldn't, not when Linea had promised to look around and sleuth for her.

Cassie took a deep breath and scooped another pile of manure with the pitchfork, glancing up to count the number of stalls she had left on this side of the aisle. Seven, then she would be halfway done.

As she tossed the manure into the cart, someone cleared their throat from outside the stall. Cassie turned slightly to see if they were trying to get her attention or merely being bothersome.

Her eyes narrowed at Theo, his dark hair and chiseled

jawline unmistakable. She'd seen him at the racetrack and at Arion, his horse unmistakable as the winner of the first race.

Would he recognize her also? The thought sent a shiver down her back.

"I was expecting my stall to be clean by now." His voice was deeply annoyed, head slightly lolled back. Cassie's eyes flicked to the last pile of manure, then back to the man.

She lowered her pitchfork to the floor and leaned on it for support. "You can wait until I'm finished, or you can lead your horse into a disgusting stall."

The flash of indignation in his eyes made Cassie swallow tightly. She was gambling on making him mad enough to leave her alone, lessening the chances of her being recognized. From what she remembered, he had mostly chatted with Selene, hardly throwing her a sideways glance.

"Have we met before?" Theo tilted his head back, his annoyance morphing into suspicion.

"Certainly not." Cassie gritted her teeth as she forced a smile, recalling how Linea had recognized her by her glare.

"You better finish this stall. Plenty of people could take your place." The threat was ominous and very, very real.

Cassie lifted her chin. He did not realize how little she cared for her current position.

"I would have been finished if you were not pestering me."

"Theodore!" A voice rang sharply. Theo maintained eye contact for another moment before breaking off.

"Yes, Judy." He rolled his eyes.

"I'll hold your horse while Miriam finishes. She is still new here and getting used to how things work." She took the reins from his hands, holding her smile as Theodore strolled off. Then she scowled at Cassie, her eyes disapproving. "This better not happen again."

Cassie refused to agree, digging her pitchfork into the last pile of manure in the stall and pushing the door open with more force than necessary. She wheeled around Judy, and the manager led the stunning horse into the stall. His coat gleamed in the low light, muscles rippling under the skin.

Moving on to the next stall, she took several deep breaths to calm herself down. Someone as entitled as Theodore did not deserve such a beautiful horse, fast enough to win races and do well in shows, which only fed his arrogance.

Judy rushed to help a student tighten a girth, and Cassie paused her work to focus on the escalating voices outside the barn.

"Conrad doesn't have any relative that would explain her." The mocking tone sent a tingle through her nerves. Had Theo recognized her? If he went to Selene to ask questions, she was done for.

"He has family living away from Desmalogo." Agnetha's voice was harsh. Cassie would have said it was full of hatred, except she didn't think the woman was capable of such jarring emotions.

"This is preposterous. No, he does not. I swear she is familiar to me and I have seen her before, but I cannot place her."

Cassie let out a breath, pushing away the strands of hair falling out of place.

"I know my husband better than you do. Miriam came to visit us, and you will not question my integrity." Agnetha's voice was steel, not bending under any pressure.

"What's her exact lineage?" Theo demanded, and silence ensued. Agnetha finally replied but too quietly for Cassie to hear. It seemed to end the conversation, though, and the blonde woman wandered into the stables.

Cassie quickly resumed her mucking, working faster than ever. Agnetha leaned against the stall door, a heavy frown on her face.

"The girls are ready to go home." Agnetha's gaze wasn't focused, eyelids fluttering.

"Ok. I'm nearly halfway finished with the stalls, but I'm sure Judy has more tasks for me." Cassie tried to make her voice as cheerful as possible, giving the stall a second glance to make sure she hadn't missed any corners.

"You'll go with us," Agnetha replied in a flat tone, her eyes meeting Cassie's. "I regret ever asking you to work here. Finish this up and let's go." She pushed away from the stall before Cassie could argue.

Cassie gripped the pitchfork, beads of sweat collecting on her forehead from the rising heat. To an extent, Judy was right, and she had been very late today. It was easier to muck in the mornings when it was still cool outside. But she was not the only person hired to do chores, and it was rude to shove so many tasks on her.

Agnetha waited with the patience that could only belong to a mother, starting the walk back to her house when Cassie joined her. She was silent, as she often was, preferring the girls' chatter to the thoughts in her mind.

"My trainer says I'm very good and have natural talent," Emine said proudly, her nose turned up in the air.

"Yes," agreed Mallika, "it takes great talent to have the horse walk in a circle around the pen." This sent Emine into a fit of giggles, and Agnetha frowned.

"Girls, run along ahead." She gave Emine a light push, and the little ones ran to the house. Conrad had returned, opening the door to greet them.

Agnetha stopped, turning to Cassie with a tight facial expression.

"Judy told me about Theo being rude to you. Don't mind him. He is simply angry at me and taking it out on you." The woman chewed on her lower lip, genuinely concerned as she shook her head. "I hate to force you to go there every day when you are treated like this. It cannot continue."

"I don't know." Cassie shrugged, hanging her head. At no other time had she felt like more of a burden than she did now. She liked having a job and tolerated the jabs thrown at her in exchange for drachmas.

"While I don't mind Vivion and that doctor handing you over, it's not fair to you. They ought to have explained themselves better." Agnetha furrowed her eyebrows.

"Can I ask why Theo—" Cassie faltered, unsure how to phrase the question.

"Theodore had an older brother, Clarence Vallumvis." A painful memory flashed behind her eyes. "He and I used to be married, but he is no longer among the living."

"Oh! I—I'm sorry." Cassie choked out the words, not sure how to comfort the older woman. Agnetha turned to meet her gaze, the smallest of smiles curling her lips upward.

"Don't be. He reaped what he sowed." She marched toward the house, an indication that the conversation was finished. She stopped at the front door, turning around to glance at Cassie. "Come along. We mustn't waste daylight."

After a hearty lunch of baby creamer potatoes paired with roast beef, Cassie sat outside with the two middle children, leaving Agnetha to whisper with her husband about what they would do with her. She had heard her name, Vivion, and Mycroft mentioned a few times before she was ushered outside to bask in the sunshine.

Cassie stretched out her legs, leaning back on her hands. Her eyes unwillingly moved to Emine and her little brother, soppy mud squelching between their fingers as mud pies took shape on the ground.

Emine let out a happy shriek, hurling her mud pie directly at the unsuspecting toddler. Dirt splattered over his shirt, droplets landing all over his body.

Cassie sighed and rolled her eyes, inching away from the

flying blobs of mud between the two children. For a moment, she tried to remember her own childhood, trying to recall if she had been unruly like Emine or calm and practical like Mallika.

No matter how hard she thought, nothing came up except a headache.

"I'll be back. I want to get some water," she informed the little ones, who both laughed at her.

"Where are you going? There's water right here." Emine pointed to the bucket next to them tainted with grass and chunks of dirt.

"To drink," Cassie clarified. Emine blinked with a shrug, not understanding the problem. Cassie would have ruffled the caramel blonde hair if it had not been decorated with brown, earthy streaks. Instead, she simply went back inside, nearly colliding with Agnetha.

"Cassie. Someone is here to see you." Agnetha motioned toward the door. Thinking it was Linea, Cassie smiled and ran to open it.

Taven stood several steps away from the doorframe, his eyes fluttering to Cassie. He took a step forward, stretching out his arms, but clasped them together after a moment of hesitation. A grin developed across his face, his eyes flicking from her blonde hair back to her eyes.

Cassie stepped outside and closed the door behind her, nervously chewing her bottom lip. She'd have to explain things to him, but she didn't want to.

Instead, she wanted him to tell her everything was alright and she could return to Thebesia.

"How are you doing?" The Ranger broke the silence, friendly as ever. Their last interaction was rough, but Cassie put that aside.

"Fine. Thebesia is better." She tried to smile but couldn't bring herself to. Taven sighed, lifting his cap and running a hand through damp hair.

"We've been trying to locate you for nearly a week now. Put all the Rangers in a panic, trying to discover if you were alright, if you were alive even." His voice trembled, and he grew quiet, avoiding her gaze.

"I had to run. And even here, I am in disguise. My name is Miriam." Her words were choppy and all in a bunch, and she took a deep breath to steady herself.

"I heard. You're staying here?" Taven's eyes darted toward the house, then met hers.

"Yes. I need to get my horse here. I'll wait until the doctor gives me the ok to move back. He was the one that helped me escape and find a new place to live," Cassie explained, a light frown on her face. "But how did you know I was here?"

"Linea." The response came in a heartbeat. "She told Luke, who was relieved to know you were safe." Taven pulled his lips into a tight smile, his eyes apologetic. "I was at Thebesia asking Henrik if he knew anything." He dragged out each word, buying time for himself.

"What's wrong?" Cassie demanded, her eyes narrowing.

"He told me Tenille broke away from her stall and is nowhere to be seen. I'm sorry, Cassie, I—" He reached out to comfort her but stopped himself.

Cassie stood frozen, horrified by the news. If Tenille broke out and was running loose, anybody could capture her. Her mind instantly went to the man from her dreams hovering close to her with a knife.

"Would the man who stole her before try to get to her again?" Her question was directed more at herself than at the Ranger, but he stepped closer with understanding.

"No, he's away from the island."

"So he escaped." Cassie frowned, her lower lip jutting out. "Do you know anything, Taven?" His eyes were the softest of browns, holding enough warmth to melt her. "Do you know if it is safe for me to return to Yvonne?"

"Cassie," Taven murmured in a low voice, taking another

step toward her and grasping her hand in his. He let out a long breath, closing his eyes as his face twisted into a painful expression. "Cassie, I—" He heaved a sigh. "Yvonne is dead."

"Dead?" Cassie echoed, her voice as empty as her mind.

No, Taven was wrong. She couldn't lose her home like that.

She tore her hand away from his, clenching her fists at her sides. Taven said nothing, wrapping her in a tight hug. She didn't have the energy to do anything but slump against him, his well-muscled torso a solid wall of warmth.

"I'm sorry," he whispered against her hair, and Cassie tilted her head against his chest, squeezing her eyes tightly against the tears spilling out. Her heart pounded wildly, blood rushing up to her head and making her lightheaded.

It was only then that she realized how close to death she had been. Had the doctor been a second later, the knife would have plunged into her. The thought made her shiver despite Taven's warm body pressed against hers.

They had their differences, but surely Yvonne did not deserve to die. And with the doctor whisking her away so quickly, she very well may have taken the knife meant for Cassie. Or the man was just so angry he had to take down anyone.

Her breath hitched in her throat, the world melting around her, only Taven's arms keeping her grounded.

"I'm so glad you're safe and away from harm. Luke and I kept this quiet. We didn't want the entire island talking about it," Taven continued, his voice rumbling in his chest.

"Thank you," Cassie whispered, tilting her head back. Taven's shirt was stained with her tears, yet he didn't seem to notice. "Do you think you could help me find my horse?" She hiccupped, and Taven nodded.

"Now that I know you are safe, I will expand my efforts to find Tenille. We'll find her and get her back to you. On that, I promise." He released her, shoving his hands into his back pockets.

Cassie sniffed, wanting to feel relieved, but she was still tense.

"Do you think it would be ok to tell Selene I am alright?" Cassie asked slowly, crossing her arms as a sudden shiver went through her. Taven took a step back from Cassie, shaking his head lightly.

"I really don't know. She has been asking about you every day, and I feel guilty keeping her in the dark. I certainly won't tell her where you are." Taven tilted his head to the side, the shadow of a smile on his face. "But I'll reassure her you are safe."

"Thank you." Cassie smiled for a moment, her momentary happiness fading when Taven faced her directly.

"As a Ranger, it is my duty to know what happened. Do you know who the attacker was?"

Cassie swallowed a sigh, the scenes from the dream filling her mind. The man who tried to steal her horse was the same as the one who entered the house, but would Taven find her dream valid?

"I have never seen him before on the island. It was a young man, maybe around twenty years of age." Cassie's voice hitched as Taven's gaze bore into her. "I do not think I'm in immediate danger, but I do think it is wrong for me to be separated from my horse."

"Your horse," Taven repeated, somewhat flatly. "We need to figure out who was threatening you and killed your foster parent, and you say you need your horse."

"Yvonne was attacked because of Tenille. He is still after her, Taven," Cassie snapped.

The Ranger sighed again, shifting his weight from one foot to the other.

"Very well. I will consult with Luke. I don't think he'll

agree to send out more Rangers, but I can try. Regardless, I will look for her."

"With four white socks and a prominent blaze who happens to be unmanageable at all times." Cassie clasped her hands together, her very soul aching at being separated from her horse for so long.

Taven managed to smile in return, even though his body language showed how much he didn't like the situation at hand. He was uncanny at reading her, and she did not like it.

"Alright, Cassie."

"Miriam," Cassie corrected with a grin.

"Miriam," Taven said, exasperated. "We'll find your horse."

She wanted to hug him on the spot, but something held her back. "Thanks, Taven."

Chapter

21

Mycroft Lykaion was often busy with his patients, but as soon as he had a free night, he saddled a horse and made his way to the Valley of Vathis in the dead of night, only the stars above guiding his way forward. Truly, the guilt over thinking she would be alright with Yvonne threatened to tear him apart, especially after he had gone through so much to keep her alive. Even in her current location, he could not be so sure she was fully away from harm, but Vallumvis had the lowest crime rate on the island.

Leaving the horse tied to a tree, the doctor was surprised when the door opened as he approached, allowing him into the house.

"Mycroft." The young man's voice did nothing to hide the emotions weaving through each word. "I've been expecting you."

Candles emitted a luminous glow across the walls, and the doctor was hesitant to enter the house. He had known he would have to answer questions about Cassie eventually, yet he had clung to the empty hope that she would never be entangled with Vathis. He was wrong.

Vivion leaned against the counter in his kitchen, the dark

pants and hoodie a jarring contrast to his usual choice of clothing.

"You've been out in town?" Mycroft presumed, settling into a chair. He was many years older than the man standing a few feet away from him, yet he did not feel it. Vivion knew everything, keeping most of it to himself. A trait that frustrated everyone around him, Mycroft especially. As an Igetis, no one could force him to share if he wished not to.

"Yes. Investigating an issue that has arisen within the Fýlax," Vivion quipped, picking up a cup of steaming tea.

"Indeed. Would you mind sharing why you were expecting me?"

"You were to stop by and tell me more about the red-haired girl you saved from death. Twice." The last word was said with a harsh pronunciation that might have made another man flinch. The doctor, however, remained irrationally calm.

"What's there to tell? I care for all my patients."

"Enough to go out of your way to create portals to bring them to safety? Mycroft, you swore you would stop using any remaining power you may possess." Vivion hid his face with a swig of tea.

"Blame the hand that controls fate. I didn't decide to have a half-dead girl appear on my hospital bed with severe head trauma." Mycroft remained comfortable; it was Vivion who started pacing the short width of his house, cozy slippers muffling the sound of his movements.

"I'd like to hear the details of the procedure." Vivion paused, his brown eyes fixating on the doctor.

"That's outside your realm of understanding," Mycroft countered, growing still as footsteps approached the door. It swung open, and a man of average stature but with a commanding presence stopped the spill of moonlight into the small house.

"Vivion, guests at this hour?" The voice was scathing, full of disrespect. Aurelian took another step inside.

"It's but the doctor." Vivion sighed, resuming his pacing.

"What does he need?" Aurelian asked with a boldness that was only seen between two Igetai.

"Vivion was simply asking if I could assist in the new investigations underway," Mycroft said, mindlessly fiddling with his hat.

"Nonsense. You have no role in anything we do here. Well, Vivion, explain yourself. How much has he been told?" Mycroft flicked his eyes toward Aurelian in the doorway, the door wide open.

"All I said was we have detected traces of a corrupted individual around the Thebesian district, which is where he resides. I wanted to know if he knew anything about it." Vivion pulled his eyebrows together, knowing he was defeated.

The hairs on the doctor's neck stood straight up as he took in the information, a breath away from being horrified. This was not what he wanted to hear, not at all.

He had thought she would be cleared of her connection if her memories were removed. But whatever was inside her was rooted very deeply and still there. He was a fool to think her powers lay in her memories instead of the bond with her horse.

"You cannot identify the individual?" Mycroft asked after a moment of collecting his thoughts.

"No. Which means that none of the trackers have ever had any contact with them. I've tried to get Jakobi to get a closer look at the traces of corruption, but he refuses."

"Interesting," the doctor noted, his fiddling with the hat no longer mindless but rather stressed. Jakobi had his reasons to refuse the case, though he supposed a man like Vivion would never understand why.

"Would *you* know anything about this individual?" Aurelian asked, his voice full of scathing distrust. Mycroft glanced up to meet Vivion's eyes, seeing the question in them.

Was Cassie the one leaving traces of corruption around Thebesia?

Maybe Vivion didn't think that and Mycroft was over-reacting.

"That's absurd," Mycroft said slowly, referring directly to Vivion. "We've managed to weed out everyone who is not of our kind."

"As expected," Aurelian said in a dangerously low tone.

"Aurelian—" Vivion tried to interject, but evidently thought better of it, gripping his teacup instead.

"You are of no help and pledged to not be with our kind due to our disciplinary actions." Aurelian repeated the words said long ago with mockery. "Mycroft, I do not wish to see you associated with my kind or even stepping foot in the Valley of Vathis. You simply cannot choose when you want to be involved and when you do not. We require full loyalty—if you refuse to uphold our law, then you must leave. You made your choice clear when you told us it was wrong to banish the Opposed."

"You left them all to suffer when many of them did nothing wrong."

"Mycroft. That is enough. You make a mockery of the Fýlax by not joining us in the Valley as is required by law."

"I am a doctor, Aurelian. And not even an Igetis can tell me what to do."

With a set face, the doctor placed the hat firmly on his head, not sparing another glance at the two men he was leaving behind.

Mycroft had gotten the information he needed, and with it he could make a better decision on what to do with Cassie. More than anything, he had to ensure she was not banished to the underworld like so many of her kind.

Or be taken captive by the last remaining Igetis of the Opposed, Lokiir.

Chapter 22

Despite Agnetha's fussing, Cassie continued her work at the stables of Vallumvis. She couldn't stay at the house all day, and being at the stables allowed her to be close to the horses.

Then there was Linea, who had a host of her own horses, some leased, and managed to keep Cassie nearby most of the time with a list of never-ending tasks. She gladly accepted the reins each time Linea handed them over, the work a distraction from her troubles. Judy frowned, but her threats were empty.

"Miriam is a fantastic rider, and I need my horses exercised." Linea put her foot down, and it was settled.

For each horse Cassie exercised, Linea's scrutinizing glance analyzed every flick of her wrist or ankle, each movement of her hands, and even the slightest reactions from the horse. She seemed to be searching for something, eyes sparkling with excitement.

Cloud, one of Cassie's favorites, became a daily partner. She loved brushing him down after her sessions, admiring his coat, the lightest of grays dipping into darker tones around his legs.

"Take him over the poles," Linea commanded, and Cassie did as she asked. Judy poked her head in, shaking it lightly.

"Linea, it would do you good to be the one riding him."

"I like to see him moving from the ground," Linea quipped in return, eyes never leaving the pair in the arena.

Cloud carried himself with a powerful momentum, his long legs creating a ground-covering stride that was, at times, difficult for Cassie to keep up with. She found herself breathless as she neared the end of the session, slowing Cloud down to a walk as they approached Linea.

"What do you think?" Linea asked, her gray eyes dancing with excitement.

"He's quite the horse. Very bold."

"You think he would do well in a show? I don't want to rush Waffles's recovery, but I need to find a different horse for Saturday." A mere two days away.

Cassie sighed. Exactly one week ago, she was in Arion living blissfully before her life had been torn away from her. And what a sad life it had been before that, lost in a whirlwind of confusion and lack of memories.

"They are your horses. You'd know better how they do in shows." For a moment she thought of Taven and wondered if he had any updates about her horse.

"Never hurts to ask for a second opinion." Linea flashed a smile.

Agnetha walked confidently across the arena, not caring that Cassie was in the middle of a session with a horse. Linea didn't argue with her cousin, knowing if Agnetha had come here, she had come with good reason. The light-haired woman handed Cassie a piece of folded paper, waiting for her to read it.

If you're not busy tonight, we can discuss how you

have been doing. Vallumvis Clinic, room ten, six o'clock. Dr. Lykaion.

"I can." Cassie nodded.

"Good. I have plenty to say to him, but I'll save it for another time." Agnetha frowned at the gray horse in front of her. "Don't overwork yourself." It was a rather scolding voice.

"I'll try." Cassie slid off Cloud and removed her helmet, handing it to Linea. "Do you think I rode Cloud well?"

"Very." Linea glanced at Agnetha retreating out of the arena. "She has a real talent with horses, you know."

"And with trouble." Agnetha shamelessly tossed the words over her shoulder.

"I'll brush him down and take him to his stall, then try to squeeze in as many chores as I can before I go to the doctor's." Cassie refused to let Agnetha's statement rile her, knowing full well it was her fault she kept attracting trouble. It reminded her of how much she did not belong with the rest of the people here on the island.

"Thank you for riding him. He loves it." Linea patted Cloud's sweaty neck, walking with Cassie to the barn.

Cassie brushed down the tall gelding, running her hands down each leg to check for any abnormalities. He was in top condition, nicely filled out without being overweight, and a soft gleam to his coat. He enjoyed the attention, nibbling on her hair whenever it was within reach. His halter was soft in her hands, delicate fibers strung together showcasing the skills of a weaver.

Cloud was housed several stalls away from Waffles, and Cassie made sure to give the pretty mare some pats before she grabbed a rake and headed toward the smaller lesson rings to run through the footing, ensuring it was free of major debris and safe for the horses.

She headed home early without checking with Judy, as the

manager was nowhere to be seen. With the show at Dionysian Falls looming ahead, the manager was slacker with how and when chores were completed as long as they were done.

Besides, with most of the horses and riders gone, no one was left to make a giant mess at the stable.

Agnetha had a hot bath waiting for her, bringing out a pretty dress that she had worn the first day there. Most days had her in breeches and a shirt, but the change was welcome. She set them on the bed and glanced at Cassie in her bathrobe, her mouth tipped into a small frown.

"Before you go, I must ask you a question."

Cassie went rigid, holding the towel that had been wrapped around her hair a moment ago in her hands.

"Ok," she breathed, forcing herself to meet Agnetha's gray-green gaze.

"Are you in any way associated with the Fýlax?" Each word was laced with a deeper meaning, and Agnetha crossed her arms against her chest.

"Associated?" Cassie sputtered, the question sending unwelcome shivers down her spine. "With the robe people?" She would never, ever want to be.

"The people that Vivion is associated with," Agnetha continued, her focus laser sharp on Cassie's every movement.

"No, I am not. At least, I don't think so. Vivion did not want me to be seen. And Yvonne wrote letters to them, letters that I read myself, saying she was in danger, and they did not care." Cassie clenched her fists at her sides, the anger surging up again. "No, they are not my friends. I do not want anything to do with them." She was angry that Agnetha would even have to ask, a small nagging thought making her wonder if perhaps she was.

Agnetha softened, her suspicion diminishing. Cassie wouldn't say it was fully gone, as Agnetha had her doubts from the beginning, but she dropped her scrutinizing gaze.

"You do know Vivion is not allowed freely in Vallumvis?" This time, her voice was a hushed whisper.

"He is not? Why?" Cassie frowned, remembering the ease with which he had entered the house and cuddled with the baby.

"We do not want any Fýlax in our city. They are dangerous and have good reason to be confined to their Valley. They tell us the dangerous ones are gone, but they are all dangerous. Vivion is only allowed to enter on occasion, as he is the younger brother of Conrad. The children love their uncle. We appreciate their work as a conservation society, as long as it does not bother us." Agnetha pressed her lips together, motioning toward the clothes on the bed. "Hurry and get dressed. I am not telling you to not trust the doctor; I am telling you to be careful if he is so deeply intertwined with those who live in the Valley." With a final pointed look at the clothes, Agnetha left Cassie alone in the room.

Cassie wanted to punch something, tearing the bathrobe off and flipping through the neat stack on the bed. She hated the knife of doubt plunged into her at every turn, leaving her breathless.

She hadn't told Taven about Vivion or the Valley, not knowing where that would lead. But had that been a mistake? Surely he had his own opinion on the matter. Yet she had not seen Agnetha be wrong about anything, and she trusted her new friend. Was the doctor aligned with dangerous people?

The doctor could travel through portals when he was in dire need. She should have told Agnetha that, but she'd changed her mind. If anything, the woman already knew.

Leaving her hair a wild, wet mess, Cassie bolted out the door to avoid any more interactions. She stifled a groan as Mallika caught up to her right outside the house and pressed a warm muffin into her hands.

"Let me know if you like it! I made it all by myself. I even gathered the blueberries from our very own bush!" She gave

Cassie a reassuring pat on the arm, as if she were the older one in the situation, before scampering back into the house.

Cassie glanced down at the muffin, still warm, her memories transporting her back to Yvonne's house. The woman would make warm bran muffins for her, ones that the horses liked but she didn't.

It wasn't her fault.

Breaking off a crumb, Cassie pressed it into her mouth, only then noticing a sticky sugar glaze on top. The flavors lingered on her tongue, reminiscent of a swig of blueberry lemonade.

Should she ever return to Thebesia Stables, she would ask Agnetha to pack her a never-ending supply of the heavenly morsels, the bright lemon contrasting against the sweetness of the blueberry, sending her straight into euphoria.

Cassie was still licking away the remnants of the muffin when she found the clinic and stepped inside. At the desk she stated she had an appointment in room ten, and the lady led her away without asking for so much as a name.

The doctor was waiting, flipping through several files of papers, a grave look on his face. It worried her deeply, as he usually wore a soft smile that put her at ease.

"Dr. Lykaion. Something is amiss." Cassie slowly climbed atop the exam table, wringing her hands together.

He gently set the papers aside, turning his full attention toward the girl.

"You've been eating more," he remarked with a nod, and Cassie dropped her gaze. She hated that her weight was still one of the top concerns for many people around her, but it only made sense. After being in a coma for so long, it was important to be on the right path to recovery.

"Agnetha," she mumbled, leaning her head back at the mere thought of the blueberry muffin. She'd eat a dozen of them, no question.

"Of course. How have you adjusted?"

"Besides hating the fact that I live under a fake name and have to work for Judy Moody, it's good. Linea is my friend. Taven visited because the Rangers were worried about me."

"Yes, by the time I filled in Luke he said he already knew." Dr. Lykaion sighed, his expression somber. "Of course, it is tragic what happened to Yvonne, and we will do what we can to keep you out of harm's way. Cassie, I know you saw Reginald in the room, but," Dr. Lykaion said, pausing to make sure Cassie was paying attention, "he is not the root of the problem. Such actions are only taken out of desperation, meaning someone else could very well be threatening him for the horse."

Cassie paled, slumping against the wall. Dr. Lykaion stood with concern, his eyes running over her. The doctor knew the man from her dream. Reginald. What a strange name.

She bolted upright. Taven had told her about Reginald. He had known all along, always watching out for her.

"Cassie, I promise everything will be alright." He took a few steps across the room, placing a hand on her shoulder. She nodded numbly, finally finding her voice.

"I—I thought I was safe if I escaped that man. But if there's a trail of people behind him." Her words ended in a hiccup, and she clasped her hands together to keep them from shaking. "I want my horse."

"Cassie, I know it's hard for you, but believe me, it is safer for you to remain in Vallumvis." The doctor hesitated, sitting back into his chair and avoiding her intense gaze.

"Why?" she demanded, needing to know.

"I'll help you get your horse there, but," he said, sighing, his eyes scanning the room as the rushed words tumbled out of him, "Vallumvis is a gated city. No one can get in or out without permission. It has better security. The Dasos Academy means many Rangers live there, for the protection of all citizens." It almost sounded like he was rambling, and

Cassie sniffled, slightly suspicious of the strange behavior from the doctor.

"Very well. I will stay in Vallumvis if you want." Cassie narrowed her eyes thoughtfully, legs swinging slightly as she leaned forward toward the doctor. "Why are you involved with the Fýlax?"

The doctor's eyes snapped toward hers, holding an emotion that seemed like dread.

"I wish I was not. And it is my goal to keep you away from them." He sounded honest enough, but also bitter, as if regrets clouded his decision.

Cassie found herself laughing lightly, jumping down from the exam table.

"Don't worry. I will not associate with anyone who ignores death threats and cannot keep anyone safe. Unless there is more to discuss, I will be on my way."

"No. You seem to be in a rush, so run along. If you have anything bothering you, your head, sickness, I am a doctor," he reminded her with a soft smile, but Cassie brushed it away.

"I am in a big rush—to find my horse."

"Cassie?" The doctor beat her to the door, reaching for the handle.

"Hm?"

"When you want to find your horse, call to her. In your mind." His voice was hardly above a whisper yet held a bold intensity that was hard to ignore.

"She is always in my mind." Smiling to herself, Cassie slipped out of the room and left the clinic. Even though the doctor told her to stay in Vallumvis, she was not forbidden from visiting other places.

And even if she had been, she would not have listened.

The next morning dawned with bright colors, not a single cloud in sight. Cassie appreciated the sun warming her as she walked toward the stable, sunny rays chasing away the damp darkness of her dreams.

She shuddered as she shoved away the murky thoughts of her horse being in danger and her narrow escape, reminding herself she was doing fine. The feelings still persisted, clinging to her skin like salty beads of sweat.

The road that led to the barn was lined with magnificent trees, their trunks sturdy but slim, guiding each visitor forward and framing the barn looming ahead. She sighed at its over-whelming presence, mentally preparing herself.

A girl nearly knocked into her, not apologizing as she scrambled away with an armload of gear. Cassie pressed her lips together and glanced around, spotting Linea near Cloud's stall.

Agnetha had told her that Dionysian Falls was close enough to Vallumvis that many riders would stay within the protection of the gated city, only heading to the showgrounds in the early morning. Linea did not agree with such senti-ments, hauling Cloud's tack across the aisle to where several packed bags stood.

"You're getting ready early," Cassie commented, folding her arms tightly together as her dream came back in pieces, a painful reminder of what had occupied her mind last night.

She had dreamed of being in the Valley, not far from Vivion's house. This time, she was stuck in the tangles of the alluring vines, screaming as they dragged her deeper into the forest. No doctor came to her rescue, not a single soul to be found anywhere. It was her and the darkness, all alone, like before.

Before? What had happened before?

The frustration of not being able to remember only caused pain, and she let go of the thought.

"You look tired. Is everything alright?" Linea placed the

stack of items on the floor, pushing her attention toward Cassie.

"I—" Cassie scrunched her nose, trying to formulate her thoughts without saying the wrong thing. "It's the strangest feeling ever. I used to only want to remember anything. But today, I learned I also want to forget some things."

"Something bad," Linea mused, tilting her head to the side. She studied Cassie for a few moments, bending down to pick up a saddlebag from the floor and swinging it over her shoulder. "I won't force you to tell me about it if you don't want."

"I had a bad dream." Cassie rubbed her temples with the tips of her fingers, unwillingly going back to the images in her mind. When Reginald had caught Tenille in the plains, the dream had been vivid. Each blade of grass whispered with the wind, rippling across the land until it met the blue sky at the horizon. Flowers had been so detailed she could count the petals on each one.

But the illusion from last night was a lot like other ones she had. There, but vague, and not as clear.

"A nightmare? Was it about your horse?" Linea asked.

"No. Not about her. If it was, I would have already left looking for her."

"You feel well enough to travel?" Linea almost smiled, clasping her hands together.

"Yes, if I need to." Cassie sighed, not particularly thrilled about leaving the safety of the city.

"You do. We leave for the show today." Linea tossed Cassie a halter, and she barely caught it in time.

"We?" Cassie questioned, a light frown on her face.

"Yes, silly. You and me. You'll ride Cloud, since you get along well. I'll be riding Nutmeg, that mare." She pointed across the aisle to a frisky mare tossing her head impatiently.

"And we're going to the Falls today?" Cassie frowned. Linea laughed, entering Cloud's stall.

"Yes. I suggest you go home and get a change of clothes, then come back. I'm almost done here." Cloud was saddled, one hind leg cocked patiently. Linea lifted the saddlebags and gently placed them over his back, nestling them right behind the saddle.

"But why?" Cassie shook her head, unable to dislodge the ominous feeling from last night. She knew it was her fears getting to her, but she couldn't deny the fact that her dreams were often linked to something happening in the real world.

"I wanted it to be a surprise, but—" Linea sighed, motioning her inside the stall. Her eyes sparkled as she dropped her voice. "We are going early to plan."

"Plan," Cassie echoed.

"Yes, plan. We will plan on how to get Tenille back where she belongs."

At that, Cassie grinned, the excitement bubbling out of her, drowning out any other emotion. Thoughts about murky dreams vanished, evaporating because of the warmth those few words brought to her.

"I'll go get some clothes and be back as quick as I can."

Cassie followed Linea back to their room, her stomach comfortably full. The room was nicely furnished, two wooden beds on opposite sides of the wall and various knickknacks throughout displaying the owner's love for horses. Cassie lifted a small statue off the dresser, admiring the intricate carvings in the smooth wood.

Several small rugs cushioned the floor and protected bare feet from the cold wood underneath. Each knot was artfully woven, sketches of horses etched into the finished product.

The washroom to the side was shared with the room adjacent to theirs, and Linea rummaged through her bags for her pajamas.

"Here they are." She pulled them out with a smile, heading into the washroom. Cassie's eyes drifted to the t-shirt and shorts she had laid out on the bed, and she sighed.

It was similar to the shirt she had been wearing when she woke up at Yvonne's, this one a gift from Agnetha. While Linea changed in the washroom, Cassie donned her clothes, folding the others away neatly inside the drawer.

At Yvonne's house, she wouldn't have considered herself to be very organized, her clothes often taking up space on the floor instead of having a place of their own. That changed at Agnetha's, when she was expected to fold all her items neatly. She was still in Mallika's room, though the girl never complained. In fact, she had taken quite a liking to Cassie.

A single tear dripped down her cheek, and she scrubbed at it furiously. She had no reason to be getting emotional over the fact that she would never return to Yvonne's house and would never see the woman again.

"Cassie? Are you alright?" Linea whispered, and Cassie whirled around to face her.

"Yes. I'm fine." She forced a deep breath, crossing the room to the window. It was a breathtaking view of the city below, framed by the mountains. In the center, a waterfall cascaded down into a pool of water, sparkling as it caught the last of the day's sunlight. It was only fitting for the city to be named after such a beautiful sight.

"Cassie," Linea said again, this time her voice bordering on something horrified. The girl at the window stiffened, her worry returning as she faced her friend. "I—" Linea swallowed, running both hands through her hair. Slowly backing away from Cassie, she slumped onto a bed, avoiding the girl's eyes.

"What's wrong now?" Cassie demanded, fear and annoyance clashing in her mind.

"You have a strange sign." Linea frowned, pointing to Cassie's leg. She turned to glance at the back of her calf, noting the faint lines that all swirled together, spread out about the size of her palm.

"Yeah, I do. The doctor told me very little about it, stating that it is best for me to not know." Cassie huffed, crossing her arms. It seemed ridiculous to even think, but she did not want something so minor as a birthmark ruining her friendship with Linea. Or anyone, for that matter, even if it meant keeping quiet about such matters around Selene and Henrik.

"You don't know? Oh, no, you wouldn't remember." Linea

caught herself, answering her own question. She finally met Cassie's pressing gaze, her nose scrunched up as she scanned the girl's face. "I probably should have guessed when you were so obsessed with your horse. I guess it makes sense, since she was the only familiar thing in this unknown land." She sighed, slumping against the wall.

"No one in Thebesia cares about bonds. They say there are horses you connect with more than all others, but there is no such thing as a deep bond that unites horse and rider."

"Who says?" Linea quickly cut in.

"Henrik, Selene, I don't know. I didn't go around the stables asking." At that, Linea laughed. Cassie tightened her arms in front of her, on the verge of leaving the room.

"That's funny. No, most people in Desmalogo are well aware of the Fýlax and their work within the community, though I suppose there are plenty of deniers."

"Their work?" Cassie frowned, her conversation with Agnetha fresh in her mind. "They are not even allowed in Vallumvis." Linea's eyes sharpened toward her, and she propped herself up on her elbows.

"I'm surprised you know so little." She adjusted herself into a crisscross position on the bed, patting the blanket next to her. "There is a place in the middle of Desmalogo called the Valley of Vathis."

"I've been there." Cassie dropped, sliding onto the bed next to her friend.

"You've been there!" Linea nearly shrieked, her eyes wide. "Like, inside, inside?" Cassie backed away, a flood of self-consciousness drowning her coherent thoughts.

"The doctor and I traveled through it. Then I came here," Cassie mumbled, wrapping her arms around her knees.

"Oh. Talk goes that they are very secretive. No one is allowed in besides some Rangers. Anyway, a few years ago, changes to the law were implemented, and a lot of people were banished from the island. They'd been trying to do this for years and couldn't get enough support. I remember it well; my dad was involved as the representative for Vallumvis. Then word came from the Valley—we were told all the corrupted riders were kicked from their ranks, leaving only those who would protect the island and live up to their name: the Conservation Society of Desmalogo." Linea sighed, a shudder running through her. "Cassie? Do you think it's possible you are one of the ones who was banished and you are not supposed to be here?"

"No," Cassie instantly shot back, her anger toward the secretive robe men heightening. "No one there knows who I am. I think if I were part of them, they would know who I am, even if I didn't remember."

"That's true." Linea softened, fingers trailing on her chin. "So you came from outside the island for sure, yet you have a mark like they do. I wonder if it matches anyone's in the Valley. But you won't find anything about them in libraries. They do not allow information about them to spread, claiming it will be twisted into lies." Linea's mouth curved into a smirk. "I think allowing people to speculate leads to worse results, but no one asked me."

"The doctor does not want me to be involved with them," Cassie lamented, resting her chin on her kneecap.

"A shame." Linea sighed, scooting to the edge of the bed and standing up with a luxurious stretch. "Because I've lost several friends to the stupid Valley and its secrets." She shook her head at the memory, leaning over to blow out the candles on the nightstand, and the room dipped into darkness.

"Goodnight, Cassie. We need to rest well before the show tomorrow." She said no more before she dove under the covers of her bed, leaving Cassie with her heart thundering harder than she ever remembered.

She would never wear shorts in public again.

"You don't mind, do you?" Linea asked, her hand on Cassie's shoulder keeping her in place. Cassie pushed past, picking up the saddle and swinging it over the numnah lying on Cloud's back. The gray gelding was to compete in the show, so Nutmeg would be able to rest for their grand plan.

"No. This time, I'm the groom and you're the rider." Cassie cinched the girth carefully, making sure it was tight but not pinching the horse.

"Ok." Linea stepped back, her hands clasped together. "Maybe you could warm him up for me. I'm feeling nervous."

"He's your horse." Cassie tossed a dubious glance over her shoulder, squatting down and running her hands over the gelding's legs one last time.

"I know. But horses can sense feelings, and I don't want my nerves to transfer to him."

Cassie straightened out and stared flatly at Linea, noting the excitement in her gaze. To her, the girl seemed to be the least nervous person on this side of the barn, but she didn't want to argue.

"Fine."

Linea clapped at her victory, handing Cassie a helmet, and briskly headed toward a ring. She held the door open and allowed Cassie to enter, climbing up on the fence post to watch the girl mount.

Cassie fidgeted with the reins, biting down on her lower lip as she tried to focus. If anyone was nervous it was her, more concerned about finding Tenille than helping Linea with her horses.

Linea would compete with Cloud, and then what? Leave?

Too many people knew her.

Really, if she didn't even seem that excited and was having Cassie do all the work, she should have saved her drachmas for another purpose and forgone the show altogether, and they could have snuck out to an abandoned Thebesia while everyone was busy here.

Cassie sighed when she remembered Linea didn't need to save her drachmas and was not limited like she was.

"He's doing great!" Linea flashed a thumbs up, the grin on her face saying more than words could. Cassie slowed down her horse, trotting by Linea for the dozenth time.

"When do we go look for Tenille?"

"After our class. We have a few hours, then we go." Linea swung her feet, humming a random tune.

"Won't Cloud be too tired to travel?"

"We'll double on Nutmeg so you can ride her back without having an extra horse."

Linea's confidence made her smile and feel better about herself. She was sure they would find Tenille, but Cassie couldn't ignore the unease gnawing at her.

She decided it was enough exercise for Cloud and led him out of the paddock. An older woman was approaching them, so Cassie took the chance to escape and walk back toward the barn.

Linea was close with her family, but Cassie preferred to keep her distance. The fewer people that knew her, the less likely she was to get into trouble.

The stables here were smaller than in Thebesia or Vallumvis but still large enough to host several dozen horses. Cassie wandered down the aisle, glancing at some of the steeds waiting for their riders. She wanted to leave and go look for Tenille now, but leaving without Linea would only result in her getting lost if she strayed off the main road too far.

Cassie headed back outside, hovering close to the Vallumvis riders but staying far away enough so that she didn't have to hear the snarky comments about a groom tagging along for the show. She had heard enough the day before when the two of them left the stables.

Cassie leaned against a tree as Linea fussed over Cloud. The girl turned and noticed Cassie, instantly brightening. With a smile she strolled over to join her friend under the shade.

"The walkthrough is soon."

"Yes," Cassie agreed half-heartedly.

"I want you to watch me walk through the course and help me count the strides between jumps, as well as point out any strategies to secure a faster time." Linea twisted her palms upward in anticipation.

"Ok." Cassie smiled. "Do you think Cloud is good enough to take the win?"

"With your help, absolutely." Linea nodded. She followed Theo to the main arena, and Cassie trailed behind. She leaned against the paddock fence a short distance away, a girl on the other side leading a gleaming black horse.

The indigo and white blanket confirmed that it was indeed Kismet sporting the colors of Thebesia Stables. Cassie swallowed against the lump in her throat, wishing she could go talk to Selene but knowing she couldn't.

How much longer would she have to live in hiding?

Cassie shivered, almost leaving the arena but remembering Linea's request. The grandstands behind her were slowly filling with people, and she adjusted her hat. She no longer had red hair that would give her away, but those who knew her would still recognize her if they looked close enough.

Linea entered the arena for the walkthrough, laughing at something the Ranger at the gate told her. Her gaze met Cassie's for a split second, and Cassie gave her the smallest of nods.

It was a complex course, with a dozen colorful obstacles set out at various angles. The first one was not too high, the perfect size to start with. Next was a jump fitted between two tree props. Two rows of poles meant she would have to take a closer lift-off to make it across.

Cassie wished she had paper to take notes but tried to keep it all in her head as Linea walked from jump to jump. Cassie started, noting the end looked like a half portal.

The bottom was curved, then glitter-covered poles were stacked on top. It seemed like a nod toward those who held power, meaning there were more than just Dr. Lykaion who could open a portal for travel.

Cassie tore her eyes away from the final jump, focusing on memorizing the order of the course. Only when she knew the pattern well enough to imagine herself competing would she feel comfortable giving Linea advice.

She remained at the fence when Theo walked in, taking much longer than Linea to get from one fence to the other. He walked the distance between the third and fourth obstacle twice, glancing over his shoulder at the hedge with poles on top before moving on. Linea joined her at the fence, fingers clasping and unclasping.

"You see where he walked twice? It's a tricky distance, because you have to circle around at the right angle." Cassie scrunched her nose instead of pointing to Theo, who was facing them but focused on the course.

"I'll remember that. Won't be hard since I requested to be the first one to go. We start in fifteen minutes," Linea quipped.

"You must get ready!" Cassie exclaimed. Linea turned to glance at her, eyes full of mischief.

"No, *we* must get ready." She grinned and beckoned for Cassie to follow her to the barn. Linea stepped into her locker, walking out with a pile of clothes identical to her own and handing them to Cassie.

"What's this?" the girl sputtered, accepting the black show jacket and crisp breeches.

"An outfit to match with me. Go and put these on. I have a fun plan for us." Linea shoved Cassie into the locker, not taking no for an answer. Cassie sighed and got dressed, her mind humming with ideas of what Linea could have thought up. She stepped out of the locker, the breeches slightly loose on her.

"Perfect!" Linea clapped her hands together, pushing past Cassie and taking a helmet off the rack. "And boots too. You need the whole outfit." As a final touch, she handed her a crop.

"Linea," Cassie began to protest, but Linea pressed a finger to her lips.

"Not now. Just do what I say." Suppressing a fit of giggles, Linea walked outside and led her to the horse. An announcement pierced the air. Three minutes until the first rider was called out.

Cassie panicked, sweat collecting on her palms as her heart rate increased.

"Linea!" she hissed.

Linea smirked, handing the reins over. "You'll do fantastic."

"I can't!" Cassie refused to take the reins, gulping down a breath of air.

"Why not? You watched the walkthrough, did you not? Surely you didn't forget already." Linea raised a dubious eyebrow, glancing around to make sure no one was too close.

"And what if someone discovers us?" Cassie demanded in a hushed whisper, more concerned about someone discovering her true identity. Linea shook her head.

"We're close enough in height, and it's only for a few minutes. I'll lead you to the entryway and wait there. As soon as you're done, dismount, and we'll walk back together. No one will talk to me at the gate, since they'll be too busy watching Linea Vallumvis's spectacular performance." She ended her statement with a proud smile as the announcer broadcasted that it was now time for the advanced class to compete in the Dionysian Falls Show. "It's now or never,

Cassie. You get a true chance to showcase your skills. This is what you've been training for! Even if you haven't been riding that much in Vallumvis, when we get your horse back, that will change." Linea offered her the reins one last time, and Cassie hesitated.

Linea had a good point. Cassie could prove to everyone, but mostly to herself, that she was capable of competing. And if everything went well, she could return to being Cassie, train with Tenille, and finally earn her place on the island.

It was one step closer to becoming like the citizens of Desmalogo, one step closer to being accepted.

Grabbing the reins from Linea, Cassie lifted her head and marched toward the arena entrance. Two Rangers stood a short distance away on either side in case something went wrong.

Linea's name blasted loudly in her ears, and the crowd roared excitedly. It was much different from the Vallumvis show where people clapped politely and there was minimal noise.

Overwhelmed, Cassie hardly noticed Linea get down on one knee to give her a step up to the saddle. She scrambled up, catching Linea whisper the word "wave" into her ear. Pushed into the arena, she made the required introductory salute, then waved to the crowd. The cheering became louder, but she tuned it out, facing the first jump.

She clicked Cloud into a canter, and the rest of the world faded around her. Her horse dutifully listened to her every command, slowing down when she asked and picking up speed when given free rein. They sailed over the jumps, clearing each with ease. Cassie turned Cloud sharply toward the hedge jump and he collected himself, launching over the poles with plenty of room to spare.

Time seemed to slow when she approached the portal obstacle, the very last one in the sequence. Cloud sensed her hesitation, his stride faltering.

Cassie clenched her teeth together, forcing all thoughts about portals and problems and doctors out of her mind. They were all distractions, things that took away her focus. She could not risk falling and being discovered, not when she was so close to the finish line.

Cassie closed her eyes, focusing wholly on her position as Cloud's powerful hind legs launched the pair into the air and they flew over the last jump in the course. The cheering returned in full effect, but Cassie was too tired to wave at anyone. She slowed Cloud to a trot, hardly passing through the gates of the arena before half sliding, half falling off the tall gelding.

Linea instantly swiped her into a hug, twirling them both around several times before letting go. Cassie opened her eyes, and it was Linea that stood by Cloud, not her, and Linea that held the reins.

The older woman that Cassie had seen many times came rushing up to her daughter, squeezing her shoulders tightly as she pressed a kiss to the girl's forehead.

"Linea, love, that was amazing! I was afraid you'd be so distraught over Waffles you wouldn't do good with Cloud, but look at you! It seems as though purchasing him for you was the right choice after all. And of course, your new trainer is wonderful as well!" The woman hardly spared Cassie a glance as she kept rambling. "I adore the matching outfits. She's very supportive."

Cassie reached up to unclip the helmet clasp, slowly moving away from Linea. She nearly ran to one of the washrooms, only then tearing the helmet off her sweaty head. Her hands shook uncontrollably when she tried to run them through her locks in an attempt to straighten them.

Splashing some water onto her face, Cassie forced herself to take several deep breaths.

She had done it, and she had done it well.

Chapter

24

Taven easily complied with Luke's request for him to remain at Arion instead of going to the show. Not once had he argued with Luke over a given instruction, and it had been one of those days that he needed peace.

Granted, a show would have provided a wonderful distraction.

Cassie would be at Dionysian Falls with Linea, and he asked Luke if he could go too. As it was, there were enough Rangers there to take care of show prep, and he was needed to manage the station in Arion.

He suspected Luke did not want him too close to Cassie when the girl was supposed to be living under an alias. He'd slipped up one too many times.

Taven sighed and dropped his heels further into the stirrups, clicking his horse into a canter. Rophon picked up the pace dutifully, oblivious to the wandering mind of his rider. Grain fields growing on the outskirts of Thebesia slowly morphed into more diverse vegetation as the road led deeper into the Arion Woodlands.

A bluebird chirped from a tree, welcoming him into the forest. Taven smiled up at it, whistling in return. The bird perked up, flitting from branch to branch as he followed the Ranger for several lengths before evidently becoming bored and flying away.

Taven jerked his head back, shocked to see a girl sitting against a tree. Her eyes were closed, her face tilted toward the sky.

Gently leaning back, Taven reversed a few steps and examined the girl on the ground. Her helmet was off-kilter, the clasps hanging at the sides and blending in with hair so blonde it glowed with a silver sheen. Her hands rested against her drawn-up knees, both of them sporting grass stains, and her clothing was dotted with patches of dust.

Plastering on his most polite smile, Taven bent toward her, the saddle leather creaking under him.

"Hello, miss. May I be of assistance?" He kept his voice kind, although it surprised him that he did not recognize her.

The girl's eyes twitched. She slowly dipped her head before her eyelids flittered open, revealing pale irises.

"I've waited for so long." Her words stretched luxuriously, her voice melodic enough to flow with the slight breeze moving through the forest. Taven's smile slipped away, guilt forming at making her wait. He'd taken his time getting ready at his apartment in Thebesia, stopping by Luke's office to make sure nothing had changed with his schedule.

Then his frown deepened. Surely if she had been lost in the forest for a considerable length of time, a different Ranger would have found her? At the very least, she should have headed toward the station or back to the city.

Unless she was hurt.

"What happened?" Taven pressed. Her eyes had fluttered shut.

"I was riding." The girl sighed deeply, slumping against the tree as she peeked up at him through her lashes. "Then my horse spooked and threw me off. She ran away." She sat up straighter, her lips shaped into an everlasting pout. "Something about these woods is concerning." Silver-blue eyes met his, and Taven tried not to shake his head. If anything about his favorite part of the island was concerning, it was the appearance of a girl with pale skin, pale hair, pale eyes, and a way of speaking that slid right under his skin.

"Are you here alone? It's always recommended to ride with a buddy for safety or let several friends know of your whereabouts." His own voice sounded hollow to him, his mind distracted by the girl stretching out her arms in front of her, twisting her wrists to get the kinks out.

"I was with my trainer. I don't know where she is." The girl made a show of glancing in both directions, craning her neck. She faced Taven with the softest of frowns, lifting a shoulder and letting it drop down. "I think I hurt my leg." She pointed down at her thigh.

"That's unfortunate," Taven said slowly. His own hesitance came as a surprise to him since he'd usually jump at the chance to be the hero to a distressed citizen.

"Could you give me a lift to the nearest hospital? The ground is damp and seeping into my bones."

Taven stared down at her, noting a flash of defiance in her eyes. She was angry he hadn't already offered, that was clear.

Keeping a steady face, Taven dismounted and approached her, sticking out his hand.

"Taven."

"Daz." Her pale hand gripped his and he helped her up, the contrast in their skin tones not sitting well with him. It looked like she hadn't seen the sun in years, if ever. Daz had a brilliant smile, showing off a row of neatly set teeth.

A shiver ran down his spine, a warning to stay away.

Only a heartless, soulless man would leave a young girl hurt and alone in the forest. Even if her story was fabricated, she did seem to be truly hurt.

Taven helped her up onto his horse, then mounted in front of her. Instantly, her hands snaked around his waist, and her chin rested on his shoulder. He swallowed tightly, turning Rophon back toward the city of Thebesia.

At least she kept quiet while they trotted along the path leading back to the capital, and Taven kept his mouth tightly shut. It was the perfect time to ask more questions, but with her dishonesty about the situation in the forest, he doubted he'd get any more information.

The road dipped down, pressing her closer to him. Her grip around him tightened, and the hairs on the back of his neck rose up in protest. There was nothing to be done now but bear the rest of the ride and drop her off at the clinic.

Rophon stopped with a snort in front of the door of the Thebesian clinic, champing against the bit. Taven leaned forward to pat his neck, and Daz slid off the horse.

He whipped his head toward her, making sure she was stable on her feet before meeting her eyes. She smiled.

"Thank you." Without a limp or a singular sign of being hurt, Daz strode through the doors of the clinic and plopped into a waiting chair.

The sweetness in her tone was enough to cause goosebumps on his forearms, bringing forth a chill that even the midday sun could not disperse, and he shivered.

No, he did not want to see her ever again.

Chapter

25

Cassie brushed down a sweaty Cloud, happy to be away from the burning sunlight and sheltered in the barn.

"You did really good." Theo narrowed his eyes at Linea as he stepped into the barn, and she tossed her head back in laughter. Her next statement was directed at Cassie, ignoring her cousin.

"Theo is not used to me doing better than him. But that's ok, he doesn't have much room left on his trophy shelf anyway." Cassie ignored how the statement bothered her as she opened the door to Nutmeg's stall. The mare had waited patiently during the show and was more than excited to leave her confinement.

"Has she been training you?" Cassie barely caught Theo's low tone but pretended she didn't hear. She fitted a bridle over Nutmeg's head and led her out of the stall.

"If anyone asks, we headed toward town to get some lemonades and we'll be back soon." Linea dodged her cousin's question and ran after Cassie outside.

Leading Nutmeg toward a paddock, Cassie used the fence posts to climb up on the horse's back, extending a hand toward Linea. The dark-haired girl clambered on in front of her and they were off, trotting away from the stables.

"You know," Cassie mumbled, the wind tearing away most of her words, "I never asked Conrad about using his stable for my horse."

"We'll figure something out." Linea stifled a laugh, pointing toward a road leading along the river in the opposite direction of Vallumvis. "Use that path. We'll cut through Ombros Silvae and go through the mountain passage toward Aetherpolis. Most people use the other road, so we'll have a low chance of being discovered."

Cassie nodded and wrapped her legs tightly around the barrel of the horse, a light tap against the side bringing her into a steady canter. They reached a wooden bridge spanning a rushing river, and Linea slowed Nutmeg down to a walk. She stepped onto the plank, the wood protesting with a creak. Cassie tightened her grip around her friend.

"The River of Naiad is fed by the Falls, and this bridge is constantly checked for structural damage. It's perfectly safe," Linea encouraged her, pressing the horse forward.

"It doesn't look safe," Cassie countered, holding her breath as Nutmeg stepped over each plank of the bridge.

"Wait until we reach the Styxis River. It's twice as deep as Naiad." Linea laughed, and Cassie grimaced.

The path here was harder to find, less trodden and, in places, overgrown by weeds. Linea traveled like she was here every day, mostly following the river to the left. The water chased after them, bubbles in the water laughing as if they wanted to join in on the fun. Several hills rolled up and down before dipping into a dense forest. Here, the trees were a mix of deciduous and coniferous that loomed overhead, blocking out most of the sun.

The temperature plunged, and Cassie shivered at the coolness sticking to her exposed skin. The road became narrower, ferns overgrowing the path. She arched her head back, admiring the trees above her, with vines snaking between the branches. She swallowed, the echo of a memory hovering close to the edge of her mind. She hated the damp and the wet, being reminded of how she felt right after she woke up in Yvonne's house.

The coldness aside, the forest was the strangest place she had ever been. What confused her was how the forest shifted with each step, trees parting to allow them to pass. The path was hardly visible in the low light, but the horse's steps were sure-footed.

"They're thinking of setting up a Ranger station here at Ombros Silvae," Linea informed Cassie, butterflies that sparkled unnaturally in the light circling around them.

"Oh. I don't like it here. It's too cold and wet." Cassie tapped her heel against Nutmeg's side, not wanting her to slow down until they left the forest. "It seems like this forest will never end."

"Only a small stretch left," Linea reassured her. The cover of trees broke, finally revealing the mountains that towered so close to the path yet were obscured by the tall foliage. Following the road, they entered the passage through the mountains that led to Aetherpolis.

When the city was within eyesight, Linea pointed to a different road and they skirted around civilization, cutting through several fields of grain for a more direct path toward Thebesia. One more bridge stood in their path, but this one was made of stone and much more trustworthy; Nutmeg steadily trotted across.

They looped around the capital city, stopping a short distance away from Thebesia Stables.

Cassie slid off Nutmeg, patting the mare's slightly sweaty neck. She glanced around with a frown.

"Taven told me she broke away from her stall. But it's possible she is roaming around here somewhere." Cassie let out a frustrated sigh, crossing her arms in front of her. She had no idea where to even start looking, and Linea was still perched atop her horse, playing with the mane with a thoughtful look.

"I don't think anyone has reported a found horse or else the Rangers would have known," Linea offered. Cassie nodded, closing her eyes against a wave of emotion. She felt Tenille close by, yet she seemed too far away.

With a start, her eyes popped open, and she glanced at her surroundings.

When she closed them again, the images in her head were similar, but different.

Helpless, she turned to Linea.

"I'm losing my mind. When my eyes are open, I see this." Cassie gestured toward the fields surrounding them, the closest cluster of trees a long distance away. "But when they are closed, I see the trees right above me, the fields are gone, I am in a paddock. A sense of safety envelops me, and I am not worried."

"Cassie?" Linea asked in a hushed whisper, fingers gripping the mane of her horse. "Do you see where your horse is in your mind?"

"My horse?" Cassie frowned, her eyes still shut. She didn't see her horse anywhere, and even when she moved her head in different directions, she saw the same image.

Cassie forced herself to take a deep breath. No, she didn't need to see her horse. She could feel her, calmly grazing the grass at her feet, curious when her rider would come back to her.

"You're right!" Cassie grinned, launching into a run without waiting for Linea. "It is my horse! She is in a paddock behind Thebesia Stables."

Call to your horse, the doctor had said. She did, feeling a pull toward the fields ahead of her. Tenille's ears perked up and she ran in the direction of her rider, powerful legs easily clearing the fence that separated them and closing the gap between the two.

Cassie collapsed against her horse, arms wrapping around the muscular neck as she buried her face into the orange mane and allowed tears to fall freely down her cheeks. Linea stopped a respectful distance away, smiling.

A missing piece of her soul clicked back into place. Cassie sighed when Tenille nickered, grabbing a handful of mane and scrambling up onto her horse. Her broad back was warm from the exposure to the sunshine, taut muscles rippling under her skin.

Tenille lifted herself into a rear, her whinny echoing throughout the surrounding valley with a clear message: no one was to come between her and her rider.

"I've never seen anything like it." Linea nodded, satisfied. "Do you think she was in the fields this whole time?"

"Yes." Cassie clicked Tenille into a walk, returning to the path that would lead her back to Vallumvis. "Someone was taking care of her, and she was safe."

"Do you think Henrik was honest when he said she broke away?" Linea asked, bringing her mare in line with Cassie's. They skirted around Thebesia Stables as much as they could but still passed by too close for comfort.

"Yes. I think she escaped and was captured by someone who kept her hidden away in the fields." Cassie urged her horse into a quicker pace. "I hope they waste the next several days trying to find her." The girl wrapped a strand of mane protectively around her finger, easily balancing on the horse's bare back.

Cassie shifted her position, an eerie sensation causing the hairs on the back of her neck to rise, and a shiver tingled down her spine. She whipped her head around, spotting a girl cleaning out a paddock a short distance away. Her movements were slow, as if she were preoccupied. Her face, though obscured by the cap on her head, was directed at Cassie. One glance at the messy hair sticking out was enough to confirm that it was Mitchie, sending Cassie's heart rate into a gallop.

Tenille sensed her anxiety, responding to the lightest of cues as she picked up her pace, kicking up a slight cloud of dust as they disappeared over a hill and headed toward the bridge that spanned the Styxis River. They dropped down to a walk behind a small cover of trees and waited for Linea to catch up. A sweaty Nutmeg and panting Linea galloped toward her a few minutes later, the girl struggling to get words out as she stopped next to Cassie.

"What happened?"

"Mitchie." Cassie scowled, ignoring how heavily her heart was hammering in her chest. "Mitchie saw us. I don't know if she recognized us, but I recognized her."

"Oh, no." Linea paled, still trying to catch her breath from the run. "We're busted."

Cassie frowned at the build up of pressure in her head. "We have to get back to Vallumvis as fast as possible, but even then. What if she tells Henrik that two girls stole Tenille?"

"You have to get back," Linea corrected. "I have to stop by Dionysian Falls and get Cloud before I am accused of abandoning my champion." Both girls snickered at that. "If someone cares enough to make a report, I'll tell Luke what truly happened. He's trustworthy."

"He is?" Cassie lifted an eyebrow, and Linea shrugged. "We've gotten into so much trouble today." Cassie changed the subject, allowing Linea to take the lead as they skirted around Aetherpolis toward the mountain passage.

"Nonsense. There's no law against switching out riders last minute. What if I was feeling unwell?" Linea said with flair, not an ounce of regret in her tone.

"Precisely what happened." Cassie agreed. "We were very honest about it too."

"You're a nobody. No one knows who you are, no one knows where you came from. They can't get you in trouble.

And if they try, I'll take the blame." Linea dropped into silence as they approached the forest. Cassie moved through the damp woods as quickly as her horse could, breathing a sigh of relief when they crossed the bridge and she was back in Dionysian Falls.

Linea was still silent when she branched off and headed into the city, leaving Cassie to fend for herself.

The road leading to Vallumvis was sprinkled with horses and riders, most not sparing her a second glance as they moved past. Cassie kept her head low when she reached the city gates. Two Rangers stood on either side, one giving her an approving nod when their eyes met.

She swallowed tightly, moving through the city until she found Agnetha's house. Emine running in circles around her baby brother gave her a sense of safety. At least the family was home.

"Wait here." Cassie kissed her horse's cheek and entered the house, slowly making her way toward the kitchen. Agnetha was elbow deep in flour with her eldest daughter, their pale hair nearly identical in color. She watched the two working in harmony, not sure how to bring up what she wanted to say, when the older woman spun around.

"Cassie! Is everything alright?"

"Yes." Cassie swallowed, her gaze trailing down to the floor. "I'm fine."

"Something is bothering you," Mallika commented lightly, her eyes glued to the little lump of flour she was kneading.

"I have a horse," Cassie blurted out.

"Indeed!" Agnetha exclaimed, walking over to the sink and washing her hands. "Where is she?"

"Outside." At that, little Mallika perked up and trotted after her mother. Cassie followed the two, standing in the doorway as Agnetha shook her head and Mallika clapped excitedly.

"A chestnut, Mama. She is a chestnut!" The girls' squeals

unnerved Tenille, who sidestepped. She tossed her orange head, silky mane flowing in the wind.

"Well. Keeping her at the stable will be too much trouble. Come along, we'll take her to Conrad's old blacksmith shop. He has two empty stalls there."

Cassie smiled, bounding over to her horse.

"Thank you," she whispered, both to the horse for showing her the path to reunion and to Agnetha for accepting her.

Chapter

26

Having reported the incident to the Head Ranger of District One, who didn't find it too important, Taven tried to forget about the girl. He couldn't explain to Luke how unsettled he was; therefore, he didn't try.

The most Luke could do was request for him to remain at the Arion station for a few days to make sure nothing else suspicious was going on, and Taven readily agreed. Instead of running errands, he scouted the forest and kept the station running, spending most of his time chatting with the visitors to the beautiful woodlands.

The sun dipped in the sky, promising to stay for a few more hours before taking its night rest. Taven had scanned each section of the forest, his patrol with Adria coming to an end.

"No sign of the girl again," Adria half asked, half commented, with a sideways glance at Taven.

"Good riddance. I don't understand what she was doing here, but no sign of anyone lurking around. Still, we should be careful." Taven shifted in the saddle, patting his horse's sweaty neck. Adria nodded in agreement, pulling ahead toward the stable. It was quaint and could only house about a dozen horses, a few empty stalls left in case of emergency.

"I'll take care of your horse," Taven offered, extending his hand toward Adria. She smiled and tossed the reins at him, twirling in a circle as she thanked him before dashing inside.

No doubt straight to the shower to wash away the dust and grime that had been collecting on them for the past few hours.

Taven picked up a crosstie and clipped it onto his horse, loosening the cinch so that Rophon would be comfortable while he dealt with Adria's mount. He took his time brushing Adria's mount, giving him plenty of reassuring pats and talking to him in a soothing voice.

Days like this reminded him of his first days being a Ranger, fresh out of the Dasos Academy, finding solace in the barn after a tough day.

One horse finished and in his stall, Taven moved on to his own mount. The sweaty horse was more than relieved to have his gear removed, asking for more scratches between the ears.

Taven grabbed a rag from a bucket and wiped down the saddles, bridles, and bits before hanging everything in its orderly place and heading back inside. He immediately went into the kitchen, where several Rangers were staring at him.

"Did you talk to her?" The Head Ranger of the Arion station raised an eyebrow.

"Who?" Taven asked, reaching for an apple on the counter.

"A white-haired girl showed up the station asking if Taven was around. We redirected her to the barn, but she said never mind."

His blood ran cold and his hand froze halfway to his mouth, fingers tightening around the piece of fruit. He knew it was too good to believe she would leave him alone. She had come here with a purpose.

"And she walked away?" Taven demanded, unsure if he should be angry at himself for not being quicker with the horses or angry with the Rangers for not telling him right away.

He should not be angry at all, as anger never helped solve a situation. Luke would be more than disappointed to hear how often he had been losing his cool with his recent cases.

"Yes." The Head Ranger nodded, and Taven tossed the fruit back on the counter.

"I need to figure out what she's up to." He scowled and ran out the front door, taking the main trail that led to Thebesia. It didn't take long to spot white hair in the distance, but he refrained from calling out her name.

She noticed soon enough, turning around with a victorious smile.

Taven slowed when she noticed him, not wanting to be anywhere close to her. She would only bring forth problems, but he would rather be the one to solve them and stop her before she did anything reckless.

His mistrust increased when she took a step forward without any trace of a limp, and mentally he calculated the distance she had to walk to the station. No horse, which meant she was either telling the truth about losing her in the forest or she had no mount. The second was more plausible, as any horse would have wandered close to the station in search of someone.

She also was not hurt, meaning she was not thrown off her horse and had staged her accident the day before.

"What do you want?" Taven demanded, doing his best to keep a relaxed posture.

Daz shook her head, her long hair swishing back and forth. She laughed lightly, managing to look down on him even though she was shorter than he was.

"Quite rude of you to speak to me in such a way when the Rangers of Desmalogo are supposed to be here to aid the citizens."

He ground his teeth at that. Something about the way she

said the word "aid" was more degrading than her mocking laugh.

"Yet you left without stating your case." Taven tried to reason with her, his patience evaporating.

He was normally a very patient man.

"This is a special case, meant only for Taven Thespios." Daz took another step forward, and Taven held his ground. He refused to be pushed around by her.

Her knowing him much better than he knew her did not sit well with him, but he was a Ranger, and that wasn't uncommon.

"I'm right here." Taven gestured to himself, goosebumps crawling over his neck when she took another step toward him.

"Like I said yesterday, my horse threw me to the ground and ran off. I'm very disappointed that she has not been found." Her gaze moved to the ground, then slowly trailed up his body to land on his eyes again. "Perhaps you'd like to help me find her?"

He could help her find the horse, but they could search separately.

"What does your horse look like?" Taven asked, slowly letting out his breath.

"He's a tall chestnut, four white socks and a prominent blaze." Daz smirked, reaching up to push her hair to the side. The silky locks went right back to how they lay before.

"He," Taven expressed with doubt. "A moment ago it was she."

"It's . . ." Daz sighed, tilting her head back to gaze at the sky. Her pale lashes fluttered closed. "A mare, of course. You would know."

"I would?" Taven dragged out the words, watching her smile grow across her face as she smiled.

"Good. We are stabled at Thebesia, so maybe you could

start there." Daz turned around and continued down the path. Taven kept himself in place.

"What's her name?" he called out. Daz completely ignored him, her steps even as she walked away from him.

He refused to chase after her, heading back to the station to show he didn't care as much as she did. He knew she turned around at some point to watch him, but he kept going.

He would go to the stables tomorrow and not waste his evening on a wild goose chase.

Instead of heading into the cabin, Taven slipped into the stable and checked each stall, making sure that all the horses were in their respective places and each one looked healthy.

Climbing onto one of the fence rails outside, Taven scanned each of the surrounding turnout paddocks. They were empty, the horses belonging to the Rangers safely in the barn, not a single sign of a missing horse that could have belonged to Daz.

With a disgruntled sigh, Taven trudged into the cabin. He found Adria in the kitchen surrounded by ingredients, and he swiped a handful of chocolate chips from the bowl. She swatted his hand away with a playful frown.

"It's for the cookies."

"I happen to like cookies." Taven sighed, opening the icebox and scanning his options.

"Did you figure out what she wanted, the girl?" Adria asked curiously, holding the mixing bowl in one hand as she turned to face him.

"Yeah." Taven picked up sandwich fixings from the shelves, tossing them near the bag of flour on the counter. "She's mad at me because I haven't found her horse yet."

"If a horse were loose in the forest, we would have spotted her by now," Adria exclaimed with surprise, rolling her eyes. "Sounds like she's fabricating things to mess with you."

"That's the concerning part. She couldn't provide any

basic information." Taven sliced himself a thick slab of bread, handing the knife back to Adria. "She doesn't even know if her horse is male or female and then refused to tell me the name."

"Maybe she's looking for someone else's horse," Adria reasoned, cracking two eggs into the bowl and continuing her mixing.

"Not mine," Taven mumbled through a mouthful of sandwich. He swallowed and slumped into a dining chair a short distance away. "A chestnut mare with four white socks and a blaze. At least, at one point she said it was a mare."

Adria lifted her head, tilting it slightly to the side.

"Wasn't Cassie's horse a mare with that very description?"

"Maybe?" Taven stilled. Each word he spoke after this was critical. None of the Rangers knew where Cassie was except that she'd left Yvonne's. Luke reassured them everything was fine and that Cassie had found herself a different place to live. Most of them hardly cared to the extent that he did, except for Adria.

She had pressed him on the issue several times, but he simply told her he knew as much as she did.

Which was a lie, of course, but for the sake of everyone he upheld his duty.

"There aren't many horses a bright chestnut color with four white legs. I remember that, but did she have a blaze?" Adria sighed. "At any rate, Cassie was at Thebesia before she moved. Might be worth looking into."

Taven forced himself to keep eating, his suspicion heightening. Now he had to deduce if Cassie and Daz were friends, if they knew each other, if one was sending the other; he sighed.

Last he had checked with Henrik, the horse, Tenille, had broken out of the stables and was nowhere to be found. Which also sounded like a fabrication due to the fact that very few horses jumped paddock fences, and even then, they stayed close by until they were stabled for the night. Horses tended to be communal creatures, preferring the company of their kind.

Stuffing the last of the food into his mouth, Taven wiped the crumbs off the table and headed outside, walking toward the tower a short way from the station. The tower housed trained personnel, someone always on duty ready to deliver hydraulic telegraphs at the discretion of the Rangers.

"Hello, Yanni." Taven tipped his hat in greeting.

"Which direction would you like the message sent?" the young man stated methodically, hardly glancing up from the notebook he was scratching away in.

"Thebesia."

Yanni responded with a curt nod, lighting the torch. Taven ran a hand through his hair, the torch casting shadows across the watch tower. He squinted in the waning light, waiting for the return signal. "Case 050, repeat situation."

Torches flickered back and forth, and Taven tilted his head back to watch the distant torch. He had once wanted to be the messenger in the watch tower before he grew bored trying to learn all the mechanics required. The sound of rushing water faded, and Taven twisted away from the window in anticipation of the return message.

The symbols dipped deeper into the water, his heart hammering with each passing second. The far torch flickered, and the post stopped moving.

"Missing horse report," Yanni stated respectfully, having no idea the weight of those words.

Had Daz already taken Tenille and was messing with him? Taven slammed his hat back on his head and thanked the messenger before scurrying down the stairs. What purpose so many people had to take her horse, he didn't know.

Most of the Rangers had retired to their rooms, save Adria in the kitchen, leaving the cabin empty.

Taven grabbed his hoodie from the foyer, pulling it over

his head. Adria poked her head out of the kitchen, flour dusting her apron.

"Inform the Head Ranger that Luke has requested me back in Thebesia to follow a lead." Taven was halfway out the door when Adria rushed toward him with a concerned face.

"Is this about Daz? If there's anything I can do to help, you need but ask." She placed a hand on his arm, and he shrugged it off.

"I will take care of this myself, thank you." His voice came out harsher than intended, shame flooding him when he realized what an effect Daz had on him. But he suspected her threats did not end with him.

Taven prepared his horse with the routine of a trained first responder, his body moving ahead of his mind, ensuring Rophon was comfortable before scrambling into his seat. His horse sensed his urgency, running with all his might toward the stables of Thebesia. They skidded to a stop, Taven finding Henrik in deep conversation with one of the grooms.

"Taven Thespios from District One. There has been a report of a missing horse?"

"Yes." The groom turned to him with a set face, her eyes narrowed. "A chestnut mare has been stolen from the stables by a girl with blonde hair. She had an accomplice, but it was the white-haired girl who did the thieving."

The words were worse than a punch to the gut. He was too late.

27

"I have a present for you," Mallika announced, flopping down on the ground next to Cassie. The older girl frowned at her.

"You shouldn't sit on the ground. Your mother wouldn't approve."

"You don't want a present?" Mallika asked, tilting her head back to admire the chestnut horse in the stall. Tenille watched the girl warily, snorting impatiently. "She looks like she wants to go on a ride."

"I'll take a blueberry muffin," Cassie mumbled, her hands folded behind her head. Truth was, she wanted to take Tenille out to stretch her legs but couldn't fathom a place where she wouldn't be seen.

"It's not." Mallika reached into her pocket and produced a lump of crumpled paper the size of her palm, placing it on Cassie's outstretched leg. Cassie frowned, unwrapping the paper to reveal a tiny wooden sculpture of a horse. She was mid-stride, little details carved into the mane and tail. But what surprised her the most was how the markings matched up perfectly with the horse in the stall across the aisle, from the wide blaze to the white stockings.

"It's perfect." Cassie gave the little girl a bear hug, holding it up for her horse to see. Tenille hardly seemed interested, flicking an ear from her spot at the hay net. "How did you get it to look exactly like her?"

"I have almost a hundred wooden horses, and each one of them is chestnut." Mallika had a sad smile. "They were presents from Mama when I lived with her sister, long ago. Papa and I picked one out that matched Tenille's color the best, then we found some white paint. He checked on her last night to make sure she was safe, and I tagged along. You were sleeping."

Cassie clutched the horse close to her heart, touched by the thoughtfulness of the family. With each passing day that she spent with them, the thought of going back to Thebesia became more difficult. Why couldn't she stay here? Her horse was here, and where her horse was, her heart was also.

The one minuscule detail was that she wanted to be Cassie, not fake Miriam hiding in the shadows for fear of something happening. And her hair. She would do anything to have her red locks back, Agnetha regularly touching up her roots to keep the blonde.

"Why don't you take her to the Ranger paddocks? They won't mind." Mallika stood, brushing off the dust and straw that clung to her clothing.

"Ranger paddocks?" Cassie questioned, glancing at the girl.

"There are a lot of paddocks around the Dasos Academy, east of all the houses. They usually have empty ones, and no one will care."

"You sure?" Cassie asked again, scrambling to her feet and grabbing a brush from the shelf of the small stable. Mallika nodded, a wistful look in her eyes. Cassie hesitated, entering the stable and glancing back at the girl. "Do you want to come with me, show me where to go?"

The way the girl's eyes lit up let her know she had made

the right choice. It brought a flashback of a memory, and Cassie stood frozen, hardly hearing Mallika telling her she would check with her mother first.

The memory evaded her, but she wasn't much older than Mallika when she had met Tenille, and she'd been so happy to be on a horse. Tenille pressed her face to the girl, sensing her frustration.

"Why can't I remember?" Cassie sighed, picking up a rope halter that had collected dust for many years and fitting it over the head of her horse.

Can't remember what?

Tenille's voice rang clearly in her mind, and Cassie felt a smile stretching over her face. Whereas she had a connection with Tenille before and they had communicated, this was as if they were having a real conversation.

"Anything, Tenille. I can't remember anything. There is so much of my past that I need to know, so much that impacts me today, yet I do not know." Cassie took a deep breath, waiting.

The silence brought forth disappointment.

"Mama said I can go," Mallika announced, her little hands clasped in front of her, two pale braids falling over her shoulders.

"Ok." Cassie unlatched the stall door, leading out an eager Tenille. The horse pranced in place as Cassie boosted the girl up on the back of the horse before climbing on herself, ducking as they left the small shed.

Mallika gripped the mane with both of her hands, pointing to the left.

"Follow the path that way, then I'll show you how to get to the Academy." They traveled silently until they reached their destination, a large stable attached to a building that was as large as a school: the Dasos Academy.

On the outskirts, round paddocks provided a place to train. Mallika slid off the horse and waited on the fence post as Cassie pushed Tenille through her movements, focusing on keeping contact with the young mare.

"She's so pretty," Mallika mused, her hands propping up her chin. "I wish someday . . ."

"Why don't you have a horse?" Cassie asked, spotting a young Ranger a short distance away coming toward them. She bit her lip, trying to decide between running away or explaining the situation.

"I'm waiting," Mallika said, picking at her fingernails. "Papa has offered many to me, but none of them are mine. One day, I'll find one as special as Tenille is to you."

Cassie smiled warmly, relaxing her stance on Tenille and letting her walk slowly around the pen. The Ranger was in better view now, about the same age as Cassie, dark tousled hair falling over his eyes.

"Hi," Mallika called out with a wave, braver than Cassie when it came to meeting new people. "We're exercising the horse."

"Ok." The boy's eyes narrowed, and his face was set in a line. "Ah, I know you. You're Agnetha's kid." He turned to Cassie, head tilted to the side. "You are allowed to ride here, but it would have been nice if you let someone know."

"Sorry," Cassie mumbled, her head hanging down in dismay.

"Can we come back?" Mallika asked, her eyes bright. The young man gave a single nod, pushing away from the fence.

He left as quickly as he had shown up, but Cassie was done. She extended a hand to the young girl and placed her in front of her, riding back to the house.

The Rangers could be trusted, but she wanted to leave before she overstayed her welcome. And besides, Agnetha would have lunch ready soon.

Cassie shoved the rest of her sandwich into her mouth, rushing past the grand entrance of Vallumvis Stables. It was well past noon, the busiest time at the stable. Having spent all morning with Tenille, she did not know how to approach Judy without getting in trouble for neglecting her morning duties.

A crowd was gathered in the entryway and comments on a horse floated through the air. Cassie dodged the people, trying to squeeze into the barn.

Someone caught her arm, and Cassie forced a smile in response to Linea's grin. She decided against telling her friend that she was already late to her chores, eyes trailing to the horse.

She bit back a gasp when Denny turned to her with a nicker, recognizing his rider from the previous stables.

"Isn't he gorgeous?" Linea asked, stepping back to stroke the golden-brown gelding.

"As if someone who mucks stalls would know anything about the conformation of a horse."

Cassie whipped around to see who the snarky comment came from and met the gaze of a young girl about her age. She was about to fire back when Linea stepped between them, handing Cassie the lead.

"Could you take him to his stall? I moved Nutmeg to a stall further down, so he will be right next to Waffles."

Grabbing the lead rope, Cassie counted her breaths as she walked toward the stall. Sometime between her first day at Vallumvis and now, she had transformed from a stable worker to Linea's personal groom.

The change she did not mind. Judy's reaction to it she did, as the woman was becoming more cross with her.

"Don't take it personally," Linea tried to reason with Cassie, catching up to her. "Some of them are rude for no reason."

Cassie ignored Linea, reaching up to untie the rope halter

from Denny. Stepping out of the stall, she hung the items on the hook.

She knew why they were rude. She was an unknown, no horse or wealth to her name.

"Henrik approached me after the show yesterday when we came back," Linea continued in a hushed whisper, falling silent when several girls walked by and tossed them curious glances. "Also, people are telling me I shouldn't be friends with a groom, but that's beside the point. He asked if I'd be interested in leasing Denny."

"Really?" Cassie frowned, considering the motivation behind Henrik's decision.

"Yes." Linea shrugged. "I think the rumors of a new groom at Vallumvis Stables have reached him. It's not hard to connect the dots."

Cassie stared, feeling her world crashing down on her. "So anyone who knows Cassie disappeared and a new groom named Miriam appeared knows I am a fraud."

"Shh, not so loud!" Linea scolded, leaning against the stall door. "Not a fraud, and not everyone. Only those that care enough about where you are. Grooms come and go. Maybe he got an update from the Rangers."

"I have no reason to be *Miriam*," Cassie snapped, folding her arms across her chest. "I could be *Cassie*. People already know."

Linea met her heated gaze with a tired sigh, pressing her hand to her forehead.

"We don't know if it is safe to do so."

"Safe!" Cassie said the word mockingly, throwing her hands into the air. "You said yourself if someone cared enough they could figure out who I am." Linea said nothing, having no counter argument for the girl. "I'm sorry, but I have to get to work." She turned to leave as Linea finally spoke.

"If you'd like to exercise him sometimes, I'd greatly appreciate it."

"Sure." Cassie couldn't pass that up, spotting Judy leaving the arena with a rider and entering the barn. She approached the manager with the most neutral face she could muster, her heart rate too elevated. Judy would not tolerate this much neglect, and it would take a miracle for Cassie to stay.

"Good evening. I am here to request the tasks that need to be done for today." Judy ignored her at first, patting the rump of a horse as a boy led him away. Cassie refused to be scared when Judy frowned down at her.

"You were supposed to be here in the morning. Agnetha told me you could work every morning. We don't pay you to slack off."

"I'm sorry," Cassie stated, not finding it in her to try to explain to the manager why she was late.

"Sorry won't do your work for you," Judy said slowly, a touch of anger in her voice. "I've received numerous complaints about your behavior and conduct in this stable, and I will say that I am far from pleased."

"I'll try harder." Cassie swallowed. She should have expected this. Judy didn't look convinced, her face twisting into an ugly frown. "Also, Agnetha wanted me to ask if she could bring her girls tomorrow instead of Tuesday?" She held her breath, counting the seconds until Judy responded.

"I have an answer for Agnetha," Judy sneered. "Tell her that her niece—" she near spat the word "—is no longer welcome to work here."

Cassie staggered back, stunned by the statement. Judy was kicking her out? She was fired? She came here expecting a scolding or double the workload, not to be kicked out.

Judy did not stay to elaborate, leaving the girl standing by herself in the aisle. Cassie clenched her fists at her sides, spinning around and marching out of the barn. Linea called out her name, although it took several tries before "Miriam" registered.

Ignoring Linea, Cassie picked up her pace once she was

on the main road, running all the way to the small stable behind Conrad's blacksmith shop. The forge was cold and coated with a thick layer of dust and grime after so many years of not being used.

Cassie entered the stable, blinking back the tears that threatened to push through. She slipped into the stall, leaning against the door and sinking to the floor. Tenille lowered her head and pressed it against the girl. Cassie wrapped her arms around her, and the tears started flowing.

She didn't know how much time had passed as she sat on the straw bedding, except that she could hardly see the outline of her horse a few steps away, slowly chewing through her net of hay. The tears had gone dry, and all that was left was rage.

Rage at the doctor who had dragged her out of Thebesia and forced her to live here under a new identity. Rage at the robe people with their secrets who refused to tell her anything about herself. Under it all, she even found herself angry at Yvonne for dying and flipping her world completely upside down.

Cassie felt a strange warmth in her palms and lifted her head from her hands. She stared, petrified, at the soft indigo-outlined lights that left her palms in sparks as they fed on her rage.

Remembering the portal that Dr. Lykaion had created with his lights, she clasped her hands together, extinguishing everything. The last thing she wanted was to create a passage to a different place and start all over again from square one, even if this situation was dire.

Was that the before? Her mind scrambled to grasp the possibility, her heart shuddering. Anything was possible. But if so, why Desmalogo? Her mind needed a reason why she had been drawn to the island.

Cassie clenched her jaw, ignoring how softly Tenille nudged against her. She would figure everything out herself, and she didn't want the doctor or anyone else telling her what to do. If she wasn't welcome at Vallumvis, she would simply move back to Thebesia and continue her life there. She would compete with Denny and Tenille like she did before, and life would be normal again.

Cassie was about to stand when she felt a hand on her head, stroking her short blonde locks.

Agnetha said nothing at first, standing silently on the other side of the door. Cassie peeled her palms apart and stared at the slightly too-pale skin, not a speck of indigo in sight.

"Vallumvis is a tightly knit community, and many of us are family. Outsiders often have a difficult time fitting in. I remember when Conrad first came here and we announced we were to be married. The wedding was small. Not many people wanted to attend." Agnetha drew in a slow breath. "I suppose I am not surprised they ran you off, though I think it is highly unfair."

"I am not going back there ever again," Cassie whispered, scrubbing at her eyes.

"And you don't have to. There's plenty to do around the house, and I can teach you how to make blueberry lemonade muffins. You can have some whenever you want."

Cassie tilted her head all the way back, the shadow of Agnetha's face hovering above her. "Truly?"

"Of course. Come along. I won't allow you to sleep in the barn."

Cassie sighed and stood, her legs aching from being in a folded position for so many hours. She pressed a kiss on Tenille's cheek and followed Agnetha back to the house.

Chapter

28

Orange horses and orange-haired girls swirled around in his dreams, and Taven jerked awake in a cold sweat, shivering in the coolness of his room.

He had stayed late at the stables, going over the details with Henrik and a groom named Mitchie. A blonde girl had taken Tenille, and the two simply rode away.

That detail didn't sit well with him. She should have struggled to wrangle Tenille, unless the horse knew the girl and trusted her. Unless Daz was right and the horse was hers, not Cassie's.

His head spun with it all, the days and nights blurring together. A knock at the door roused him from his half sleep, the pale pink light spilling into the room an indication that it was early morning.

Taven accepted the notice with a mutter of thanks, cracking open the Desmaligan Rangers seal and reading the note out loud.

"Update on the case. Horse has been found." He shook his head. "You sure, Luke?"

Daz was dangerous and cunning and knew too much about Desmalogo to be new to the island. So unlike Cassie, who struggled with each step to find steady footing. He could imagine Daz sending a note about a horse or fabricating a message. But no, Luke seemed to know more than he was saying in the note.

It seemed so unfair to him that he had left Cassie to fend for herself in a city where she knew no one. He had told her he would find her horse, and that statement alone created a knot of twisted guilt. He had let her down, failed her, just like he had failed Elara.

Taven shoved his feet into his boots. Dwelling on things he couldn't change was a waste of time, and he had work to do. He took a step outside, and each already-tightened nerve inside his body screamed.

The figure sitting at the bottom of the steps turned slowly, her white hair cascading like a waterfall around her. An upturned smile played across her features, a hand reaching up to toss several locks of hair to the other side of her head.

"Good morning," Daz said cheerfully, still sitting. Taven tried his best not to gape at her, everything in his system telling him to go back inside his house and hide. If she had the horse, what else could she want? His mind scrambled for a suitable explanation. The link between Cassie and her horse was a possible answer.

No, if Daz did anything to Cassie, he would never forgive himself. Or Luke, for telling him to stay away.

"Daz," Taven choked out, eyes darting to the stable across the road. Rophon munched on his hay, bringing him a sense of comfort. She hadn't touched his mount.

"You don't like me." Daz stated the obvious, standing up from the step and brushing dust off her white breeches. She still had the air of an equestrian, though he had not seen her ride on a horse yet. She gave him a concerned glance and took a step backward, making her level with the cobblestone street.

"What are you doing at—here?" Taven almost said "at my

house" but didn't want to give away more information than necessary. Would it change anything, if she had managed to track him here anyway? He furrowed his eyebrows in concern, and Daz tossed him a pointed look.

"I'm only here because I need something. As soon as I have it I'll leave and won't bother you anymore." Daz tilted her head back with a small shake, and his focus moved to her hair again. In the light of day, it seemed to almost glow. It was stunning, though he hated to admit it.

"What is it?" His tone came out flat and disinterested, the opposite of what the girl was aiming for. She pursed her lips, crossing her slender arms against her chest.

"The horse, obviously." Daz's eyes bore into him, an unsettling shade of gray that looked more like a shadow than an actual color.

"Horse," Taven repeated stiffly, unsure what tricks she was playing now. "Did you not take her from the stables yesterday?"

"No. I was too late." Daz looked away, sending a wave of relief over him. Her eyes held him like a spell, and he hated it. "She had already been moved from Thebesia Stables when I arrived."

"Cassie." The name came out in a whisper as his mind connected the dots. Cassie was blonde now. Naturally Mitchie wouldn't recognize her from a distance. Daz's head snapped back at him, eyes sparkling at the information he'd revealed.

"I suppose yes, she took her away. It would be a shame if she was hurt." Daz puckered her lips, eyes shifting from side to side. "As a Ranger, it is your responsibility to keep the citizens safe. Unless you can't fulfill your duties?" Her smile expanded into a grin as his blood ran cold. Was this who had killed Yvonne? It brought new light to his investigation, and Taven hardened his gaze. She would not get away with this.

"You cannot have her horse."

"And how do you know the horse is truly Cassie's? There

was another owner before her, and the horse must be returned to its rightful place. She is not to be sold on a whim." Daz turned her attention to her fingernails, captivated by the rays of light catching on the painted sparkles.

Taven searched his mind for an answer. If Cassie was indeed the one who partook in the heist, who was the girl with medium brown hair on a smaller chestnut mare? A friend of Cassie's?

Linea.

Linea would have told Luke, hence the message.

"I don't know where the horse is," Taven finally said. At least that part was true. Daz scoffed.

"The girl at the stables said you do."

"Which girl?" Taven demanded, wanting to take a step closer to her but holding his ground.

"One of the grooms. Short hair sticking out of a cap. That was the first place I went looking for her, and she told me the girl and horse were gone and the Ranger would probably know where she is cause she heard you and the stables owner talking about her." Daz shrugged one shoulder, her eyes half closed as if this were the most boring statement she had made in her life.

"Mitchie?" Taven sighed, running a hand through his hair. That was the only person who knew of the case besides Henrik, unless more people had overhead and gossip was rampant.

"Yes. I was there yesterday though, late in the day after the show. One of the girls said she knew who Cassie was and that Taven would be able to help me find her. That's—" Daz lifted her hand and counted out with her fingers "—two people who have directed me to you."

And no wonder. With the odd vibe that followed Daz around, Taven wanted to applaud the girls for directing the nuisance to someone they thought could manage her. Except that he wasn't sure if he could. He needed Luke.

If Daz tracked him down so easily, what was stopping her from doing the same to Cassie? He shivered, facing the girl directly.

"I can only help you if you promise not to lay a finger on Cassie or cause her damage of any kind."

"Heroic." Daz smirked, but she nodded. "Very well. You find the horse and lead her to me, and I will not harm the girl." She extended her hand to make a pact. Taven swallowed, knowing nothing good could come of this. He accepted the handshake, her skin cool and damp. He was treading on very thin ice, but for now, it held him up.

"How do I lead her to you?"

"The horse is a monster. She's very hard to wrangle. But if she trusts you, then it won't be difficult to lead her to Arion where we first met."

"And how will you know if I am there?" Taven challenged, finding the whole ordeal more confusing by the second.

"I'll notice soon enough." Daz winked at him, turning down the street. Taven watched her leave. He blinked once and she was gone.

Vanished.

He scowled, crossing the cobblestone to where his horse was stabled. Daz unsettled him more than anyone, but an air of importance cloaked her.

Was she from the Valley? If so, it would be stupid to not give her what she wanted. He needed to consult with Luke.

Taven entered the Head Ranger's room with a racing heart, pausing by the door. Luke was not alone, deep in conversation with a dark-haired girl sitting across the table. She tilted her head back with a soft laugh.

"Come in." Luke waved his hand. "You're not interrupting anything."

"Hi, Linea." Taven tipped his hat toward her, leaning on the desk between the two. "Luke, Daz showed up at my doorstep."

"Who's Daz?" Linea asked curiously, her focus shifting from Luke to Taven.

"We do not know yet," Luke replied curtly, taking another swig of his coffee. "What was it this time?"

"She wants Cassie's horse."

"Nonsense!" Linea interjected again, and both Luke and Taven withheld a retort. Linea had wanted to become a Ranger, but her parents had a different path set out for her. Despite that, she tried to stay as close to the Rangers as she could. "Cassie cannot live without Tenille."

"I would have come earlier, but Daz takes a while to leave. Does Henrik know?"

A certain kind of defiance flashed through Linea's gaze, but she gave in.

"Yes, we felt it was only fair to give him a brief update. It was only right for us to take her back, and Cassie is safe within the limits of Vallumvis." Linea dropped her gaze for a moment before it flitted back to Luke. "It's supposed to be a secret, but I won't keep it from the Rangers."

"Why does Daz want the horse?" Luke asked, the least rattled of the three. Taven wondered if he was ever shaken by anything.

"She claims the horse did not always belong to Cassie and must be given back."

"No." Linea stretched out the word, casting a pleading glance at Luke. "Cassie and the horse stay together."

"For what it's worth, we can look into the history of the horse, even though there is no information about any sales within Desmalogo, and—"

"No," Linea repeated, standing up from her chair. "I won't watch another person lose their horse over something they cannot control. She is safe in Vallumvis." Her lower lip trembled as she paused. "Cassie is part of the Opposed."

Luke hardly even blinked, his lips pressed in a thin line. Taven held his breath, his heartbeat escalating until he could no longer stand the silence in the room. An Opposed. With Daz after her horse, was she a Favored? The law would govern he hand over the horse to a Favored, but he would not bring himself to betray Cassie like that.

"You are right. She is safe in Vallumvis and can continue to live there." Luke shook his head. "Unless discovered."

"And the matter with the horse, sir?" Taven blurted out, eyes searching Luke's deadpan facial expression. He ignored the way Linea's eyes flashed at him, needing an answer before he moved on.

"There is no matter. Tell Daz she cannot have the horse."

"But." Taven's shoulders slumped, regret eating at him for striking a deal with Daz before he knew anything. "I agreed to give her the horse and in exchange she would not hurt Cassie. She kept threatening me. She follows me around incessantly, I do not know what to do." There. Now Luke knew what a failure he was.

"As of right now, you know nothing," Luke said slowly, finishing his coffee and setting his mug to the side. "You'll be searching for the horse until we figure out more about Daz's affiliations and how we can effectively tell her to take a hike." The Head Ranger of the Thebesian district grimaced, his eyes on the papers on his desk. "It won't be easy, Taven."

"I'll manage."

"You think Daz is stalking you?" Luke pressed.

Taven winced. "Probably."

"Then I suggest you stay away from Cassie." Luke said it in such a no-nonsense way, ignoring how Taven's face fell. Taven needed to check on her, to make sure she was still doing alright.

Linea steepled her fingers together, head tilted to the side.

"He can stop by. I'll get Cassie to hide her horse for the time being. It'll do her good to hang out with someone she is familiar with. I think she misses her friends from Thebesia." She turned to glance at Taven.

"No." Luke shook his head. "If Taven goes to Cassie, he will lead Daz right to her. Cassie is in a difficult position through no fault of her own, and though I hate to bend the law like this, we can decide what to do with her after the Daz situation is settled. Understood?" Luke met Taven's eye, and the Ranger knew well that Luke could see the raging emotions beneath his stoic exterior.

"Yes. Sir." He choked on the words, swallowing stiffly.

"I'm off to get a refill on my coffee. I'd like you to run to Bucephala and check on the interns at the stables."

"Yes, sir." Taven stepped outside and shrugged off the feeling of being watched, untying his horse from the post and taking the road south toward the small city. The Ranger station there always attracted the least attention, and internship spots were usually taken by members of different cities. Luke often avoided such trivial duties, preferring to send Taven instead.

Bucephala was the opposite direction from Vallumvis, and if Daz asked, he was checking everywhere for the girl and her horse.

Chapter

29

T he silence in the room was deafening, and Vivion counted his breaths before Aurelian, the Igetis Ílios, decided it was time to speak. As the oldest of the three Favored Igetai, his self-prescribed position as the most important man in the Valley was well respected.

By most people, at least. Vivion's mind darted back to the tense conversation with Mycroft, knowing well that Aurelian had plenty of reasons to be jealous of the doctor, enough to kick him out for good. Or attempt to; the doctor would return.

"I hope everyone is doing well." Aurelian brought his hands together, the long sleeves of his robe swishing and echoing in the silence. Vivion sat to his left, sitting very still and hoping his thoughts had not traveled outside of his mouth. There was a quiet rustling in the crowd, but no one dared to speak unless explicitly asked by an Igetis.

"As we have been discussing, there is an unknown presence of an Opposed on our blessed island of Desmalogo. The land has been good to us, and it our moral duty to be kind to the land in return." Aurelian paused, the hood over his head obscuring most of his face, bringing forth shadows to distort it. "As such, it is our duty—" he put an extra emphasis on the last word, and Vivion felt a flick of eyes at him "—to ensure that all of those who are aligned with the Opposed are sent to where they belong." Aurelian paused again, humming beneath his breath. It was a low sound, echoing throughout the chambers as an audible presentation of the aged man's thoughts.

"Nora, please step forward." A girl in a pale white robe stood from the crowd, the gold stitching catching rays of light and sending sparkles through the air. Vivion did his best to hide his distaste; he and Nora did not get along. She was far too prim, too obsessed with making sure every rule, every law, was followed exactly how it was written.

Exceptions did not exist in her world.

Nora crossed the room to the table standing at the center, dramatically pulling a handful of leaves, dirt, and sticks from within her robe and placing it on the table. She faced the Igetis Ílios, bowing low to him before giving a smaller bow to Vivion and the third Igetis, Phaedra. After her ceremonious presentation, she backed away to her seat.

Vivion did nothing. He refused to nod at her when he did not know what kind of evidence she was bringing forth. If he was lucky, this would be over in a day. If not, the possibility of remaining on this case for a week sent a groan through him that he was forced to suppress.

Aurelian noticed anyway, a light tsk of his tongue reminding Vivion of his place as the youngest Igetis in the history of the Fýlax, which translated to power without power. Not a single Mito came close to wielding as much power as he had; not a single one could see as far into the future.

"We have discovered the presence of an Opposed in our beautiful Arion Woodlands and lurking around Thebesia Stables. It is critical for us to identify this individual," Aurelian stated. "Everyone associated with the Kleros Yi, please stand." A dozen people complied, the rustling of fabric against the stone floor echoing in the small chamber. Vivion dared to look at his best friend, but the boy's eyes were downcast. As if sensing Vivion's searching gaze, Jakobi pushed his hood forward, obscuring his face completely.

Vivion swallowed a sigh.

"I want everyone to go through and see if you can recognize the Opposed who is bringing corruption and darkness to our harmonious island. Identify if this is someone from Lokiir's band or if this is a citizen trying to hide their true identity."

Vivion gritted his teeth. The statement was unfair. Not all the Opposed wanted to bring trouble. Many didn't even care for the powers they could wield. But this would go down like any other trial.

The Opposed would be discovered, tracked down, and brought to the Valley. There would be lengthy meetings in which the individual would be accused of carrying evil everywhere they went, tainting the island with their corruption.

Then they would be banished and never see the light of the earth again.

He had seen the process too many times, and each time he was reminded of how unjust it was.

A man in a dark-colored robe shuffled toward the front, palms up as he called forth indigo-framed lights. He bent over the pile of nature, the light consuming the pile as he studied it intently.

The room dipped back into darkness, and the man shook his head. Silently, he returned to his place and sat down. Aurelian called out the next Yi, then leaned over to Vivion.

"I expect that if I call out Jakobi, he won't give me much trouble?"

Vivion feigned not hearing, staying silent until the older man straightened in his chair.

He couldn't make decisions for his friend. At times, he couldn't even influence him into something he strongly believed in himself. Aurelian never understood that, thinking that since Jakobi had followed him to the Valley of Vathis, he would do whatever Vivion wanted. No, Jakobi was not here willingly.

"Jakobi? Please step forward," Aurelian commanded. The audience strained with tension as everyone waited to see what the young man would do.

Several sighs of relief followed as Jakobi strolled forward, his hands in his pockets. He stood in front of the stone table, head bent enough so that Vivion could only see the tips of his sandy brown hair poking out from under his hood. His fingers trailed along the length of the table, then moved to the center. Only then did the shimmering blue-purple illumination project from his palms and engulf the table. He stood very still, his hand outstretched over the pile of debris as he searched.

Aurelian shifted in the seat next to Vivion, calculating his next move. Only if nothing was familiar at all did a Yi move on immediately, as to not waste time with something worthless. If Jakobi was searching, there was still a chance.

Jakobi pushed apart the pile, picking up a singular branch. Aurelian frowned, leaning forward to interject. It was against the law to touch anything with bare hands that was brought forth as evidence, as Jakobi's trace would cover up the previous one, dampening its effect.

He tossed the branch to the side, retracting his hands into the warm folds of fabric enclosing his body. Head lowered and eyes downcast, he stood behind the table.

Jakobi was to speak, yet he waited for Aurelian to allow it. Aurelian stayed silent, expecting Jakobi to speak first.

Vivion waited for another minute, then decided to put them both out of their misery.

"Has there been a discovery?" Vivion asked, his voice echoing across the chamber. It wasn't often he spoke, living his life under the ever-threatening presence of Aurelian and Phaedra. Jakobi nodded, flipping his palms upward. A collection of glowing lights traveled to the very branch he had tossed aside, then returned with a greater intensity. Tilting his hands toward each other, a portal began to form. The images were hazy, and Vivion thought he saw a flash of red hair.

When the image focused, a white-haired girl materialized, leaning against a tree in the Arion forest. Her eyes were following someone intently, a haze of indigo light surrounding her.

"Daz," Vivion said, glancing at Aurelian.

"Yes, yes, I remember her case. So she has returned to Desmalogo yet again. Do we know what she is up to?" Aurelian let out a short breath, turning to consult with Phaedra, who sat on the other side of him.

"At the moment, she seems to be looking for someone," Jakobi uttered. The images became hazy again, and he slammed the portal closed. Vivion stared, shocked at the outburst. Once this meeting was over, he had a list of questions he needed to ask.

With his hands firmly clasped together and his cheeks a shade of pink, Jakobi dared to meet Aurelian's gaze. "I'll track Daz down to where she entered the island, which might aid in our search for Lokiir."

"There is no need." Aurelian waved his hand. "Finding a Skiá is impossible, and she will leave soon. Instead, we need to focus on why she is here." He turned to Vivion. "I want you two to spend the next few days outside the Valley to determine what you can, then come back and report." He stood, and the quiet whispering in the crowd dropped off.

"The summit is dismissed."

Vivion wasted no time leaving his dais, following Jakobi out of the room. Nora was right outside, catching Jakobi's arm.

"Why did you touch the branch?" She had a little upturned nose and a talent for bothering Jakobi, who hated her.

"The traces on all the nature were very weak. I could

hardly connect to the strongest trace of her." Jakobi pried his hand away, giving Vivion a helpless look. Nora had a smug smile, satisfied.

"I always knew your connection to Rhiza was weaker than mine." She moved away before either man could respond, and Jakobi shook his head.

"She is a waste of time. Come, we must get ready. Meet you at the west exit." Jakobi said nothing more, running across the small clearing to his house.

Vivion watched him, then entered his own cottage. He swapped his robe for a pair of dark pants and a thick white sweater, pulling the hood over his head out of habit.

Jakobi kept his mouth shut too much inside the Valley, and leaving Vathis was oftentimes the only way to get him to open up. Vivion's thoughts went back to Jakobi's flustered face as he had slammed the portal closed, shaking his head as he left the house to meet his friend.

"I lied." Jakobi said flatly, his mount bare but for a rope halter strung over the nose and ears, a singular rope leading back to the boy. Vivion glanced down at his own saddle and made a face.

"About what?"

"The weak connection to the pile of rubbish on the table." Jakobi tossed the hood off his head, clicking his mount into a steady canter. Vivion matched his pace, his thoughts scattered.

"Was it not Daz?"

"No, that part was true. Daz is here and lurking, and I know exactly what she wants." Jakobi glanced behind him as if scared he was being followed. No, not scared. Cautious. Jakobi did not fear anyone in the Valley, taking his role as a Yi like a burden that needed to be carried.

"Is she hunting down another horse?" Vivion asked, and Jakobi nodded. "Strange. It usually only takes her a few hours, then she leaves."

"A very strange case, because she is tracking a horse who cannot be tracked." Jakobi's voice was calm, only serving to agitate his friend even more.

"You don't make any sense," Vivion complained, pulling up to a halt next to Jakobi and dismounting. His friend had brought him to the biggest clinic on this side of the island, the Thebesian clinic.

"Daz's trail was only on the tree branch, but every single item brought in had a trace of darkness." Jakobi tied the rope hastily to the post outside and headed inside without waiting for Vivion.

Unsure why his friend was in such a rush, Vivion tied his horse next to Jakobi's and rushed after him, glancing left and right to find him halfway down a hallway.

"Is this part of looking for why Daz is here, or something else?" Vivion asked, exasperated, only to be met with silence. Jakobi knocked on an office door, and it swung open in a moment.

"Jakobi and Vivion. A welcome surprise." Mycroft stepped aside and allowed the duo to enter his office. Jakobi flopped into a chair, his head craning backward as he looked at the ceiling.

"Every day her connection grows stronger. It is only a matter of time before she discovers who she truly is." Jakobi sighed, leaving Vivion gaping at him.

"You haven't told him anything?" The doctor seemed impressed, half sitting on a corner of his desk.

"No. There was no point until now." Jakobi tossed his hands into the air. "And now he's pestering me about everything."

"Good." Mycroft nodded, pleased. "The fewer people who know, the better."

"Know what?" Vivion demanded, his head swinging between the two schemers.

"It was supposed to be a onetime event, but this has escalated beyond what we expected." Mycroft turned his attention toward Jakobi. "And we're still sure her memories are not returning?"

"I got rid of as much as I could about the bonds, but it's no use. Anything that I removed seems to be floating back up. The fact that she can't remember her family must be the damage done from the prolonged water exposure. Her memories are gone, but not her identity."

Vivion stared, his mouth dropping open as he connected the dots.

"Cassie?" he sputtered, leaning forward out of his chair. "Cassie is part of the Opposed?" Two nods, one tense and the other relieved that he finally caught on. "And we are helping her?" It was hard to mask the disgust in his tone, and Jakobi lost his bashful look.

"Yes, Vivion, we are helping her because she has nowhere else to go. While she bears the mark of an Opposed, she is not from Desmalogo. When I healed her I caught a glimpse of her memories, but they were fleeting, already partially gone. I would have recognized if any of them were from Desmalogo. However, she has the mark of an Ánemos, and with the ways things are going, I wouldn't be surprised if her connection strengthened enough to cause destruction." Jakobi eyed him warily; even Mycroft looked a little uncomfortable. "I do not know if she had any abilities before the incident with the water."

"This is treason," Vivion said flatly, his head spinning. He knew Jakobi had a mind of his own, but to go and heal someone who was to be banished by law if discovered?

Jakobi shook his head, his jaw clenched. "Treason, Mycroft. Treason for helping a girl dying in the water. Treason for helping a poor soul with no family and nowhere to go.

Treason!" The words were full of mockery, and Vivion shrunk back. "What do you suggest we do with her now?"

"Well," Vivion said, clasping his hands together to avoid fidgeting with his sleeve. "We could tell Aurelian about her so he knows that she is the one leaving traces of corruption all over Desmalogo."

"And you think Aurelian would spare her?" Mycroft asked softly, his eyes narrowing.

"If we explain the situation and let him know that Cassie is not connected to Rhiza."

"But she is," Jakobi interjected. "I can track her."

"How?" Vivion frowned. "How can you but not Nora?"

Jakobi tensed, pulling a lock of red hair from his pocket.

"I cleared her memories and bond from her horse, but they are returning." He placed the lock back into his pocket, a flush running across his cheeks under Vivion's intense gaze.

Jakobi frowned and formed a small portal between his hands, watching it intently. Vivion leaned over to stare at the watery surface. A blur of red hair flickered across, but nothing else. The man was patient as the images slowly cleared, showing a girl in a stable with a horse. She leaned against her, stroking the soft neck and whispering something as her choppy blonde hair swung back and forth with a furious shake of the head.

The portal vanished, and Jakobi glanced at Mycroft with wide eyes.

"I can track her horse."

"No." Mycroft moved off the table, running a hand through his hair. "It's too soon. We still don't know how to deal with this."

"Clear as day, this means she's tried something. Someone must get to her immediately and ask questions." Jakobi turned to Vivion, his expression begging for an answer.

"She's now trackable?" Vivion guessed, and his friend nodded.

"I knew I couldn't hold it off forever, but now she will be banished." Jakobi fell silent, his eyes on the floor. Mycroft cleared his throat, raising an eyebrow at Vivion.

"Do you think you could look into her future? See what happens?"

"I don't know. There are risks." Vivion sighed, lowering his head into his hands. It was only fair to allow the other two to know what would happen. He lifted his head, and Jakobi handed him the lock of red hair. He sighed again, fingers hovering over the strands. With a brush of contact, the connection to the girl built up inside him, lights flickering from his palms. A portal began to form between his hands, blank and hazy.

He narrowed his focus, making the portal smaller and visible only to him. The men with him waited, silence engulfing the room.

"Nothing shows up," Vivion grumbled, not used to having to struggle.

"More evidence her powers have developed. She is of your opposing Kleros."

"An Ánemos?" Vivion groaned, his attention moving away from the portal. He tilted his head from side to side, then glanced at the indigo sparkles.

Mycroft and Jakobi leaned forward as the blood drained from Vivion's face.

"Is it bad?" Jakobi pressed in a whisper. Vivion sat frozen, yet when Jakobi glanced into the portal, it was hazy again.

"I saw it," Vivion said in a hushed voice, his face incredibly pale. "I saw what happened."

T he run in with the Ranger combined with her being barred from Vallumvis Stables sent both horse and girl into a state of distress. She helped Agnetha around the house, learned to braid Emine's unruly hair, made muffins with the assistance of Mallika, anything to occupy her mind.

But none of it could replace the longing inside of her, demanding her return to the barn with its comfort, to be on a horse with the rippling power beneath. Night fell, and a plan formed in Cassie's mind.

"I will take Tenille out for a run around the city. There are fewer people who can complain about me in the dark."

"Very well." Agnetha pursed her lips with a light shake of her head. "Do not stray far or be gone long."

"I won't." Cassie couldn't stop smiling as she ran to Conrad's blacksmith shop a few blocks from the house and swung the stable door open.

She was sorry, truly, to leave Agnetha and her family like this. But she had no choice, not when everything around her was threatening to suffocate her. Tenille nickered, her eyes gleaming in the low light.

Where are we going?

Cassie swallowed her nerves and pulled herself onto Tenille's broad back, clicking her horse out of the stable. She allowed her mount to trot at a steady pace until they were halfway through the city, then kicked her into a swifter gait.

"The closest thing that feels like home to me." It was an answer for her more than her horse, who would follow her wherever she led.

Tenille tossed her head in excitement, racing toward the city gates. They had a few minutes until the gates would close for the night. They would only be opened at the request of a visitor, and then only if the Ranger on post granted their request.

Stupid, stupid, stupid.

The words rang through her mind as she offered her friendliest wave to the Ranger, taking the path that led to Arion Woodlands. She would prefer to take the northern route, the passage through the southern area of the island harboring too many memories.

She doubted she was easily recognized with her blonde hair even though Linea made it sound like Henrik knew it was her who came to take her horse away.

It was stupid to leave without telling anyone. Foolish to be wandering at night in places she only had limited memory of.

Cassie slowed Tenille when they reached Arion, following the path along the river. Here, the break of trees overhead allowed the moon to shine with all its brilliance, lighting her path forward.

Tenille nickered, and a horse answered her call. Cassie shrugged, shaking off the fear that gripped her. It was a Ranger, most likely, on night patrol. If asked, she was on her way home.

She spotted the Ranger sitting on the bank at the edge of the river, and she leaned back to cue a halt. Tenille ignored her, moving forward until they stood a few steps away from Taven.

"Cassie!" He set his fishing rod to the side, scrambling to his feet. They were bare, wet from the river. "What happened?"

"Nothing." She mustered a smile, waving her hand dismissively. "I am simply enjoying a ride with my mount."

"At this hour?" Taven raised an eyebrow, crossing the distance between them and laying a hand on Tenille's muscular neck. At her silence, he pried further. "Cassie. You are running away."

"I can't stay." Cassie dropped her head, embarrassed at the shame flooding her. "I was fired from my job, no one likes me there, and I have to be someone else. I hate it, Taven. I hate it so much."

The Ranger was silent, only serving to unnerve her more.

"Come, sit by me."

She complied, sliding off Tenille and allowing her mare to drift closer to Taven's horse, who snorted in greeting. Taven went back to the bank, submerging his feet again in the cool stream. Cassie lowered herself onto the soft grass, drawing her knees to her chest. Her jaw clenched as she gazed at the trees across the river.

"The Styxis River runs almost the whole width of the island. It starts in the mountains close by, flowing through Arion, past Thebesia, and emptying out into the ocean near Aetherpolis. Many kinds of fish love it here, so close to the source in the mountains." Taven stared at the empty basket next to him, lips pulled back into a frown. "I haven't fished in three years."

"Why?" His statement piqued her interest, washing away the wall of stubbornness she was so determined to keep between them.

"Three years ago." His voice was husky, and he cleared his throat before continuing. "Three years ago I graduated from the Dasos Academy. I had recently turned eighteen, and my father was so proud of me for continuing our family legacy."

The silence stretched on, and Taven set the rod to the side, turning to fully face her. Moonlight framed his features, his eyes masking a pain that was not far from her own. Cassie's breath hitched, and she leaned closer to the Ranger as his voice dropped.

"I had a sister, Elara. We went fishing afterward to celebrate. She had been given an apprenticeship as a nurse assistant at the Thebesian clinic. At sixteen, it was quite the feat." Taven drew in a ragged breath. "The springtime currents can be quite strong, even though she was a good swimmer. She loved the water, climbing in while I dug around for some worms." He paused, his eyes developing a glassy film. "I don't even know how it happened. I turned my head for one second and heard a shout. She was struggling against the flow of the river, the current stronger than she expected. I jumped in after her, realizing how futile it was when I could hardly hold my own footing. The rocks on the bottom were very slippery, though I doubt she could reach them as she was quite a bit shorter than me. Then she disappeared from my sight. I backed out of the water and chased after her along the bank, but I wasn't fast enough. Her head hit a rock." His eyes squeezed shut. "There was so much blood. I rushed her to the clinic as soon as I pulled her out of the water, but it was too late. She was already gone when we reached the doors." He choked back a sob, tears cascading down his cheeks.

Cassie did not know how to comfort him, so she leaned closer and allowed her forehead to rest on his. His story carried so much raw emotion, and though he did not say it, Cassie knew he was thinking of her. How close she had come to death. How lucky she was to survive. How she never truly thanked the doctor for his work in bringing her back.

"I'm sorry, Taven." She placed a hand on his knee, a connection humming between them.

"So you see, I know what it is to lose someone you care for deeply. Your family, even if you don't remember. Your horse, how fiercely you are fighting for her." These words carried admiration that warmed Cassie's heart. "You've become special to me, Cassie. I'd hate—" He swallowed hard, his eyes meeting hers in the dark. "I'd hate to lose you. Please, return to Vallumvis. You are much safer there than in Thebesia with the enemy still lurking close by."

Even these words penetrated her softened exterior, and Cassie couldn't find it in herself to argue.

"Very well. I will return."

He nodded grimly, offering his hand and pulling her up with him when she accepted.

"I'll escort you back."

Agnetha said nothing of her late return, sending her promptly to bed. Cassie snuggled into the covers, waking up to an empty and very peaceful house. Slowly, she adjusted to the shouts of children outside and smiled at Agnetha's thoughtfulncss.

Yesterday's adventure felt like a dream, a realistic, detailed dream that refused to depart from her mind. The burning emotion in Taven's gaze and the gently whispered story about his sister lingered.

Cassie pulled on her clothes for the day. A firm knock on the door announced the arrival of the morning postman. She swung the door wide, mumbling a sleepy greeting.

"Good morning! I have a message for Miriam. I believe she resides here."

"I am Miriam." She hoped it was a message from Linea, not having heard from her friend in several days. The postman smiled at Cassie, handing her a thick sheet of brown paper. It was silky and luxurious, of high quality. On top was an inscription in a loopy font that read "Desmaligan Rangers Association."

"If you'd like to write a return message, I'll wait for you. It might be urgent."

Cassie nodded and broke the indigo seal, unfolding the paper.

> Dear "Miriam,"
> I hope you are doing well at Agnetha's and that the island is treating you well. If you are not busy this afternoon, I would like to propose a picnic at the foot of the mountains near Thebesia's Crown. It is walking distance from the house; no need to bring your mount.
> Hope to see you there,
> Taven Thespios

Cassie covered her grin with the paper as she glanced at the postman and told him she'd be right back. She skidded around the corner, careful with the door as she entered Conrad's office. He had nice paper too, but it was incomparable to the ones the Rangers used. She pulled out the inkwell and a pen, quickly scratching out an agreement to the proposition. Waving it around for a few moments to allow the ink to dry, she melted some wax under the candle and folded the letter roughly, sealing the point where all corners met.

She raced back to the door, finding Emine shrieking in laughter at something the postman had said. The girls had wasted no time entering the house upon his arrival, collecting the mail being one of their favorite tasks.

"Here," Cassie gasped, extending her own letter to him. He accepted with a curious glint in his eyes, then waved to the little girls, whistling as he walked down the pathway to his horse waiting outside the fenced front yard.

"Who sent you a letter?" Emine piped up curiously, tilting her head to the side as she stood on her tippy toes to get a better look at Taven's message. Cassie folded it in half, treasuring his words for herself.

"She can't read." Mallika laughed. "And she's too stubborn to try."

"I can too read!" Emine stomped her foot, running off to complain to Agnetha that her sister was being rude. Cassie caught Mallika's green eyes, the color not far off from her own.

In that moment, something connected the two of them. Something sisterly, she supposed, a single glance with so much meaning. Mallika was the oldest of the girls, and though she was much younger than Cassie, she possessed enough understanding for Cassie to want to share details from her personal life.

"It's from Taven! He is a Ranger at Arion."

"Is he your friend?" Mallika asked dreamily, her pale lashes fluttering. Cassie tilted her head to the side, contemplating. Was he her friend? Perhaps, in a way. "Friend" didn't seem quite right after last night.

"I think so. He was the Ranger who found me in the water."

A curious "ooh" escaped from the lips of the girl, and she pointed to the letter. "What did he want?"

"He wants us to go on a picnic." Cassie smiled, unprepared for the way Mallika wrinkled her nose with a growing smirk.

"How quaint," the girl said, reaching out and grabbing Cassie's hand. "We need to ask Mama to lend you a pretty dress."

"I don't need anything." Cassie tried to argue but allowed herself to be dragged halfway across the house and outside to the back, where Agnetha was tending to her gardens.

"Mama!" Mallika pushed Emine aside, her blonde hair a

perfect replica of her mother's as she whispered into Agnetha's ear. The older lady smiled and led Cassie back inside.

They started by rummaging through a handful of sundresses, deciding on a dark green linen with intricate silver-white stitching along the hem. Then Agnetha smoothed out Cassie's cropped blonde hair, her hands trailing along the silver chain of her necklace.

"It's a unique construction I haven't seen the likes of in Desmalogo," Agnetha commented, glancing in the mirror again. She played with several different hairstyles, and Cassie picked out the one she liked best. It was still early to get fully ready, but she kept the dress on for the next few hours, watching Agnetha prepare lunch in the kitchen.

Each detail about her pointed to the same conclusion that she was not from this island. But what if she wanted to stay? The magic of the place called to her, beckoning for her to remain. Even when she tried to run, something had brought her back. Taven, the doctor. Cassie let out a pent-up breath, unable to argue that she belonged in Vallumvis for now.

Yet Thebesia held many perfect memories: the stables, training with Henrik, and finding a sense of purpose. She even missed the jealous and sometimes hateful glances thrown at her by some of the students that took riding very seriously, upset that a newcomer had taken some of Henrik's attention away from them.

Was it possible to find a place to call home between the two opposing sides of the island? Cassie was not ready to make that decision for herself.

She allowed Agnetha to fuss over her, not complaining when Emine brought a white bow for her to wear in her hair, and had wrapped herself up into a bundle of nerves by the time Taven showed up at the doorstep. He was still in his Ranger uniform, but his hair was combed neatly to the side.

Nothing about him reminded her of the previous night when his hair had been tousled and his feet bare.

"Cassie, hello." His greeting was warm, his grip on their handshake firm. Cassie stepped out into the sunshine, closing the door when she heard giggles. The little girls seemed almost as excited as she was.

"Taven. How have you been?" She took his arm and matched his pace. He tilted his head to glance at her, not showing a single sign of unease. In turn, her own tension faded away, more so than ever with him.

"Being a Ranger, sometimes life gets so busy I don't have time to question how I'm doing, as long as I keep pushing forward. There have been many things that come up, keeping me on my toes." He sighed, pointing to the mountains looming ahead. "A trail leads to the path. It's about a half-hour walk, but we'll get a beautiful view of the city from there."

"Are horses not allowed up there?" Cassie only meant the question out of curiosity, but the way he faltered did not sit well with her.

"They are. But if you were on horseback, I couldn't be a gentleman and have you on my arm." He turned to her with a wink, and Cassie blushed.

She hadn't anticipated the rush of heat, very aware of the point of contact between their arms. His gentle smile and kind eyes were almost painful to look at, so different from last night when they were torn with memories. Now, he radiated happiness like he usually did. His shield was back in place.

Her thoughts scattered when they reached their destination, as beautiful as he had promised. But what made her pause and stare was the assortment of pastries and finger foods arranged neatly around a blanket, a bouquet of wildflowers in the center. A few pillows invited her to sit on the ground, and she turned to Taven, her eyes wide with bewilderment.

He shuffled, hiding a smile as he spoke. "Please, sit down."

She did, folding her knees under her, still at a loss for words. Several paces behind them, a black iron gate marked the border of Vallumvis. Ahead, rows of civilian houses stood neatly, and beyond them the racetrack loomed in all its glory.

"Would you like some tea?" Taven offered, and Cassie nodded. She picked up her cup and extended it, and he poured a fruity tea out of the teapot. Cassie brought it to her nose, taking in the summery aroma. "Did you sleep well?"

"Yes, thank you." Cassie reached for a muffin, breaking off a piece and allowing it to settle on her tongue. "And you?"

"Decently." Taven shrugged, his mouth a playful smirk. "Though I did worry that you snuck away behind my back."

"I wouldn't." Cassie shook her head with a grimace. "No matter how tempting. I didn't even know where I was going, and—"

"You have very pretty eyes. Has anyone told you that?" He said this in a slightly bashful tone, and something warm flickered in her heart. It was a sincere statement, distracting her from her mess of muddled thoughts.

Taven let out a slow breath, pulling out a flower from the bouquet and twirling it between his fingers. When Cassie met his gaze again, he extended it to her, their fingertips brushing when she accepted. "I spoke with Linea this morning on how to help you settle into Vallumvis better, to find you some other purpose besides the stable work. She suggested I do something special for you, a proper welcome to the Island of Desmalogo." He smiled, the gesture warmer than the rays of sun she looked forward to every day. Cassie dropped her gaze, her heart swelling with happiness at his words.

Maybe she wouldn't get along with everyone, but there would still be those who cared about her. Truly cared, not like Yvonne.

"Thank you." Her voice came out a little hoarse, and she cleared it. "I truly appreciate this." Cassie gestured around the blanket, leaning forward to get a sandwich off the platter. Taven selected one as well, setting it on his plate instead of taking a bite.

"Cassie? Can I ask you something?"

"Yes." She agreed rather hesitantly, popping a few blueberries into her mouth.

"Do you know anybody named Daz?" Taven asked, leaning a little closer to her. Cassie felt caught in his scrutinizing gaze, and she quickly shook her head.

"It doesn't sound familiar."

"Maybe you just don't remember?" he proposed, catching the blueberry that Cassie tossed at him.

"No. I would have recognized the name, even if I didn't remember who she was. Why?"

"Ah, I just wanted to know." Taven gazed out into the city below them, and Cassie couldn't decide if he believed her or not. "She showed up in a case a few days ago, and nobody in our station seems to recognize her. I was curious if there was any connection."

"Certainly not," Cassie confirmed. "I would know, like I know I do not have any sisters. It's just me, I think." This caught Taven's attention, his eyes flicking toward her. She drew in a breath, her mind going to Elara. "I'm sorry, I didn't mean to mention anything."

"It's ok." Taven gave her a smile that was more pained than his typical one. He tilted his head to the side, looking bashful again. "Linea wanted me to ask you something while we were here, a favor." After all the effort she put into creating such a whimsical evening, it would be blatantly rude to ignore the request. She could at least hear him out, even if she didn't want to do it.

"She would like to know if you are interested in competing at the Vallumvis Open Show this Saturday, riding Denny," Taven said each word slowly, watching as her facial expression dipped into a frown.

"No one likes me there. They all think Miriam is a weird girl who shouldn't be friends with Linea."

"Ah, Cassie." Taven smiled with a hidden secret. "You don't understand. She doesn't want you to go as Miriam. She wants you to compete as Cassie, with Denny, to do what you two wanted to do at the Vallumvis Debut Show all those weeks ago and show the island what you are capable of."

"Cassie?" She scrambled to her feet, staring down at Taven. "I can be Cassie again? Yes, yes, yes!" She wanted nothing more than to stop hiding and just be who she was meant to be.

"Think of it like a test, to see if you will be targeted again after revealing your location. Don't worry, though. We have several Rangers who will be placed on alert." Taven reached out to right the cup she had knocked over in her haste, dabbing at the spilled tea with a napkin.

She pushed past the worry, twirling around in her dress and walking around the blanket. Taven caught her in a hug, letting go when she squirmed out of his grasp, a sudden flush crawling up her neck.

"Yes, tell Linea I absolutely will do that." Cassie returned to her previous spot, hyperaware of his gaze on her.

"Very well. I am afraid I must return to my duties soon. After we get this cleaned up, I will see you back to your house."

Chapter

31

Within a few hours, all of Vallumvis knew that Cassie was competing that day, a heroic return with Denny to the place she stood a month ago to reclaim her failed attempt. Some marveled at the orange horse that had whisked her away and hoped to see her again, but Linea reassured everyone that Cassie would only be competing with Denny.

At that, Cassie frowned. It was almost as if Linea didn't want anyone to ask about Tenille, but her statements were too forced to be natural. Did she think that pretending Tenille didn't exist would minimize the risk of her being taken away?

Cassie stood in the center of the showgrounds, her mind spinning at the number of people who would be watching her today.

"Does Henrik know?" Cassie asked tentatively, and Linea nodded.

"He's known for a while, which is why he let Denny go so easily, knowing you're here." Linea handed her the reins, pointing out a ring she could practice in. She had reassured the girl earlier that she had taken care of all entry fees, and all

Cassie needed to be concerned about was Denny and their performance.

It had made her slightly upset to leave Tenille in a small stall for the entire day, but she had promised to make it up to her horse the very next day. Or night, so long as she stayed within the city walls.

Tenille would be fine. Conrad promised to check on her every now and then and alert Cassie if anything went wrong, and Conrad was someone Cassie trusted.

Cassie entered the empty ring and tested out Denny's gaits, making sure he walked and trotted smoothly before pushing him into a faster pace. She had one chance to get this right, to redeem herself.

She didn't think the citizens of the island would approve of anyone who had two botched attempts at a show. Knowing nothing about her life before Desmalogo, she might be here forever. The mere thought sent a trickle of foreboding down her spine, the anticipation of the day looming overhead.

Linea watched Denny while Cassie walked the course, avoiding as many people as she could there and back. She was registered and the course was walked. The waiting game began.

Cassie kept her helmet on her head, her blonde hair hidden under the protective gear. She didn't want her identity questioned when Cassie was supposed to be a redhead.

Horse after horse went into the arena, each trying to prove they could outperform the rest. Cassie watched each one carefully, noting where they did well and the mistakes that were made.

Soon, Linea's number was called, and she headed toward the ring with Waffles in tow. The horse had made a nice recovery from the Arion incident, and it would be their first show together since.

"Best of luck," Cassie whispered to herself, watching the two enter the ring. Linea seemed hesitant to begin, cautiously approaching the first jump. They cleared it without effort and moved on, Waffles doing well, albeit going slowly.

Cassie frowned when the pair took the wrong turn at the fifth jump, wincing when the judge loudly announced that the girl was disqualified. She wanted to rush toward her friend but didn't want to interrupt Linea's moment with her mother.

She perked up when Selene was called into the ring, her familiar black horse gleaming in the bright sun. The loud cheering for her made it evident that she was a popular rider and had a good shot at taking a placement. They finished the round without a fault, causing the crowds to cheer even louder. Cassie smiled, happy for her friend and proud of Selene for beating the riders before her and placing herself as first overall.

"Here, you're up in a few riders." Linea handed Cassie a blueberry lemonade, defeat and unease chasing each other across her face.

"You started off well," Cassie tried to say, but Linea waved her off.

"It's my fault. I didn't walk the course." Linea grimaced, reaching out to pat Denny's neck. "I thought I could follow it from the paper, but, whatever." She laughed at herself, straightening when Cassie's name was announced by the commentator.

"Amaze them." Linea smacked Denny's rump.

Cassie mounted her horse and led him toward the entry gate. A Ranger opened the door, and she was slightly disappointed that it wasn't Taven.

The crowd was dead silent as Cassie stood in the ring, almost as if they unanimously held their breath. The question hung in the air: would she do well or be interrupted like last time and be carried off on an orange horse?

Cassie took a deep breath. She could do this. She would complete the course and place well. No disqualifications allowed.

Adjusting her grip on the reins, Cassie clicked Denny forward. His ears perked up, and they swiftly cantered toward the first jump. It was lower than most, so Cassie allowed a freer rein. She asked Denny to lengthen his stride a little, and they sailed over the second jump without a problem. The sharp turn toward the third jump did not faze the pair, and they executed the jump perfectly. Loud cheering from the grandstands faded into the background, leaving her mind with nothing but the connection between her and her horse, trust flowing between them. Denny was alert to her slightest cue, not airheaded like he sometimes was when training.

As they headed for the final, highest jump, everything Henrik had told her flooded her mind. Not too fast, but don't lose impulsion, proper strides. Denny's muscular back legs pushed against the arena ground, and Cassie leaned forward with him. He tucked his forelegs neatly under him and folded his back ones after. Cassie leaned back to prepare for the landing, relief flooding her when it was soft.

The crowd erupted into wild cheering, and Cassie strained to hear the time announced. Her heart leapt in joy when she heard that she was the fastest, taking a solid lead over Selene.

Denny trotted out of the arena, a slight sweat gathering in places. She hopped off her horse and loosened the girth, patting him for such a wonderful performance.

Adrenaline still coursed through her veins, and amidst the chaos, she realized one thing could have made this moment better.

If only Denny had been her lovely orange horse.

"Amazing!" Linea rushed up and gave her a quick hug, her eyes scanning the surrounding area. She left as quickly, sending a bolt of confusion through Cassie.

Cassie walked with Denny to cool him off, knowing she was probably done for the day. If too many riders had a similar time, an additional jump off would be requested, so Denny would remain tacked until the results were out. She loosened the girth a few notches for comfort, stroking his neatly trimmed mane.

"Have you seen Theo?" Linea asked absentmindedly, flashing Cassie a giant thumbs up as she walked past again. Cassie shook her head, moving closer to the arena fence to watch the next rider. Her heart thudded rapidly in her chest as the pair flew over the last jump in the course. The announced time allowed her to take a deep breath again.

She still held the lead with only a handful of riders left. If they didn't beat her time, Cassie would take the win. Another girl walked past, and Cassie hardly noticed her until she stopped.

Cassie nearly yelped in excitement, tightly hugging her friend.

"Selene!"

"Once I saw your name in the roster, I had to come find you. Taven told me some things, but I knew the Rangers were hiding something." Selene stepped back, shaking her head lightly as her hands lingered on Cassie, and her voice dropped to a whisper. "It's so good to see you alive and well. I know Yvonne was murdered, even though they didn't report it as so. Oh, Cassie! I was so scared they had gotten to you as well."

"He did not," Cassie spat in a furious whisper. "The coward ran from the island as soon as the deed was done, and I was forced to find refuge in Vallumvis. I miss you terribly and want to go back, but I cannot. Not until we get to the bottom of what's going on. I've been safe here, don't worry. Taven might not be sharing everything, but he is doing good." The mere mention of his name brought a flush to her cheeks, but with her face so sweaty she doubted Selene would notice.

Her friend nodded, biting her lip with worry. "Mitchie ratted out to Henrik about someone stealing your horse. Henrik was trying to keep her safe, and how you both walked away peacefully, it had to have been you. She would have thrown off anyone else for trying."

"Henrik kept her safe?" Cassie whispered, gratitude flooding through her. She closed her eyes and tilted her head back, listening to the announcer call out the time for the previous rider. A smile cracked her expression when he confirmed she was still in the lead.

"Yes. She is safe now?"

Cassie nodded furiously to Selene's question, her attention on the judges talking amongst themselves.

"What happened?" Cassie asked Linea, who leaned against the fence next to her.

"Theo was supposed to go, but he is nowhere to be seen. I hope he's alright." Linea frowned. "I've been searching for nearly an hour and no one has seen him, so he has been disqualified."

"I won?" Cassie gasped, staring at Linea with shock. The girl smiled widely, but it was clear she was still concerned about her cousin.

"We'll know for sure when they announce it." With a cautious look at Selene, Linea left the two.

"You did amazing! Henrik is very proud of you for holding a lead over me." Selene smiled, genuinely happy for her friend. "If it wasn't for your help with Kismet, I don't know if I could have done half as well."

Cassie ducked her head, smiling at the compliment. She had missed being useful at the stables, where Henrik and Selene treated her much better than anyone at this stable. Except Linea, and even then she was hidden in her shadow.

The announcements of the top three resulted in more cheering from the crowd. Selene and Cassie exchanged a glance, noting a very proud Henrik standing on the opposite side of the arena.

Cassie felt all eyes on her as she walked across the arena to accept her prize from the judge. She followed shortly after Selene, her heart thumping loudly in her chest. Not her first win, but her first time feeling the press of the cold metal to her palms. She shivered with a mixture of excitement and apprehension.

"That was an amazing performance," the judge said kindly, her eyes twinkling.

Cassie could barely find her voice as she stood face to face with Linea's mother. Surely the woman knew that Cassie was not actually competing with Thebesia Stables and instead cowering in Vallumvis.

"Thank you." Cassie sighed, turning to face the crowd and lifting her trophy. The cheering intensified, her heart skipping a beat when she realized how many people were watching her. A trickle of fear trailed down her spine, pleading for her to run.

Cassie's smile faded away, confused by her train of thought. She didn't have stage fright. In fact she reveled at the idea of so many people cheering for her.

Something still tugged at her mind, begging her to leave the arena and go.

Cassie nearly dropped her trophy in the midst of her confusion, ignoring her raging mind long enough to walk normally to Denny. Linea was standing near her mount, about to congratulate her. Cassie shoved the trophy into her hands, taking off at a sprint across the grounds of Vallumvis Stables and toward the shop where Conrad did his smithy work.

The stable was dark, and not a single sound greeted her when she entered.

Her horse was gone.

Chapter

32

Taven had a couple errands to run before he could make it to the Vallumvis Open Show, but as soon as those were out of the way he headed toward the grounds. He wanted to watch Cassie's performance and see if Linea had managed to pull off what she had wanted.

Passing through the familiar city gates, a chill prickled at his skin, and he reached up to adjust his hat. For some uncanny reason, he felt like a pair of cold eyes followed him wherever he went, and he wanted to place the blame on Daz. He had spent years in Vallumvis during his Academy years. He was supposed to be as comfortable here as anywhere else. A flash of white hair should not flip the script so easily.

There she stood in front of a store that sold baked goods, a sticky bun in her hands.

Taven groaned. He couldn't go more than a few days without the girl appearing like a ghost out of thin air, and today she had found her target. He tried to ignore her, pretending like he didn't see. A low whistle escaping from her lips caught the attention of his mount, and the horse tilted his head toward her.

Plastering on his best smile, Taven tipped his hat at the girl.

"You might want to take Cassie away from here."

Taven stilled, listening to what she might add on to that statement. But she didn't, which only served to infuriate him further. "What happened?" he finally asked when Daz made it crystal clear she would not speak a word to him unless he pried it out of her.

Her gaze was on the sticky bun, fingers tearing it into bits as she savored it. "There is a man who took her horse to a place where she will not be easily discovered. He is looking into her past as we speak and has come to the conclusion that Cassie is part of the Opposed."

Chills ran down his spine, his body screaming in alarm. No Fýlax of any kind were allowed in Vallumvis without explicit permission, but an Opposed was an even bigger danger. Still, Cassie belonging to that society did not make any sense to him, and he had almost forgotten the information Linea had shared a while back. Besides, other than her sometimes prickly personality, he couldn't possibly fathom the girl doing any damage.

"The Opposed are not allowed within Desmalogo."

"Precisely. She will be banished if discovered." Daz stuffed the last bit of the bun into her mouth, slowly licking the sugary coating off her fingers. She caught Taven's eye, a slow smirk forming on her face. "But you must return."

"Return?" Taven scowled, staring down at the girl.

"Yes. You'll have the honors of taking the horse from whoever that man is and leading her to me. As per our agreement, then I will not hurt Cassie." In an instant, her face went from playful, almost flirting, to something deadly.

"Yes, yes, of course." Taven nodded, knowing he had no other choice. He would do as Daz said, and everyone would be safe. Cassie could buy another horse, one identical to Tenille. He'd look through every steed in Desmalogo and find her one that suited her just as nicely. She'd understand, surely, when Taven explained the situation to her.

Daz walked down the street as if to leave the city, and Taven pushed on toward the show. Loud cheering flooded his ears, and he walked into the stable to drop off his horse. Linea stood in the center, her hands on her hips as she angrily stared at her cousin.

"Theo, where have you been?" she demanded, and the man simply shrugged, staring at a horse in a stall.

"Around."

"Around?" Linea echoed, fully upset. "You missed the show."

Theo hardly reacted, tapping his finger against his chin. "Look, Linea, I don't have time for this. I'm busy." He waved her away, and the upset girl left the stable. Taven almost went after her, but he stayed, removing the gear from his horse to look occupied. Theo milled around the stable, glancing into each stall, then eventually left the barn.

Taven watched him go, fingers clenching his reins. If Theo dared harm Cassie, he'd have to reckon with the Rangers first.

He needed to get her out of here, but he could not risk anyone seeing them leave.

Chapter 33

Cassie scrubbed at her eyes, leaning against the stall door. Her fists were clenched in anger at the family who had housed her for so long.

Her horse was gone, not a trace to be found. Her soul had been torn away from her yet again, and now she had no one to turn to.

Everyone had known she would be at the show. They all told her to leave her horse behind. They'd said her horse would be safe, watched over. Taven had ushered her back, promising she was better here. Linea had her compete as Cassie and reveal her location.

The pain of betrayal hit deeply, a double wound when coupled with the fact that her horse was gone.

She could stay here no longer, lied to about everything. She had nothing to take with her, most items were borrowed and not her own. This time she truly would run away, and no one would stop her. Not Taven, not the doctor. She would run to Thebesia and ask Henrik for refuge while she searched for her horse.

Cassie stayed at the stall until nightfall, waiting until it was too dark to see clearly before she stepped outside. She never wanted to see anyone from the household again if they were complicit in Tenille's disappearance. Eventually, Agnetha would come here in search of her. Or maybe she wouldn't.

Cassie frowned, keeping to the trees as she crept away from the stable and the old forge, taking the road back to the house. She'd quickly make sure Tenille wasn't there, and if she wasn't, Cassie would leave Vallumvis for good.

She did not care for the stupid iron gate that dictated who could enter and who could leave. If the Rangers tried to stop her, she'd tell them exactly what she thought of the city behind her.

A low light cast a hazy glow around the house, and Cassie caught sight of horse legs standing near the horse gate.

Her heart leapt out of her chest and she rushed out of the cover of trees, realizing too late that it was not her horse. She ducked down, picking up voices.

"No? We assumed she would be at the show." That was Agnetha.

"Is it possible she went to town then for some snacks and got lost along the way?" Taven's voice made her smile before it quickly vanished. What was he doing here?

"I wouldn't know. We've been home all day. Conrad was called out to reshoe a horse in Dionysian Falls. She might be at Conrad's old forge. Check there."

"Thank you." The door closed and Taven walked back to his horse. Cassie panicked, as there was nowhere to hide. She closed her eyes, listening to her heart beat in her chest as she squatted near Taven's horse, out of sight from anybody in the house.

"Cassie?" Taven's voice was hushed, and he lowered himself to match her position. "What happened?"

It took her a few moments to find her voice, and even then, she was sure if she spoke, a dam of tears would be unleashed.

No. She would not cry. She would find who took her horse, and that person would pay.

"Tenille is gone. Everyone told me to keep her back here, for it would be safer, and now she is gone. The door was closed, meaning someone took her away. If she broke out, the door would have been open."

Taven was silent for a few moments, placing his hands firmly on her upper arms. Cassie lowered her head, tired of having to decipher who was on her side and who was not.

I'm a Ranger. I help people. He had said it so many times, Cassie felt inclined to believe it.

"I'm sorry, Cassie. If I had come earlier, we could have escaped together."

"Escaped?" Cassie lifted her head, eyes wet with tears. "You've come to take me away?"

Taven nodded, a sad smile on his face.

Cassie stood abruptly, not caring anymore if anyone saw.

"Good. Let's leave this stupid city. I am never coming back."

Taven mounted his horse, extending his hand to her. Cassie felt a grin growing on her face as she grasped his hand tightly and clambered on behind him. She wrapped her arms around his waist and leaned her head against his muscular back.

Taven cared. He cared enough to come for her and take her away from those who would hurt her. Together, they would get Tenille back and move to Thebesia, and no one would bother her ever again.

The horse remained at a steady trot as they neared the gates of the city. Cassie's heartbeat escalated with each step closer, and she pressed herself tightly against Taven. His body was a warm solace, a beam of comfort she could rely on.

He paused near the Rangers, and she stilled completely.

"And where are you two headed?" It was a teasing, playful tone, yet it did nothing to calm her.

"A sunset ride, climb one of the trails on the mountain." Not a lie, but not the full truth.

"Mm. Safe travels!" A second voice chimed in, and Taven tipped his hat as they moved forward. Cassie loosened her grip around him, whispering sorry. Taven said nothing, placing a hand on top of hers and clicking his mount into a swifter pace.

The sun was now set, the road dark. Rophon was sure-footed, having traveled this road many times before. Cassie's breathing regulated, knowing she was fully entrusting herself to the Ranger.

The same Ranger who had found her in the water and rescued her, the same one who stopped her plan of escape, here again to take her away from harm. The Arion Wood-lands were so dark she couldn't see anything, and her eyes might as well have been closed the entire trip. Only when they neared Thebesia did the city lights provide a beacon of direction.

Rophon perked at the lights, knowing his home was a short distance ahead. He had a new resolve in his step, his pace steady until Taven slowed him down on the cobblestone. He paused in front of a small apartment, sliding off the horse. Rushing to the door, he unlocked it.

"I keep him right across the street. Go inside, and I'll join you in a moment," Taven whispered, and Cassie nodded. She stepped into the small apartment, finding it on par with Yvonne's old house.

A small kitchen nestled into the corner, from which the main room was visible. A narrow hallway led to several rooms, and not knowing where to go, Cassie stood in the entryway as she waited for Taven. He nearly bumped into her as he walked in, shedding his hat and shoes near the door.

"You can have my room. It's the one straight down the hall. If you want a snack, feel free to help yourself to whatever

I have. Doesn't matter to me." Taven paused, running his hand through his hair. "For now, try to get some sleep. The first ferry leaves at five o'clock sharp, and I don't want to miss it."

"Where are we going?" Cassie peeked curiously into the kitchen, and her gaze traveled back to the disheveled-looking man in front of her. He offered a slightly lopsided smile.

"Sparta's Hoof. It's pretty desolate, and timed ferries going back and forth allow at least some communication with the mainland. I'll let the captain know to be extra careful with who he allows onto the ferry tomorrow. No one will hurt you, I promise." His eyes matched his statement, dependable and steady.

Cassie dropped her gaze to the floor, a rush of comfortable heat coursing through her. He was too kind.

"I'm not hungry," she lied, clasping her hands behind her.

"If you're sure, then ok." Taven led her down the hall, opening the door to his room. He grimaced at the piles of clothes on the floor, rubbing the back of his head. "Um, excuse the mess."

"It's ok," Cassie said, edging past him into the room. "My room was always a mess at Yvonne's. Not at Agnetha's though. She picks up clothes before they even fall to the floor."

Taven laughed, a beautiful sound echoing in the small room. Cassie smiled to herself, pleased that he found her amusing.

"Good night, Cassie. We'll talk more in the morning."

He closed the door, and Cassie made herself comfortable under the covers, anticipation for the next day preventing sleep from coming anytime soon.

Cassie awoke with a pounding headache, her mind and thoughts fuzzy from her patchy sleep. It took her a minute to readjust to her surroundings, the window outside still dark.

The knock at the door came again, firmer this time. Cassie nearly tripped over the sheets, stumbling to open the door.

"I'm awake."

"Good. We have time for a quick breakfast, then we have to be going. We cannot miss the ferry. The next one won't run until seven. I must be back at my post by then." Taven was already dressed in full uniform, bright-eyed and showing no signs of sleepiness. The polar opposite of Cassie.

"Ok," she mumbled, following him out to the kitchen. The icebox and cabinets were sparse, giving them limited options to choose from.

"There should be a pan in that drawer." Taven gestured toward a cabinet, and Cassie dug through until she found the object, handing it out to him. He placed a pat of butter onto it, taking a few eggs from the basket on the counter. "I should say I don't usually eat at home, so I'm sorry if it's not what you're used to." He opened the window above the sink, allowing a breeze into the house. The slightest hints of pink were beginning to show on the horizon, preparing for the day ahead.

"It's ok." Cassie stifled a yawn, leaning sleepily against the counter. Her thoughts moved to her horse, eyes squeezing shut in focus as she tried to pick up on clues to where she was. In a stall, angry and confused at being torn away, but where?

Taven plated the eggs, then tossed two slices of bread onto the pan.

"Coffee?" He arched an eyebrow, and Cassie shook her head. She didn't think it was worth the hassle of making, and it wasn't something she enjoyed anyway.

"I usually only drink blueberry lemonades."

Taven smiled, his eyes crinkling at the corners.

"I'll try to remember that."

314

The simple words were as welcome as a ray of sun, pene-
trating the darkness of worry inside her. She didn't realize
how much warmth it brought forth, knowing someone cared
enough to tuck away pieces to remember later. She stared at
Taven handing her the plate of food, wondering how she
could take a piece of him, too, to learn something he liked, to
remember a favorite of his.

They ate for a few minutes in silence, except for the
clinking of utensils against plates, before Cassie spoke up.

"Why can't we search for Tenille together?"

"It's not safe." Taven glanced up, blinking slowly. Cassie
clenched her fork tighter, tired of hearing the same thing over
and over. "And truly this time. The people after your horse,
they will not hesitate to get you out of their way."

"Fine." Cassie stared down at her plate, forcing herself to
finish for Taven's sake. He looked like he wanted to say more,
but Cassie did not give him a chance. She stood and walked
toward the sink, washing her plate clean and drying it off.

Like a dutiful child, she stood by the door with her arms
crossed, waiting until the Ranger gave her the go ahead to go
outside.

"You don't understand. You and your horse are being
actively hunted. I don't want to worry you, but you must
understand. I've been followed for weeks, and either I give
away your horse peacefully, or they will come after you
themselves."

"You traded my horse for my safety!" Cassie shrieked, her
breathing shallow as she stared at Taven a few steps away
from her. Her world was collapsing all around her. The very
man she thought would keep her safe, the very man who
moments ago shone like a ray of sun, had stabbed her in the
back.

"No, I did not. Not yet." Taven ground his jaw, his arms
tense as he crossed them over his chest. His words rang in her
head. *Not yet. Not yet.*

"Is Tenille in Vallumvis?" Cassie asked, clenching her teeth to curb the desire to scream at him.

"I don't know where she is. I was searching for you, and it's more important for you to be safe first, then I will search for her," Taven explained quietly, his eyes locking onto hers.

"She's in Vallumvis. I'm going to go get her." Cassie whipped around, her hand on the doorknob.

"You can't!" Taven yelped, grabbing her shoulders. When Cassie turned to face him, the panic in his eyes was clear. "Daz will kill you."

"Daz?" Cassie questioned, her eyes narrowing. "The girl you asked me about during the picnic?"

"Yes," Taven said breathlessly, still holding her in place. "Please, Cassie. We have to get you to Pax Valles. We are wasting time by arguing."

"She can try to kill me," Cassie said defiantly, lifting her chin. "I don't think she'd be successful."

"Cassie? Have you ever considered getting another horse?" Taven's voice was low, which did nothing to calm the rage that the question flared up in the girl. "Not . . . Tenille?"

"No, never. She is my only reason to keep going, and if I can't have her, I have no reason to—"

"Cassie!" Taven sputtered, taking a step back from the girl. He shook his head furiously.

"I want my horse. I need her." How many times would she have to say it before he understood? She'd do anything to get her back.

"I'll take you to Pax Valles, then come back and look for her." Taven reached for his shoes, slipping them on. Cassie stood like a statue, waiting until Taven met her gaze again.

"I hate you." Each word she said slowly, wanting the statement to cut through him. His face fell, and she knew he knew that she did not believe them.

"Hate is a powerful emotion. It causes you to act irrationally. Let's go." He opened the door, waiting for her to go through before locking it behind him. Cassie followed him across the street to the small stable housing several horses. She helped him brush down his horse quickly, passing the tack to him without being asked. His words burned in her chest, the accusation that powerful emotions were causing her to act irrationally. Perhaps they were, because she couldn't deny that the emotions raging inside her were powerful.

Taven's lips were still pressed into a thin line, and he was silent. He didn't look at her, not even when he extended his hand down and helped her climb onto the horse behind him.

Cassie balanced on the horse, not holding on to the Ranger in front of her. Touching him would make her mind think she could trust him, but he had traded her horse away.

She knew she had hurt him, but it was nothing compared to the hurt she felt when separated from her horse. If Tenille was taken away for good, she would surely die.

Rophon kept a steady pace through the city, and Cassie respected the Ranger for not rushing his horse too fast, even if they were running a little late. She shoved the thought away. Taven should not get any respect if he did not care for Tenille.

The ferry was not far from the city of Thebesia, the edge of the sea coming into view soon. Cassie couldn't help but think the ocean was beautiful, with the rolling waves and endless sky. She took a deep breath of the salty sea air and tried to forget about the idiot sitting in front of her. An idiot who willingly gave away her horse at the first available chance.

They reached the docks as the captain was coming down to close the gate of the ferry.

"Where you headed, son?" He glanced at them with a kind expression, reaching toward the reins as Taven waited for Cassie to slide off.

"Pax Valles, sir. Meeting up with some Rangers there." Taven flashed a grin, not as bright as before. Cassie's heart twisted seeing him like this, and she wished she could apologize. But she couldn't, not when she didn't know if he would live up to his promise.

The captain closed the gate and walked to the main cabin. Desperate to get away from Taven, Cassie followed the older man up the stairs, marveling at the view.

"If it isn't the same girl," the captain suddenly said in awe, sparing her a glance before going back to the wheel of the ship. "Almost didn't recognize you with the change of hair, but it must be you."

"Are you the one who found me out in this sea?" Cassie asked softly, sitting down in the chair next to him. The captain nodded, pointing out to the far waters.

"Aye, out there. I should say, never in my forty years of captaining ships had I seen such a sight." He shook his head slightly, carefully steering the ship toward the island that loomed in the distance. It appeared to be of high elevation, the side they were headed to having tall cliffs that obscured the rest of the view.

"It seems like a nice job," Cassie commented lightly.

"That it is, the sea is a wonderful creature. Could I ask, miss, how you ended up in the middle of it?" The captain glanced at her, then down at the deck to ensure everything was in order.

"I'll be honest, Captain, and say I don't know. No one knows, really. When I recovered consciousness, I couldn't remember," Cassie explained, at ease with the older man. The captain glanced at her sympathetically.

"Miss, that's sorry to hear. Perhaps the fresh sea air will help remind you." He pointed out the docks coming into view. "That'll be your destination. Have fun with the boy; he's a good one." The captain gave her a smile. Cassie gritted her teeth and gave him a stiff smile in return, then walked out of the room, resisting every urge to slam something. The boy was an idiot; there was nothing good about him. She blocked the memories of his kindness, his branding words returning. *Hate is a powerful emotion.*

The ship docked slowly, the sun peeking over the horizon to welcome the new day ahead. Cassie hesitantly stepped out on the ratchet docks, the wooden boards slimy under her feet. The nails creaked when Taven led his mount across to the land. He looked like he wanted to say something, but one glance at her face kept him quiet.

"Thank you!" Cassie forced a smile, waving goodbye to the captain. He tipped his hat at her, a smile on his aged face. She scampered after Taven, accepting his hand and settling on the horse right behind him, leaving just an inch of space between them.

They followed a dirt path weaving upward through the cliffs, each step increasing their elevation. The cliffs around them towered high in the sky, but once they reached the top, Cassie marveled at the sight before her.

The plains rolled out in front of her, the trees so sparse she could count each one. A city stood far down the path to the left, and the path to the right went on until it dipped into a valley that hid its final destination.

The grass rolled with the wind, nearly whispering her name.

Cassie . . . Cassie.

She jerked her head up. This was the very same grass from her dream where Tenille had been stolen and led away.

Was this where she had come from? It was possible. No, likely.

"I'll take you to town." Taven's voice was rough, but Cassie shook her head furiously as she slid off the horse.

"I remember something about this place. You go find Tenille."

He didn't have the chance to argue as Cassie took off at a run down the path away from the city. The stable had been behind her, which meant she had to stray off the path and run into the grass. Taven called after her once, but after that, silence.

Cassie turned, noting he had left. She had dipped into a particularly high patch of grass, reaching almost to her chest. She oriented herself against the barn. It was still the same distance away. She kept running, grasping at anything that could remind her of the past.

Was this another dream? It felt surreal, with the beautiful pink of the horizon, the soft green of the flora, the same stable that stood so far away, yet every time she glanced at it, she felt that neither she nor the stable had moved.

How could this be, when she was sure Tenille had been right here in the dream? Had she fallen off the cliffs into the water?

"Tenille!" she called out, her voice high-pitched and laced with sorrow. The empty plains echoed the word, bringing it back to her with greater force. No one else responded, and her voice faded away.

Tenille was not here, and she had been foolish to run off like she had.

Collapsing to her knees, Cassie choked back a sob. It was no use, and the tears flowed without an answer. She wanted her horse back, no matter what she had to do to get her.

Her calf pulsed, and Cassie hiked up her pants, staring through bleary eyes at the mark that glowed with the most beautiful indigo light she had ever seen. It was like the same light that had radiated out of her palms in sparks when she had been in the stall with Tenille.

Cassie stood, shaking her palms. She wanted to call to the indigo, see what it would do. The world hushed around her, not a single critter making a sound. Even the wind quieted to help the girl focus as an image of Tenille formed in her head.

And then something shattered in her mind, the pain nearly causing her knees to buckle. Sparks erupted from her palms, and she could feel her horse's presence very close yet far away.

"Tenille," she whispered, clutching her hands when she heard the whinny of her horse, "where are you?"

Here. The response was clear as day in her mind, yet she heard it like an outside voice.

"Please come back."

I will.

Chapter

34

Taven rode back to the ferry with a frown, scared to leave Cassie like that. He hoped she wouldn't do anything to harm herself, and now he had to figure out how to undo what he had done.

Daz and Cassie were not friends, that much was clear.

Cassie would never forgive him if he was responsible for her horse going missing or being given away.

He had promised to give Daz the horse in exchange for keeping Cassie safe.

Taven rubbed at his temples, a breath away from running to Luke's office and asking him what to do. But he wouldn't, not when he had dug this hole for himself. Luke couldn't help him choose between two evils.

Instead, he headed straight to Vallumvis Stables and led Rophon into a stall. Linea stomped up to him, flames in her eyes.

"Where is Cassie?" she demanded, her hands on her hips, eyes narrowed with suspicion. Taven mirrored her expression.

"Where is the horse?"

"Theo has her, and he won't give her back. He says that Cassie took the horse illegally, and no one will take my side."

Linea tossed her hands in the air. "Of course everyone sides with Theo over Cassie. I don't even know why he has the horse."

"Cousin, but you do know." Theo's voice was almost like a purr as he slid into the conversation. His eyes fluttered, and he looked at Taven with a brighter smile. "Ranger, tell me what the Desmaligan law looks like. Are Fýlax allowed to be in Vallumvis without explicit permission?"

"No." Taven swallowed at his own betrayal. She had every right to hate him.

"They cause damage and harm. You've seen firsthand how wild and unpredictable the girl is, and her horse only makes it worse. She's in a stall and will be taken care of separately. And you, Ranger, will find the girl and we will ensure she does not taint our city ever again. We do not accept any Fýlax whatsoever, therefore turning her over to the Valley is the best choice here. I had my suspicions the very moment she stepped into the stable with her bogus claims, and if my deduction is wrong, please correct me." Theo shook his head, flicking a piece of hay off his shoulder.

Taven gripped his reins a little more firmly, annoyance prickling his skin at the condescending tone. But Theo was right. Anyone bearing the mark of Rhiza was only allowed to live in the Valley of Vathis, which was specifically built for them and by them. But Cassie was an Opposed, belonging to the half of the society that had split away and were banned for their treasons. Which ones, Taven did not know. He could never take her there, to hand her over to a shadowy demise.

"I do not recall being a servant to your fantasies. A request like that would require the approval of Edmunds, who you know well, and—"

"Nonsense. If you cannot refute my claims, then I am correct." Theo waved him off dismissively, "But if it is Edmunds you want, it is Edmunds you'll get." A satisfied smirk pulled at his lips, and Taven watched him depart with a sinking stomach. He didn't want to stay long enough to see what Theo had up his sleeve.

"Where is she? The horse?" Taven whispered. He had to find Tenille and return her to Cassie, then he would go look for Daz. He would tell her the deal was broken, and Cassie was under the protection of the Rangers. Even if dangerous, she'd surely give up if no one was on her side.

Cassie didn't deserve to live in a shadowed valley of a secret society. She would hate it there.

"In the stable, a few stalls down." Linea gestured down the aisle, and Taven handed the reins of his horse to Linea, quickly making his way toward the stall.

Tenille was pacing back and forth, tossing her head. She let out a shrill whinny. A call for Cassie.

He tried to imagine what it would be like to be separated from something he loved dearly, something close to his own heart. Painful memories surfaced, replaying the scenes. Elara going cold, her blood trickling down his arms. His stricken parents when they heard the news. They didn't blame him, no. No one blamed him like he did himself.

Cassie was distraught, running away as if that would help. He had run too, burying himself in any task Luke tossed in his direction, anything to distract himself from the ache growing stronger every day.

The horse was agitated, the whites of her eyes visible as she started throwing a fit in the stable, rearing up into the air and kicking her feet.

He couldn't watch, couldn't bear it. He couldn't bring Elara back, but he could bring Cassie and Tenille together.

Taven took a deep breath, checked both sides of the aisle to find it mostly empty, then reached forward to undo the latch. He hardly had time to open the stall door, Tenille bursting out like a cannonball, nearly running him over.

Taven stumbled backward, falling smack on his bottom. A groom dodged out of the way, cursing under his breath.

"You should not have let her go, idiot."

"I didn't know what else to do."

Tenille galloped out of the stables, her tail high in her pursuit of freedom.

The groom rolled his eyes. "Some Ranger you are. Go get her now."

Taven jumped to his feet, chasing the horse down the aisle. He didn't get far, Edmunds blocking the entrance to the barn.

"Taven, what is the meaning of this?" He gestured his arm in a circle, flanked by two Rangers of his own. Taven swallowed, his throat drying. He never, ever broke the law.

Until today.

It was only deserved, for no transgressions were tolerated in the land of Desmalogo. His chin dipped in shame, and he had nothing to say.

"Come along, then. We shall discuss this privately." Edmunds sighed, waiting for Taven to approach before leading him out of the stable. Taven felt like a criminal, flanked by the other two.

But worse was Linea staring at him with a helpless expression, still holding the reins of his mount. He only ever wanted to help Cassie, who had done no wrong. Instead, he had let them all down with his rash behavior.

Another Ranger rode up to them on his horse, pulling the steed to a sharp stop.

"Edmunds, the horse has escaped through the fence gates. Rangers are now pursuing her, but I doubt it will be a swift operation."

"Thank you." Edmunds shook his head, walking down the city road until he reached the main Ranger office. He opened the door and allowed the two Rangers to follow in after Taven, the mounted patrolman leaving to his other duties.

The lobby was empty, and instead of taking the stairs to the second story where Edmunds had his office, the group entered a room on the right. The windows were minimal, candlelight flashing shadows across everything.

Another handful of Rangers were in the room, as well as Theo. And Daz.

The last one made his stomach drop, but at least she was here and not where Cassie was. She scowled at him, only breaking off to give the same treatment to Theo.

Taven straightened out, his eyes flashing with indignation. Was everyone here because of Cassie and Tenille or was something else going on?

"I don't understand why I'm here," he said lightly, trying to make the best of the situation. Edmunds leaned against one of the chairs, rubbing his eyes with one hand.

"Taven. I've hired you and trusted you as one of my best Rangers. Your recent behavior is confusing, and you are here to explain yourself against your accusers." The statement about him being one of the best made him swell with pride. Whatever had happened, he would set it right. "Theo," Edmunds stated, turning to the young man. "Tell us what you saw."

"The Ranger took the girl away from her home against her will, leaving the city and returning alone. When he returned, he also released my horse from the stable, posing a danger to our society."

"Is this true?" Edmunds peered at Taven, and he swallowed uncomfortably.

"It was not against her will." Not fully, at least. "Cassie is under witness protection of the Desmaligan Rangers and needed to be moved."

"We don't have her listed in the files as someone with those specs," Edmunds said slowly, crossing his arms against his chest. "I want to believe you, but there are simply no records. However, I am well aware of the situation between the girl and this horse at the very first show. That doesn't explain the claims of that girl." He waved a weary hand at Daz in the corner of the room.

Taven took a deep breath, scrambling for a way to prove that Cassie and Tenille belonged together, that separating them would be just like ripping apart a family. Edmunds had originally requested he find the owner of the horse, and he had done just that.

"I'd like to speak with Luke," Taven muttered, running a hand through his hair. Edmunds tapped his finger against his arm, his gaze landing on Daz.

"Please repeat your claims to the man here."

"The horse does not belong to Theo." Her voice was cold enough to bring a chill into the room. "Reginald was supposed to deliver her to Lokiir before he ran like the coward he is."

Edmunds stared at her in disbelief, taking a few moments to consider the situation.

"None of this adds up. We can't have everyone claiming the horse is theirs."

"She's Cassie's," Taven said, "and that's where she went. It is cruel to separate the girl and the horse when they have clearly forged an unbreakable bond."

"Nonsense," Theo cut in. "She has been harboring the horse like a criminal, no paperwork, no identification. How can she legally own a horse without being a citizen? And, don't forget that time when she stole the horse from Henrik's grounds." Theo crossed his arms with a light shrug as if that would settle the debate.

Taven rubbed his temples, his head aching from the number of accusations and finger pointing. He needed to find a way to solve this and make everyone happy.

Surely Theo would understand that the horse was truly Cassie's, and with Daz refusing to explain how she thought the horse was hers, he couldn't support her wishes.

"Can we please bring Luke into the conversation?" Taven

requested again. Edmunds started to nod, freezing up when the ground shook beneath them.

"Looks like an earthquake. We'll continue this later." Edmunds's voice was sharp, and he ran toward the door. Taven dove under the table, pressing up against Daz. He gritted his teeth and closed his eyes.

The shaking only intensified, and part of the building came crumbling down. The candles all went out, and darkness flooded the room.

Then, the softest string of indigo lights wrapped around him.

Chapter 35

She felt her horse running across the plains, crossing through the mountain passage, plunging into the water that separated the two of them. The horse moved at an unnatural speed, her body barely visible under all the sparkles of light that illuminated her.

Cassie ran toward the edge of the water, her own feet moving under her at a speed that was not normal for a young girl. She shouted in excitement when her horse stepped out of the water, dripping wet and rearing.

Cassie rushed toward her, her fingers brushing against the damp hair that matched her own. Something inside her clicked back into place; their connection had been restored.

"Tenille, I'm so glad to have you back. We'll go back to Thebesia and live there with Henrik, and we'll be Cassie and Tenille, and win all the shows, and——"

Cassie. Taven released me from the stall.

"And?" Cassie frowned, pressing a kiss to her horse's cheek.

He was taken away by the Rangers.

"You think we should go look for him?" Cassie was dubious, but Tenille gestured toward her back with encouragement. Cassie clambered on with a sigh, threading her fingers through the horse's mane. She still had fragments of indigo light brushing against her palms, and she nibbled on her lip in her focus.

She needed to get to Vallumvis as fast as possible, as quickly as Tenille had gotten here. On cue, her mind wrapped the two in indigo lights, and the horse took off at a run toward the gated city.

Cassie gasped as they plunged into the water, Tenille's powerful legs kicking against the water and moving through it within the next minute. Tenille didn't even shake off the excess water, taking the path through Arion and toward Vallumvis.

Only when she saw the city gates did Cassie slow down, collecting the lights with her palms and hiding them away. Tenille still galloped, but it felt like a walk compared to how the two moved before.

"You!" The Ranger at the gate leapt up, his horse tossing its head in surprise. "You're the one who stole the horse."

"I did not." Cassie lifted her chin. "Where is Taven?"

"He was taken away to be questioned," the other man said, his horse sidestepping as they moved further from the gate. "Let her go. They can clear it up all together."

"Fine." He waved her through with a grimace. Cassie instantly went to the stable, seeking out Linea. The girl was there, deep in conversation with Adria.

"Cassie!" Linea spotted her, running over with the Ranger. "Cassie, is everything alright? Taven stole you away and I was so worried, and Theo took the horse from right under our noses like the nuisance he is, and now they're all arguing, and we don't know what to do." Linea paused her rambling to take a deep breath, and Adria cut in.

"He's at their headquarters in the city. It's the large building right across the street from city hall."

"I'm going." Cassie clicked to her horse, turning her around and heading away from the stable. She'd seen city hall before and knew where to find it. She needed to find Taven alone, without Linea and Adria tagging along.

Dark clouds gathered in the sky overhead, and Cassie tilted back to glance at them. The wind picked up and called out to her.

Cassie gasped as the wind gathered under her fingertips, sparkles lacing each breath let out by the clouds. It was her wind, fueled by her anger at the situation and the dire necessity to get Taven out of the building before he was framed for helping her.

She did not want peace, not when those who took away Taven would not be kind to her.

The wind grew stronger, whipping her hair around her face and making it hard to see. Cassie pushed forward, spotting the building ahead. It was almost too easy to direct the wind toward the old brick and mortar, the pressure building up against one side and cracking the wall.

She closed her eyes as parts of it came crumbling down, and she panicked internally. Taven. She had to keep Taven safe.

The indigo lights that she had subconsciously gathered around her dashed toward the building, finding her target and blanketing him in a protective halo. She didn't know who else was there or if they would be hurt.

It was too late to reverse the path of destruction, and a final gust of wind brought down another chunk of the building, blocking the entrance. It was akin to thunder, booming across the buildings and rumbling far away. The action made her weak, and she slumped forward against Tenille, her head spinning wildly.

"You can't be out here. It's dangerous!" A male voice came from behind her, shouting over the wind whirling around them. "Get away from the buildings before they all collapse."

"They won't," Cassie whispered, sick to her stomach at what she had done. If anyone had been hurt, it was all on her. Her pent-up emotions had gotten the best of her, ruling her mind.

They were all right. She was dangerous, and she didn't belong here.

Slipping off her horse, Cassie ran toward the half-broken building, shouting Taven's name. The man who had ridden up to her looped a rope around Tenille, tying her to his own mount as he ran after the girl.

"Taven!" Cassie repeated, dropping to all fours as she scaled the pile of bricks in search of familiar straw-blond hair. He emerged from the darkness, his face blank and as white as the wall. Cassie didn't hesitate, throwing her arms around him and burying her face in his chest. She wanted to apologize for everything she had said, that she didn't hate him and she understood everything he had done for her. Through it all, he was the one who wanted to help her. "Are you alright?" She lifted her face toward him, noting the way he blinked slowly.

"Is this . . . real?" Taven whispered, stuck in a trance. He glanced down at his hands, then at Cassie. All evidence of indigo-colored lights was gone, only the hint of a memory floating around. His breaths came slow, arms moving to tighten around Cassie.

"Oh, Taven, you were so concerned about my safety you forgot your own." Cassie blinked back tears, telling herself to stop being emotional. Hate was a strong emotion, but it was far from hate brewing inside her now. "I'm sorry." The words just spilled out. "I'm sorry that I said I hate you. I really don't, truly, and—"

"It's ok," Taven whispered, his hand moving up to rest on the back of her head. "I'll take care of the girl. Luke, you can survey the damage."

"Is it bad?" Luke asked softly, and Taven remained silent. Cassie felt him tense under her, and she kept her eyes shut from utter shame.

She didn't want to pull away from him, finding solace in his strong embrace. His forehead tilted toward hers, sending a flutter of emotions through her. Whatever this feeling was, it was new to her, not something she had felt before. It wasn't even familiar.

"You two look cute." A voice broke through the peace of the moment, and disappointment filled her when Taven released her immediately, spinning toward a girl with white hair. It almost glowed in the summer light, her smile as brilliant as her eyes.

"You're a disgusting human, Daz." Taven's face had turned to stone, his voice angry.

"I know." She shrugged, glancing at the two horses standing on the street. "But I still need the horse." She walked past calmly, stepping over some of the rubble.

"Horse?" Cassie nearly shrieked the word, taking one step to follow her.

"Yes, yours." Daz turned with the most repulsively sweet smile that Cassie had ever seen, and the rush of emotions from before returned with stronger force.

"If you can pry her from my cold, dead hands," Cassie spat, turning to Taven. "Is this the girl that followed you around everywhere?"

Taven nodded, his jaw set.

Cassie turned back to the girl, but she was gone. No one had moved, but the girl had vanished from their sight. It was too late to return the indigo lights streaming from her palms, aimed at the very spot the girl had been standing. They gravitated to a singular spot, fading out for a moment.

A scream pierced the air and Daz tumbled to the ground, the lights flickering brightly before waning. Her limbs were askew, akin to someone being dropped out of the air. She sat limp, her scream fading out, horror flooding her face.

Cassie stepped back, bumping into Taven. She didn't know, didn't even want to know, what the bright indigo lights had done to the girl.

"What did you do to her?" Taven gasped, stepping away from Cassie. He glanced at Daz, torn between the two.

"You broke me," Daz whimpered, glancing up at Cassie. Their eyes crashed together, one pair terrified and the other full of despair. "You broke my power."

She stood on shaky feet, her appearance no longer striking. Her hair lost its glow, her face twisted in anguish. Cassie watched her go, her feet rooted to the spot. Her own power had broken someone else's like it had broken the building. She needed to leave the city as quickly as she could. Sticking around would only lead to trouble with the law.

"I had no idea." The words caught in her throat, and she rushed toward her horse to mask the pain. Taven didn't follow her, standing close to the building.

The wind had died down; not a single breeze ruffled the air. Fluffy white clouds replaced the dark ones, painting a picturesque image outside. If she turned her head away from the damage, it would have been impossible to tell that a storm had raged through a handful of minutes ago.

Cassie still had her head pressed against her horse's neck when she felt the lightest of taps on her shoulder. She let out a sigh and turned to see Dr. Lykaion surveying the building with a frown pulled tight against his face.

"Cassie? How are you feeling?"

"Not bad. Good, actually." It was shameful to admit that she was feeling better after letting her rage out on the surrounding buildings and people. "I'm sorry."

"We'll deal with you. I want you to tell me everything that happened, but not now. Later." The doctor adjusted his hat, striding away to meet with Luke.

"Death count of five." Luke kept his voice low, but Cassie heard. She froze, unable to breathe as her heart constricted inside her chest and her lungs failed her. The doctor noticed her reaction, appearing at her side again.

"Cassie, don't panic. I don't blame you." He placed a hand on her shoulder, the other one dragging down his face. Luke pressed his lips together, silent as another figure approached.

The older man was the spitting image of Linea, and the girl was right behind him. He stroked his chin as he surveyed the people, his gaze landing on Taven, who hadn't moved.

"It seems as though there has been a natural disaster here." Luke's voice thundered against the buildings, much louder than necessary. Cassie shrank back against her horse, and Tenille nickered to comfort her. She felt Linea's eyes searching for her but was too ashamed to meet them. "Edmunds was found dead under the rubble."

"Edmunds." The man, presumably Linea's father, arched an eyebrow. "That puts us in a difficult situation. The Rangers cannot continue without a Proedros to manage them. Luke, I authorize you to take his position and clean this mess up. We'll set up the ceremony on Saturday to move people around and pick a new Proedros. What do you suggest we do about the building?"

"We'll move all operations to Thebesia. I'll be more organized there." Luke's voice was firm, disregarding the man's pinched lips.

"Very well."

Luke stepped forward and shook the man's hand, and Cassie lost interest in the conversation. She turned to the doctor, her mind disoriented.

"Can I return home?"

"Home?" Dr. Lykaion almost smiled, but the concern in his expression maintained its hold.

"Thebesia. I want to go back."

"Yes." He let out a small sigh. "You can go."

Without a look backward, Cassie pulled herself onto Tenille's bare back and tossed the rope Luke had placed on her to the side. She was about to ride off when Taven appeared at her side, placing a hand on her thigh as he glanced up at her.

"No helmet?"

"I'll be fine." Her breath hitched. For Taven to see everything she had done, to have a front-row seat to the damage caused, and still care about her safety warmed her heart deeply. "You'll visit me in Thebesia?"

"Of course." He patted her, a gesture conveying how reluctant he was to leave, his honey-brown eyes searching hers. Cassie leaned down closer, a whisper away from his face.

"Have I ever thanked you for everything you did?"

"I don't think so." Taven spoke barely above a whisper, his lips brushing hers. It was the most tempting invitation, the action heightening her awareness of how many people were watching them. Cassie drew back, a smile playing across her lips.

"I must go." She turned one last time to catch Linea's eyes, sharing a sad smile as the girl moved closer to her father. Linea mouthed the word "go," waving her hand in a discreet manner. Cassie nodded and urged Tenille forward, the clip-clop of the hooves echoing through the alleyway.

It was not a natural disaster, but with so many people willing to cover up for her, she would not ruin the moment.

The iron gates loomed ahead of her, the two Rangers still at their post.

"Is everything alright?" one asked, clearly dying of curiosity.

"There has been a natural disaster, and I was told to go home." She smiled as the words hit her lips, bringing forth a sense of familiarity.

She still had not remembered a single thing from her life

before, but now she was more confident in her life here on Desmalogo.

Putting the events behind her, literally and mentally, Cassie leaned forward on her horse.

"Run, girl. Run how you'd like, as if you have all the freedom in the world."

Chapter

36

The coffee met his lips, scalding him as he waited. Waited and waited, frustration picking at his skin. How long would it take her to get the blasted horse?

Mnemosyne landed on his shoulder, her talons digging in to his shirt. "She has returned without a horse."

"Why?" Lokiir lowered his cup of coffee, tilting his head to meet her beady eyes.

"She's on the edge of the island. Send Merel to portal her."

"You go bother that twit."

The bird took off, swooping into one of the cabins. He waited for a few moments, and the portal crystalized in front of him.

Daz stepped across, not looking like herself. He leaned closer to peer at her, aghast to see her face stained with tears. She rubbed at her cheek, sniffling.

"What is the meaning of this?" He was in no mood for her games, clever as they might be.

"She broke me." Daz's voice was no more than a whisper, hardly heard above the rocking of the waves against the ship. "I had no idea someone could be broken."

"What do you mean, broke?" Lokiir gripped his cup, anger flashing in his eyes. Mnemosyne landed on his shoulder again, feathers ruffling with indignation.

"She has a strong connection to Rhiza. It flits into her fingers as easily as thoughts. I struggled to keep myself hidden, and she controls the wind like it's her breath. She is dangerous, very dangerous."

"And the Fýlax allow this?"

"They do not know of her. From what I gathered, she was untraceable at first, though I suppose that has changed." Daz slowly ran her tongue along her bottom lip, her eyes fluttering. "I no longer have a place here with you. I am broken and cannot be tracked. Send me back to Desmalogo and I will spy for you." Her eyes flicked up toward him, void of their usual charm.

Daz was an anomaly, harboring a power that seemed to enhance her very features. Losing everything was a massive blow, shown in the way she knelt on the ground before him lacking her usual flirtatious manner.

He considered the proposition, downing the rest of his coffee. Truly, if she could not be tracked and could not be hunted, sending her to the island was his best option.

But it also provided a chance for her to stab him in the back, which no doubt she would do after how he had treated her the past year on this forsaken ship.

"Very well." A brutish smile pulled at his mouth. "You may return, but only on one condition."

"Yes?"

"Find a way to get back at the girl."

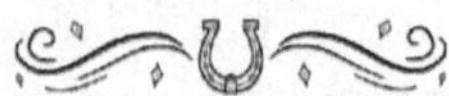

Vivion grimaced at the portal in front of him, annoyed to find it blank. Cassie's power was diminishing his own.

No, not diminishing. Balancing. The three Favored Kleros and the three Opposed Kleros balanced each other like day and night, black and white, order and chaos, calm and storm.

Life did not exist without storms, and too much calm placated the citizens. Life could not exist without a night to give it rest, summer would not come without winter.

Vivion slammed the portal shut with his palms and opened a new one. Instead of Cassie, he turned his attention to Jakobi. His eyes sharpened as the images cleared, and Aurelian stood before him, berating his friend. Jakobi stood with his hands bound behind his back, a trial taking place.

His gasp echoed through the trees, hands shaking away the remains of the portal as he ran across the path to where his friend lived.

A trial for Jakobi meant that Aurelian had discovered it was he who had healed Cassie, betraying his own kind, shattering the trust he had worked so hard to build within the Valley.

"Jakobi!" His voice came as a furious whisper as he swung open the door to the house. It was dark, all storage components torn open and void of things.

Either someone had raided his home or Jakobi had done what he had wanted to do for years: flee.

"Cassie?" Henrik dashed across the stable grounds with a wide grin. "What a surprise!"

"I've come to live here now," Cassie stated, sliding off her horse. Tenille nickered at Henrik, who extended his hand toward her.

"I'm so glad to see you reunited again. I kept her safe for as long as I could, but I knew eventually you would come back."

"Selene told me, thank you." Cassie tossed her hands around Henrik's waist, too happy to care if a hug was acceptable. He patted her back gently, a soft sigh escaping from his lips.

"Cassie, you still don't remember?"

She shook her head.

"You can have a place here. Do you think Tenille would like being stabled next to Kismet?"

"Yes!" Cassie accepted the halter Henrik gave her, fitting it gently over her horse's face. Tenille was calmer than usual, her hind leg propped up.

The barn was as busy as ever, several people tossing her curious glances as she proudly led her horse through the aisle and into the designated stall. Kismet tilted his head toward Tenille, snorting a greeting through his nostrils.

"They have very similar conformation," Cassie noted, their neck placement and arched heads making them look of the same breed.

"Yes, both are equally beautiful. Selene will be here soon, but in the meantime, we can find you a room." Cassie followed the owner to the lodging house next to the stables, giddy excitement flowing over her. She waved at a few familiar faces as she went up the stairs and down a hallway.

"You'll have Mitchie next door if you need anything." Henrik pointed to the door to the left before opening the one that led to her room. "And we'll get you something to do at the stables so you can have some drachmas to spend for yourself. Perhaps you can train privately like you did for Selene. I think many riders will look up to you after your win with Denny."

"Even if I lied and said I was riding with Thebesia Stables?"

"Cassie! You didn't lie. You've always belonged here."

His words made her heart leap with delight, and as she scanned the small room, she could very much imagine this being her home.

"Thank you." The bed was appropriately sized for her, the bed covers a lovely indigo color that made her shiver when she remembered the light that could leave her palms on a whim. She clenched her fists closed as if that would help, turning to Henrik.

"I don't really have much to my name, but I truly appreciate everything you've done for me."

He smiled, his arms crossed over his chest. "Don't ever doubt it, Cassie. You were brought to this island for a reason. We'll get you settled in and have you registered as an official citizen of Desmalogo. Then, no one can question if you truly are supposed to be here."

"Thank you." Cassie blinked back tears. All she wanted was to fit in, and citizenship was a step in that direction.

"Dinner is in half an hour. Wash up and we'll meet you downstairs." Henrik gave her a single nod, then left the room.

Cassie peeked out of the hallway, noting the washroom at the end of the hall and making her way there. She did her best to wash the dirt and grime off her face and hands, but there was no saving her tattered clothes or the mess of blonde hair on her head. Even the brush had a hard time detangling it.

She felt a little better afterward, heading downstairs and noting the table where all the grooms were sitting. Mitchie sat in the center, talking animatedly.

Cassie slid into a seat at a table behind her, not ready to have a conversation about her stealing Tenille. Dinner was served shortly, and after taking her plate to the kitchen, Cassie headed back to the barn.

Tenille nibbled on her fingers through the bars that separated them, ears flicking back and forth. Cassie noted a spark of indigo lights between them fading into the night, and she swallowed stiffly.

She wanted to put whatever had happened in Vallumvis behind her, but if the lights had followed her here, then the consequences surely would as well. Bidding her horse another farewell as she left the stable, she ran over in her mind what she needed to do. Some of her items were at Yvonne's. She'd never asked anyone about their current whereabouts. There were also a handful of clothes and items given to her at Agnetha's, though she was unsure if she was still entitled to them.

A strange proceeding at the entryway to the stable caught her eye, led by a familiar Ranger. Taven spotted her, his horse ambling in her direction. Behind him, several people clothed in robes followed slowly. She wanted to be excited to see him, but his presence was tainted with the very people that she knew brought forth trouble.

Cassie sucked in a gasp and whipped around. If she pretended not to see them, maybe they would leave. The secret people unnerved her, and she had seen enough when Vivion and the doctor moved her around.

Deep down, she knew she was part of them, but she refused to acknowledge it.

"Cassie." Taven stood at the entrance of the stable, holding his horse to the side. His eyes harbored pain deep inside him, and Cassie knew he saw this as a failure of his promise to keep her safe. All those weeks hiding away at Vallumvis only for them to claim her as soon she stepped out of the gated city. "The law of the island states that if you are one of the Fýlax, you must go with them."

"No." She grabbed on to the door of the stable, grasping for anything to keep her away from the creepy darkness of the valley. She did not want to be stuck in a cabin for the rest of her life, each movement restricted. "I will not go."

Cassie stared at Tenille, their connection humming in her mind. *We can make a run for it.*

Tenille was silent at first, patiently chewing through another mouthful of hay.

We will get tired of running.

Cassie stumbled back in shock, hurt that her own horse would betray her like this.

Find out what they want, and we can go home.

Her mouth dropped open.

"Home?" she asked. "How do you know where that is?"

Taven placed a hand on her shoulder, making her jump.

"I won't let them hurt you, but you must go."

Cassie alternated her gaze between her horse, the Ranger, and the group of people heading toward her. She felt trapped, constricted, and on the verge of simply running away.

But Tenille was right, as painful as it was to admit. She

could not run forever. Her head dropped in defeat, not looking at the people steadily approaching her.

"Greetings, Cassie. My name is Aurelian."

She stilled when she heard the name, the letter from Yvonne's house written clearly in her mind.

"You are to come with us."

ACKNOWLEDGMENTS

First and foremost, I would like to thank God for being with me every step of this incredible journey. His timing is always right, and even though this book took me longer to finish than expected, I trust there was a reason for it.

For my sister and best friend, thank you for being my biggest fan and my OG alpha reader. You encouraged me to write even when I had my doubts, and your support means more to me than you realize.

For Emily, thank you for being one of the reasons my stories went from spoken words to sentences on paper. I still remember the unfinished chapters we swapped as teenagers, both through digital platforms and the handwritten fan fiction. So much has changed since then, but you still serve as an inspiration to me.

For Jessica, my amazingly talented editor who taught me so much about the process of editing and made hundreds if not thousands of comments on how to improve my writing. I appreciate every single one of them, and am grateful to have you along on the journey.

For my beta readers: Kristina, Kasey, Sarah, and Jennifer. I appreciate all of your comments and suggestions to improve this story and polish any glaring issues before handing it over to my editor.

For the indie authors of the world, thank you for showing me that publishing my own book, once a faraway dream, was possible. You all are amazing.

And last but not least, for you, dear reader. Your support means the world to me, and it's an honor to know that you chose to read my story.

ALSO BY STELLA MCAFEE

<u>Desmaligan Archives</u>

Unbreakable Bond

Unbreakable Soul (coming soon)

ABOUT THE AUTHOR

Stella McAfee is an indie author who has been sharing stories with those around her for as long as she can remember. She has a bachelor's degree in management from her local university but prefers writing to working. When not drafting a story, she enjoys exploring the outdoors when the weather is warm, with a special love for evergreen forests and looming mountains of the Pacific Northwest. She runs off caffeine—in the form of iced lattes—and the grace of Jesus.

Her debut novel, *Unbreakable Bond*, was inspired by her love for horses and passion for adventure set in a world where people live at a slower pace and appreciate the nature around them.

Connect with Stella on her website, www.authorstellamcafee.com, or on her Instagram page, @authorstellamcafee.